Jane,
    May this Southern to

God Bless,
Jill Smith Entrik

1

Star of Flint

Star of Flint

Jill Smith Entrekin

Amy Bell, Editor

Room 272 Press

To Holly and Amy, my daughters and champions, who served as my conscience for every page of this story.

To Dana, my very own knight in shining armor, who believed in me and my story even when I did not.

Finally, to the memories of Daddy and my "big" sister Dawn, whose lives provided the inspiration for this story.

Acknowledgments

Because my mother taught me that a Southern lady always sends a handwritten thank-you note, I doubt she would think the following acknowledgements are adequate. Forgive me, Mama. Nonetheless, I am forever grateful to each of these dear people:

- Gene Kilgore, posthumously, for offering his vast knowledge and wonderful stories about the newspaper business during the 1960's.
- James Lackey, posthumously, for sharing his memories about working in the cotton mills and for painting me a picture of mill village life.
- Mama (Mildred Smith) for doing her best to impart her Southern lady graces even though I was often a reluctant student.
- Rob Bell, my Army veteran son-in-law, for providing his military knowledge to assure the authenticity of references to the Vietnam War.
- Janet Lackey Hill, my BFF (even before there was such an acronym), for helping me to fill in the blanks when my memory was hazy.
- Joyce McKinney Duncan and Beverly Sessions Crum for being such good sports about my revealing childhood secrets.
- Barbara Roy for sharing her godly wisdom, much of which made it into my story.
- Connie Bryant and Karen Davis for serving as my very honest literary critics.
- My sisterhood of prayer warriors for their spiritual support during this journey.
- Merilee Giddings, Jodi Rassett, Mary Catherine Domaleski, and Carla Brown, my World Gym fitness gurus, who kept my body strong so that my brain would function.
- Tonja Lucio for being a magician with a blow dryer and a makeup brush.
- Emma Edwards and Marissa Shockley for sharing their precious feet on the cover.
- Rachael Weaver for her ability to interpret my imagination's eye and to capture the perfect cover shot through her camera lens.
- Keaton Taylor for his graphic design creativity on my cover.
- My two beautiful and amazingly talented daughters: Holly Wasson for donating both her time and her marketing genius and Amy Bell for spending countless hours so that not a single wrong word got past her editing expertise.
- My devoted husband and best friend Dana Entrekin for sharing his firsthand knowledge about the game of football and always having another sales angle for my story.
- David Anders and *Room 272 Press* for taking a chance on me and for expertly guiding me through every step of this process.

2009

Prologue

The swing on the front-screened porch of the Kingston Road house offered my favorite place to sit and ponder. The porch was the only room to escape Aunt Bird and Uncle Hoyt's remodeling over the years. Aunt Bird had added some updated patio furniture with bright cushions, but she'd left the old swing, refurbished, so it wasn't dangerous for someone preferring its comfortable sway.

The September day had been warm, even by Georgia's standards. But now, as the first stars twinkled in the dark, cloudless sky, a hint of autumn breeze drifted across the front yard. Except for the hum of the air conditioner inside, a quiet stillness permeated the night. Typical for a weeknight in Flintville, I thought.

Emma and Aunt Bird were finishing up the dishes in the kitchen. My Emma had driven down from Atlanta yesterday in time to greet Walt and me when we arrived this morning. Hopefully, Cece would get here before tomorrow's ceremony. Her plane had been delayed in Honolulu due to a tropical storm brewing in the Pacific.

As if reading my mind, Emma, expertly managing wine glasses and a bottle of Chardonnay, burst onto the porch in excitement. "Guess what, Mama? Cece just called; she's already in L.A. and trying to make a connection to Atlanta. I can't wait to see her!"

She grinned, her bright brown eyes glowing, and flopped down in one of the comfortable, new porch chairs. "Aunt Bird went to bed. She's got a hair appointment at 8:00 A.M. What hairdresser starts that early? In Atlanta, I'm lucky if I can book an appointment before noon. Daddy's out with Uncle Hoyt in his workshop admiring that old car Uncle Hoyt's rebuilding. Why would anybody want to refurbish an ugly old Studebaker? Did you know Uncle Hoyt keeps a refrigerator stocked with Miller Lite out there? He tucked away this bottle of Chardonnay for us yesterday. I know you said we should always respect Aunt Bird's 'teetotaling' beliefs while in her house, but we are on the porch. I guess it's okay to uncork this since Aunt Bird's in bed, don't you think?"

Emma paused to take a breath and operate the corkscrew. The light from the living room window fell upon her chair, and I gazed at this beautiful, intelligent, passionate young woman. Her soft, dark hair and deep chocolate eyes reflected the Cherokee Indian blood in Walt's family line. We had rightfully named her after Emmaline, the Cherokee Indian wife of Walt's great, great grandfather Oscar Madigan.

"Mama, are you all right?" Emma interrupted my thoughts.

"Perfect! I'm sitting in my favorite chair in the world and talking to my favorite daughter in the world," I smiled as she handed me a glass of deliciously cold Chardonnay.

"Mama, I'm your only daughter," Emma giggled. "Have you figured out what you're going to say at the ceremony tomorrow?"

"Not exactly, but I'll think of something."

"Yeah, right. I bet you tried out a dozen different versions of your speech while you and Daddy drove up here. He's probably hanging out with Uncle Hoyt so he doesn't have to listen to the thirteenth revision."

Emma knew me too well. "You're probably right. At least while Uncle Hoyt has your daddy occupied, you and I can visit. What's your next assignment?"

"I'm not sure, but it may take me to the naval base in Jacksonville. Wouldn't that be great! I could drive up to see y'all in Savannah on weekends. My editor's still working out the details. Don't tell Daddy, though. I don't want to disappoint him if it falls through," she warned.

"Oh, Emma, we'd be thrilled! I promise to keep mum until you know for sure, or your daddy will drive me crazy."

An investigative researcher and writer for CNN, Emma had traveled the globe in the past five years on one assignment after another. Luckily, she'd never been sent to any of the hotspots like Iraq or Afghanistan although it wasn't because she hadn't begged for the opportunity. Her editor said she was still "wet behind the ears" and needed a few more years of experience; I blessed her editor every evening in my prayers.

"I got an e-mail from Martin last week. He's spending the next two months in Savannah. He wants me to join him for a gig when I'm in town. Daddy would love that, wouldn't he?"

Martin Raymond, Emma's best buddy from high school, divided his time between writing scores for Off Broadway musicals in New York and playing sets at his own river-front piano bar within walking distance of our antebellum home on one of Savannah's historic squares. Emma and Martin had been high school costars in every musical production from *The Wiz* to *Evita*. The realization Emma's best friend was black was somewhat difficult for my "good ol' boy" husband to digest at first, but Walt had come around especially when he realized Emma and Martin's relationship was purely platonic. Walt and Martin had actually become good friends, which seemed to grow out of their shared passion for fishing the Savannah coast.

Emma herself was quite a musician, a gift she'd received from Aunt Bird, whose melodic voice still carried the church choir every Sunday. "So, what are you going to sing tomorrow?"

"I'm not sure. I kind of want Cece's approval before I make up my mind. I pulled out my guitar and 'jammed' with Aunt Bird in the kitchen when we finished the dishes. I told her she should be the one singing tomorrow, but she said singing alone these days makes her too nervous. She prefers a choir surrounding her even if some of them sing off key," Emma laughed.

"Hopefully, Cece will arrive in time to help you choose the right song. I'm so anxious to see her. It's been far too long, hasn't it?"

Emma offered me a little more wine and sat down beside me on the swing. "Yes, Mama, it's been almost five years since we saw Cece. Do you remember the promise you made me then?"

"What promise?" Knowing full well my promise, I took Emma's hand in mine. I'd agreed to share my sister's entire story one day when the pain subsided. I knew it was time.

Emma turned off her cell phone. "Mama, I don't think there could be a better time than now or a better place than here. Don't you agree?"

Emma was right. The years had softened the pain as time does in its kindness for those who grieve. We were sitting in the very place where my memories of Cece and Diddy always delivered me. And so, I began.

Part One
1961

Chapter One

I was sitting on the curb of Kingston Road popping tar bubbles with my bare toes. Cece was in the front porch swing painting her toenails.

"Allie, git out of that tar before you git it all over those new bermudas," she yawned in her big sister tone.

Cece was always bossing me around these days. She was fourteen; I was not quite ten—only four years difference, but these days we seemed centuries apart.

"I bet it's 98 degrees out here today. Hey, Cece, go git an egg and let's see if it'll fry on the sidewalk!"

"I'm not wasting a good egg, Allie. Don't be so immature!"

"That's not what you said last summer when we cracked two right out here on the curb."

"Oh shut up! That was last summer. Anyways, the temperature's only 92. They just said so on WSFT, and stop playing in that tar." Ninety-degree weather was typical for a summer day in middle Georgia. No one got worked up unless the mercury rose into triple digits.

If my best friend Josie McClendon had been in town, she'd have gone down the street to her house and sneaked a couple of eggs from the kitchen when her maid Lorna wasn't looking. But Josie had gone to visit her cousin in LaGrange for our first week of summer vacation, so Cece was all I had. Last summer Cece would've been popping tar bubbles with me, but something had happened to her in the past six months. All she cared about was listening to Bobby Goldsboro and the Lettermen on Flintville's local radio station, painting her nails with the latest Cutex shade from Mackey's Dime Store, and trying to get her hair to grow in a flip like Doris Day's.

Aunt Bird said Cece was on the threshold of puberty; at least that's how she explained it to me last winter when she took Cece to Nash Franklin's Department Store to buy her first brassiere. While she helped Cece fasten it in the dressing room, Aunt Bird called it a "training bra." I asked Cece what she was trying to train her "titties" to do.

Cece turned beet red, and Aunt Bird looked at me reproachfully, her freshly permed red curls just a jiggling, "Don't say 'titties,' Allie. That's undignified."

"Maybe I don't want to be dignified," I mumbled as I sat on the small bench behind the dressing room curtain and picked a scab on my knee.

Aunt Bird ignored my comment. "Call them breasts, please. You should always refer to the parts of your anatomy with the proper terminology." Aunt Bird, a high school English teacher who could even beat Diddy in **Scrabble**, had the broadest vocabulary of anybody I knew and never failed to impart new words upon me whether I liked it or not. "There now, Cecile, how does that feel?" Aunt Bird asked as she adjusted the straps on the brassiere.

Cece pulled her shoulders back, sucked in her stomach, and jutted her chest out as she stared at her reflection in the dressing room mirror. She seemed so proud to have that stupid thing on. I had to admit her body had changed in the past year. Standing in the new brassiere and a pair of white cotton Carter's panties, her legs, which had always been long and lithe like a dancer's, had a slight curve at the thighs now, and her waistline was no longer straight but had a cinched in look like she was wearing a belt buckled a little too tight. Her blonde hair, pulled up in a ponytail, had a soft sheen against her olive, smooth as a baby's butt complexion. Even her face had changed shape and lost its pudginess, so her cheekbones seemed higher. She reminded me of the mantel picture of our mama in her wedding dress.

"Well, it looks ridiculous to me!" I chimed. "Why, your tit—," an admonishing look from Aunt Bird again, "I mean your breasts ain't no bigger than mosquito bites!"

Cece blushed again and in hushed tones snarled, "Shut up, Allie, just shut up!"

"Okay, that's enough, girls. Cecile is just starting to bud. But one day soon she'll be fully developed like me." She brushed Cece's blonde bangs out of her blue eyes.

I pushed my glasses up, a habit I'd developed over the years because the frames always slid down the bridge of my freckled nose, and looked at Aunt Bird. She was my daddy's younger sister by seven years, and she was beautiful to me. Her real name was Ophelia, but the family had nicknamed her "Bird" when they discovered her voice was as sweet as a nightingale's. At the tender age of four, she could sing every song on the radio's *Hit Parade*. Although the rest of the world referred to her as Ophelia, she would always remain "Bird" to the Sinclair family. She had curly red hair and deep green eyes. That day she was wearing a straight wool skirt and a sweater set with pearly buttons, and she had some Big Titties! Somehow I couldn't imagine Cece with titties that big.

I loved my Aunt Bird more than anybody in the world, except for my daddy, whom Cece and I referred to as "Diddy." Aunt Bird was the closest thing to a mama I'd ever known. Our real mama died in the big fire at the Winecoff Hotel in Atlanta when I was barely three. The art teacher at Flintville High School, Mama had taken the school's art club for a weekend tour of some Atlanta exhibits. She and the school's counselor had shared a room at the hotel, and they, along with three students from the art club, perished in the fire.

"Now, Allie, while Cecile gets dressed, why don't you take this dime around the corner to Mackey's and buy a bag of chocolate covered peanuts. We'll meet you there in five minutes. I think it's time you had some nylon panties, Cece." Aunt Bird knew what to say to make me happy; I loved chocolate covered peanuts almost as much as I loved aggravating Cece. As I clutched the dime in my hand and skipped out of the dressing room, I heard Aunt Bird say something about my feeling a little inadequate at the moment, and I noticed a look of relief on Cece's face. I guess they were both glad to be rid of me for a while.

Anyway, ever since that day, Cece'd been different, I guess because of puberty, which Aunt Bird defined as "a maiden's miraculous blossoming into womanhood." Whatever that meant, I wasn't exactly sure. The one thing I was sure about was that puberty seemed stupid to me, and I hoped I never got it.

"Allison Sinclair, I said stop playing in that tar, or I'll tell Diddy when he gits home!" Cece snapped at me as she screwed the top back on to her bottle of nail polish.

"Yeh, you do, and I'll tell Diddy and Aunt Bird what I saw you and Ned Davis doing out behind the car shed!" I snapped back.

"That was way last spring, and I haven't spoken to that square since. Besides, what I do is none of your business, Allie! Anyways, we were just experimenting."

"Experimenting, huh? It looked more like French kissing to me—eeeww yuk! Why you'd ever want to put your tongue in some stupid boy's mouth is a mystery to me."

I heard Cece slam the screen door of the porch and head across the front lawn towards me, but I didn't look up from the tar bubbles. I knew I had her. Pink sponge rollers dangled from the ends of her blonde hair as she tried to walk on her heels so the grass wouldn't stick to her wet toenails. She looked ridiculous. "Come on, Allie, you wouldn't tell Diddy on me!"

"It'll cost you," I replied as I picked up a stick and stirred the melted tar.

"Okay, how much?"

"A dollar."

"A dollar? You little twit! That's my entire week's allowance, and you know it!"

I happened to look up just in time to see Mrs. Clara Davis, Ned's mother, backing her station wagon out of her driveway. "Hey, look, here comes Miz Clara now. I bet she'd love to hear what her little Ned's been doing with his next door neighbor."

Cece was furious. I could tell by the red splotches appearing on her neck, but her voice remained calm. "All right, Allie, how about 25 cents a week for the next month?"

I dropped the stick in the tar goop and looked up at Cece. "You got a deal! And I'll take my first payment now."

I followed her back into the house just in time to hear Tommy Edwards whine, "Many a tear has to fall, but it's all in the game" on the radio.

Chapter Two

With a quarter in my pocket, I decided to walk downtown to Hastings Drug Store and spend a nickel on an ice cream cone. I yelled to Cece that I'd be back before 4:30, but she was too busy teasing her hair and spraying it with *Aqua Net* to care.

As long as I was home by the time Aunt Bird got off work at the county library, I wouldn't get in trouble. Aunt Bird worked there in the summer to supplement her teaching salary. I don't know why; she really didn't need the money. She'd lived with us ever since Mama died, and Diddy wouldn't allow her to spend a dime on anything concerning the house or the family. He said Aunt Bird's devotion to us was payment enough.

My aunt had a standing appointment every Saturday morning at 9:00 with Miss Thelma Boswell at Charm Beauty Shop, and I learned at a very young age never to schedule anything requiring Aunt Bird's assistance during her hair appointment. She had a love/hate relationship with her mass of red curls, which never behaved exactly the way she wanted them. She claimed Miss Thelma was the only person on earth who could tame her mane. To maintain her perfectly styled hairdo between appointments, Aunt Bird wrapped her entire head in toilet tissue and topped it with a huge hair bonnet at bedtime. She was a sight!

Although she was a redhead, Aunt Bird didn't have the temperament of one. She rarely lost her temper with me or Cece, and the closest thing to a cuss word I'd ever heard her say was "Heavenly Father above!" It wasn't in her nature to preach or belittle us. Diddy said she had the patience of Job, but she did become impatient if we weren't on time.

In the summertime the one rule Aunt Bird enforced with an iron hand was for Cece and me to be home when she got home from the library each afternoon. Once she'd seen us safe and sound, we were free to take off again as long as we were at the supper table on time.

Today, I had close to two hours before Aunt Bird would be home, so I laced up my Keds and started "footin' it." If Josie had been with me, we would've ridden our bicycles, but I'd made a pact with her not to do any riding until she came home. We'd both received bike odometers for Christmas that year and had vowed to put 500 miles on them before summer's end. We were up to 197 miles each, and it wouldn't be fair for me to top 200 with Josie gone even if I had to put on shoes to go to town. Josie and I did most of our riding in my neighborhood and hers, so we could ride barefoot. However, I knew Aunt Bird or Diddy either one would tear the seat out of my pants if they caught me in bare feet on the town square.

I crossed Kingston Road and headed up Birdsong Street. I started to stop by and say hey to Miz Gertrude Stansell, who lived at the top of Birdsong, but her car wasn't in her garage. Miz Gertie was a widow two times over and was loaded with money. Her first husband, Mr. Arlen Stansell, had owned the Ford dealership in town; when he died, Miz Gertie married Mr. Arlen's younger brother, who owned the Chevrolet dealership in town. He died a couple of years later, and Miz Gertie sold both dealerships and made a fortune. Too bad there wasn't another Stansell brother to own the Studebaker dealership.

Josie and I knew we could always count on Miz Gertie to invite us in when we showed up at her front door all hot and sweaty from a bike ride. She never failed to offer us a *7-Up* to drink as long as we'd sit and visit for a while. I didn't mind making small talk with Miz Gertie since Aunt Bird didn't believe in our having soft drinks much. Besides that, Miz Gertie had central air conditioning.

Miz Gertie was always dressed like she was going to church even in the middle of the week. I think she was right lonely even with all that money. The only child she had was a grown retarded boy who lived in an institution up north and came to visit once a year, but I don't think poor Roscoe Ray was much company to her. All he did was sit on Miz Gertie's back terrace in his Zorro outfit and look at comic books.

Remembering the blackmail quarter burning a hole in my pocket, I passed Miz Gertie's house and started the half-mile walk to town. At the edge of town stood the First Baptist Church, a sprawling brick building painted white and taking up almost an entire block. First Baptist had been a part of my family's life as long as I could remember. Diddy taught the ten-year-old boy's Sunday school class, and Aunt Bird sang in the choir at the morning services every Sunday of my life.

Cece and I weren't allowed to sit with our friends during the morning service. Instead we sat in the left transept on the second row with Diddy. I liked the singing part of church because Aunt Bird had a magnificent voice, but I usually dozed on Diddy's shoulder during Brother Clayton's sermon.

Cece and I also went to Sunday evening Baptist training union while Aunt Bird attended choir practice. I hated training union except when we had "Sword Drills" to locate the books of the Bible. If it ran over, we'd always miss the first act on Ed Sullivan. No amount of begging earned us a reprieve from training union. Sunday evening was Diddy's time to sit in a porch rocker and read the Sunday **Atlanta Journal and Constitution** without interruption.

I walked past the church, crossed at the traffic light, and turned left into Hastings Drug Store. David Estes was running the soda fountain. David was sixteen, tall and skinny, and covered in freckles. He reminded me of a giant Howdy Doody. I jumped up on the nearest stool and set my quarter on the counter.

"Hi squirt, what'll you have today?" David grinned as he wiped off the counter in front of me. Normally, I'd be offended by the term "squirt," but I let it slide. I knew what he'd ask next. "Where's that pretty big sister of yours?" Bingo! David was hopelessly in love with Cece, who wouldn't give him the time of day.

"She's at home painting her toenails and listening to the radio," I replied. "I'll have a single dip of chocolate ripple on a cone," I added. I knew if I kept talking about Cece while David filled my cone, he'd give me a ten cent double dip but only charge me a nickel for a single.

"Oh really? Is she getting ready to go to the dance at Weaver Park pavilion tonight?" David whined in a hopeful voice. All the time he kept packing fudge ripple into that cone.

"Uh, I think so. She's been talking about it, but I'm not certain she has permission to go. You know, she's only fourteen." Cece had been talking with Margaret about nothing else but the dance for the past week. For months, Cece'd been campaigning to double date once she turned fifteen, and now her birthday was only a week away. Of course, the way David Estes mooned over her, he was probably willing to wait. David rang me up, only charging me a nickel for the double dip, handed me my ice cream, and leaned into the counter to give me the third degree about Cece when he was interrupted by Mr. Hastings, the druggist and owner, who needed David to make a delivery.

Besides working the soda fountain, David occasionally made deliveries on a little red moped with Hastings Drugs painted on a sign attached to its basket. One Saturday afternoon about a month ago, he'd puttered up our drive with a big box wrapped in white paper. Josie and I were in the driveway pumping air into our bicycle tires.

"What's in the box, David? Is it a gift for Cece?" I asked as I winked at Josie. She giggled, and David's face turned beet red.

"Uh, no. Uh, is your aunt here? She ordered this um, um package from the drugstore. I'll um just leave it on the front porch if that's okay with you," he stammered. David set the package on the front steps, practically ran back to his moped, and took off.

"What was that all about? He acts like he's scared of us!" Josie laughed.

"Who knows? Boys are so stupid. Let's see what's in the box."

I carefully removed the Scotch tape and pulled the paper away from the box's edge so I could get a peek and then reseal the paper. The blue box was labeled *KOTEX SANITARY NAPKINS*. "What are these? I wonder if Aunt Bird is having her bridge club for dinner and wants fancy napkins to use on her table."

"No, that's not what those are," Josie informed me in a superior tone. "Those are to wear when you get your cycle."

"What cycle? Aunt Bird doesn't ride any kind of cycle." I added.

"Not a cycle with wheels," Josie explained. "It's a monthly cycle of some kind. Kind of like the moon, I guess. My mama has a box just like it up in the top of the bathroom closet, and when I asked Lorna what they were, she said, 'They's for women to wear when they's got the monthly curse just likes the cycle of the moon.'"

Josie's family had a fulltime maid because Josie's mama was a bank teller at Flintville Savings and Loan and worked from 9 to 5 every day.

Now as David cranked the moped parked out front, I hoped he wasn't making another delivery to our house. I was glad to sit in the comfort of the air-conditioned store and enjoy my fudge ripple cone without listening to him moon over my big sister.

Chapter Three

I had a full hour left before Aunt Bird would get home, so I decided to stroll around the courthouse square and do a little window-shopping. I ambled up Church Street and peeked in the windows of Edgar's Pool Room.

I was forbidden to enter this establishment where on any given day a passer-by could see several young men dressed in jeans and white t-shirts shooting pool and smoking cigarettes. Usually, I didn't recognize any of these fellows; Cece told me they were mostly mill workers who worked the four to midnight shift at the cotton mill. They'd come into town before their shift to shoot pool and have a burger. Edgar's was renowned for having the best hamburgers in Flint County; once Diddy brought a bag home for supper when Aunt Bird was at a choir convention. They were delicious! Of course, that was the only time I'd ever had one because, according to Aunt Bird, young ladies were not allowed in the place even just to sit at the counter and have a hamburger. I thought it was a stupid rule.

Past the pool room was Paris's Dress Shoppe, Cece's favorite place to shop when she was occasionally allowed to purchase a store-bought outfit. Most of our clothes were made by Mimi, our maternal grandmother, who was an expert seamstress in Atlanta. Every season Aunt Bird would take our measurements and mail them to Mimi. A few weeks later Cece and I would each receive a box filled with new outfits stitched by our grandmother. Mimi always kept up with the latest fashions, so Cece became the envy of her friends as she modeled her custom made *Villager* skirts and *Lady Bug* blouses.

A few doors down was Norwood's, another dress shop that catered to the teenaged girls in town. Aunt Bird forbade Cece from going into this shop. Aunt Bird didn't care for Mrs. Norwood, who always sent her teenaged shoppers home with a bag full of outfits "just to try".

As I passed Mackey's Five and Dime, I had a sudden pang of remorse for blackmailing Cece. I knew she'd had her eye on a new shade of nail polish in Mackey's, so in a charitable moment, I decided to use part of my "spoils" to buy it. There was only one bottle of *Cutex's Pink Sunset* left.

With a nickel and thirty minutes to spare, I decided to stop by the newspaper office one block off the square. I could use my nickel to buy a Strawberry Nehi from the drink box in the pressroom. Since it was Tuesday, the office was closed to the public. The paper came out on Monday, Wednesday, and Friday, so Diddy gave his workers Tuesday afternoons off.

The front door was locked, but I knew Diddy would be there working on his weekly column, which was filled with funny tidbits about local residents and an occasional homespun Southern word of wisdom. Diddy named his column "Not Responsible" so the people he mentioned in it couldn't take offense at what he'd written. I couldn't think of anyone who took offense since most locals were quite flattered to make it into the paper.

Since Mama died, Diddy had been married to his work. He seemed to spend every waking hour at the paper. He appeared totally uninterested in remarrying although Miss Blanche Bledsoe down at the Blue Goose Café flirted with him when he went in for coffee. Diddy paid her no mind. Maybe it was because Miss Blanche was a smoker. Diddy didn't smoke and wasn't much of a drinker either because he was a diabetic. He kept a case of *Pabst Blue Ribbon* beer in the crawl space under our house. On Saturdays when he came home from the paper, Diddy would ice one can of beer, or two cans if Uncle Hoyt was coming for supper. That was the extent of his drinking.

The front door of the newspaper office was locked, so I walked up the alley behind the building. Diddy's 1951 Studebaker, which looked like a blue bullet, was parked there, so I knew he was inside. The back doors were chained loosely together with a padlock; because I was small for my age, I'd mastered the art of squeezing through the opening between the two doors. Sometimes, Uncle Hoyt would be in the back repairing a machine or setting type for advertisements.

Although he wasn't really our uncle, I'd called him "Uncle Hoyt" all my life. He and Diddy had been best friends since they were basic training bunkmates at Ft. Benning in 1943. They were both handpicked for pilot training, but during a routine physical, the Army discovered Diddy had diabetes. Diddy spent the entire war in an office in Washington, D.C. where he wrote for *The Stars and Stripes*. Uncle Hoyt became a paratrooper. He jumped over Normandy on D-day, landed in a tree, shattered his leg, and spent the rest of the war in a military hospital. He still walked with a limp.

After the war, Diddy returned to Flintville where he worked his way up at the newspaper. Once I asked him why he wanted to be a journalist in a little town like Flintville after working in Washington, D.C. for a big publication read by the U.S. Army. He explained that he wanted to return to his roots and write for the people he'd known all his life. Diddy and Aunt Bird had grown up in Milltown, a neighborhood in East Flintville.

After Uncle Hoyt graduated from Georgia Tech with an engineering degree, he visited Flintville in search of job opportunities. Diddy was just finalizing a deal to buy out the newspaper—all he needed was a partner to help fund the purchase and keep the presses running. Uncle Hoyt fit the bill.

It wasn't long before Uncle Hoyt was courting Aunt Bird, the prettiest redhead in the county. They became fast friends at choir practice since their melodic voices harmonized perfectly together. The Christmas before my mama died, Uncle Hoyt gave Aunt Bird an engagement ring. The wedding was planned for the following summer, but when Aunt Bird moved in to help Diddy take care of my sister and me, the wedding was postponed. It had been on hold for seven years now.

Thinking about Aunt Bird reminded me that I needed to get home before she showed up. I squeezed through the opening between the two doors and was in the pressroom. The big presses were quiet now, but tomorrow they would be humming with the latest news in Flint County. I loved the sound of the presses and the smell of printer's ink. Evenings when I'd greet Diddy in our driveway as he climbed out of his Studebaker, I always knew if he'd been working on the presses because he would smell like printer's ink mingled with the aroma of Clove chewing gum, which he chewed constantly. I loved that fragrance. Diddy said I had printer's ink in my blood.

On the other hand, Cece couldn't care less about the newspaper business except to look at the fashion section in the Sunday Atlanta paper. She was a talented artist, just as our mama had been, and she'd already won every art prize in the county as well as some state medals. Cece and I were total opposites in every way.

A single light bulb burned over the drink box in the corner of the pressroom. I dropped my nickel in the box and opened the top. I was in luck. There was a solitary Strawberry Nehi left, so I slid it through the slots and pulled it out. I heard Diddy pecking away on his old Underwood in his office adjacent to the pressroom, so I decided I'd ease out instead of disturbing him. Being careful not to spill any of my Nehi, I squeezed myself through the pair of chained doors and scurried back down the alley.

Just as I rounded the corner that led to the front of the building, I saw Sheriff Brady, clad in his official uniform, tapping on the front door of the newspaper. A large man in both height and width, Sheriff Brady's presence was enough to scare any would-be lawbreaker. I wondered what he wanted with Diddy. I bet he had some juicy story for tomorrow's edition. A robbery? Perhaps a wreck? Or maybe a murder? There'd never been a murder in Flintville, at least in my lifetime.

My curiosity quickly overcame my better judgment. I scooted back around the corner, scurried up the alley, and silently squeezed into the pressroom. It was one of the biggest mistakes of my life.

Chapter Four

At the tender age of ten, I had three bad habits: biting my nails, shoving my glasses up on my nose, and (my deadliest sin) being an incurable snoop.

I'd lost count of the times I'd been punished for not minding my own business. I'd argue that I wanted to be a journalist, that journalists had to be curious to get the story, and that I was just honing my skills at an early age. My argument never worked, and both Diddy and Aunt Bird had lectured me countless times.

Nevertheless, my curiosity got the better of me when I saw the sheriff at the newspaper office. I crept over to the drink box, climbed atop it, and held my ear to the wall. Sheriff Brady was in Diddy's office; I heard the scrape of a chair as the sheriff sat down, and Diddy's typewriter fell silent.

"A.L., here's the file on that mill girl I've been telling you about," I heard the sheriff say. Diddy's full name was Albert Lemuel, but everybody in town called him by his initials.

"I don't know why you want to get me involved with this," Diddy replied as the rollers on his desk chair squeaked. "You know it's going to be just like last time. The girl's word against his."

"Couldn't you just go out to Milltown and talk to the girl's family?" Sheriff Brady said.

"Why can't you send one of your boys out there, Hilton?" Diddy asked in an exasperated tone.

"You know as well as I do what will happen. Those folks out in Milltown will take one look at a deputy's uniform, circle the wagons, and keep their mouths shut. But you're one of them. You grew up out there. Anyway, it's high time these town folk realize folks in Milltown aren't just a bunch of 'lint heads;' they're human beings, too. Whadda you say, A.L.?"

This was getting interesting. There was a small ventilation window a few feet above my head; if I could reach it, I could peek in and see Diddy and the sheriff. I slid off the drink box and discovered three old bottle crates resting in a nearby corner. Quietly, I stacked the three crates on top of the drink box, jumped back up, and climbed atop them.

If I stood on tiptoes, I could see in the window. Diddy had his back to the wall, but I could see Sheriff Brady's face. He was handing a manila folder to Diddy with *CONFIDENTIAL* stamped in big red letters on the front of it. Diddy took it reluctantly, opened it, and read the contents.

"Damn it, Sheriff! This guy's got to be stopped even if we both get run out of town on a rail. All right, I'll take a ride out there, but I make no promises I'll be much help." The backs of Diddy's ears were red, which I recognized as a sign of anger. I'd never heard my daddy cuss before, but the sheriff looked relieved.

Who was this guy they were talking about, and what did he need to be stopped from doing? Just then the back door of the pressroom swung open and bright sunlight blinded me. I took a step backward from my wobbly perch; the next moment I landed on the floor as bottle crates tumbled on top of me.

"Allie, are you all right?" Uncle Hoyt stood over me. "What were you doing on top of the drink box? Are you hurt?"

One of the crates had smacked me right in my forehead. I could already feel a big goose egg growing. Diddy walked through the door leading from the front office. "Allie, what are you doing back here? Are you all right?"

"Uh, I just stopped by to get a Nehi, and somehow I stumbled over all these old bottle crates," I replied innocently while I brushed myself off. I glanced at Uncle Hoyt, but he didn't say anything.

"You know you're not supposed to come back here without permission." Diddy looked peeved. "Did you squeeze through the doors again, or did Hoyt let you in?"

I figured one fib was enough, so I looked Diddy in the eye with an honest answer. "No, he wasn't back here, so I slid in through the crack." Again I glanced sideways at Uncle Hoyt, who remained mute, his arms folded and a look of amusement on his face. Uncle Hoyt, who was tall and muscular, towered over my daddy, who had a short, wiry build. Uncle Hoyt had a slow, gentle voice for a big man while Diddy's speech was crisp and impatient.

Diddy ran his hand across the top of his crew cut, a habit when he was thinking or agitated. "How'd you get to town? Did you ride your bike up here? Does your sister know you're in town?" He rained questions on me like he was interviewing me for a front-page story.

"No sir, I walked. I was just about to head home. It's my night to set the table."

"Well, from the looks of that knot on your head, you don't need to be walking home. We're not finished with this discussion, but I've still got some work to do..."

"I'm heading out, A.L. I'll run her home. I've got some choir music I need to give Bird anyway," Uncle Hoyt offered.

"Thanks, Hoyt. Allie, have your aunt put some ice on that goose egg. We'll talk later," Diddy added as he headed back to his office.

With my head hung low, I followed Uncle Hoyt out the back door. I didn't have to squeeze through the opening, but I still felt like I was in one tight spot.

14

I slid into Uncle Hoyt's pickup as he turned on the radio. "Thanks for not squealing on me."

He sighed. "I've never been much for tattle telling. But what were you doing on top of the drink box, Allie? You could have really hurt yourself."

"I know," I mumbled as I fingered the knot on my head. It felt as big as a ping-pong ball, and I knew by tomorrow it would be black and blue.

"You *know* what?" Uncle Hoyt continued.

"Well, I know I shouldn't have been up there, but I was just making sure Diddy was okay. He and Sheriff Brady were talking about some important file with big red letters stamped on the front of it."

"I doubt that file had anything to do with you, Miss Allison. I also doubt your daddy wants you eavesdropping on his business conversations," he added as he pulled into our driveway.

We climbed the back steps and came in through the kitchen. Aunt Bird was already battering cubed steak to fry.

"Well, Hoyt, I didn't know you were coming for supper," Aunt Bird exclaimed before she took a good look at me. "Allison Sinclair, what is wrong with your head? Lands sake, child, get over here." She sat down at the kitchen table and pulled me to her in one full swoop.

"She had a little spill at the newspaper, but she's all right," Uncle Hoyt interjected.

Aunt Bird had already pulled down the ice compress from a cabinet and was filling it with ice cubes. She put it in my hand, which she guided to my forehead. "Now hold it there for a few minutes, honey. Hoyt, stay for dinner anyway; you know I always have plenty."

"Thanks sweetheart, but I need to get home and mow the lawn before it gets dark. My neighbors are starting to complain. I did want to show you this new rendition of 'What a Friend We Have in Jesus.' Brother Haynie thought it'd make a nice duet for us." Uncle Hoyt stared down at my aunt with the sweetest loving eyes. He adored her, and she him. His blonde flat top and deep blue eyes made him a handsome man. He and Aunt Bird would have beautiful children if they ever got married. Cece said it was our fault because Aunt Bird couldn't bear to leave us even if it meant sacrificing marriage.

Uncle Hoyt didn't seem to mind their arrangement. They usually went to a movie on Friday nights, and the table was always set with an extra plate for him after church each Sunday. It seemed like a pretty good setup to me. I'd explained all this to Cece, who laughed and told me I didn't have a clue about true love.

As Uncle Hoyt headed to the back door, he tousled my hair and smiled. "Stay away from bottle crates from now on, Miss Allie. See you later."

"Allie, do you need an aspirin? Cece, Cece!" Aunt Bird yelled down the hall toward the bathroom. "Get the bottle of Bayer from the medicine cabinet and bring it in here, please! Oh Allie, that is going to leave a big bruise. Thank goodness, you didn't break your glasses."

Cece padded down the hall in her bare feet with the aspirin bottle in her hand. She looked at me with the ice pack planted on my forehead. "Ouch, who'd you run into?"

"She took a spill at the newspaper," Aunt Bird explained as she poured me a glass of water and handed me an aspirin. "Cece, can you set the table tonight?"

"Anything to get out of chores, baby brat!" Cece smirked as she took down plates from the cabinet. Her hair was in those sponge rollers again, and I could tell she had applied as much makeup as Aunt Bird allowed. This included pink blush, pink lipstick, and some mascara. She was obviously getting ready to go somewhere.

"I saw David Estes down at Hastings Drugstore. He wanted to know if you were going to the dance tonight. He was all moon-eyed and drooling all over himself when he said your name."

"Oh, shut up, Allie. He's a nice guy." Cece argued.

"That boy's got freckles from head to toe. I bet his butt is covered in freckles!" I giggled.

"Enough, Allie. That's rude, crude, and uncouth! I won't have such talk in this house!" Aunt Bird ordered.

I stuck my tongue out at Cece, who sneered at me. "Aunt Bird, do I have to wait on Diddy to eat? Margaret's mother is picking me up at 7:00, and I don't want to be late."

"Now, Cece, you know your daddy will be home and seated at this table by 6:01. I think you can spare fifteen minutes so we can eat together like a civilized family," Aunt Bird replied as she mashed the potatoes.

My daddy was a creature of habit when it came to mealtime. He ate breakfast at 7 A.M., lunch at 12 noon, and supper the minute he stepped through the door. We could set our clocks by his evening arrival. Aunt Bird was usually pouring up the iced tea when he walked in the door.

I followed Cece down the hall and into the bathroom.

"Why'd you roll your hair up in curlers again? When I left for town, you were teasing it into a rat's nest," I ventured trying to distract her from questions about my swollen forehead.

"I was just practicing this afternoon to make certain it would look right. Anyway, as hot as it's been, even my Dippity-do wouldn't hold this curl for more than an hour or two." She had a large jar of the green sticky-looking substance resting on the sink.

"Do you have a date for the dance?"

"You know Diddy won't allow me in a car with a boy until I'm fifteen even if it's just a week away. Anyway, Margaret and I want to check out all the single guys who'll be attending Flintville High." She expertly patted her rat's nest down into a smooth flip. It did look like Doris Day's.

"You mean there are some married boys in high school?" I asked in sincere confusion.

"No, silly. By single, I mean they're not going with anybody," Cece explained.

"Going where?" I ventured.

Cece gave her flip one last spray of *Aqua Net*. "Going with somebody means you're dating one particular person. Usually a senior boy will give the girl he wants to 'go with' his class ring or a gold football to wear on a chain. That way all the other boys know she's off limits for asking out."

"Well what if you get tired of the person you're going with? Then what happens?" I was sitting on the toilet lid watching Cece add a pink satin ribbon to her perfect flip. She laid it across the top of her head, tucked it under the base of her neck, and tied it in a small knot that couldn't be seen once her hair was in place.

"In that case, they break up, and the girl returns his jewelry. It's just that simple," she added as she turned off the bathroom light.

I followed Cece into the bedroom we shared. She rubbed some Jergen's lotion on her hands and feet and slipped on a pair of penny loafers.

My ice pack had become soggy, so I set it on the floor and fingered my knot. The swelling had gone down some, and it felt more like a marble than a ping pong ball now.

Cece stood in front of the full length mirror in the corner of our bedroom. She did look pretty. She had on navy bermudas and a soft pink sleeveless blouse with tucks down the front, compliments of Mimi's handiwork.

The pink blouse reminded me of the surprise I had for Cece. "Oh I forgot. I bought you something." I'd tucked the bottle of Cutex *Pink Sunset* in my pocket. Luckily, it hadn't shattered when I suffered my fall.

Cece looked surprised. "Well, now, Miss Baby Brat, you were busy in town this afternoon," she teased. "After smacking that noggin' of yours, how did you ever have the time to think of me?" She leaned over me where I sat on the edge of the bed, pulled my glasses off, and brushed my bangs out of the way to get a better look at my bulbous forehead. "Are you going to tell me the truth about this little accident, or am I going to have to put Nancy Drew on the case?"

"Oh Cece, it was nothing. I just fell over some old crates in the pressroom."

"Yeah, sure. You're not fooling me, baby sister. I doubt you'll fool Diddy either with that story."

At the mention of his name, Diddy's Studebaker rounded the corner of Birdsong and Kingston. We could always hear him coming as he shifted gears. As much as I loved country-fried steak and mashed potatoes, I was dreading this meal. It could be my last supper.

Chapter Six

Diddy was already drying his hands on a kitchen towel, so Cece and I took our places at the round oak table. Diddy gave me a stern look as he placed his napkin in his lap. "Is your head all right, Allie?" I nodded as Aunt Bird sat down between Cece and me.

We bowed our heads as Diddy offered thanks. I knew I was safe at the supper table because suppertime was a time to talk about the pleasures, not the disasters, of the day. Usually I was bubbling over with conversation about my day's events. Tonight, however, I remained focused on chewing my fried steak and watching the gravy float on top of my potatoes. Diddy seemed quiet and preoccupied himself; I reckoned he was considering my punishment.

"So, Cece, your first summer dance at Weaver Park. Are you excited?" Aunt Bird asked.

Diddy recovered from his private thoughts. "A dance? Tonight? Who are you going with? What time is it over? Are you sure they'll allow someone your age in the dance pavilion?"

"Oh, Diddy," Cece moaned. "Of course they will. This is the first summer dance, and all the freshmen go. It's a tradition. Tell him, Aunt Bird." She gave our aunt a pleading look.

"She's right, brother. Don't worry, the high school will have chaperones there, and the thing is over by 9:45. Cece will be home and in bed by 10:00."

Diddy hadn't adjusted to the reality that he had a daughter old enough to be in high school, much less out dancing with boys. He shrugged his shoulders in surrender and looked at Cece closely for the first time that evening. "You look mighty pretty, Cece. You'll be fighting those boys off with a broom."

After supper, we heard a horn honk out front just as Cece and I were clearing the table. Cece checked her reflection in the hall mirror and was out the door.

Once I'd scraped all the plates and cleared everything from the table, I decided to stay in the kitchen while Aunt Bird did the dishes. I felt I'd be safer if I remained close to her.

"Aunt Bird, what does confidential mean?" I asked as I dried a plate.

"Well, let's break this word apart, Allie. What's the root word?"

"Confidence, I think."

"Excellent! To have confidence means to feel certain about something or to be sure of one's self," Aunt Bird explained. "Confidential is an adjective derived from the root word confidence, which can also mean 'a secret which one confides.' Do you understand?" Aunt Bird looked at me.

"So, I guess confidential means secretive?" I asked.

"That's exactly what it means." This answer came from Diddy, who was standing in the hallway.

Uh oh, I thought. I'd sealed my own doom with a vocabulary lesson.

"Come on back to the sun porch, Allie. You and I need to have a talk." Diddy headed down the hall toward our side porch as I hesitated.

By the time I made it to the porch, Diddy was sitting in his favorite rocker with a copy of the latest issue of *Life* in his lap. I slunk in and sat down on a metal porch chair. It was the most uncomfortable piece of furniture in the room but situated farthest away from Diddy.

"Well, Allison, what do you have to say for yourself?" Diddy looked me squarely in the face.

No matter what I said, I knew I was in deep doo doo, so I opted for the truth. I recounted my original trip to the newspaper and explained why I'd returned. I ended with my "just wanting to make sure you were okay" excuse.

Diddy listened intently. When I finished, he sat quietly; the only sound was the creak of his rocker and the chirp of crickets from our yard. "Allie, you never need to worry about my safety. I'm a grown man, and I've been taking care of myself for a long time. Now let's move on to the real crux of this matter. Being a snoop is as bad as being a gossip; neither quality will earn you friends. And don't start your argument about becoming a better journalist. A good journalist does his research, goes to the source, and asks direct questions. You'll find people are much more apt to talk to you if they feel you're being sincere with them, not spying on them. Do you understand, Allie?"

"Yes sir," I replied with my eyes glued to the floor.

"So, beginning tomorrow, you'll accompany your aunt to the library for the morning hours. I want you to do some research on mental retardation," Diddy began.

"But Diddy, I'm not retarded! I just did a stupid thing today, and I'm sorry."

Diddy smiled for the first time all night. "No, Allie, you've definitely got all the brain cells you need. That's not why I'm giving you this assignment."

"Why then?"

"Have you been by to visit Miss Gertie since Roscoe Ray's been in town?" Diddy began. I averted my eyes to a roly-poly crawling across the floor. "Miss Clara said she saw you and Josie peeking through Miss Gertie's shrubs and giggling. Is that true?"

Caught once again, I could do nothing but respond with another "yes sir."

"Allie, that poor young man cannot help his plight in life, and Miss Gertie, God bless her, has done everything in her power to see that Roscoe has the best care possible. Did you know that Roscoe is not even Miss Gertie's son?" I shook my head in disbelief. "He's her stepson by Miss Gertie's second husband. When the second Mr. Stansell passed away fifteen years ago, Miss Gertie took care of Roscoe night and day until the doctor said she was too old to shoulder the responsibility. It broke her heart to send Roscoe away, but she found the best institution available in Philadelphia. She's too old to drive up there, so she has him brought here each summer for a visit. You know, we humans can't understand why God blesses some of us on earth more than others, but I can assure you that the Lord loves Roscoe Ray as much as he loves me and you. Miss Gertie has earned herself a special place in heaven."

As Diddy continued, I picked up the roly-poly, opened the screen door, and set him on the steps outside. Diddy stopped long enough to ask. "Why'd you do that, Allie?"

"Well, if that roly-poly stays inside, somebody's bound to stomp on him," I explained.

"Don't you think Roscoe deserves the same respect you're giving one of God's smallest creatures?"

"Yes sir, I do." I was so ashamed of spying on poor Roscoe. "What kind of retardation does Roscoe have? How'd he get it?"

"It's called Down's Syndrome. You can research it when you go to the library with Aunt Bird tomorrow. Consider it your first journalistic exercise," he added.

"Now let me have a good look at that bump on your head." Diddy drew me towards him and pulled me into his lap. "My goodness, child, it's a good thing you're hardheaded like me. From now on, if you want to come by the newspaper when it's closed, just knock on the front door. You're getting too big to squeeze through the back doors."

I sat in his lap while we read a story about Russia's space program in *Life*. I didn't mention the file folder with the big red *CONFIDENTIAL* stamped on it; neither did he. I figured it was none of my business.

Chapter Seven

The next morning I was choking down a piece of toast slathered in grape jelly when Cece, clad in shorty pajamas and frilly hair net, made her entrance. She yawned, opened the refrigerator, and reached for the milk bottle.

Rubbing sleep from her eyes, she focused on me. "Why are you all dressed up? Why are you wearing shoes? Don't you know school doesn't start for another two months?"

"I'm going to the library with Aunt Bird today," I replied glumly. Cece gave me one of her "I told you so" looks.

"And I'm leaving in five minutes, so stop playing with that toast and start eating it," Aunt Bird interrupted. Getting me to eat breakfast at such a God-awful hour was a constant battle between Aunt Bird and me. She wouldn't allow me up from the table until I choked down something. So, I began to chew.

"How many mornings do I have to spend in the library?" I moaned as I saw summer days ticking away before my eyes.

"When you've completed your research and written a report to my satisfaction," Aunt Bird explained.

Since it was so early when we arrived, the library was empty. I headed straight to the reference section and pulled the "D" encyclopedia for both the *World Book* and the *Britannica* editions. If I got busy, I could have this research knocked out by lunch and not lose another precious day of summer. Aunt Bird squelched my intentions.

"Just a minute, Allie," she began. "Keep in mind that encyclopedias only skim the surface of information available in this library. You may use two encyclopedias, but I expect three other sources which offer more in-depth information. Use the *Reader's Guide* to locate those sources."

I was probably the only ten-year-old in Flint County who knew what the *Reader's Guide to Periodicals* was, much less how to use it. I had learned about it simply from the lack of anything better to do. Every day after school, Cece and I walked up the street from the elementary school to the high school where we waited for Aunt Bird to finish her last class. As she explained the details of research to her sixth period, I received an early lesson on how to use the *Reader's Guide* and the card catalogue.

I also mastered the art of creating a bibliography during Lester Duncan's after-school sessions. Lester seemed to have a standing detention date with Aunt Bird because he was always sleeping in class. I guess he was tired because he worked a part-time shift at the mill in the evenings.

He was a crackerjack mechanic and could not only repair mill equipment but could also keep any automobile running. Town boys kept Lester busy on the weekend with repairs to their hotrods. Although he was the best grease monkey in the county, Lester was a miserable English student.

Once I asked Aunt Bird why Lester didn't quit school and open a mechanic shop. Aunt Bird sighed, "Because he wants to better himself, Allie. He wants to join the Air Force and become an airplane mechanic, but that requires a high school diploma." While most teachers made their detention inmates sit quietly for thirty minutes, Aunt Bird used her sessions for remedial practice.

I found some sources in the *Reader's Guide* and settled in for several hours of study. I discovered that Down's Syndrome was a birth defect named after the doctor who discovered it. Although some people only display a few of the symptoms, poor Roscoe Ray seemed to carry almost all of them, based on what Josie and I had observed from behind Miss Gertie's shrubs. I couldn't be certain that he had an enlarged tongue because I'd never talked to him, and I didn't know if he had an excessive space between his big toe and his second toe because I'd never seen him barefooted. All the other symptoms fit, and there was no doubt that Roscoe Ray had a full-fledged case of Down's Syndrome.

As I studied a medical reference book, I noticed a group of five and six-year-olds gathering around the children's book section. Mrs. Meriweather, the fulltime librarian, was corralling the children into a circle on the floor for story time. She'd chosen "Jack and the Beanstalk" and explained the story was about a giant. A little redheaded girl exclaimed, "I don't like monsters!"

"Don't worry, my dear," Mrs. Meriweather reassured her. "This is just a story. There are no monsters in real life."

I snickered under my breath and thought to myself that Mrs. Meriweather had not introduced the children to the library's very own in-house monster. Her name was Miss Benton, and she was without a doubt, the meanest creature I knew.

She lived in a glass office situated smack dab in the middle of the library. High school students referred to her office as "the cage." Because she'd suffered from polio as a child, she wore heavy braces on her legs and walked with metal crutches. On rare occasions when she emerged from the cage, everyone in the library would look up. Pulling herself up from her leather desk chair, snapping her heavy metal braces into place, and fumbling with her crutches created a noisy ordeal that never failed to interrupt the quiet of the library. Every eye would follow her excruciatingly slow journey as she hobbled down the aisle while the rubber tips of her crutches made a "pink, pink" sound on the hardwood floor with each agonizingly deliberate step she took. She had a sharp, cackling voice she used to bark commands from her cage to other librarians or student aides.

Miss Benton believed a library should maintain absolute silence. She expected every student to have their nose stuck so far down in a book that the voice of God himself couldn't rouse them.

Luckily, for me and the little redheaded girl who hated monsters, the glass cage was empty on this day. I guess Miss Benton had sense enough to take summers off. I went back to studying another kind of monster. I needed only two more references to satisfy Aunt Bird's requirements, so I made my way back to the *Reader's Guide*. As I was thumbing through one of the larger guides, I heard that unmistakable "pink pinking" across the hardwood floor. It was Miss Benton headed directly towards the *Reader's Guide* section. I became so flustered that I dropped the heavy reference guide. The enormous book created a resounding thud that drew the children's attention away from "Jack and the Beanstalk." As I leaned down to retrieve it, I found myself eye level with the protective rubber caps of Miss Benton's crutches and saw the glint of her leg braces in the artificial light. There was nowhere for me to escape; my only hope was to stand and fight like a man (or girl, in my case.)

"Young lady," she began in that witch-like tone, "do you not realize there is a rule of silence in this library?"

"Yes ma'am, I accidentally dropped this book," I stammered as I stood up. This was the first time I'd been so close to the un-caged fiend. Miss Benton wasn't much taller than me. She was bent and shriveled in body, but she had a look of wrath in her eyes.

"There's no excuse for making any kind of noise in this library," she snapped. "You're Miss Sinclair's niece, aren't you?" Before I could answer, she continued, "What are you doing in here on this pretty summer day? You are far too old to participate in the children's reading hour. Speak up, child!"

"Uh, I'm uh doing some research on Down's Syndrome." My hands and forehead began to perspire, and my glasses slid down my sweaty nose.

"Down's Syndrome? Humph—what does a child your age need to know about Down's Syndrome?"

"Well, uh, my daddy wanted me to do the research," I mumbled as I readjusted my glasses.

"Nonsense! Don't lie to me, young lady!" She shook a gnarled finger at my face as she leaned on her crutches.

"No ma'am, I'm not lying. Really, just ask my aunt!" Seeing Aunt Bird approaching us, I exhaled for the first time since Miss Benton had started her interrogation.

"Well, good morning, Miss Benton! I thought you were taking the week off. Isn't your sister visiting from Birmingham?" Seemingly unafraid with a smile on her face, Aunt Bird used her sweetest Sunday school voice as she talked to the mean, old hag.

"My sister went back to Birmingham early," Miss Benton said in a dismissive tone. I didn't blame the old bat's sister, I thought to myself. "Miss Sinclair, your niece is creating commotion in my library, and I shall not have it!"

Before I could plead my case, Aunt Bird intervened. "I'm so sorry. Allison has been doing some research. It's my fault. I guess she's a little young to be using the *Reader's Guide* on her own, but you've always told me it's the best source for locating the most valuable information. Now let me help you to your office; that new book on the Impressionists came in our delivery today. I was saving it for you to review since you're the art expert." Aunt Bird delivered this in a soothing tone as she guided Miss Benton to her cage.

I shrank back toward my table in the corner of the library. I was in reverent awe of how Aunt Bird had totally commanded the situation without smacking that hateful old biddy across the face. Aunt Bird always seemed to have the charm to remedy any situation. She was definitely my hero that morning.

On the way home for lunch, I asked Aunt Bird why Miss Benton was so evil.

"She's not evil, Allie, just unhappy," Aunt Bird began.

"I've never heard her utter a single pleasant word to anybody. No wonder they all call her the 'cage creature,'" I added.

"Allie, I don't want to hear you call Miss Benton that. It's cruel and disrespectful," Aunt Bird lectured.

"I don't see why I have to be respectful to her when every word she spits out of her mouth is ugly!"

"First of all, she's an old woman, and you should always respect your elders. Secondly, because of her handicap, she could stay home and wallow in self-pity, but instead, she plugs along doing the best she can."

"Well, the library would be a much more pleasant place if she stayed home," I mumbled under my breath.

"Shame on you, Allie! Instead of looking at Miss Benton through your eyes, try seeing her as the Lord sees her."

"How do you think the Lord sees her?"

"Probably the way she was when I first knew her. When your mama and I were in high school, Miss Benton was the art teacher."

"Could she walk then?"

"No, but she was more mobile. She hadn't developed the crippling arthritis she has now. She was an amazing artist and a gifted teacher. She took a liking to your mama; she saw true potential in her talent. She was instrumental in getting your mama into the University of Georgia. Miss Benton quietly submitted some of your mama's watercolor prints to the university's school of art and wrote several letters to professors in the art department. That's how your mama received a scholarship." I'd seen some of my mama's watercolors. Cece often pulled them out of a cedar chest in our attic to study them before she painted something.

"She sounds like she was a sweet person then. What happened?"

"Well, she developed rheumatoid arthritis. Eventually, Miss Benton couldn't even hold a paintbrush in her hand anymore, so the school created a job for her in the library. When your mama graduated, she came back to Flintville and was hired as the school's art teacher. She and Miss Benton were dear friends. They went to art shows in Atlanta and discussed books about art. I think Miss Benton's heart broke when your mama died. She withdrew more and more and became bitter. First she'd lost her own ability to paint and then she lost the one kindred spirit who shared her love for beauty." Aunt Bird wiped a tear from her eye as she pulled into our driveway. "I think the Lord sees Miss Benton as she was when she was a whole person. That's the way I try to see her."

Later, I asked Cece about Mama's early watercolors. "Can I have a couple of them?" I asked.

"I guess so," Cece replied. "There are several she did in high school; I don't need them all. Do you want to study some of them?"

"Not really, but I know somebody who would."

The next day I slid a large manila envelope with three of Mama's prettiest water colors under Miss Benton's cage door. Maybe they would remind her of a better time in her life, and maybe that would help me see Miss Benton the way God saw her.

Chapter Eight

After two more mornings of library research and painstakingly writing the report in ink, skipping every other line as Aunt Bird required, my work was complete. Aunt Bird appeared satisfied with the content although she pointed out two misspelled words and something she called a dangling participle.

"Well, Allie, we might make a writer out of you after all!" she smiled. "Now run along and get some sunshine while there's still some left."

Sunday evening when I returned from training union, I rushed to my room to change into my pajamas so I wouldn't miss any of Ed Sullivan. Lying on my bed was my report; its cover page had a note scrawled in Diddy's handwriting:

> *Allie, I am impressed with your thorough research because investigation is the backbone of good reporting. I am even more impressed with your ability to convert the scientific information into a humane understanding of Roscoe Ray's condition. With a few more years of training, I'm convinced you will make a formidable investigative reporter. –Diddy-*

Although I had to look up *formidable* in the dictionary, I knew Diddy had paid me a compliment.

Monday morning Josie was standing at our kitchen door before I'd even finished breakfast. We packed sack lunches so we could bike all the way to Weaver Park and back.

As I made a peanut butter and jelly sandwich, I filled Josie in on the events of last week. She was most interested in Diddy's knowledge of our spying on Roscoe Ray.

Josie made a whistling sound between the small gap in her two front teeth, a talent I still hadn't achieved. "Oh no," she sighed. "I hope your daddy doesn't tell my folks!"

"Aww, he's forgotten all about it by now. Besides, unless Diddy runs into your mama at the bank, they rarely see each other since we don't go to church together." Josie's family belonged to the Methodist church, and her daddy's dry goods store was out the Atlanta Highway instead of in town.

Josie sighed. "I hope you're right. I can't afford to get in any trouble now."

"Why now? I thought there was no time we could afford getting in trouble!"

"My folks told me if I kept a good report card next year and behaved myself, they'd consider buying me a horse of my own and keeping it at my uncle's stable in LaGrange."

Although Josie and I were best friends who did almost everything together, I did not share her infatuation with horses. They were such big four-legged creatures, and I was such a squatty two-legged one. Josie, on the other hand, had long, skinny legs and arms. When she climbed upon her mount, she looked like an equestrian goddess.

By Thursday, Josie and I had added almost fifty miles to our odometers. On Friday, we planned to ride all the way to Crystal Hill and back until I awakened to the sound of thunder. It stormed so hard all morning that Cece and I had to pull every window almost shut to keep rain from blowing in. By mid-afternoon the rain stopped and the sun peeked through the clouds, but the house was hot and sticky. We retreated to the side porch, the coolest place we could find. I played a solitary game of *Pickup Stix* while Cece worked with charcoal in her sketchbook.

As I attempted to withdraw the last yellow stick from a pile of blue and red ones, the telephone rang and shattered my concentration. "I'll get it," Cece said as she covered her drawing with a thin sheet of protective paper.

A minute later Cece returned to the porch. "It was Miz Gertie. She needs you up at her house."

I moaned. "It's probably Zsa Zsa. I hope she's not in the storm drain again."

Named after Zsa Zsa Gabor, Miz Gertie's white, fluffy cat was constantly getting stuck in places she didn't belong. As I rode my bicycle up Miz Gertie's drive, I wasn't looking forward to any rescue efforts.

Miz Gertie met me at her front door with Zsa Zsa circling her feet. "Oh good, Allie. Thanks so much for coming. I have just enough time to get to the bank before it closes. Roscoe Ray is visiting, and he's on the back patio. He's been cooped up inside all day, and I just hate to make him get in the car now that the sun is finally out. Could you keep him company for about thirty minutes?"

Getting to study a live specimen after all that research was a dream come true. "Sure, Miz Gertie. I've been cooped up all day, too, so I don't mind at all."

She led me through the house to the sliding glass door off of her den. Roscoe Ray was sitting in a lawn chair peering through a View Master. Instead of a Zorro costume, he was clad in a plaid shirt and tan bermudas. I thought I'd get to study his big toe and second toe because he was wearing sandals, but then I noticed he had on socks. He must have picked that habit up from the people at his school in Pennsylvania since Yankees were the only fools who wore socks with sandals.

"Roscoe, this is Allie." Miz Gertie gently pulled the View Master away from his eyes. "Can you say hello?"

He peered at me through glasses so thick that they magnified his eyes. "Hi Allie," he said in a childlike voice. Although he spoke like a child, he looked like a young man, very much like the senior boys in Aunt Bird's class.

I stopped staring long enough to answer. "Hi, what're you looking at?" I pointed to the View Master and sat down beside him.

"Now that you're acquainted, I'll be on my way," Miz Gertie chirped. "Allie, there's *7-Up* in the refrigerator. You just help yourself, now. I'll be back shortly." I heard her head out to the carport with her keys.

"You want a *7-Up*, Roscoe?" He'd not taken his eyes off me since I had first spoken to him.

"You've got glasses like me!" He pointed from my face to his.

"Yeah, I guess I do," I answered as I pushed my own glasses, with lenses not half as thick, back up on my nose. "Dr. Johnston says I have astigmatism."

Roscoe Ray looked confused. "A stick of what?"

I giggled. "It means when I try to read words, they all run together. My glasses help my eyes spread the words apart so I can read. What's wrong with your eyes?"

"I don't know, but my glasses don't help me read any better. I can read *Dick and Jane* stories, but I don't like them anymore. They're for babies, and I'm *not* a baby."

"Well, what do you like to read, then?" I queried.

"Mostly my comic books. I like Batman and Superman best of all! But they're too hard to read. Miss Betsy at my school reads them to us all the time, and she knows all the voices, too. Mama Gertie can't make the voices. Can you make the voices?" He looked up with a pleading expression.

"I could try. Why don't you go pick out your favorite comic book while I get us a drink." By the time I'd opened two bottles of *7-Up* and returned to the patio, Roscoe Ray had not only retrieved his favorite Batman comic but had also donned his Batman mask.

Obviously, I was pretty good at the voices because Roscoe Ray listened so intently we didn't hear Miz Gertie drive up. I was finishing the last page of *Batman and the Case of the Joker's Crime Circus* when she slid open the door and peeked out. "How are you two?"

Roscoe Ray hopped up out of his chair. "Mama Gertie! She can read the parts as good as Miss Betsy. I like Allie. Can she live with us until I go back to school?"

Miz Gertie winked at me. "Well, we don't have room for her to stay here, but perhaps we can persuade her to visit on occasion. What do you say, Allie?"

How could I say no? Roscoe Ray had no friends in Flintville, especially none who'd researched his condition like I had. Seeing Roscoe Ray peer through his Batman mask with a hopeful smile on his face, I was convinced. "Sure, Miz Gertie. I can come on days you need to run errands."

"Yeah, and next time, you can read Superman!" Roscoe Ray chimed in with excitement. "I've got a real Superman cape and everything!"

Miz Gertie walked me to the front door. "Allie, thank you so much. Roscoe Ray has been lonesome here without his friends from school. He's a good, sweet boy, but he needs the companionship of someone besides an old lady." She tried to slip a dollar into my hand. "Will that be enough of a sitting fee?"

For a fleeting moment, I considered pocketing the dollar. It was rare that I had folding money. But I thought of something Diddy had said and reconsidered. "Oh no, Miss Gertie. I can't take your money. A *7-Up* is payment enough. Call me next week when you need to go out, and I'll visit Roscoe Ray again."

After being with Roscoe Ray for just an hour, I now understood what Diddy meant when he said Miz Gertie was earning herself a special place in heaven. I figured Roscoe Ray was the perfect opportunity for me to work on my own salvation.

Chapter Nine

By the middle of June, I'd settled into a summer routine. Josie and I rode our bicycles every morning while the air was still cool. If we could get a ride with Cece and some of her friends, we'd go to Parker's Pool for the afternoon. If not, we'd go to Potato Creek, a tributary of the Flint River that flowed through the wooded area behind Josie's subdivision.

In the shade of oaks, Josie and I waded into the cool water and squished our toes in the white clay bottom. Since Georgia is renowned for red clay, we considered this watering spot with its unique white clay bottom a real find. We'd sit for hours on the edge of the creek and design little clay pots and clay animals.

On Friday afternoons, Roscoe Ray and I read every Superman and Batman comic book ever published while Miz Gertie ran her errands. Sometimes Josie would tag along. We discovered that Roscoe Ray, who couldn't read anything past a primary reader, had a knack for dressing like the comic book character of the week. Once he came to the door clad from head to toe in an authentic-looking Robin costume. He even had a Clark Kent wardrobe, and when I'd read the part where Clark would jump in a phone both, Roscoe Ray would hop up, throw off his glasses, and pull off his jacket to reveal his Superman shirt.

Since Josie's mama had signed her up for weekly horseback riding lessons, I was left to my own diversions on Tuesday afternoons. I decided to take Diddy up on his offer and visit him when his office was closed. Each Tuesday after lunch, I'd make the short walk into town. Diddy began leaving the front door unlocked for me even though there was a "Closed" sign on the door.

On Tuesdays, Diddy had lunch with his Kiwanis Club at the Hotel Flintville, the biggest building in town. Although it housed only a handful of tenants, the hotel managed wedding receptions in its large banquet hall and catered to the local organizations that met during the lunch hour.

The Andersons, who ran the hotel, offered a buffet luncheon renowned throughout the county. Miz Anderson made the best potato salad in all of Middle Georgia while Mr. Anderson was known for his chocolate meringue pies. They had a fat white English bulldog named Miss Georgia, who lay around on the cool marble floor of the hotel lobby. Supposedly, she was a direct descendant of Uga, the mascot for the University of Georgia, and she was the Andersons' pride and joy.

I'd arrive at the newspaper on Tuesday afternoons and meet Diddy just as he was returning from his Kiwanis meeting.

By the time I reached the newspaper one Tuesday, a single light burned from Diddy's office; he'd already returned. I found Diddy sitting in his chair with one pants leg rolled up above his knee. He was drawing insulin from a bottle.

"Whaddya doing, Diddy? I thought you took your shot in the mornings before breakfast." Many early mornings when I'd stumble by his bedroom, I'd see Diddy seated on the edge of his bed giving himself his injection.

"Hi, Allie. I did take my insulin this morning, but I needed a little extra today." He swabbed his upper thigh with an alcohol soaked cotton ball.

"Why?" I quizzed. I was curious about Diddy's disease.

"If I eat too much, my body sometimes requires an extra dose," he explained as he expertly jabbed himself and emptied the syringe. "Today, Mr. Anderson had a fresh batch of lemon meringue pies. I can resist his chocolate, but lemon meringue is my favorite. It was almost as good as my mama used to make." He rolled down his pants leg.

"I never had Mommie's lemon meringue pie, but I do remember her tea cakes. I miss those at family reunions."

"So do I, and I miss her, too," Diddy replied. He replaced the syringe and insulin bottle in the small, monogrammed leather case, which he always carried in his coat pocket. It was odd to hear my daddy talk about his mother; I guess I couldn't imagine him as a little boy.

"Why does eating too much make you have to take more insulin?"

Diddy grinned. "Aren't you the curious one! There's an organ in our bodies called the pancreas. It produces insulin, which is needed to help digest our foods properly. My pancreas doesn't produce insulin, so I have to help it along by injecting some into my bloodstream."

"What if you didn't take your insulin shots each day?"

"I could become very sick and would eventually die." Diddy always gave me a truthful explanation. "But you needn't worry; I carry insulin with me wherever I go. Now, it's time for me to work on my column." He turned toward his Underwood.

I spent the next two hours typing on Miss Opal's typewriter in the outer office. Diddy had taught me months ago where to keep my fingers on the keyboard, and I'd almost mastered typing without looking down at the keys. Around 4:15, I was rolling a tenth sheet of yellow typing paper into the typewriter when Diddy turned off his office light and pulled his door shut. He never left the office this early unless he had a story to cover. I thought maybe there was a trial going on at the courthouse. "Are you going up the street?" I asked.

"No, I need to make a trip out to Milltown. I thought we might stop by and visit Aunt Rosebud while we're out there. Are you interested?"

Of course I was. Aunt Rosebud was Diddy's mother's sister and one of the best cooks I knew. Her kitchen always smelled of something freshly baked, and she always offered me a sample.

The drive out to Milltown was a short one. Two miles out the Atlanta Highway, we came to a traffic light. There were mill villages to the right and to the left. Instead of turning left and heading toward Aunt Rosebud's, Diddy took a right down a street I'd never traveled.

"Where are we going?"

"I have an appointment with someone who lives in this area," Diddy turned down another street named East Mill. I gazed out at row upon row of houses. These mill houses didn't look like the one where Aunt Rosebud lived. These were smaller and dingier; in almost every front yard there were three or four children in all forms of play. Diddy pulled up to the curb at one house where a little redheaded girl was playing a game of jacks on the sidewalk. Diddy opened his door, so I started to get out on my side. "No, Allie, you need to stay in the car. I'll just be a little while." Diddy nodded and smiled at the little girl and walked across the yard to the front door.

Even though I had my window rolled down, the car was stifling. I opened the door in hopes of getting more of a breeze. I watched the redheaded girl as she bounced the ball and did her "threesies." She didn't miss a single jack. "You wanna play?" The girl looked up at me and smiled.

I figured Diddy wouldn't mind if I stayed on the sidewalk right by his car especially since I was suffocating. "Sure," I replied.

She beat me four times in a row before she asked me my name. "Allie Sinclair. What's yours?"

"Essie Dunn. Do you live around here? I've never seen you on Mill Street before."

"Uh, no. I live in town," I replied.

Essie eyed me suspiciously. "Oh," was all she answered. She threw the jacks again and bounced the little rubber ball.

I tried again. "So, do you have any brothers or sisters?"

Her eyes concentrated on the jacks as she bounced the ball for her twosies. "Yeah, I have a big sister."

"I have an older sister, too, She'll be a freshman in high school this year. She's so boring; all she does is talk about boys and curl her hair," I added in hopes that Essie would commiserate with me. When she didn't, I continued. "So, is your sister in high school?"

"No," Essie replied without missing a bounce of the ball. "She quit last year to work at the mill."

I'd never known anyone who quit high school, and I was intrigued. "You mean your mama and daddy let her quit school?"

"We ain't got no daddy. He died last year, and Mama needed my sister to go to work. She wants to go back to school this year. Mama says the only way she can do that is if she gets a job on the 4:00 to midnight shift. Then she can work and go to school." I tried to imagine how someone worked eight hours, got home after midnight, and then came to school at 8:00 A.M. When did they do their homework?

"Macy's always messing with her hair, too," Essie interrupted my thoughts, and I realized that she was talking about her sister. "She gets so much lint in it at the mill that she thinks she needs to wash it in the kitchen sink every day."

"The kitchen sink?" I giggled. "My Aunt Bird would kill me or Cece if we washed our hair in her kitchen sink. She has a phobia about hair getting on food. We have to take care of that kind of stuff in the bathroom, and Cece's in there so much that Diddy and I barely get a chance for ourselves!"

"Well, we only get five minutes a piece in the morning, or Mr. Tate gets mad," Essie explained.

"Who's Mr. Tate? The water man?"

Essie looked at me as though I had no brain. "No, stupid! He and his family live on the other side of our house. We take turns using the bathroom. Our time is from 6:00 until 6:30 in the mornings and 6:00 until 6:30 in the evenings for baths and things. If there's an emergency, Mama says always knock before grabbing the doorknob. One time I ate too many green plums and couldn't get in the bathroom because Mrs. Johnson was taking a shower."

"What did you do? Did you go behind a bush or something?"

"I ran next door to the Henry's house. They were both at work, but their son let me in. It was close, though! Anyway, Macy curls her hair in front of a mirror in our bedroom. She sticks those big rollers in her head and then climbs in bed with me. One night I rolled over and scratched my nose on one of those prickly curlers."

"Yeah, Cece and I share a bedroom, too, but we have two beds in there. I couldn't stand having to sleep with her with all that sticky stuff she puts in her hair," I moaned.

Essie looked at me as though I came from another planet. "Well, we have two beds in our bedroom, too. That's where Mama sleeps. Don't you have another bed in the bedroom for your mama and daddy?"

"Uh, no. My daddy has his own bedroom," I tried to explain. How could I possibly admit that we had a third bedroom for Aunt Bird?

Before I had time to tackle that problem, Diddy was standing over us. "Allie, I thought I told you to stay in the car," he peered down at where we sat on the sidewalk.

"It was really hot, and Essie asked if I wanted to play jacks."

"That was nice of Essie," Diddy smiled at my new friend. "It's time for us to go, Allie."

Diddy pulled a nickel from his pocket and handed it to Essie. "Why don't you treat yourself to an ice cream at Rome's Drugstore down the street? Make certain you tell your mama where you're going." He climbed into the car.

Essie grinned and took off skipping toward the house. I wasn't even jealous that Diddy didn't offer me a nickel. At least I didn't have to share my bathroom with our neighbors.

We stopped by Aunt Rosebud's, but she'd already left for her supper club. As we made our way back into town, I asked, "Diddy, does Aunt Rosebud share her bathroom with anyone?"

"Yes, with her son Elmo and his wife." Elmo and Estelle had lived with Aunt Rosebud for as long as I could remember. "Why do you ask?" Diddy seemed puzzled.

"Essie says she has to share her bathroom with the Tate family. And she only has one bedroom for her entire family! That's weird, isn't it?"

"When Aunt Bird and I were children, the first mill house we lived in was just like Essie's house. We had one bathroom to share with the Stokes. Mr. Stokes had a stop watch and would start beating on the door if we stayed in the bathroom over ten minutes."

My eyes grew wide. "Did you ever run over your time?"

"I didn't, but your Aunt Bird did on many occasions. So, she started bartering for some of my bathroom time. I gladly sold it to her for a penny a minute until Mommie got a good look behind my ears one morning on the way to church. We both got a whipping, and Aunt Bird learned to manage her bathroom time more economically after that! Later on, we were able to afford a one family dwelling. Luckily, by the time your Aunt Bird was a teenager, she only had to share the bathroom with Sinclairs!"

I giggled. "Diddy, why do town folk call people like Essie's sister a 'lint head'? I think it's a hurtful term," I added when Diddy gave me a stern look.

"It is a hurtful term. Allie, if it weren't for the mill and its workers, we wouldn't have a town at all. Those mill people spend their hard-earned money in our town. There's no shame to having lint in your hair, dirt on your boots, or ink on your fingers as long as you're doing honest work. The Lord loves us each the same no matter what kind of work we do. Now, who have you heard using the term 'lint head'?"

"Josie said she heard her mama say Miz Norwood called a mill worker a 'lint head' when she came in her dress shop," I admitted.

"I wouldn't pay attention to idle gossip especially if you still aspire to be a reporter."

"Yes sir," I mumbled. I felt a little guilty for not being completely honest. I myself had heard Sheriff Brady say "lint head" in Diddy's office that afternoon when I was standing atop the drink box, but I felt it best I didn't remind Diddy of any already forgiven transgressions.

I suddenly remembered the confidential file folder Sheriff Brady handed Diddy that fateful day. Meeting Essie Dunn must have triggered my memory. A vision came flooding back to me as though I was still teetering on the drink box and peering into Diddy's office. Scrawled in pencil above the red "Confidential" on the folder was the name "Macy Dunn."

That night as I sat on my bed and watched Cece entwine sections of her sun-bleached locks onto sponge rollers, I told her about my visit with Essie. She was most fascinated with the "community" bathroom. "Eww, gross!" she exclaimed. "Can you imagine having to share a bathroom with Miss Clara and Ned? I bet he'd leave pubes all over the bathtub!"

I pushed my glasses back up on my nose and raised my eyebrows. "What are pubes?"

Cece giggled. "You know, pubic hair—down there." She pointed to the little patch I could see beneath her white shorty pajama bottoms. I dreaded the day when I'd have hair sprout in such places, but Cece didn't seem to mind it.

"That's disgusting, Cece! Maybe I won't get any hair in those places if I'm lucky." I placed my glasses on the nightstand between our beds.

Cece turned on the nightstand's lamp and opened her new copy of *Ingenue Magazine*. "Oh, you will. You can't be a tomboy forever."

I hadn't told her about Essie's older sister or about the mysterious file folder that carried her name.

"Cece, do you know Macy Dunn?" I asked nonchalantly.

"Yeah, she dated Margaret's cousin Bud last year, but then Macy quit school last spring. Margaret said Bud's parents didn't want him dating a dropout, so they broke up. Why? Is she Essie's sister? Is that who Diddy went to interview?" Cece seemed intrigued.

I didn't reveal too much because I knew Diddy would frown upon it. "Uh, yeah, she's the one. She had to quit school because her daddy died, and her mother needed her to go to work." I feigned a yawn to avoid any more questions.

"That's sad," Cece commented. "You know, we're fortunate to have Diddy and Aunt Bird." Cece switched off the lamp between us. "Nighty-night, baby brat."

I pretended to be asleep, but I couldn't stop wondering about Macy Dunn. I hoped she wasn't in any kind of trouble.

Chapter Ten

Diddy and Aunt Bird decided to throw a cookout on the Fourth of July. By mid-afternoon, we had a real celebration underway. Miz Gertie brought a case of *Seven-Up,* and Uncle Hoyt iced it down in a metal tub. Cece patted out hamburgers as Diddy heated up the grill. Aunt Bird sliced peaches for her homemade ice cream while I rummaged around in the attic for decorations. By the time Josie and her folks arrived with potato salad and baked beans, there were hot dogs and hamburgers sizzling on the grill. I'd found three dusty Uncle Sam top hats and a full box of sparklers in the attic.

By late afternoon everyone was stuffed. Diddy, Uncle Hoyt, and Mr. McClendon took turns cranking the ice cream churn while the ladies cleaned up. Cece disappeared; I figured she'd escaped to our bedroom to read or draw. Margaret was out of town, so Cece probably felt a little left out. Although Roscoe Ray was closer to her age, he was quite content with the company of Josie and me.

When the three of us realized the ice cream wasn't ready, we asked permission to take a bike ride. Roscoe Ray had asthma and couldn't ride his bike in the heat of the day. Since the sun was low in the sky and the day had cooled, Miz Gertie allowed him to go. We hopped on our bikes and made our way down Avalon Road to Greenwood. "Whaddya think, Allie? Should we show Roscoe Ray our secret place?" Josie grinned slyly.

"Why not?" I agreed. "Follow us, Roscoe." I turned down Cherokee Road toward Potato Creek. We laid our bikes against the curb and walked the short distance through the brush.

Josie, who was barefoot like I was, slid down the bank to the cool water, but Roscoe hesitated. "Wait a minute, Roscoe, you need to take off your shoes." I helped him unbuckle his sandals. He seemed a little afraid, so I held his hand and together we waded in towards Josie until the water touched our knees. "Squish your toes, Roscoe. Doesn't it feel good?"

Roscoe grinned from ear to ear. "This is the first time I've ever been swimming! Wait 'til I tell my buddies at school. They won't believe it." He'd be leaving the following Saturday, and I found myself feeling a little sad.

The sun fell quickly, and I realized Miz Gertie would be worried if we didn't hurry. We helped Roscoe Ray dry his feet and replace his socks and sandals. In all the rush, I'd forgotten to see if Roscoe had an excessive space between his big toe and second toe. Somehow, examining his toes no longer seemed important to me.

We arrived in our backyard just as Aunt Bird scooped the first spoon of ice cream from the churn. She'd also baked a batch of her mama's famous teacakes. They were a taste of heaven.

As I licked the last drop of ice cream from my plastic spoon, I heard firecrackers popping in the distance. "Oh, I forgot all about the sparklers!" I darted inside to retrieve them and a book of matches. As Josie, Roscoe, and I each held one in our hands, Cece lit them for us. We stood in our dark front yard waving the sparkling candles in the night.

As we returned to the porch for a second sparkler, Sheriff Brady pulled up to the curb. Dressed in his uniform, the sheriff emerged from his car and ambled across our front lawn. "Well, well, well! I thought I'd run across a UFO for a minute!" he joked. Since *Life Magazine* had published a story about unidentified flying objects a few months earlier, the sheriff received several calls a week from Flintville citizens claiming to have spotted alien aircraft.

"Oh no, Sheriff. It's just our fourth of July sparklers," I explained.

"Is your daddy home?"

"Yessir, he's out back," Cece walked down the front steps. "I'll take you to him."

As Sheriff Brady followed Cece to the backyard, I blew out my sparkler. "Come on, Josie. Let's see what's going on." Roscoe Ray wasn't interested, so we left him sitting on the front steps with his sparkler. Josie and I crept through the house to the kitchen's back door. The kitchen was dark, and we kneeled down beside the screen door. We sat still as church mice.

We could hear the chatter of the adults sitting at the picnic table under the one big oak tree in our backyard. Aunt Bird offered the sheriff some ice cream, but he declined. Diddy excused himself from the group and walked toward the back steps to talk with Sheriff Brady. Josie and I held our breath as Diddy sat down on the steps, his back just inches from the screen door. Sheriff Brady faced him.

"There's been a drowning down at the river," the sheriff began. This didn't shock us much because at least once a year, somebody drowned on Flint River.

Diddy scratched the top of his head. "When will they ever learn that the river can be dangerous? Who was it this time? A drunken boy or an amateur canoeist?"

I could see Sheriff Brady shake his head. "Neither," he replied. "This time it's a girl."

"A girl?" Diddy said in disbelief. "What was a girl doing down at the river?" I saw him shaking his head in dismay.

"I don't know, but some fishermen found her body washed up near Spruell Bluff. Looks like she'd been dead for a while, but I won't know for sure until the doc takes a look."

"Is she a local?" Diddy's tone had converted to that of a reporter.

The sheriff studied the river mud on his boots. He cleared his throat as Diddy, Josie, and I waited for an answer. "It's that Dunn girl. Macy Dunn."

I gasped loud enough for everyone to hear.

"Allie, is that you? Come out here, right now!" Diddy ordered.

I pushed open the screen door. "Diddy, is it Essie's sister? Is it, Diddy?" My voice choked as I held back tears. Josie just stood there staring at me with her mouth agape.

"I'm afraid so, Allie," Diddy answered. He didn't even fuss at me for my eavesdropping. Instead he called to my aunt. "Bird, I'm going out with the sheriff for a while." He patted me on my head, and walked around the house with Sheriff Brady.

"It's time Roscoe and I went home anyway." Miz Gertie hooked her arm into Roscoe Ray's and steered him in the direction of their house. Still in shock from the sheriff's news, I stood in a daze while the McClendons loaded up their car with their belongings. I barely said goodbye to Josie. I knew if I tried to explain, I'd burst into tears.

I sat on the back porch steps as Uncle Hoyt helped Aunt Bird clear the picnic table. Climbing the steps to the kitchen, Uncle Hoyt gazed down at me. "Allie, are you okay?"

"I suspect between all those carbonated soft drinks and sweets, she's nursing a stomachache," Aunt Bird kidded as she felt my forehead. It dawned on me that the adults hadn't heard the sheriff's sickening news. My eyes welled with tears as a shiver ran over me. "Honey, are you okay? You aren't chilled, are you?" Aunt Bird squatted beside me.

"Uh, no ma'am. A cat just ran over my grave. I'm tired; I guess I'll go on to bed." Diddy could be the bearer of bad news.

Cece was sitting on her bed thumbing through an art book when I skulked into our room. "What's up, baby brat? Did you run out of sparklers? What did the sheriff want with Diddy?"

"Somebody drowned. Somebody I know." By the time these words spilled from my lips, tears began to spill, too.

Cece looked stunned. In an instant she engulfed me in her arms. "It's okay, Allie. It's going to be all right." Her sweet, soothing voice and comforting hug inspired my tears to turn into sobs. I buried my face in her shoulder and wailed. She rocked and patted me until my shaking subsided and my tears were spent.

"Do you feel better, Allie?" I'd never before seen Cece have such a look of genuine concern for me. She handed me a tissue.

I blew my nose and took a deep breath. "Yeah, I guess. It just doesn't seem right for a young person to die. I mean, when old people die, you know they're probably ready, but why does God want somebody like Macy?" I looked at Cece hoping she could explain this mystery to me.

"Aunt Bird says we don't always understand God's plan, but when we get to heaven, all our questions will be answered. Until then, we just have to trust He knows what He's doing." She rubbed my back. "Allie, who is Macy?"

"Macy Dunn. You know, the girl I told you about a few weeks ago. The one Diddy went to visit out in Milltown."

"Oh my God! How horrible! I wonder if Margaret's cousin knows. What in the world was she doing out at the river?"

"I guess she went swimming out there last night," I suggested.

Cece frowned. "No, Allie, nice girls don't go out to the river at night unless they want to earn a bad reputation. But I know Macy was a nice girl or Margaret would have told me different."

I was confused. "What do you mean by a 'nice girl'? Do you mean a girl who says 'yessir' and 'yes ma'am' and that kind of stuff?"

Cece managed a tiny grin. "Not exactly, Allie. You're a little young to understand. Nice girls are girls who act properly around boys. Bad girls do things they shouldn't do with boys."

"Like what?"

Cece hesitated. "Well, like bad girls will go out to the river and drink beer and smoke cigarettes with the boys. They might even let a boy go all the way with them."

"Go all the way where?"

"No, Allie. Go all the way means having sex." Cece rattled this explanation off in a hurry.

I knew what sex was. I'd read about it in a book Aunt Bird gave me when I'd asked her about the sanitary napkin delivery. "I don't think Macy was doing that kind of stuff, or Essie would have told me," I said. "She was in trouble, though, some kind of trouble."

Cece looked at me intently. "How do you know she was in trouble, Allie? Did her sister tell you something?"

I avoided looking at Cece eyes. "No, not exactly. I just know something was wrong."

Cece gently lifted my chin. "Look at me, Allie. I know when you're hiding something, so you might as well tell me."

I knew Cece would needle me until I told her the truth, and I was so worn out from the day's drama that I gave it all up. I told her everything I knew about Macy and Essie Dunn beginning with the mysterious file folder and how I came to know about it. By the time I finished, my voice was quivering, and my body was trembling again. "Please don't tell Diddy, please Cece," I begged.

Cece held me close. "Don't worry, honey. It's going to be okay. Diddy and the sheriff know what they're doing. If Macy was in trouble, they'll get to the bottom of it. I promise you. Now go to sleep. You'll feel better in the morning."

The funeral was scheduled for Wednesday at the Milltown Baptist Church. Although Diddy couldn't attend because it was a press day, he and I drove out to Milltown on Tuesday afternoon. Aunt Bird had baked one of her chocolate cakes for the Dunns. Essie was on the porch this time, but she wasn't playing jacks. She was dressed in a clean, pressed Sunday school dress, and her red pigtails were tied with yellow ribbons. Diddy went inside to pay his respects to her mama while Essie and I sat in the porch swing.

It was 98 degrees in the shade that day. Aunt Bird had insisted I wear my Sunday dress of starched blue organdy that made me itch. My feet were sweating in my Sunday socks and shoes. I felt miserable, but poor Essie looked even more miserable. Although Cece and I argued occasionally and her prissy ways irritated me, I couldn't imagine going through a single day without her. It put such a lump in my throat that all I could say was "I'm so sorry, Essie."

Essie sniffed and nodded. I think she'd used up all of her tears. Her eyes were red and swollen, her shoulders sagged, her entire face appeared limp. We sat on the swing in silence for a long while.

All of a sudden, Essie began to talk. "My sister was a good swimmer. I seen her swim the entire length of Parker's Pool a hundred times. They say the water in the river can have undercurrents and pull even a good swimmer under. She was all excited because she had the week off from the mill. Mama let her buy a new swimsuit, and she and her friends were going over to Callaway Gardens on Sunday. But she never came home on Saturday night. She's always home by midnight. She went to the movie with some of her friends, and then they went by the drugstore for an ice cream. Her friend Alice said Macy decided to walk home because it's just a block from our house. But she never came home. Mama called the sheriff Sunday morning, and he sent a patrol car looking for her. Some fishermen found her Sunday afternoon. They say she smelled like beer, but I don't believe that. She hated beer because that's what killed our daddy. She said she'd never take a drink in her life and that she'd tan me if she ever caught me drinking." Essie stopped as a tear dropped on her pretty yellow dress. "Well, I guess now I'll have the bed to myself."

She grew quiet again. She'd said her piece and didn't say another word. I couldn't think of anything to say to make her feel better, so I just held her hand and rocked in the swing with her.

The headline of the **Star** read "River Claims One of Flintville's Own." According to Diddy's article, Macy's body had washed ashore about two miles south of Riverview Estates. Riverview Estates was situated atop Spruell Bluff overlooking the Flint River. The bluff boasted the biggest mansions in the county where the richest of the rich lived.

Most of the homes belonged to the Hamiltons and anyone married to a Hamilton. The Hamiltons owned every textile mill in Flintville. I really didn't know many of them because the Hamilton children were sent away to boarding school.

The previous summer I'd been invited to Juliet Hamilton's ninth birthday party, hosted by her mother Mrs. Daphne Hamilton. Juliet was home from boarding school at the time. She was a pretty girl with long dark hair and big blue eyes. Her bedroom was the most magnificent room I'd ever seen with her own adjoining bathroom. She had a canopy bed, something I thought only existed in fairy tales. Their kitchen boasted a crushed ice machine, and we were allowed to help ourselves to as much ice for our Cokes as we desired.

Diddy and Aunt Bird said the Hamiltons were good people who brought industry to our town. I couldn't help but think how much Essie would love to sleep in a canopy bed and have her very own bathroom.

The rest of Diddy's article detailed the discovery of Macy Dunn's body. It included a quote from Sheriff Brady, who said the coroner had ruled drowning as the cause of death. The sheriff added that the investigation would remain open until they determined if the drowning was the result of an accident or foul play. My heart ached when I read the final sentence: "Miss Dunn is survived by her mother Katherine Dunn and sister Essie Dunn."

By summer's end, it seemed that everybody in Flintville had forgotten all about the Dunns and their loss. I never forgot, but it would be many years before I'd see Essie again.

Chapter 11

By late August, Josie and my bicycle odometers registered 485 miles, just fifteen miles from our mileage goal. Since Josie's mama was taking her to Atlanta on Saturday to shop for school clothes, this would be our final day to ride.

"I don't know how we can put in fifteen miles by just riding around the neighborhood," I groaned as we squirted oil on our bike chains.

"Wait a minute! I've got an idea!" Josie's face lit up, and she whistled through her teeth. I frowned. Usually, Josie's great ideas either caused us bodily injury or a whipping by our parents. "Let's ride out to Lincoln Village. I've been out there with Mama to take Lorna home lots of times. It's about seven miles out there. The round trip would add a total of fourteen miles."

Lincoln Village was home to Flintville's Negro population. Although I'd never been warned by Diddy or Aunt Bird that it was off limits, I had the distinct feeling it was. Josie saw my expression and continued her sales pitch. "Look, nobody's gonna see us. Mama took a vacation day from the bank to help Daddy with inventory at the store; they'll be up to their eyeballs counting socks and underwear. Lorna took the afternoon off, and isn't your aunt back at school this week?" Josie added when she caught a relenting expression in my eyes.

"Yeah, she's putting up her bulletin boards. Diddy's at a press convention in Atlanta, but Cece's around."

"Oh, you know Cece and Margaret are so worked up about starting high school in a few days, they're not going to notice us," Josie argued.

Josie was right about Cece. Yesterday the postman delivered a large box from Atlanta. The box, compliments of Mimi, contained a dozen school outfits for both Cece and me. Cece had squealed in delight and couldn't wait to try on every item. Aunt Bird coaxed me into one of my new dresses to make certain the length was correct. Fortunately, the dress fit perfectly, and I was spared of trying on the others.

The thought of school looming around the corner unraveled my last thread of common sense, and I yielded to Josie's suggestion. A short climb up Birdsong and we were on Green Street. Looking both ways, Josie took off towards Lincoln Village as I pedaled after her. As we approached a "Lincoln Village" sign, the road narrowed and turned from asphalt to gravel. As the gravel slowed our progress, we both started sweating.

Farther into the village, the road narrowed again and turned from gravel into red clay. The faster and harder we pedaled, the more red dust we stirred. Another mile and I was obliged to stop to wipe dust from my glasses.

"You ready to turn around, Josie?"

"Just a little further. According to my odometer, we've only been five miles." We began twisting and turning up and down roads in the village. There seemed to be a rooster and several chickens clucking and pecking in almost every yard, and in one yard we saw some children, barefooted and covered in red dirt, playing on a tire swing. They waved at us and smiled.

Another mile and it became obvious that Josie had lost her bearings. When we slowed to brake for another stop sign, Josie hesitated. "Maybe we'd better turn around," I suggested.

"Turn around which way?" Josie quipped, and I knew we were lost. "Look, see that smoke rising in the distance? Let's head up that hill. I bet there'll be somebody who can direct us back to Green Street." It was the steepest hill I'd ever pulled on my bike, and the muscles in my calves began to quiver.

When we reached the summit, we stopped to catch our breath. A single farmhouse stood nestled about a mile away in the distance. "I guess that's our best hope," Josie sighed. "Are you ready, Allie?" Josie always asked that question each time we topped the hill on Avalon Road. Then we would plummet downhill as fast as we could. Whoever reached the bottom first claimed bragging rights. For every one victory I captured, Josie had five. My squatty legs were just no match for her long limbs on most days. This hill was different, though, because neither of us had ever ridden down it.

I grinned, screamed "Geronimo," and took off with my legs churning on my pedals as hard as I could. Josie was right behind me, but I had the advantage with my quick start. Just as the incline leveled, I looked back at Josie with victory in my eyes. That's when it happened. My front tire hit an enormous pothole. I slammed on my brakes too late. Flying over my handlebars, I fell face down in the hard, red clay. Josie, skidding to a halt directly in front of me, screamed, "Allie, are you okay?"

When I finally recovered my senses, I looked up to see both Josie and an old Negro man peering at me. The old man held his wrinkled, callused hand down to mine. With one strong yank, he hoisted me to my feet and smiled kindly. "Lord, chile, you'se done's took quite a tumble!"

Although every bone in my body ached, my pride pained me the most. I quickly brushed myself off and recovered my glasses, partially buried in the dirt. The old man pulled a bandana from a pocket of his overalls and handed it to me. "Here, chile, wipe that dirt off your glasses so you'se can see where you'se going." He smiled again.

Josie groaned. "Allie, I think your front tire's flat, and both your elbows and knees are bleeding. Those are some of the worst road burns I've ever seen!" She gave a low whistle through her teeth.

The old man pulled off his straw hat and rubbed the white stubble on his head. "Where you chilluns ride from? Lordy, do yo' folks know where you is?" Before we could answer, he came to a decision. "Come on, chile, I'll take you up to the house and let Berthie have a look at you." He picked up my bike and examined the tire. "Don't worry, I can fix this tire out in the barn."

The old man headed down the road with Josie pushing her bike and me hobbling after them both. By the time we reached the front porch, the skin on my knees and elbows began to sting as my sweat mixed with my blood. The old man opened the screened door and hollered. "Berthie, where is you? Git out here on the porch. We'se gots some company."

A moment later, a rather large Negro woman appeared. She wore a spotless white apron around her waist and a red bandana tied around her head just like Aunt Jemima on the syrup bottle. "Lawd have mercy! What's done happened to you, chile? Git in this here house right now and let Berthie clean you up," she instructed in a commanding but somehow gentle voice.

Although I'd never been in a Negro person's house before and wasn't sure that I should be in one now, I had no choice but to follow. Josie and I trailed Berthie down the shotgun hall to a kitchen. Soon, she had me sitting atop her kitchen table as she soothingly wiped my elbows and knees with a cool, wet cloth.

She pulled a bottle of orange merthiolate from a cabinet. "Now, honey, this here's gonna sting a mite, but it'll keep down infection." She beckoned Josie over beside us. "I tell you what. I'll paint while you blow on your friend's skint places, you hear?" Josie nodded in obedience, and the procedure began.

After an agonizing eternity, Berthie screwed the cap back on the bottle of merthiolate, brushed my bangs out of my face, picked me up and set me on the floor. "All done, chile. You sho is brave. I used to have to chase my boys around the yard and almost hogtie 'em to doctor on 'em." She smiled down at me with big white teeth except for one gold one right in the middle of her mouth.

"I reckons you chillun can use some refreshment. Now just set down at that table and let Berthie see what she can find." In a moment she returned with two bowls of warm rice pudding. "Now you'se enjoy while I fetch some cool water from our well. It's better than the tap water."

Josie and I silently dug into the pudding, the best I'd ever eaten. Once I regained my strength, I eyed Josie. "Do you know these people? They sure are friendly."

Josie took another bite before replying. "I think they're kin to Lorna because I've heard her mention an Aunt Berthie. I just hope her husband can fix your tire, or we're gonna be in deep doo doo!"

Before we could discuss an escape plan, Berthie returned from the well with a bucket of cold water. She pulled two fruit jars from her cabinet and filled them to the top. I didn't realize how thirsty I was or how wonderful well water tasted.

Berthie stared intently at me. "You'se gotta be Miss Allie Sinclair! Why you'se the spittin image of yo grandmamma, Miss Louise. How's she gittin along these days?"

I realized that Berthie was talking about Mimi, my mama's mother. "She's fine. She just sent me some new school clothes that she made us. How do you know my Mimi?"

"I works for your grandmamma and her husband, Mr. Tyrone, longs before they's had your mama. Your granddaddy had the first grocery store in Flintville that sold fresh produce. It was called the Depot Market, and Mr. Tyrone had fresh fruit and vegetables brought in on the train. Why I's remember when your mama, Miss Cecile, was born. It took two days of hard labor for her to deliver Miss Cecile. Lawd, Miss Louise was so tuckered, she didn't have no breast milk. We fed that baby from a sugar teat until Miss Louise was stronger. When Baby Cecile got big enough, your grandmamma opened a little seamstress shop in the back of the market. Mr. Tyrone ran the market, and I's cooked and cleaned for them." Berthie shoveled more pudding into our bowls.

I was mesmerized by the history lesson on my mama's ancestors.

"The last time I'se seen you, you'se just a baby. Miss Cecile brought you and your big sister out here rights before Christmas. She was always sweet to remember us at Christmas. That's the last time I'se seen her alive," Berthie sighed. "I'se sorry. I hope I didn't upset you none. Them's just sweet memories for me. Now who's your friend?" Berthie pointed to Josie.

Josie looked up with rice pudding all over her mouth. "I'm Josie McClendon. I think you know my maid Lorna."

"Land's sakes, Lorna's my brother's child. Do she know you'se be riding bicycles way out here?"

Josie and I exchanged glances. "No, my mama gave Lorna the day off."

Berthie smiled. "I bet that Lorna keeps you'se in line when yo' folks be working. She was always a tough one."

Josie hung her head. "If she finds out and tells our parents, we're going to be in a heap of trouble."

"Well, I tells you what. Let's just keep your little adventure between us'n. What Miss Lorna don'ts know won't hurt her." Josie and I simultaneously breathed a sigh of relief.

By the time we made it to the front porch, Moses had replaced my bike's tire and straightened out my front fender. It was almost three o'clock, and I knew I'd better get home before Aunt Bird did. "Mr. Moses, can you tell us the shortest way to get through Lincoln Village and back to Green Street?"

"I'se sho can. Now you'se just follow this road back up the hill. When you'se get to the first crossroads, take a right. That'll take you straight to Green Street." He and Berthie waved goodbye to us.

Moses' shortcut saved us, and we headed up Green Street with time to spare. "What're you going to tell your aunt about all your skint up places?" Josie queried with a look of fear.

"I'll tell her we were racing down Avalon, and I hit a loose piece of gravel. I know I'll get a lecture about racing where cars travel, but I guess I deserve some punishment."

Josie whistled through her teeth as we pulled up to my house. "That's the best pudding I've ever had. Maybe we'll go visit Berthie and Moses again someday if you can keep your butt on the bicycle seat and out of the dirt."

Josie headed home and was almost out of sight when I heard her brakes skid to a halt. "Hey, Allie, check out your mileage! We did it!" As I looked down to see 501 miles registering on my odometer, all the stiffness in my elbows and knees melted away.

My story about a bike wreck on Avalon Road satisfied Aunt Bird although she was most upset that my new school dresses would be adorned with scabby knees and elbows. After dinner on Sunday, she reminded me to compose a thank you note for Mimi. I tried to sneak out the back door to read the Sunday funnies, but Aunt Bird intercepted me. "Not until you've completed your letter. Remember, do not seal it until I've proofread it."

Thirty minutes later I knocked on Aunt Bird's bedroom door with Mimi's thank you note in hand. "Finished already, are you? Let me see." She read and returned it with an approving smile. "Very well done, Allie. You'll need to address the envelope."

"Should I address it to Mimi or do I need to use her real name?" I questioned.

Aunt Bird smiled. "I know she's Mimi to you, but to the post office she's Mrs. Louise Banks."

"Aunt Bird, why does Mimi live in Atlanta? Didn't she grow up in Flintville?"

"She just needed a change after your mama was gone. She had a cousin looking for a partner in the seamstress business, and it was a good opportunity for her."

I continued nonchalantly. "Didn't she have a grocery store in Flintville?"

"Mr. Banks owned Depot Market when I was a little girl, but he died when your mama wasn't much older than you."

"What'd he die from?"

"I believe your mama said he had a bad heart. Besides the market, he owned some peach orchards. He even had his own label on the packing boxes. I think there are some of those old labels in the cedar chest. Would you like one?" Aunt Bird opened the chest where she stored family mementos.

She returned to the bed with a picture album. My mama's maiden name, Cecile Louise Banks, was engraved in gold letters on the front. Inside, I found Mama's birth certificate and her picture in front of the Depot Market when she was about five or six. Mimi and the grandfather I never knew were standing behind her.

As we studied photos from my mama's teenage years, I realized how much Cece resembled her. The final page held a snapshot of my mama with Diddy at an Atlanta nightspot on their honeymoon. Diddy had on a white sports coat and a bright, open collared shirt, and Mama wore a tropical sundress and a big pink camellia in her hair. She was absolutely stunning, and anyone could tell that my daddy adored her.

Aunt Bird remarked, "Your mama was a beautiful woman, wasn't she? I always thought she and my brother were the perfect couple."

"Do you think Diddy will ever remarry?"

Aunt Bird sighed. "Allie, for people like your mama and daddy, love comes only once. Once a person has experienced the kind of total devotion they had, there's no settling for second best. Don't you worry, though, your mama's memory is enough to sustain your daddy for a lifetime." Aunt Bird's voice quivered for a moment. She quickly turned to the back of the album and pulled out a large envelope. "Here they are! I knew your daddy had stashed these labels somewhere." She handed me one of them.

The label sported a large, bright peach in its middle. Above the peach was a photo of my grandmother's face with the title *Lucie Sweet Brand*. Printed at the bottom were the words "Georgia Elbertas: Grown, Packed, and Shipped by Tyrone Banks, Flintville, Georgia."

Aunt Bird peered over my shoulder. "Lucie was Mr. Banks' nickname for your grandmother. My, my, Allie, look how much you resemble your grandmother. You have the same eyebrows, and your face is shaped like hers. I remember her even back then as a petite little lady with a lot of spunk, just like you! Here, keep one of these labels. You might want to start a scrapbook for yourself." She gave me a quick peck on my cheek, patted my backside, and sent me on my way.

After training union that night, I went straight to my bedroom to change into my pajamas so that I'd have time for one television program before my mandatory school bedtime. Diddy, as usual, was on the side porch buried in the latest edition of *U.S. News and World Report*. When I turned on the lamp, I discovered a small box with a folded notecard lying on my bed. In Diddy's undeniable scrawl was the following message:

> *Allie,*
> *Aunt Bird tells me you have taken an interest in your mama's family.*
> *When your sister turned ten, I gave her a pearl necklace belonging to your mama. In the box you will find a bracelet, which I presented to your mama on the day you were born—September 12, 1951. Just like you, there's not another like it in the world. It's yours now. Take care of it and cherish it as I do you.*
> *Love,*
> *Diddy*

Inside the box atop a pillow of cotton was a delicate silver bracelet. At intervals along the bracelet tiny diamonds alternated with teardrop gems of sapphire, my birthstone.

I'd never been much for jewelry, but the bracelet was the most exquisite object I'd ever held in my hand. As I studied it, I began to understand the uniqueness of the love my parents shared. I realized why Diddy rarely talked about Mama; mere words could never explain his devotion to her.

Underneath my bed was a pink and white jewelry box given to me by Aunt Bird in her campaign to develop my interest in "prissy" stuff. Inside I'd stored my Girl Scout pocketknife and two nearly perfect Indian arrow heads. I rearranged those items to make room for my new gifts.

I folded the "Lucie Sweet" peach label until it fit in the bottom. Next, I lay Diddy's note inside the box. Finally, so that it would always be the first item I saw whenever I opened the box, I tenderly positioned my mama's bracelet, still swaddled in cotton, on top. Perhaps one day I would want to wear it, but for now I was content to know I owned a symbol of Mama and Diddy's love.

Chapter 12

The piercing clang of Cece's alarm clock tore me from a sound sleep. When I lifted one eyelid, I discovered Cece, sponge curlers dangling from her head, sitting up. "Whadda ya doing, Cece? It's the middle of the night," I moaned through a sleepy haze.

Cece silenced the alarm. "Don't you remember, Allie? It's the first day of school!" She danced out the door towards the bathroom.

I buried my face in my pillow. I guess Cece needed extra time to primp before making her freshman debut at Flintville High. Just as I drifted off again, Diddy snatched the covers off me and bellowed, "I want to hear two warm feet hit that cold floor!" With those words, summer was officially over.

Diddy agreed to drop me off at Flintville Elementary on his way to the newspaper. Cece, clad in a navy A-line skirt and a yellow and blue print blouse, was putting the finishing touches on her hair when I stumbled into the bathroom to brush my teeth. "Hurry up, squirt! I promised Aunt Bird I'd tame that mop of yours before we leave for school," she remarked way too cheerfully.

Aunt Bird had promised to forego my usual smelly home permanent if I'd allow Cece to tend to my hair each morning. "Hold still, Allie, you're squirming like a worm," Cece complained as she pulled my bangs back in a barrette.

"I don't know why I can't just keep it in a pixie cut for school. Ouch, Cece, that hurts."

"Now, Allie, you don't want to look like a boy at school. Okay, I'm done. How do you like it?" Cece handed me my glasses and turned me around to face the bathroom mirror.

I had to admit she was a miracle worker. "Thanks, Cece. I like it, and you look really pretty."

"A compliment from baby brat! You feeling all right?" She smiled down at me as she sprayed the top of my head with Aqua Net. Her blonde hair was held away from her face with a navy headband. Her olive skin was still tan from a summer at Parker's Pool, and her eyes gleamed with anticipation. Cece would be the prettiest freshman girl at Flintville High School.

The reality that Cece and I wouldn't be at the same school dawned on me, and for a brief moment, my heart fluttered with sadness. That moment was quickly shattered by Aunt Bird's stern warning from the kitchen. "Allie Sinclair, if you don't get in this kitchen and eat some breakfast, I'm going to skin you alive!"

By the time Diddy dropped me off, the auditorium was packed with children and parents scanning classroom assignments posted on the walls. I located Josie standing under the fifth grade sign. She gave a low whistle through her teeth as she delivered the bad news. "We're both assigned to Miss Pridmore's class. At least we can suffer together." My heart sank.

I soon found myself sitting on the front row of Miss Eunice Pridmore's fifth grade class. Josie was assigned to a back row desk. Because I was short and had astigmatism, I never escaped the front of the room. With a reputation as the strictest teacher in all of Flintville Elementary School, Miss Pridmore reminded me of the frumpy old maid on the playing cards.

For the first thirty minutes of the day, we were subjected to Miss Pridmore's infinite list of class rules, which we had to copy from the board as she wrote them in perfectly formed cursive letters. Although she was "Olive Oyl" skinny, the loose flesh on her arm jiggled as she wrote on the board. Every single rule began with "Students will not..."

After twenty-five such directives, I wondered if we'd be allowed to breathe. "For each rule infraction, you will receive a demerit, which I shall post on the deportment chart. After a total of five demerits, your deportment grade automatically drops a letter grade," she explained in a stern, unfriendly tone as she gazed at us with dark, beady eyes.

Miss Pridmore then gave us a social studies assignment, which included reading an entire chapter in silence and answering fifty questions in complete sentences. "You will have one hour to complete this assignment, so get busy!" She wound a little timer on her desk. It was going to be a long year.

Halfway through my reading about Aztec Indians, someone tapped me on my shoulder. The tapper was Daniel McSwain, a chubby boy who picked his nose in Sunday school. I hoped he wasn't wiping a booger on my back. He handed me a note folded into a paper football. On the outside was written "Old Maid Pridmore" in Josie's handwriting. I dropped the still-folded note into my lap and went back to the Aztec Indians.

When Miss Pridmore turned her back to erase the board, I unfolded the note as quietly as possible. Josie had drawn a wonderful likeness of our new warden. It included her long, pointed nose on her pinched face as well as her menacing, evil eyes. Atop Miss Pridmore's curly head, Josie had colored in a pair of devil's horns, and she had flames pouring out of the old dragon's mouth. I giggled, slid the picture into my notebook, and went back to work.

When the timer on Miss Pridmore's desk sounded, I still had eight questions to complete. Miss Pridmore screeched, "Close your books immediately!" We all did as we were told. She opened her roll book, peered down at it, and then scanned the class. Her voice possessed a high-pitched, nasal quality that grated on my ears. "When I call your name, stand up, read the question and your answer in its entirety. We'll begin with Randall Abercrombie." She directed her gaze towards Randall and waited.

The exercise continued down each row. If a student gave an incorrect answer, Miss Pridmore would smirk disgustedly and issue the same edict: "You will stay in during recess and write the correct answer ten times."

Miss Pridmore reached my row and ordered shrilly, "Allie Sinclair, stand and complete question 13!" Confident I had answered the question correctly, I jumped up quickly from my seat. As I did so, my notebook slid off the desk onto the floor, and Josie's note fell out. I bent over hurriedly to recover it, but Miss Pridmore was fast for an old lady. She retrieved the note just as my fingers touched it. "Proceed with your answer, Allie!"

My voice quivered as I proceeded. Just as I completed reading my response, the lunch bell rang. "Class, remember rule number five: 'Students will not talk in the lunch line!' You are dismissed. Allie Sinclair, stay seated!" As everyone else filed out the door, Josie glanced at me fearfully; I knew she was worried I'd give her up.

When the room was empty, Miss Pridmore pulled the drawing from her roll book and studied it closely. "If you are going to depict me, be accurate. My eyes are brown, not blue. Allie Sinclair, read rule number twelve from your notebook."

"Yes ma'am." I thumbed back a few pages. "Students will not pass notes during class."

"From whom did you receive this note?" she growled.

"Nobody, Miss Pridmore. I was drawing it, but I didn't have time to finish before the buzzer went off." My stomach rumbled, but I kept a straight face.

"Very well. When I catch two people breaking a rule, the partners in crime divide the punishment. Would you like to change your mind about what happened?"

I took a deep breath. "Uh, no ma'am. I had no partner in crime."

She glared at me again, went to the board, and wrote my name on the deportment chart. Beside my name, she drew a big slash. "Not a good way to start off. I remember your sister to be a lovely student who never disobeyed a rule. You should look to her as an example. Now go to lunch!"

Silently hating my perfect sister, I trudged toward the cafeteria. Josie had saved me a seat at her table. "Don't worry; you're not in trouble," I whispered as I set down my tray. The look of gratitude on her face made my rather premature fall from grace bearable.

At supper that night, Cece talked nonstop about her first day of high school. She and Margaret had four classes together. "And you won't believe the freedom we have at lunch. We just take off to the cafeteria with absolutely no supervision. I already know I want to join the Art Club, and I might run for freshman representative on the Student Council. Everybody loved my printed blouse; nobody had one like it since mine was custom-made by Mimi. Suzie Sims and Cathy Ethridge had on identical Villager skirts from Norwood's. And there's a sock hop after the football game on Friday." She stopped long enough to gulp some iced tea before adding casually, "Margaret and I plan to go together unless, of course, we get asked on a date."

Diddy had a journalist's ability to filter out nonsense and home in on the important information. He looked up from his half-eaten pork chop. "A date? I'm not certain you're ready for that, Cece. Let's take things slowly now. Remember you have four entire years of high school. Don't try to do everything in the first week." He went back to his pork chop.

Diddy's interruption provided Cece with enough time to refuel her air supply. As children we'd learned once Diddy made a decision concerning us, the discussion was over. However, in the past year, Cece had begun holding her ground and arguing with him. Aunt Bird explained that Cece's newfound courage was part of puberty. Obviously I was nowhere close to puberty because my knees still quaked any time I was in trouble with Diddy.

"But, Diddy, I'm fifteen now. This summer we agreed that once I turned fifteen, I could double date. Are you going back on your promise?" Cece delivered all of this in a calm but determined voice without a hint of fear.

Diddy wiped his mouth and folded his napkin under his plate. He pushed his chair away from the table and scratched the top of his head. "Okay, Cece. A promise is a promise. But only double dates with someone we know. We'll discuss curfews when the situation arises."

Aunt Bird, who'd remained mute during this discussion, found her voice. "Well, now, who wants some orange sherbet? I have some in the freezer." As she removed dishes from the table, I caught Aunt Bird give Cece a quick wink.

"None for me, Bird. Dinner was quite enough." Diddy picked up the Atlanta paper and headed toward the bathroom. As he passed my chair, he patted me on the head. "Allie, when you finish helping with the dishes, why don't you come out to the porch and tell me about fifth grade? You didn't have a chance at the table tonight."

After a day with Miss Pridmore, I was in no mood to talk about fifth grade. Despite torturing us throughout the school day, the old bat had the audacity to assign math homework on the first night. It was a review of our multiplication tables with twenty-five problems to work. The only thing I despised more than Miss Pridmore herself was multiplication. Somehow, the Lord forgot to bless me with number skills.

After finishing the dishes, I slunk down the hall toward my bedroom. I'd almost made it to my door when Diddy called out to me. "Allie, your aunt said someone needed to check your math homework. Bring it out here."

I dutifully carried my homework to the sun porch. Diddy checked over it, and much to his and my surprise, I'd made no mistakes. "I knew your brain would catch up to multiplication before too long! Now tell me about your day." Diddy seemed eager to hear about school from a ten year old's perspective.

His genuine interest in my pathetic life was more than I could bear, and I burst into tears. Between gulps for air, I poured out every miserable detail including the fact that I was the first recipient of a demerit. I blubbered, "And Cece's not there anymore. She used to always listen to me when I had a bad day. She doesn't care about me anymore."

Diddy pulled a handkerchief from his back pocket and waited for me to blow my nose and readjust my glasses. Then he pulled me close to him. "Cece always has time for you. Just give her a while to get over the newness of high school." He brushed away my bangs, which had escaped my barrette. "As for the demerit, I understand your reason for not wanting to implicate Josie. You were being loyal to your friend, and loyalty is an admirable trait. However, you must learn to distinguish between loyalty and self-preservation."

"What's self-preservation?" I inquired.

"Self-preservation is the ability to take care of your own hide. There'll be times when suffering the consequences alone can be painful as well as unfair. You'll have to determine when loyalty must take a bow to honesty. Do you understand?"

"I think so. I guess Josie was just as much at fault as I was, and we both needed to take responsibility," I admitted. "But I can't stand a tattletale."

Diddy smiled at me. "Nobody appreciates a tattletale, but there's a difference in offering unsolicited information and telling the truth when asked."

"Yessir, but Miss Pridmore's still the meanest teacher I've ever had. She has so many rules we can barely breathe!"

"Well, I heard of no fifth grader suffocating today, and that would be news! Perhaps Miss Pridmore will relax some of her commandments after she's whipped the fifth grade into shape. In the meantime, I expect for you to bear up and remember what my daddy used to tell me when I faced a difficult situation."

"What did he tell you?"

"If it doesn't kill you, it will make you a better man," Diddy responded.

"Well, I'm not certain I want to be a man. As a matter of fact, I'm not even sure I want to be a woman!" I confessed.

Diddy laughed. "You have plenty of time to make up your mind, but I kind of like you as my little girl. I can only handle one daughter becoming a young woman at a time. As for Miss Pridmore, talk to your sister. Maybe she'll offer some survival tips." He hugged me tight and sent me on my way.

As I climbed into bed, Cece was getting her clothes in order for tomorrow. She had selected a madras plaid skirt and a pink blouse with a Peter Pan collar on which Mimi had embroidered Cece's initials.

While mine seemed to remain the same, Cece's world had changed practically overnight. I wondered if she thought about anything other than clothes, hair, and boys. I missed the old Cece. She must have read my thoughts because she sat down on the edge of my bed to tuck me in. "So, you and Josie are both in Miss Prune Face Pridmore's class, huh?"

"Prune Face!" I giggled. "That's perfect; she looks just like a prune. She's awful, Cece, but she thinks you're perfect because you never broke one of her stupid rules."

"I just never was caught. I'll let you in on a little secret about Miss Pridmore," she whispered.

I was all ears. "What?"

"She has two little Chihuahuas named Mickey and Minnie. She dotes on them like they were babies. For Christmas the year I was in her class, I drew a charcoal portrait of her dogs. She adored me after that."

I groaned. "But I can't draw like you, and she already hates me."

"She doesn't hate you. She just needed a victim to serve as an example for the first day, and you were an easy target. Maybe you can compose a poem about her dogs. Now go to sleep; tomorrow's another school day!"

She had to remind me. At least tomorrow I'd get to walk to Diddy's office since Aunt Bird had yearbook meetings on Tuesdays. Diddy said the arrangement suited him fine; he'd grown accustomed to my company on Tuesday when the office was empty. I fell asleep dreaming of words that rhymed with Mickey and Minnie.

Chapter 13

By October, I'd fallen into the routine of school although I still despised Miss Pridmore and her deportment chart. While I battled Prune Face and long division, Cece conquered high school with elegant ease. She was elected secretary of the Art Club and Student Council representative.

One evening as I prepared for bed, I watched Cece open a large manila envelope and dump a wad of dollars and a pile of coins onto her bed. "Wow, where'd you get all the loot?"

Cece stopped counting to explain. "It's not mine. It's for the Macy Dunn scholarship. I'm collecting donations in my homeroom." The Student Council, along with the marching band, were soliciting funds for a Macy Dunn music scholarship. Cece had learned that Macy Dunn, an accomplished musician, captured first chair in the flute section during her sophomore year.

The mention of Macy Dunn caused my heart to ache, and I wondered how little Essie Dunn was faring. "Can I make a donation?" I crawled halfway under my bed to retrieve my jewelry box. Along with the precious items in the box, I'd added the allowance I'd been saving for a bigger bicycle. I handed Cece a pink envelope containing a total of twelve dollars and thirty-five cents.

"You don't want to give all of this, do you?" Cece raised her eyebrows. "I thought you had your eye on that new bike in Johnson's Hardware."

I lay my glasses on our night table and crawled under the covers. "Yeah, I did, but somehow having a new bicycle doesn't seem that important anymore."

Cece tucked me in and kissed me atop my forehead. "Did anyone ever tell you that you have one of the kindest hearts in the world, Allie?" She had tears in her eyes. I drifted off to sleep with an image of Essie Dunn without the big sister I still had.

The following Tuesday when I arrived at the newspaper office, I discovered a young colored man tapping on the front door. He was dressed in a Sunday suit and carried an official looking document, so I figured he did some kind of business with Diddy. I grabbed the handle of the door. "Oh, it's not locked. If you're looking for Mr. Sinclair, he's in there. He leaves it unlocked for me on Tuesday afternoons." When the colored man eyed me curiously, I added, "It's okay; I'm his daughter." He followed me into the office where we literally bumped into Diddy who'd obviously heard the tapping.

"Hi Allie," he grinned as he tousled my hair. "If it isn't Elijah Atwell! Back in Flintville, I hear." Diddy shook the colored man's hand with enthusiasm.

"Yes sir, I'm finished with seminary and returning to take over my daddy's pulpit if he'll let me." The colored man spoke with crisp, proper grammar.

Diddy offered Elijah a chair. "How is your daddy? Is he still working that farm by himself?"

"Daddy's doing tolerable. My brother Isaiah is helping out on the farm. You know we've got two acres of pecan trees we're cultivating for Mr. Blackwell."

"Sure enough? I bet he'll be glad that you're home to help out. And how is Berthie? Still cooking, I bet. That woman makes the best sweet potato soufflé I've ever eaten."

At the mention of Berthie's name, my heart began to pound. Could it be the same Berthie who ministered to my wounds on my and Josie's perilous bicycle journey through Lincoln Village?

"Yes sir, Mama's been trying to fatten me up," Elijah patted his stomach. "She could give those cafeteria cooks at Morehouse a lesson or two." He cleared his throat. "Mr. Sinclair, I'm sorry to disturb you on your afternoon off, but Daddy was hoping you could put these announcements in tomorrow's paper if it's not too late."

"It's not too late, and I'll be happy to. Do you have a copy to take to Mr. Higgins at the radio station? The Ebony Bulletin Board airs at noon on Wednesdays," Diddy scanned the handwritten announcements.

"Oh, yes sir. Mr. Higgins is allowing me to work that spot. He said my elocution was as good as any of his other announcers," Elijah grinned with pride. "Now, you need to bring your girls out to see my mama. She just loves to pull out old photos of when she worked for Miss Cecile's parents; she does miss your sweet wife."

Before I'd recovered from my shock, Elijah Atwell was out the door. When Diddy began typing out Elijah's announcements, I queried, "Who's that man? Did Mama know him?"

Diddy smiled. "He's the son of Berthie, the woman who practically raised your mama. Elijah just finished seminary school, and he's returned to head the Lincoln Village A.M.E. Church. His father Moses has been pastor there for the past fifty years. They're good people. Their son Joshua is in the army, and their daughter Ruth is a school teacher."

"Why are all their children named after people from the Bible?" I wondered aloud.

Diddy laughed. "Reverend Atwell told me he named his children after Biblical characters in the hope they'd strive to build lives worthy of their names. It seems to have worked. Now, don't you have some arithmetic to do?"

I sighed and opened my notebook. Diddy, tired of my running into his office for help with my long division problems, had long since placed a small table by his desk so that he was nearby when I had a question. Somehow having him close to me was such reassurance that I needed less and less help.

My time with Diddy turned into two afternoons instead of just one. Since I had Girl Scouts on Wednesdays, Aunt Bird allowed me to walk the short distance from the Girl Scout hut to the newspaper and ride home with Diddy. Wednesday was press day, but by 5:30 when I arrived, the paper was on the street, and everyone but Diddy had cleared out for the night.

I so enjoyed these quiet afternoons with Diddy. The aroma of his ever-present Clove chewing gum and the pecking of his old typewriter lulled me into contentment. Heading home one evening, Diddy turned on the radio to catch the final newscast of the day. There was a plea to local businesses for donations to the

Macy Dunn scholarship. As Diddy changed gears, he glanced at me. "I hear someone in the Sinclair household made quite a generous donation to the Macy Dunn fund. That was quite magnanimous of you, Allie."

I wasn't certain what magnanimous meant, but the tone of Diddy's voice assured me it was a compliment. "Diddy, could we drive out to see Essie sometime soon? I haven't seen her since the funeral."

"I'm sorry, Allie. I didn't think to tell you. Essie and her mama moved to Griffin about a month ago."

I was shocked. I couldn't imagine losing my sister and then having to pick up and leave the only home I'd ever known. My voice quivered a little, "Why'd they move, Diddy?"

"Once the coroner's report came out, I think Mrs. Dunn just decided she and Essie needed a new start. She moved in with an aunt who got her a job at the Carter's underwear factory in Griffin," he continued as he pulled into our driveway.

I remembered Diddy's front-page article about the coroner's findings. There was enough alcohol in Macy's bloodstream to classify her as legally drunk, and her lungs were filled with water, which indicated she'd drowned. Mrs. Dunn continued to maintain that Macy did not drink. Alongside the article was a school photograph of Macy Dunn. A pretty girl with red hair and big eyes just like her younger sister, Macy wore a blouse sporting a collar pin in the shape of a flute.

The coroner had ruled the death an accidental drowning, and the case was closed. Nonetheless, that very afternoon I had noticed the Macy Dunn folder, with its red *Confidential* stamped upon it, tucked under the ink blotter on Diddy's desk. Maybe Diddy believed Mrs. Dunn, or maybe he knew something the coroner didn't. Whatever the reason, the Macy Dunn case remained open to my daddy.

For the final Girl Scout meeting before Christmas vacation, Mrs. Ellison, our troop leader, requested that each scout bring a scrubbed-out Campbell's soup can for our Christmas craft. She provided rickrack, glitter, and paint so we could create a pencil holder for a loved one. I knew right away that I'd design a holder for Diddy to put on his desk.

Though never much of an artist, I worked with painstaking care on the project by first spraying my can with bright green paint and then decorating it in Christmas trees drawn with glue and covered with glitter. My final touch was rickrack glued around the top edge. I was quite pleased with my finished product and so anxious for Diddy to see it that I planned to present it to him when I walked to his office after our scout meeting.

Before we adjourned, Mrs. Ellison asked each scout to display her decorated can for everyone to view. Somehow, the cans of all the other scouts appeared much more professionally decorated than mine. Their rickrack trimmed the top of their cans in perfect symmetry while mine was lopsided and sported traces of smeared glue. The glitter on the other scouts' cans rested in all the correct spots whereas mine appeared to have fallen wherever it wanted making my glitter Christmas trees look more like glitter globs.

When my turn arrived to display my can, Rachel Fountain, the meanest, tallest girl in our troop, giggled. "I'll bet your daddy throws that right in the garbage when you aren't looking!"

I felt my face color in humiliation. Josie whispered, "Don't pay any attention to her. She's stupid." But the damage was done; I was crushed.

A wintry wind hit my face as I left the warmth of the Girl Scout hut with my pitiful pencil holder dangling in my hand. By the time I walked the three blocks to Diddy's office, my face was red and chapped with burning tears.

Diddy had the radio playing since he was alone. Christmas carols blasted over the air, and I could hear him whistling as he completed a paste-up of an advertisement for tomorrow's edition. He grinned as I entered. "Am I glad to see you, Allie. I can certainly use some of your sunshine on this cloudy day!"

His greeting just added to the misery of my heart, a heart totally devoid of any sunshine on this day. Too devastated to even reply, I shoved my tacky offering towards him at the layout desk. "It's supposed to be a pencil holder, but you don't have to use it if it's too ugly," I mumbled as a tear hit the yellow bow tie of my scout uniform.

Diddy picked up the can and turned it around in his hand. "Well, well, there's no way I'm using this for pencils." My heart sank into sheer agony as he carried the holder to his office. "No, ma'am, I've a better idea." I watched as he loaded my can up with sticks of Clove chewing gum. "Now that's just perfect. There's nothing better than a heart gift," he added as he handed me his handkerchief.

I wiped the fog from my glasses and blew my nose. "What do you mean by a heart gift, Diddy?"

"Any gift that comes from the heart. I know you made this with me in mind, and you wanted it to be something I'd enjoy using. Thank you for my early Christmas present. I'll always cherish it." He buttoned up my coat and placed his warm hand in mine. In that quiet moment, I realized the simplicity of real love.

Chapter 14

Christmas vacation arrived just in time. If I'd been forced to spend another day in Prune Face Pridmore's class, I would have exploded.

Just days before Christmas, Diddy, Cece, and I made our annual trip to Atlanta to visit Mimi. Aunt Bird drove Cece and me to the newspaper office where we stowed our overnight bags in the trunk of Diddy's Studebaker. While we were away, Aunt Bird would make the most of her time in preparation for the Sinclair Christmas.

I knew she would prepare her famous nine-layer chocolate cake, my absolute favorite. I'd long since presented my Christmas wish list to her and Diddy. Among other things, the list included a transistor radio, a bicycle basket, and a mini ice cream maker I'd spotted in the Sears and Roebuck catalogue. Although I knew Josie would probably get a twenty-four inch bicycle like the one in Johnson's Hardware, I didn't dare ask for such an extravagant gift.

Since we'd had no supper, Diddy stopped north of town at Porky's BBQ Shack, Flintville's drive-in barbecue eatery. We ate barbecue sandwiches while Diddy drove and listened to the news on WSB.

The drone of the evening news lulled me to sleep. Seconds later, it seemed, Cece was gently shaking me. "Wake up, Allie, wake up! You're going to miss the great tree!" I sat up, rubbed my eyes, readjusted my glasses, and peered out the window. We were traveling through downtown Atlanta, and atop Rich's Department Store stood the great Christmas tree. It towered twenty feet over the roof of the ten-story building and sparkled with hundreds of lights.

Mimi lived in a two-story duplex in the Virginia Highlands neighborhood. Her apartment made up the top floor while Miss Inez, her old-maid cousin, inhabited the bottom level. Together the two ladies owned *Southern Styles*, a dressmaking business housed in Miss Inez's extra bedroom. By the time we arrived, I felt drunk from lack of sleep. Luckily, Mimi had already prepared the sofa hide-a-bed for Cece and me to share. I climbed in and was immediately asleep.

When I awoke the following morning, Diddy had already left for his annual checkup at the VA hospital, and Mimi placed the "Closed" sign on the downstairs window so that she could entertain Cece and me. Both Cece and I had brought a Sunday dress and shoes for this occasion. Mimi had on a wool suit with matching hat; she wore high heels and carried a pair of white gloves in her hand.

We took the trolley car to Little Five Points, where Mimi did her marketing. She allowed me to choose one candy treat. I chose a king sized Baby Ruth, which cost an entire dime. Cece rolled her eyes. "I hope you don't get a stomachache from all of that, Allie. You know we're going to have lunch at Rich's." I just smirked and bit into the tremendous log of nectar, nuts, and chocolate as we boarded the trolley for Forsyth Street.

Rich's Department Store was the grandest in all of Georgia. Of course, Cece wanted to head straight to the Junior Girls' department. "Mimi, may I please ride the elevator to the roof and see the great tree?" I pleaded. "I've done it with you for the past five years. I know the way, I promise."

Mimi finally acquiesced. "Now, Allie, you be back here by 11:30, or we'll miss our reservation in the Magnolia Room," she warned as I scooted toward the elevator.

When the elevator opened, a colored woman pulled back a gate as she softly warned, "Watch your step, please. Going up." Dressed in a brown uniform with a Rich's label sewn on her pocket, she sat on a little wooden stool as she operated the buttons panel. When the elevator stopped, she stood up from her stool, opened the gate, and announced: "Second floor—linens, fine china, ladies' lingerie, and infants' clothing. Watch your step, please!" This litany continued as we made our way up until we finally reached the roof. Although by now no one was left on the elevator but the colored woman and me, she announced: "Tenth floor—Rich's great Christmas tree and the Pink Pig! Watch your step."

As she opened the gate, I paused to question her. "What's a pink pig? A new toy?"

The colored woman grinned for the first time and looked me in the eye. "Why, no chile. It's a train; you go see. Watch your step, now!"

The Pink Pig turned out to be a pink roller coaster with an engine that looked like the head of a pig. The roller coaster traveled around the great tree. I ended up sitting in a car with a pudgy, freckled face boy. He wore a cap with earflaps that reminded me of Elmer Fudd. Before the train made its first turn, the fat boy screamed, "Stop! I'm going to throw up!" The conductor obviously couldn't stop the roller coaster until it circled the entire tree. By the time we traveled the full circle, "Elmer" had vomited all over my Sunday black patent leather Mary Janes. I jumped out of the car before he spewed again.

As I made my way back to the Junior Girls' Department, I received several looks from other shoppers as they covered their noses in disgust. Poor Mimi saw no alternative but to purchase me a new pair of shoes. Luckily, the shoe department had one Sunday pair left in my size.

The Magnolia Room, the most elegant dining hall I'd ever seen, was jammed with ladies of all sizes and ages dressed in their Sunday finery. As I studied the menu, I glanced at Cece. "Wow, look at what a chicken salad plate costs! The Andersons at the Hotel Flintville could make a fortune if they charged that much!" Mimi gave me a disapproving look while Cece kicked me under the table.

The chicken salad plate was accompanied by two cheese straws and an itty bitty cucumber sandwich. I devoured every single morsel and applauded myself for choosing the giant Baby Ruth earlier in the day. On the trolley ride back to Mimi's house, she and Cece chattered on and on about the delightful luncheon and the new spring fashions. Would I ever belong to this world of hats and gloves and cucumber sandwiches? The thought just made me tired.

We headed home to Flintville with so many Christmas packages from Mimi stuffed in Diddy's Studebaker that he had to tie down the trunk. I drifted off to sleep in the back seat and dreamt I was at a tea party in the Magnolia Room. All the other guests were little pink pigs wearing gloves and hats.

Christmas Eve was my absolute favorite night of the year. Aunt Bird always served turkey and cornbread dressing. For dessert we had a choice of warm pecan pie or my aunt's chocolate cake.

After everyone was stuffed, we adjourned to the sun porch. It had been such a warm December that we'd placed our Christmas tree on the porch this year. We gathered our chairs around the tree for Diddy to read the Christmas story from the Sinclair family Bible. Then, Uncle Hoyt strummed his guitar as he and Aunt Bird harmonized to "Silent Night." The only lights on the porch came from our tree, and I could see the stars twinkling in the cloudless, winter night.

The following morning I was the first one up, but we had a rule that no one could open presents until we all assembled. Since Uncle Hoyt wouldn't arrive for another hour, Diddy relented and allowed us to get started. As I predicted, my packages from Mimi consisted of two wool skirts, two hand-knitted sweaters, and a corduroy jacket with tiny brass buttons. The final package from Mimi was a family tree book, which allowed me to trace my heritage on both the Sinclair side as well as the Banks side. She had included some photos of my mama when she was about my age.

Although I no longer believed in Santa, Diddy and Aunt Bird still laid out our "Santa" gifts unwrapped under the tree. There was the transistor radio as well as the ice cream maker. I was a little disappointed that I found no new bicycle basket among my gifts, but there was a Magic 8-Ball, which I'd admired at Mackey's Dime Store.

Aunt Bird headed to the kitchen to prepare a Christmas breakfast of link sausage and homemade biscuits slathered in butter and fresh peach preserves. Although I heard Uncle Hoyt come in the kitchen's back door and smelled the delicious breakfast aromas, I was intent on putting together my ice cream maker. Diddy called me three times before I dragged myself away from the tree.

Everyone was already seated. As I made my way to the table, I discovered a ribbon tied to my chair. "What's this?" I asked as everyone smiled at me. The ribbon led out the back door where I discovered something that made my heart stop. It was the twenty-four inch blue Schwinn with a shiny new basket already attached. I screamed in delight, ran to Diddy and hugged him, kissed Aunt Bird on the cheek, and then headed back outside to give the bike a test ride. It was almost as tall as me, and I had to stand on my toes to reach the pedals. With a look of concern on his face, Diddy watched as I took a spin around the backyard. "Don't worry, Diddy, by summer I bet I'll be an inch taller."

After several threats that I would catch a cold if I stayed outside in my pajamas, Diddy and Aunt Bird coaxed me back to the breakfast table. Between bites of sausage and biscuits, I exclaimed, "I don't think anything could make this Christmas more perfect!"

Uncle Hoyt cleared his throat. "Well, I don't know, Allie. There might be one thing. How would you like for me to be your real uncle?"

Cece jumped up and started screaming and hugging Aunt Bird. "You're getting married, aren't you? I knew it! I just knew it! I could tell something was going on! When? Where?"

Aunt Bird smiled as she took Uncle Hoyt's hand in hers. "Well, we're planning a June wedding. Hoyt is finally going to build a house on that property in Johnston Heights."

Diddy stood up and hugged his sister. Then he slapped Uncle Hoyt on the back. "Welcome to the family, Slick! It's about time."

I was stunned. Aunt Bird was leaving us? How could we survive without her? My heart sank into my stomach. Aunt Bird must have noticed. "Allie, honey, are you okay? Is this too much excitement for you?"

How could I tell her that I didn't want her to leave? She seemed to read my mind. "It's okay, baby. Now you'll have both an aunt and an uncle to love you!"

As I watched her and Uncle Hoyt wrapped in one another's arms, I knew that was where they belonged. Somehow I felt sure they would fit me in, too.

Chapter 15

During the final hour of school on a sunny Tuesday in February, our class sat quietly completing geography questions over the Amazon River. The assignment seemed more daunting than usual as we listened to the fourth grade celebrating Valentine's Day with a party. The fifth grade teachers had determined we were too old for such frivolity although they would allow us to trade Valentine cards. Ten minutes before the end of the school day, we would place our Valentines in mailbags strung on clothesline underneath the blackboard.

Valentine's Day was my least favorite of holidays. I had no sweethearts myself although some of the girls, whom Aunt Bird called "early bloomers," would receive cards from sixth grade boys. It was even rumored that Dede Upton had a beau in the seventh grade. Dede was the only girl in our class who wore a bra.

At breakfast that morning, Cece had been all a-chatter. The Student Council had sponsored a "Secret Admirer" fundraiser where students could purchase a single carnation and have it secretly delivered to their "sweetheart." Cece received a half dozen carnations from different admirers, and they were arranged in a vase on the kitchen table.

"I just can't imagine who sent me these," Cece babbled between bites of Rice Krispies. "I know the pink one came from David Estes. Margaret says he has me a box of chocolates, too. She saw him buying it yesterday in Hastings Drugstore."

Diddy looked up from his coffee. "He shouldn't be spending his hard earned money on such nonsense. The flower was enough."

Cece rolled her eyes. "Oh Diddy! I bet you bought candy and flowers for girls when you were in high school. Don't forget, I'm going to the Valentine's banquet tonight." When a frown appeared across Diddy's brow, Cece added, "Don't worry; it's over at 9:00 since it's a school night."

Diddy shrugged his shoulders and went back to his coffee. Aunt Bird winked at Cece as she buttered a slice of toast. Then she turned to me. "Allie, did you get your Valentines addressed?"

"Yes ma'am, I did them even though I think they're stupid." I hated the silly little sayings like "Cool Cat" and "You're the Tops" written on them.

"Now come on, Allie. I know you have at least one sweetheart in the fifth grade," Cece teased. "Who's that special card going to? That handmade one I saw you working on last night? Come on, tell us!" she prodded.

My ears burned with embarrassment. I'd intended the card to remain a secret, but Cece had spoiled my surprise. As I reached into my book satchel, I frowned at Cece. "It's not for any dumb boy!" I pulled the handmade card from my satchel and presented it to Diddy. "Here Diddy, I was going to sneak this under your windshield wiper before you left for work, but Cece ruined it!"

The card, constructed from red paper and a white doily, was cut into the shape of a heart. Remembering my artistic disaster with the Christmas pencil holder, I opted not to decorate the heart in glitter. Instead, I'd composed a little verse for Diddy:

> A "heart gift" should go to the one we love
> Whether on earth or way up above
> To the one whose heart is always true
> Dear Diddy, this Valentine is for you.

> Love,
> Allie

Diddy opened the folded heart and read the verse to himself. When he looked up at me, I glimpsed a tear in his eye. "Why, Allie, that's just... just... really special." He leaned over and kissed me atop my head. Then he refolded the heart and placed it in his coat pocket. "I'll keep this close to my heart today," he added gently as he headed out the door.

I knew Cece would be overwhelmed with Valentines on this day. Aunt Bird was even aflutter that Uncle Hoyt had made reservations at a new restaurant in Macon, and she was looking forward to a night of romance instead of another evening spent in the kitchen as she prepared a meal. That left Diddy and me sharing membership in the "Lonely Hearts Club." Except for feeling jealous that Cece would be loaded down with chocolates, I couldn't have cared less about having a sweetheart. However, something told me that special days like this reminded my daddy of the love that had been snatched away from him far too soon.

The early dismissal bell interrupted my musings, and I hurried out with the rest of my classmates to deliver my Valentines. Afterwards, Josie and I tarried on the front steps of the school and studied the contents of our mailbags. Miss Pridmore, the prune herself, had filled each bag with a small box of conversation hearts. Josie and I spent a half hour sharing the silly slogans and then popping the sweet candy into our mouths.

After dawdling so long with Josie, I arrived at the newspaper office almost an hour late. Although the "Closed" sign swung prominently from the front door, Diddy, as usual, had left it unlocked for me. There were no clacking sounds from his old Underwood though I could see a light burning in his office. I figured he was in the pressroom or had run next door to the office supply store.

I started to pile my book satchel and coat in its usual place, a chair beside Miss Opal's desk in the outer office. A big, red heart-shaped candy box was already resting on the chair. Taped to the top of the box was a note in Diddy's undeniable scrawl:

> Allie,
> May you always remain my little sweetheart. Happy
> Valentine's Day!
>   Love,
>   Diddy

Boy, was I thrilled! An entire box of chocolates just for me! I dug in immediately. I stuffed myself with a chocolate covered cherry, a chocolate covered nougat, and a chocolate covered peanut butter bar before coming up for air.

Then I realized I needed to thank my "secret sweetheart." Licking my fingers clean of chocolate, I headed past Diddy's office to the pressroom. Just as I was about to open the door leading to the pressroom, something inside Diddy's glass office caught my eye. My daddy was slumped over his desk, seemingly asleep. I tapped on the window to awaken him, but there was no response.

I'd never seen Diddy take a nap at work. Since it was almost time to go home anyway, I decided he'd be upset if I didn't wake him. So as not to startle him, I eased slowly up to his chair and patted him on the shoulder. "Diddy, it's time to go home. Diddy?" He didn't move. I realized he wasn't breathing. "Diddy, Diddy, what's wrong?" I shook his shoulder as hard as I could.

My heart was pounding in my throat as I ran out the front door and up to the office supply company. Uncle Hoyt literally bumped into me as he came out the front door all dressed for his evening with Aunt Bird. I opened my mouth but no words came out. "What is it, Allie? What's wrong?" I ran back toward the newspaper with Uncle Hoyt on my heels.

The remainder of that evening and the next few days, I felt as if I were swimming underwater. I remember the sound of the sirens, the ambulance pulling up to the front of the newspaper, Sheriff Brady standing over me. I remember riding in Uncle Hoyt's truck to the hospital, sitting on a cold, metal chair outside the emergency room, seeing both Cece and Aunt Bird rushing in with fear and bewilderment on their faces. I saw Doctor Justice speaking to Aunt Bird, but although I was only a foot away, I couldn't hear what he was saying. Perhaps, I chose not to hear what the doctor was telling Aunt Bird and Cece, who was dressed in a soft pink sweater and gray wool skirt for her Valentine banquet. I watched as my beautiful sister crumpled up into a little pink ball.

Two days later we buried Alfred Lemuel Sinclair beside his beloved bride Cecile Banks Sinclair as a cold rain blew across the cemetery. The funeral was held at the First Baptist Church of Flintville and officiated by Preacher Clayton. The church was so packed with people that there was standing room only. When I walked in with the family, I remember seeing Josie sitting with her parents and wondered why she wasn't in school. I cannot recall a single word spoken during the service, but I do remember when Uncle Hoyt sang "The Old Rugged Cross" without any accompaniment. His deep, resonating voice pierced my heart until I shook. They said later that there was not a dry eye in the entire congregation. Except maybe for mine.

After the burial, we returned to our house where an endless flow of friends and neighbors paraded to pay their respects. I thought if I heard one more person say Diddy was in a better place now, I would throw up. He wasn't here with me anymore, so how could that be a better place? I found myself hating God.

When I could no longer stand the parade, I drifted to the kitchen. Never had I seen such delicious food that made me feel so absolutely nauseous. There was fried chicken that Josie's maid Lorna had brought, potato salad and chocolate meringue pie from the hotel, several hams, a dozen congealed salads, ten cakes, and a tremendous pan of barbeque from Porky's Park. Berthie Atwell had delivered a sweet potato soufflé, and I thought how much Diddy would have enjoyed a big serving of it.

As the sun began to set, I found myself sitting on the back stoop off the kitchen door. It was the only place where someone wasn't telling me that it was okay to cry or trying to shove food in my face. Miz Gertie, an apron over her Sunday dress, appeared; I realized that I'd seen her in our kitchen before breakfast. "Allie, can you help me carry some dishes back over to my house? I walked over here this morning because there was no place to park." She handed me a grocery box of empty bowls, and I followed her down the steps.

The quiet of Miss Gertie's kitchen had a calming effect upon me. Suddenly, I felt completely exhausted as well as famished. Miz Gertie opened a cold bottle of 7-Up for me and suggested she make me a sandwich. "You know, when Roscoe Ray feels bad, his favorite thing is a grilled cheese and a bowl of tomato soup. How does that sound?"

Since I offered no resistance, Miz Gertie puttered around the kitchen as she prepared our little supper. When the food was ready, she set two bowls of piping soup and sandwiches on the table and sat down beside me. "I'm right hungry myself. I served food all day but didn't have a chance to eat any."

The remainder of our meal was eaten in silence, something I needed. Once I was full, my eyelids felt like they were connected to weights. "Miz Gertie, can I take a nap over here? It's just too noisy at my house," I explained. The last thing I remember was feeling the warmth of a blanket tucked under my chin as I sank into darkness and swam away from the pain.

The aroma of bacon frying had me fighting my way back to consciousness. Where was I? What day was it? Then I heard Miz Gertie humming in the kitchen, and I realized that my life would never be the same. I dragged myself off her couch and found my way to the kitchen. Miz Gertie looked as though she'd been up for quite some time, and when I read the clock over her stove, I realized it was 10:00 in the morning.

"There you are, Allie. I figured the smell of a hot breakfast might wake you." She sent me to the guest bath to wash up, and when I returned, breakfast was awaiting me. I didn't have the heart to tell her I wasn't much of a breakfast eater; however, with the first bite of bacon, I felt as if I had not eaten in months and devoured everything on my plate.

When I finished, Miz Gertie suggested that she walk me home. As I stalled for time, she sat down beside me and held my face in her hands. "Don't worry, Allie. Everyone's gone home, now. I know yesterday was just more than you could take. People mean well, but they just don't always say the right things, do they? I've lost two babies in miscarriages and buried two husbands, so I know a little something about grief. Each of us must find our own way to cope, and having people tell us that losing a loved one was the Lord's will is not what we want to hear. It may be the Lord's will, but it's not always our will, and that can make us angry. It's okay to be angry, Allie. Now let's get you home." Even though I'd walked the short distance from Miz Gertie's to my house many times by myself, I allowed Miz Gertie to escort me back to the house that was far too empty now.

According to Doctor Fenwick, the coroner, my daddy had suffered a massive stroke. A blood clot hit his heart, and he was gone in seconds. Uncle Hoyt, Aunt Bird, Cece, and I sat in the living room as Dr. Fenwick, accompanied by Doctor Justice, delivered the news. We really did not know Dr. Fenwick, who served as coroner for the tri-county area and resided in Meriwether County. I didn't like the way he looked. He was a nervous man with thinning hair, twitchy eyes, and fingers stained with tobacco. I knew Doctor Justice had come along to make us feel more comfortable.

I berated myself for not arriving at the newspaper on time that day. Perhaps if I'd been there, I could have gotten medical treatment for Diddy. But Dr. Justice assured me the blood clot would have killed Diddy no matter what. This assurance did little to make me feel better.

By mid-March our household had returned to a feigned normalcy. Each morning we headed to school as was expected. On Tuesdays, I would walk to the high school to wait on Aunt Bird, and Josie's mother drove me home from Girl Scouts on Wednesdays. Many nights I would lie in bed and listen to Cece cry herself to sleep. Although Aunt Bird kept a stiff upper lip around us, once on a midnight trek to the bathroom, I discovered her sobbing as she sat in Diddy's chair on the sun porch. I slipped past her and back to bed without her hearing me.

As for me, I was still too angry to cry. I took my anger out on the people who loved me the most. Completing my arithmetic homework became a battle of epic proportions between Aunt Bird and me. Although I'd complete all other assignments, I couldn't bring myself to work the long division problems that Diddy had always walked me through.

One night as Aunt Bird was leaving for a PTA meeting, she caught me watching television. "Allie, did you finish your arithmetic? You know that there's no television until all homework is completed."

At that moment, some other being inhabited my body, and I screamed, "No, I'm not going to do my arithmetic, and you can't make me! You're not my mama or my daddy!"

Aunt Bird's eyes filled with tears, and she bit her lip. "You're right, Allie. I'm neither your mother nor your father, but I am your guardian." She cleared her throat and when she spoke again, the tone was that of a teacher's instead of the aunt I knew. "There will be no television for the remainder of the week. And starting tomorrow, you'll stay with Miss Pridmore for thirty minutes after school to complete your arithmetic." I stormed into my room and flung open my arithmetic book. Cece was rolling her hair while she waited for the bathtub to fill. I gave her a look daring her to reproach me. She just shook her head at me and continued her hair ritual.

Miz Gertie had been right; each of us has our own way of dealing with loss. Cece suffered her grief in silence. She rarely spoke Diddy's name, but I discovered a sketch pad of charcoals depicting Diddy in the many poses of his life: sitting at his typewriter in his office, reading the newspaper on our sun porch, setting type at one of the presses. When I told her the sketches were the best she'd ever drawn, she sighed and placed the pad under her bed.

As she stood up from the dressing table, I noticed how thin she had grown. Her willowy arms and legs were losing their shapeliness, and her sunken cheeks accentuated dark circles beneath her eyes. Aunt Bird had noticed, too, because just yesterday I'd overheard her scheduling an appointment for Cece with Doctor Justice. Now as Cece padded toward the bathroom, I broke the point on my pencil. "Crap, that's my last pencil!" I exclaimed throwing it across the floor.

Cece froze and glared at me. "Allie! I don't want to hear you use such language again. Profanity does not become a young lady!"

Her holier than thou attitude infuriated me. I followed her towards the bathroom. When I discovered she'd shut the door, I stood outside with my acid retort. "Kiss my ass, you high falutin bitch! Who are you to tell me how to behave?" I waited for her reaction to my foul mouth, but there was no response. All I could hear was the water running.

My anger spent, I withdrew to my room to complete my homework. Ten minutes later when I headed to the kitchen for some lemonade, I could still hear bath water running. I banged on the bathroom door. "How about saving me a little hot water, Miss Priss Pot!" When there was no response, I banged on the door once more.

My feet grew wet, and I realized that water was flooding under the door into the hall. Luckily, she had not locked the door, so I opened it and adjusted my eyes to the steam-filled room. "Cece, you idiot! Are you trying to flood the entire house?" Cece was not in the tub, but instead lay naked and motionless on the bathroom floor. For a moment, I had an eerie feeling that I'd been suspended in time, a February evening and my daddy's lifeless body lay slumped over. The water on my ankles brought me back, and I quickly turned off the faucet. I touched Cece's neck and could feel a pulse. She's not dead, she's not dead, I told myself. Get help!

Miz Gertie was at the front door within two minutes of my call. She'd called an ambulance on her way out. She covered Cece in a blanket and told me to put on some dry shoes. I was shaking from head to toe as I heard the shrill scream of the ambulance and saw its lights blinking through our living room window.

Swimming underwater again, I obediently changed my socks and shoes. When I returned to the hall, the ambulance attendants were rolling Cece out on a gurney. Still covered in the blanket, the sight of Cece's pale, gaunt, lifeless body took the breath from my lungs. I was drowning.

Far above, at the surface of my sea of agony, I heard Miz Gertie. "Allie, stand up, honey. Come on. We'll follow the ambulance to the hospital. I called Hoyt, and he and your Aunt Ophelia will meet us there. Allie, dear, do you hear me?"

I gulped for air and returned to the world as Miz Gertie pulled me up from the hallway floor where I had sunk. The next moment I found myself once again in the narrow waiting area outside the emergency room. The only place to sit was the same, cold metal chair where I'd sat just a few weeks earlier. I chose to stand.

Just before daybreak, I felt strong arms pick me up from the waiting area's floor where I'd fallen asleep. Struggling to return to a conscious state, I discovered Uncle Hoyt loading me into his pickup. "It's okay, Allie. Let's get you home and to bed. Everything's going to be all right," he reassured me as he tucked a hospital blanket under my chin.

As Uncle Hoyt pulled into our driveway, my senses returned to me. I managed to whisper the unimaginable. "Uncle Hoyt, is Cece gone? Is she dead, Uncle Hoyt, is she?"

Uncle Hoyt wrapped his big arms around me. "No, she's not dead, Allie. She's going to be just fine. Doctor Justice thinks she had some kind of seizure. She was awake when we left the hospital, but the doc wants to run a few tests before he lets her go home. Your quick thinking probably saved her, Allie. If you hadn't called Miz Gertie when you did, we could have lost Cece."

Filled with shame, I couldn't bear to tell Uncle Hoyt that I was the cause of Cece's seizure. As I crawled into my own bed, I thanked God that my cruel words were not the last thing Cece would ever hear. Then I thanked God for sparing Cece; I guess God figured He could do without another Sinclair for the time being. By the time I finished my prayer of thanksgiving, I realized that the Lord and I had some unfinished business. As humbly as I could, I begged God to forgive me for hating Him and promised never to feel that way again.

The aroma of onions awakened me, and when I looked at the clock on our night table, I was shocked to see it was after noon. I stumbled into the kitchen to find Uncle Hoyt with a bag of burgers and fries from England's Poolroom. "I thought you might be hungry. I hope you don't mind poolroom hamburgers; they're much better than anything I could cook," he grinned as I dug into the bag.

After we finished lunch, Uncle Hoyt suggested I accompany him to the newspaper. "Your aunt wants to stay at the hospital until they've finished with the tests. You feel like going with me?" When I hesitated, Uncle Hoyt added, "Ophelia didn't think your being home by yourself all afternoon was a good idea."

I had not been to the newspaper office since the afternoon I'd discovered Diddy, and the thought of returning caused my stomach to flip flop. Uncle Hoyt, patting me on the shoulder, reassured me. "It's okay, Allie. We'll park in the alley and go in through the pressroom. One of the presses is on the blink, and I need to repair it for tomorrow's run. You can stay in the back with me."

Relieved that I wouldn't have to see Diddy's office, I reluctantly agreed to accompany Uncle Hoyt. Since it was Tuesday, there was no one working at the newspaper anyway. Although I'd dreaded this moment, once I was in the pressroom, the smell of ink and the rolls of newsprint comforted me.

At first, I hung close to Uncle Hoyt as he repaired the press, but after a while, I grew restless and began to wander among the giant rolls of paper and the other presses. Before long, I was standing in the doorway of Diddy's office.

The room appeared undisturbed as though waiting for Diddy's return. I turned on the overhead light and ventured inside the glass enclosure. I glanced at my little homework table, still snuggled beside Diddy's big oak desk.

My eyes traveled toward Diddy's old Underwood. If I closed my eyes, I could almost hear the tap, tap, tapping of the typewriter's keys. An object sparkling in the light drew my attention; it was the glitter from the Campbell soup can I'd decorated for Diddy. The can was stocked to the brim with his chewing gum. Behind his desk was a coat rack, which still held the jacket Diddy wore on his final day with me. I lovingly lifted the jacket from its resting place and held it close to my face. I could smell Diddy—his printer's ink, his chewing gum, his hair tonic.

Something rattled inside the breast pocket of his jacket. I retrieved the rattling paper; it was my Valentine, the one he'd promised to keep close to his heart on that fateful day. As I held the Valentine to my chest, the dam in my heart burst. The tears trickled slowly at first, but by the time Uncle Hoyt discovered me, I was heaving gigantic sobs. I buried my face in Uncle Hoyt's chest as I finally surrendered my grief.

Chapter 16

Cece's seizure was caused by an imbalance in her blood sugar. Dr. Justice diagnosed Cece with juvenile diabetes and began a regimen of insulin injections that she must endure for the rest of her life, just as Diddy had.

One early Saturday morning in late April, I stumbled into the kitchen to find Aunt Bird and Dr. Justice in deep conversation. For the past six weeks, Dr. Justice had stopped by each morning to give Cece her injection. This arrangement would soon come to an end, and Dr. Justice expressed his concern. "Cece's learned to inject herself without even flinching; she's one steady-handed young lady. But, if she does it herself, she'll have to inject the insulin in her upper thigh. I'm concerned that the thigh muscle is not completely matured in her body yet, and constant injections could damage muscle tissue and cause scarring. She's not happy about that."

"Where is the best place for the injection, then?" Aunt Bird poured Dr. Justice another cup of coffee.

"Well, the optimum location is in her buttocks where I have been injecting it, but she can't reach that area herself. So, we need someone who's willing to give Cece her shots each day at least for the next eighteen months. By then she can try injections in her thigh muscle. What do you think? Are you up to the task?"

Aunt Bird's face lost its color. "Oh, Dr. Justice, you know how I hate needles. The last time Nurse Stovall gave me my polio shot, I fainted." Aunt Bird's voice quivered. "I'm willing to try, but I just don't know if I can do it."

"Now, now, Ophelia, don't you go getting all upset. You've done a fine job of keeping this family together and helping Cece deal with her condition. We'll think of something."

Up until this point, I'd been pretending to examine the choices of cereal in our pantry. Before I could stop myself, I volunteered. "I could do it, Aunt Bird. I used to watch Diddy stick himself, and it didn't bother me at all."

Both adults turned around with startled looks. Aunt Bird smiled tenderly at me. "No, Allie, you're too young for such a responsibility. I'll just have to overcome my cowardice."

Dr. Justice removed a large syringe sporting a needle from his black bag. "Well, let's give it a try, Ophelia. Do you have any oranges in the refrigerator? That's a good way to practice."

Aunt Bird's eyes grew wide with panic as she studied the syringe in Dr. Justice's hand. As she stood up from the table to retrieve an orange, her knees buckled. Dr. Justice caught her before she collapsed on the floor. He grinned as he helped Aunt Bird back into her chair.

"Why, Ophelia, I'd forgotten just how squeamish you are. Now, I remember one time when you were about thirteen and cut yourself on a barbed wire fence. I chased you around the examining table to give you a tetanus shot." I giggled out loud, and Dr. Justice turned to me. "Allie, do you really think you can do this?"

"I know I can! Just give me a chance. Please, Aunt Bird," I begged. With Dr. Justice on my side and Aunt Bird's knees still quaking, she relented.

Within an hour, I'd mastered shooting sugar water into every orange in our refrigerator bin. I just hoped Cece's butt would be as easy a target. On Monday morning, it took Dr. Justice and Aunt Bird to convince Cece that I was ready to serve as her nurse. As she leaned over the bed and grimaced, she gave me a warning. "Okay, baby brat, remember, my rear end is not a dart board." Aunt Bird covered her eyes and everyone held a collective breath as I took a deep one and plunged the needle into Cece's fanny. Dr. Justice congratulated me on my expertise, and Cece admitted it was practically painless. Thus began a new chapter in the relationship between my big sister and me.

Each morning before breakfast, Cece would call me into the bathroom where she would already have the syringe filled with her insulin. I'd dab her backside with an alcohol-soaked cotton ball, aim, and fire. Although the entire procedure caused me no discomfort, being stuck in the butt every morning was no picnic for Cece. She never once complained until one morning when I sleepily straggled into the bathroom without my glasses.

Blindly aiming at Cece's butt, I shot her a little high, and she squealed in pain. "Ouch, that really hurt, Allie! Are you finished?" She rubbed her backside and discovered a pinprick of blood.

Devastated that I'd caused her more suffering than necessary, I burst into tears. "I'm sorry, Cece. Are you okay? I'm sorry I hurt you, I'm sorry you have diabetes, I'm sorry it's you and not me, I'm sorry I called you a bitch that night you got sick. I didn't mean it; I love you so much, Cece. Please don't ever leave me. Please don't die! I couldn't bear to live without you!" My pent-up confession tumbled out between my gasping sobs.

Cece enveloped me in her long, willowy arms and pulled me close to her. She stroked my hair as I wailed into her shoulder. I could smell her soft bath powder, and her clean fragrance and soothing voice calmed me. "It's okay, Allie. You didn't hurt me that much; I'm fine. I'm not about to die right now. After surviving algebra this year, diabetes is nothing. And I'll never ever leave you, I promise." She lifted my chin and gazed into my face. "We're sisters, we're family, and family sticks together. Don't you ever forget that. Now wash your face and get dressed before you make us late for school." She handed me the soap, and then hesitated. "Just one thing, Allie. When did you ever call me the 'B' word?"

It dawned on me that Cece hadn't heard my tirade the night of her seizure. She must have already been unconscious, so I'd confessed for nothing. I began brushing my teeth to avoid answering her. Of course, Aunt Bird would have maintained that the Lord gave me this opportunity to come completely clean of my sins. She would have been right. For the first time in months, my heart began to lose its heaviness.

Cece held true to her declaration that she was a survivor. She handled her diabetes with quiet grace. She made a rule that none of her friends except Margaret were to know of her condition. Adhering to her insulin regimen as well as a strict diet, Cece determined to live as normal a teenage life as possible.

In May, she tried out and made the varsity cheerleading squad, a position captured by only the best upcoming sophomores since most of the squad was junior and senior girls. A soft, vibrant fullness replaced the gaunt, strained look her face had carried all winter, she began to create pastels of all the spring flowers in bloom, and she returned to chatting with Margaret on the phone for hours at a time. The sister I cherished had returned.

Squaring things with Cece helped me begin my own healing process. The anger that had crippled me in the months since Diddy died began to evaporate. As summer neared, I actually anticipated long, lazy bike rides with Josie and Friday afternoons with Roscoe Ray.

But before I could truly feel whole again, I needed to make amends with my Aunt Bird. Since the nightmarish evening of Cece's collapse, we hadn't mentioned my display of cruel disrespect. I felt the tension of unspoken apologies hovering between me and the aunt who had sacrificed so much to keep our family together.

The Friday before the last week of school found my aunt and me home alone. Cece was at a cheerleading clinic for the weekend, and Uncle Hoyt had gone fishing with an old army buddy. I stayed up to watch *The Twilight Zone* while Aunt Bird graded her final set of term papers. At 11:00 P.M., I suddenly remembered I'd volunteered her chocolate cake for a Saturday bake sale sponsored by Brownie Scout Troop 225.

When I told her, Aunt Bird had a conniption! I knew my Aunt Bird as a good Christian woman who had the patience of Job. So, I was shocked when she threw up her hands as in supplication, did a little stamping dance, and screamed, "Heavenly Father above, how can I possibly bake that cake, get it iced, and still make my hair appointment with Miss Thelma?"

I dared not agitate her any more than I already had. "Aw, Aunt Bird, I'll just tell Miz Edwards you didn't have time to bake one...or you could wash your own hair tomorrow afternoon instead of going to the beauty shop," I softly suggested.

"First of all, Allie, once you make a commitment to someone, you should never break it. Mrs. Edwards is depending on that cake to sell, and I won't let her down. Secondly, if I do my own hair, I'll look like a red porcupine for Sunday's service, and I have a solo to sing. Miss Thelma is the only person on earth who can tame this unruly mop. Now, go on to bed and I'll take care of things," she huffed as I followed her into the kitchen and watched her pull eggs and milk from the refrigerator. I felt miserable as I slunked off to bed.

At 3:00 A.M. when I crept into the kitchen for a glass of water, I found Aunt Bird icing the last of nine layers with her famous chocolate frosting. As she used her elbow to brush a stray red curl from her eyes, I could see that her cheeks were flushed from the heat of the kitchen. My heart melted as I watched this beautiful, selfless woman at work.

"Oh, Aunt Bird, I'm sorry you had to stay up so late. It's all my fault!" The magical aroma of her chocolate frosting hit my nose. "I believe that's the prettiest nine layer you've ever made!" I remarked in total sincerity as I reached out to swipe a little frosting.

"Don't you dare!" she warned as she pinned back the straggling red curl. Her anger was replaced with an exhausted look of satisfaction. She smiled, "It is a good one. Perhaps I should do all my baking in the middle of the night when you girls aren't distracting me." She handed me a spatula and a pot of unused frosting. One taste put me in chocolate heaven.

"Don't make yourself sick, you hear," she added sleepily as she untied her apron and headed towards her bedroom.

Before she made it down the hall, I caught her and began to hug her around her waist. "Aunt Bird, you're the best aunt in the whole world. I love you as much as I loved Diddy. Can you ever forgive me for the mean things I said?" I begged as tears welled in my eyes.

Aunt Bird squatted down so that we were eye level. "Allie, don't you know I forgave you the moment those words were spoken? I knew it wasn't you speaking; it was your grief, your pain. I know you love me, honey. And I could never ever stop loving you, so I guess we're stuck with each other." She smiled, hugged me close, and then retreated for a few hours of sleep.

I padded back to the kitchen and the warm chocolate frosting. The night was so peaceful and the world so silent that I could hear Diddy's voice as though he were sitting beside me at the kitchen table. "Everything's going to be all right now, Allie." I knew his words, spoken so softly to my heart, were true.

Part II
1962-1965

Chapter 17

One early June evening, I discovered Aunt Bird sitting in Diddy's favorite chair on the sun porch, engrossed in a book of poetry.

"Whatcha reading?" I asked

She smiled. "The works of Robert Frost,"

"Oh, yeah. He wrote that poem about the snow in the woods, the one I had to memorize last year."

Aunt Bird seemed impressed. "You're talking about 'Stopping by Woods on a Snowy Evening,' aren't you?"

The title sparked my memory. "I liked the last lines:

> *The woods are lovely, dark, and deep*
> *But I have promises to keep*
> *And miles to go before I sleep.*"

"Do you know what those lines mean?" I was about to receive a literature lesson.

"I think he was ready to lie down and go to sleep, and Mrs. Crenshaw told us the word 'sleep' could mean an endless sleep. So, he must have wanted to give up and die, but he had some other traveling to do."

Aunt Bird nodded in agreement. "What do you think those 'miles' in the poem represent?"

I watched the fireflies in our yard. "Maybe 'miles' represents all the traveling he had left in his life before he was ready for the next life up in heaven."

My aunt beamed. "I may need you as a guest speaker for my poetry unit next fall."

Her voice faltered. "When your daddy died, I felt like the speaker in Mr. Frost's poem. I wanted to crawl in a hole and give up. One sleepless night I sat in this chair and had a good, long cry. Then I picked up a book of poetry and discovered the comfort I needed from another poem by Mr. Frost."

Aunt Bird thumbed through the book until she came to a poem entitled "—Out, Out," and she read it aloud. It was about a young boy working in his family's sawmill. His job was to feed the logs into the saw. When his sister called him to supper, the boy became distracted and fed his own arm into the saw. Then the boy lost so much blood that he died.

I was shocked at its ending as the family watched the boy take his last breaths:

> *Little, less, nothing—no more to build on there,*
> *And they, since they were not the one dead,*
> *Turned to their affairs.*

"That's so cruel," I remarked. "The rest of the family just went on back to work like nothing happened."

Aunt Bird smiled at me. "That's certainly one interpretation. Maybe, Mr. Frost was telling us that death is a part of life, and that there comes a time when those of us who remain on earth must move on with our lives."

The lump in my throat allowed me no response, and Aunt Bird continued, "Allie, we've all mourned long enough. It's time to start living again."

Aunt Bird's explanation stuck with me, and as the summer unfolded, each of us, in our own way, returned to the living.

Aunt Bird took over as fulltime librarian for the summer when Miz Meriweather requested a leave of absence. Cece landed a position at Paris's Dress Shoppe, where her artistic abilities gained her the responsibility of changing the window displays.

To serve as fulltime editor of the *Star*, Uncle Hoyt turned over management of the office supply store to Ellis Parks, Miz Opal's husband. Uncle Hoyt covered all the news stories while Chuck Purdy, the paper's sports editor, also sold advertising for the paper.

On evenings before the paper went to press, Uncle Hoyt would appear in time for supper with a rough copy of tomorrow's stories in his hands and a look of utter appeal upon his face. After supper, he and Aunt Bird would sit at the cleared kitchen table for an editing session. Although Uncle Hoyt considered himself more of an engineer than a journalist, with Aunt Bird's guidance, he soon proved to be an acceptable writer.

My hopes of surpassing last summer's accumulated bicycle mileage were dashed when Josie announced she'd be spending six weeks in LaGrange to attend a horse camp near her uncle's farm. As I began to consider how much I could get into without the watchful eyes of an adult, my attitude brightened. At least until Aunt Bird offered some alternatives to my plans. She had a sixth sense about youngsters left alone with idle time.

The following Monday I stood amid the upcoming sixth graders outside the First Baptist Church as we lined up for the daily march into the sanctuary that heralded each day of Vacation Bible School. Not only was I forced to put on a dress and shoes, but I must also endure four hours of utter misery.

Standing in the sweltering sun, I studied the other sixth graders, none with whom I shared much in common. As Mrs. Braswell, the sixth grade leader, waved the flag to begin our march, I cursed Josie and all horses under my breath.

When the morning devotional ended, we filed out to our respective classes where we could choose between the arts and crafts table, the books of the Bible table, or the inspiration table. After a while, Mrs. Braswell would ring a bell for us to rotate to a new location. Everyone darted for the arts and crafts table where we could paint a variety of ceramic models including crucifixes or scenes of the last supper. There were only five seats at this table and fifteen sixth graders, so the fastest five always landed there first. The rest of us would scurry to the next table where a high school student drilled us on the books of the Bible.

The least desirable location was the inspiration table, managed by Mrs. Minnie Braswell. Mrs. Braswell was considered the most Christian woman in the church. She was there whenever the doors opened for any kind of meeting, and on rare occasions when there was no meeting, Mrs. Braswell could always find a need for one. She was head of the primary children's training union, director of the Girls' Auxiliary, and superintendent of the junior Sunday school classes.

Although adults admired her devotion to the church's youth, we youngsters didn't share this admiration. Mrs. Braswell kept her eyes opened during prayer to see if any child's head wasn't bowed in reverence. She chastised us for playing outside on Sunday afternoons and often prayed aloud for high school students who attended dances.

Cece explained to me this devout woman's strict beliefs. "She was raised a Primitive Baptist. I hear she's never owned a pair of slacks. Rumor is she can speak in the tongues. If the Holy Ghost comes over her, you might get to hear her."

I'd heard of people who could speak in the tongues but had never observed such in the First Baptist Church of Flintville. Aunt Bird explained that our Baptist traditions were moderate as opposed to the "hard-shell" Baptist churches that followed more fundamentalist traditions. When I asked her which kind of Baptist was the right kind, Aunt Bird smiled. "Well, neither church is totally right or totally wrong. The best way to worship is to follow your own heart, Allie."

I insisted I could best follow my heart by discontinuing my week of Bible school, but Aunt Bird was relentless.

I landed at the inspiration table where I sat between Pammie Reese and Daniel McSwain. When I observed Daniel picking his nose and looking for a place to park his treasure, I scooted my chair closer to Pammie.

We waited in silence as Mrs. Braswell returned to the table with her daily inspiration. "I want you to raise your hand if you are saved," she began, and all five of our hands went in the air. Mrs. Braswell scowled at us. "Let me rephrase the question: raise your hand if you've been baptized." This time both Pammie's and my hand stayed down.

How I wished I'd lied and raised my hand. For the next hour, Mrs. Braswell gave Pammie and me her "testimony," told us we were covered in sin, and informed us that the only way to spare ourselves an eternity of hellfire was to be reborn through baptism. By the end of the hour, poor Pammie was shaking all over, and Mrs. Braswell had arranged for us to be baptized on Sunday morning.

By Friday afternoon I'd devised a plot for skipping the Sunday service. I'd pick all the green plums off Miz Clara's bush up the street, eat them on Saturday, and have a whopper of a stomachache before Sunday school.

Before I could implement my operation, Aunt Bird announced at supper that Mrs. Braswell had paid a visit to the library. "So, Allie, you're going to baptized? That's wonderful news! Goodness, child, you look scared to death!"

I glanced at Cece for help, but she appeared in a state of shock. "I don't see why I need to be baptized. Josie says the Methodist preacher just sprinkled some water on her head when she was a baby, and she's going to heaven. Mrs. Braswell makes it sound like the only way to escape burning for eternity is to be dunked in water. The Lord knows I'm a Christian. Can't He see everything in my heart?"

Aunt Bird appeared as shocked as Cece. "I'd no idea Mrs. Braswell pressured you. Being baptized is a personal decision, and I don't want you to feel forced into it." She patted me on my hand and went back to her potato salad.

My reprieve was short-lived, however. When the church bulletin arrived Saturday afternoon, an announcement appeared on the inside cover:

> *The church is pleased to announce the baptism of*
> *Pamela Anne Reese and Allison Louise Sinclair*
> *at Sunday's service.*

Since Uncle Hoyt had driven Aunt Bird to Callaway Gardens for a picnic, she didn't see the bulletin. It was the first thing I showed Cece when she came home from work. She was furious. "That Mrs. Braswell has some nerve, doesn't she?"

"What should I do, Cece?"

Cece sighed. "Now if you don't go through with the baptism, Aunt Bird will certainly be embarrassed. Anyway, you're going to be baptized sooner or later, aren't you?" When I gave no response, she eyed me suspiciously.

I mustered up a protest. "I bet Diddy would tell me not to worry about what anybody else thought."

Cece lovingly pushed my glasses back up on my nose. "You're probably right, but sometimes, we do things to make it easier for those we love. Hold on a minute; I want to show you something."

Cece headed down the hall and returned carrying the Sinclair family Bible. "Baptism is a tradition our family has followed for generations. If it was good enough for our mama and our daddy, for Aunt Bird, and for me, don't you think it's good enough for you?"

Thumbing to the Bible's back pages, she located a chart entitled "Sinclair Family History." The first name at the top of the page was Britton Sinclair. "He was Diddy's great-great granddaddy," Cece explained. Beside Britton Sinclair's name were four important dates: his birth, his baptism, his marriage, and his death. As I studied the history, I realized I was the only Sinclair without a date by the line labeled "baptism."

Sunday morning, I stood with Pammie on the steps leading down into the baptistery, located behind the choir loft. We were both clad in white robes borrowed from the children's choir. Dressed in their Sunday finest, Aunt Bird and Uncle Hoyt sat with Cece on the front pew.

As we watched Preacher Clayton, clad in a pair of fisherman waders, make his way into the water, Pammie quivered all over. "You go first, Allie. I can't swim too well. I hate the water."

I headed down the steps toward Preacher Clayton, who had me fold my arms across my chest. Laying a strong hand against my back, he raised his other hand over my head and pronounced, "I baptize you, Allison Louise Sinclair, in the name of the Father, the Son, and the Holy Ghost." Then he pushed me under with his free hand, and in a matter of seconds, I was cleansed of all my iniquities.

Mrs. Braswell was waiting on the other side of the baptistery to hand us a towel and gloat over her two new "disciples." I was toweling dry my hair when Pammie emerged coughing and sputtering from the dunking. As she stumbled up the steps, poor Pammie threw up all over Mrs. Braswell's blue linen dress.

Her face coloring in anger, Mrs. Braswell gasped. I thought she was about to be overtaken by the Holy Ghost and begin speaking in tongues. Instead, she stormed towards the bathroom leaving her "disciples" to fend for ourselves.

I slipped into the sanctuary and slid between Uncle Hoyt and Aunt Bird just as Preacher Clayton began his sermon. The entire baptismal process was completely painless, at least for me. I felt not one iota different than I had before I was dunked.

After Sunday dinner that afternoon, Aunt Bird retrieved the Sinclair family Bible and turned to the very page that I had studied with Cece on Saturday. Next to my name with her best black fountain pen, Aunt Bird neatly recorded the date of my baptism.

Somehow seeing baptismal dates by the names of my beloved family gave me a sense of peace and belonging. I reckoned when the roll was called, every Sinclair would now be present.

Chapter 18

One morning at breakfast, Cece announced, "Aunt Bird, I've had my learner's permit for almost six months, but I've yet to sit behind a steering wheel. If I don't learn to drive this summer, I'll never have a chance once school starts again."

Aunt Bird dished out scrambled eggs. "I know, Cece. Your daddy's Studebaker is gathering dust, and Hoyt says it needs to be driven before the tires rot. The car is yours if you can learn to drive it. I haven't driven a car with a manual clutch and straight stick since I was a teenager, and I don't have the nerves to teach you myself."

Both my and Cece's mouths fell open. A car of her own! "But how am I going to learn to drive a straight stick?" Cece asked.

Aunt Bird stirred her coffee. "Cece, I admit I've been stalling on this issue. Hoyt knows my reservations about teaching you myself and has volunteered his services."

Cece squealed in delight. The following Tuesday, Cece and I prepared the old Studebaker for her first lesson. We scrubbed and buffed every last inch of the exterior, used steel wool on the dirty whitewalls, and then went to work on the interior. By the time Uncle Hoyt arrived, the "blue bullet" was shining inside and out.

"It looks like it just rolled off the assembly line! I remember when your daddy bought this car." He grinned as he pointed to me. "It was a week before this little squirt blossom here was born."

I giggled. "Is it okay if I ride in the back seat? I promise to be quiet," I begged.

Cece rolled her eyes in disgust, but Uncle Hoyt sided with me. "Actually, Cece, I think it's a good idea for Allie to learn along with you." When Cece rolled her eyes again, he added, "Since Bird is afraid of a manual clutch, there could be an emergency when Allie would have to drive." My mind returned to the horrible night of Cece's seizure as Cece held the bench seat forward for me to climb into the back.

Every Tuesday, Uncle Hoyt drove us to the parking lot at the county fairgrounds, where he turned over the wheel to Cece. She was a terrible driver. We'd bump and skid stirring up red dust as Uncle Hoyt reminded Cece to "ease off the clutch slowly." The man had more patience than Job himself.

Our lessons lasted one hour each week. Cece had the wheel for the first forty-five minutes; the final fifteen minutes were reserved for me. Though my legs just reached the pedals, I couldn't quite see over the steering wheel, so I borrowed two fat encyclopedias from the living room bookshelf. Uncle Hoyt would position them in the driver's seat and turn the "bullet" over to me.

As I expertly captained my vessel around the dirt lot, Cece would fume. "I don't understand why it's so easy for Allie! She'll have her license before I do!"

Cece grew more determined. Evenings after supper, I'd discover her sitting in the Studebaker as she practiced her foot technique on the accelerator and clutch.

One hot July Tuesday, Uncle Hoyt announced, "I think it's time we took this old jalopy on the road, Cece! Why don't you drive us to the Dairy Queen, and I'll treat us all."

While color drained from Cece's face, I could already taste a large vanilla cone dipped in warm chocolate. Cece stuttered, "I ...I...I... don't know, Uncle Hoyt. What if I mess up? Chester Talley works at the Dairy Queen. I'd just die if I did something stupid in front of him."

Uncle Hoyt appeared shocked. "Cece, I've watched you conquer so many mountains this year. And this—it's not even a molehill. Now you turn this car around and take us to the Dairy Queen. I need a milkshake!" He folded his arms and waited.

Cece clenched the steering wheel until her knuckles were white. After several deep breaths, she turned the ignition and reassured herself. "Okay, I'm ready. I can do this."

Ten minutes later we were enjoying our cold treats in the parking lot of Dairy Queen. Cece had delivered us without a single bobble, jerk, or screech. I licked all the chocolate off my cone as Uncle Hoyt and I sat atop a picnic table in the shade. Cece remained in the Studebaker while Chester Talley hung onto the driver's window admiring her vehicle.

As Cece chatted with Chester, she fluttered her animated blue eyes and tossed her sun-bleached ponytail. I reveled in her stunning beauty. I wondered what her next challenge would be. A mountain? A molehill? A star football player? Whatever the task, I knew she'd persevere.

The following week Roscoe Ray arrived. Was I glad to see him! With Josie at horse camp, I'd grown tired of finding ways to entertain myself.

I visited him that Friday while Miz Gertie ran some errands in town. Clad in a madras shirt, khaki bermudas, and sandals with those ridiculous white socks, Roscoe Ray had changed little in a year. However, I discovered he had retired all of his Batman costumes.

"Miss Mason, my teacher, says I'm too grown up to wear those costumes anymore. She says it's okay to keep my comic books, that lots of grownups collect comic books, but only children dress up. Allie, I want you to read my whole collection while I'm here 'cause this will be the last time I come to visit. I'm going to have a new home soon."

I thought he was confused. "What do you mean, Roscoe Ray? Miz Gertie's not moving anywhere. Why do you need a new home?"

Roscoe Ray looked at me like I had no sense. "Mama Gertie's not going with me, but I've got a printer's ship, so I have to move."

His comment only muddied the waters more. "A ship? Are you joining the navy?"

He smiled. "No, silly, I have a printer's ship to learn to make furniture. Miss Mason said I was so good at carving things, I could get a job. This man in North Carolina wants me to live with him and his wife and learn how to make furniture.

That's what a printer's ship is, silly." He was still explaining when Miz Gertie returned.

She patted Roscoe Ray lovingly on his shoulder. "Roscoe Ray means he has an *apprenticeship* in Hickory, North Carolina, where they're known for their handcrafted furniture. It's a wonderful opportunity for him," she added.

Each week when I visited with Roscoe Ray, I'd read my weekly letter from Josie. He loved hearing about her horse camp activities, which included every aspect of caring for a horse from grooming to feeding to shoveling manure.

"What's manure?" Roscoe Ray asked one day.

I'd learned from Aunt Bird that a simple question deserves a simple, honest answer. "It's horse doo doo, Roscoe."

"Eww!" he squealed. "I bet that really stinks. I share a room with Earnest Jones at school. He's big and fat, and his doo doo stinks bad, and he's not half as big as a horse."

When the mail arrived one Friday, Roscoe Ray accompanied me across the street to see if I had any correspondence from Josie. I found instead an envelope with no return address. My name and address were printed neatly in pencil.

We sat on the curb to read my letter.

Dear Allie,

Last week my mama's best friend from Flintville came to visit us in Griffin. She told me your daddy died in February. I am so sorry that he died. I know how sad you must be because my heart felt like someone was jumping up and down on it when my sister died. I still miss her, but I'm not as sad anymore. Mama says time makes grief easier to bear. I guess she's right.

We live in a house with my aunt now. I don't have to share the bathroom with anyone except my mama. I have my own bed now, too. But I'd be happy to share it with Macy if she was alive.

Your friend,
Essie Dunn

As I folded the letter and returned it to the envelope, my hands shook and a tear splashed on the penciled address. For a few minutes, I sat speechless on the curb.

I forgot Roscoe Ray was sitting beside me until he put an arm around my shoulder. "You miss your daddy, don't you? I miss my mama and daddy sometimes, too. One night just after my daddy went to heaven, I got really sad because I had a dream about him taking me fishing. Then I woke up and remembered he couldn't take me fishing ever again 'cause he was in heaven. I got out of bed and went to my window. There were a whole lot of stars in the sky, and I remembered one time when I was a really little boy before my daddy married Mama Gertie. He took me camping, and one night we could see all the stars up in heaven. Daddy found the brightest star in the sky and told me it was my mama looking down on me, and if I ever got lonely, all I had to do was to look up at the stars and find the brightest one and I'd never be lonely. So that night I found another bright star right next to my mama's star, and I knew it was my daddy looking down on me, too. So, now I'm never alone anymore."

Roscoe Ray made me feel better than any adult could have. That night I placed Essie's letter in the box under my bed. Maybe one day we'd meet again.

When Uncle Hoyt invited me to go fishing, he suggested I bring a friend along. I invited Roscoe Ray. Miz Gertie insisted on packing us a picnic lunch.

Just as the sun was coming up, the three of us, crammed into the cab of Uncle Hoyt's pickup, puttered down a dirt road toward his favorite fishing spot. By noon, both Roscoe Ray and I had caught two catfish apiece, while Uncle Hoyt had hooked a five-pound bass.

After lunch, Roscoe Ray and I decided we'd had our fill of fishing and opted to play along the banks near the whitewater. Since we would be in yelling distance of Uncle Hoyt, he agreed.

Soon we were up to our knees in the cool, crystal clear water. Roscoe Ray picked up rocks from the river's bed. "I like these black ones. They're the prettiest." He pocketed a handful of the smooth black rocks. We began a game of finding the prettiest shapes and sizes of black rocks. Uncle Hoyt washed out a bait pail and let us dump our finds into it. "Look at these black rocks, Uncle Hoyt. Aren't they shiny? Roscoe Ray thinks he can carve them into special shapes."

"That kind of rock was good enough for the Indians in this area, so I bet they'll work for Roscoe Ray just fine." Uncle Hoyt studied a few of our specimens.

The mention of Indians brought Roscoe Ray to life. "What kind of Indians? Do they have bows and arrows?" he asked in a frightened voice.

Uncle Hoyt chuckled. "Don't worry, Roscoe Ray. The Indians have been gone from these parts for years, but, when they lived here, they used these black rocks to make blades for their knives and arrowheads for their arrows. Do you know what kind of rocks these are?"

Both of us shook our heads.

Uncle Hoyt sat down in the clearing and dumped our pail of shiny black rocks on the tablecloth. "It's a variety of quartz from the family of crypto-crystalline silicates."

Roscoe Ray whistled softly. "That's a long name for a rock!"

"Well, that's what my geology professor at Georgia Tech called them, but we folks from Flintville call them flint rocks. They're abundant in the Flint River. Thus the name of our river as well as our town," Uncle Hoyt explained.

"I'll be," I exclaimed. "No teacher ever taught me that, Uncle Hoyt."

We gathered our belongings and headed home. Roscoe Ray drifted off to sleep as I watched the sun set over the river and listened to Uncle Hoyt whistle. I was beginning to think Uncle Hoyt was almost as smart as Diddy.

Two weeks later, I was thrilled when Miz Gertie invited me to accompany her and Roscoe Ray to the Atlanta Airport. At the airport, we waited at the gate with Roscoe Ray until it was time for him to board. A really pretty stewardess with a pillbox hat assured Miz Gertie that she'd stay with Roscoe Ray until his new employer arrived at the gate in Charlotte. With tears in her eyes, Miz Gertie wrapped her arms around her stepson. "You go have a good life, Roscoe Ray. I'm always here for you."

Roscoe Ray smiled and held Miz Gertie in a bear hug. "I love you, Mama Gertie. You come to see me in Hickory, and I'll make you some furniture."

Then he turned to me and pulled something from his coat pocket. "This is for you, Allie. Mr. Hoyt was right about that flint; it was easy to carve." He handed me something wrapped in white tissue and tied with a blue ribbon. Inside lay two perfectly formed stars, carved from the black flint rocks we'd discovered in the river.

"They're beautiful, Roscoe Ray." I was amazed at the perfection of each star.

"I made them to remind you of your mama and daddy. Just pick out the brightest stars, remember," he smiled down at me, and then he was gone.

Before I went to sleep that night, I once again removed the box from beneath my bed. I opened the smaller box where Mama's sapphire bracelet lay swathed in cotton. Inside the circle of the bracelet, I deposited my stars of flint.

Chapter 19

The final Saturday of the summer, Josie and I sat on the highest limb in Miz Gertie's mimosa tree and watched the cars line the curb on Kingston Road. Aunt Bird was hosting a baby shower, and every lady in Flintville was invited. The sweltering heat and heavy humidity had not discouraged a single guest from dressing in her finest attire.

We saw Sunday dresses in every shade of pastel, white gloves adorning each pair of hands, and hats ranging from big-brimmed straw ones decorated with wide bands of ribbon to more modest small styles covered in netting. Of course, every single lady was wearing high heels and stockings. "Can you imagine putting on all of that stuff on a day like today," Josie groaned.

"Yeah, and underneath, they've got long-line brassieres and girdles to hold up those nylon hose. Then on top of that a long nylon slip. I bet they're all sweating like mules."

Josie whistled softly through her teeth. "I wonder if Miz Parker has on a girdle, her being all swollen up like she is." Frances Tyler Parker was the guest of honor and Aunt Bird's best friend since high school.

Although Aunt Bird had invited me to attend, I bowed out. Having to put on my Sunday attire for church was all I could handle. I wanted to enjoy our last moments of summer in bare feet and without a care in the world.

As we sat in the tree, I filled Josie in on events she'd missed while away at horse camp. I included every impressive detail of my trip to the the Atlanta Airport with Roscoe Ray and Miz Gertie and told her about my letter from Essie Dunn.

Josie readjusted her position on a branch just above mine, "What did you say when you wrote her back?"

I sighed. "She didn't include a return address."

Just as we decided to descend our perches, the party broke up, and ladies in all shapes and sizes of summer colors poured out the front door. "Come on, Josie. Let's ride around the block."

We slid down the trunk of the mimosa, grabbed our bicycles, and were about to tear off in the opposite direction when Josie's mother spotted us. "Now, Josie, you come on home right now. You need to wash that hair for church tomorrow, you hear?"

Josie shrugged in defeat. "I'll see you at school Monday, Allie. Keep your fingers crossed we're in the same class again this year!" With her painful reminder that sixth grade began in less than forty-eight hours, I gloomily pedaled home by myself.

All the guests had vanished, but a mixture of soft, perfumed scents still lingered in the air. Cece was helping Aunt Bird return furniture to its proper location. Since they were in deep conversation, I remained in the kitchen to sample the leftover refreshments.

Settling at the kitchen table with a glass of punch and a miniature iced cake, I overheard Cece and Aunt Bird's discussion, which had progressed into an argument.

"But, if you don't get married soon, you'll be too old to have children of your own."

"Now, Cece, when I marry is for me to decide," Aunt Bird replied in her schoolteacher tone. "Allie needs my full attention these days; she's immature, and that makes her vulnerable. She's had enough change in her life for right now. She's about to enter puberty, whether she likes it or not, and she's going to need us both to help her deal with the reality that she'll soon be a young woman."

Cece giggled. "Deal with the reality that she can't be a tomboy for the rest of her life? We'll have to drag her kicking and screaming! But, what about you and Uncle Hoyt? It's not fair for either of you."

I held my breath for Aunt Bird's reply. "Cece. life isn't always fair. I'm where the Lord wants me to be, and if Hoyt really loves me, he'll wait for me."

As quietly as possible, I eased out the back door. I hopped on my bike and pedaled down to the creek. As I wiggled my toes in the white Georgia clay, I wondered if I was the one stepping block to Aunt Bird's happiness. And what did *vulnerable* mean? If it would grant Aunt Bird the marriage and family she so deserved, I'd try to mature. Before I headed home, I promised I'd prove my sister wrong. I'd travel into that world of femininity as gracefully as possible, without kicking and screaming.

By the time the dogwoods and azaleas burst into color the spring of sixth grade, I'd totally forgotten my mission to behave maturely. While most girls our age were studying fashion magazines, Josie and I took up skateboarding. With the help of Uncle Hoyt, we designed a homemade skateboard from a piece of plywood and wheels from an old roller skate. Although my board was a unique creation, it traveled downhill just as fast as Josie's sleek board from Johnson's Hardware.

One Wednesday at a scout meeting, Miz Edwards announced our troop would sponsor a rummage sale in two weeks. She asked us to pencil in our names on a signup sheet by the hour we would work. Josie and I decided a morning slot would leave us some playtime in the afternoon.

By the time we reached the signup board, all those slots were taken. "Hey, would anybody like to swap out times with Josie and me?" I asked.

Roxie Carmichael responded, "No, I can't! I'm getting my hair done at 2:00 that Saturday."

With a pleading look in my eyes, I turned to my old baptismal buddy Pammie Reese. She hesitated before turning me down. "I'm sorry, Allie, but I have a hair appointment too, and then we have to pick up the shoes I'm having dyed to match my dress for the party."

Josie and I exchanged confused glances. "Dyed shoes?" I snickered. "What party?"

Before Pammie could answer, Roxie shushed her. Pammie's face colored as her gaze fell to the floor.

Josie took a more aggressive approach. "Roxie, what's going on here?"

Roxie stammered as Pammie continued to stare at the ground. Josie and I, both with our hands on our hips, waited for an answer. Just then, "Miss Smarty Pants" Rachel Fountain stormed into our circle. "Oh, I'm sorry, girls. We were trying to keep my party a little secret. You know, it's going to be the first boy/girl party ever. I figured you two wouldn't be interested. We'll be dancing and playing spin the bottle—things tomboys don't enjoy. Sorry," she added in a sugary tone.

Now it was time for my face to color and for Josie to stammer. Although Pammie and Roxie seemed embarrassed, they didn't want to cross Rachel. I guess they figured she might un-invite them. Totally humiliated, Josie and I signed up for the late afternoon slot so all the other girls could prepare for the party from which we'd been banned.

Waiting for Josie's mother to pick us up, I put on a good front. "Who needs them?" I began. "They're all so prissy and snotty." When Josie hung her head and offered no response, I was devastated. I knew she would've been invited if it weren't for her alliance with me. Josie had matured over the year; she'd shyly shown me the little lacy bra and panty set her mother gave her for Christmas. She'd even remarked that her mom suggested she shave her legs once summer arrived. I, on the other hand, was still completely hairless and flat-chested.

Two days later, the sixth grade held its annual field day. The three sixth grade classes competed against one another in athletic events. Since Josie had the stride of a gazelle, she always participated in the 100-yard dash. I was inevitably selected for the sack race since my legs were the only pair still short enough to fit in the feed bag.

Waiting for events to be called, we sat with our classmates on the grassy hill overlooking the athletic field. Josie had just headed to the track to warm up for her race. The remaining nine girls in my class sat in front of eight boys in the warm May sun. Buddy Harlowe instigated a game. He and two other boys began going down the line of girls and popping their bra straps. When they arrived at me, all I had to offer was the strap of my Carter's cotton undershirt.

"Hey, look!" Buddy exclaimed. "Allie Sinclair's got four eyes but no titties!" I felt my ears and neck heat up as they reddened. Then I broke out in an embarrassed sweat, causing my glasses to slide down my nose.

His cruel words and giggles from my classmates so destroyed me that I didn't witness Josie cross the finish line first. When she returned to sit beside me, she could tell something was wrong, but I wasn't talking. By then the boys had moved on to some other tomfoolery.

When Cece entered our bedroom unexpectedly that night, she caught me standing topless before the mirror. "What are you doing, Allie?" she exclaimed.

I quickly folded my arms across my chest and muttered, "Nothing," but Cece caught the quiver in my voice.

As I retrieved my pajama top, Cece sat down on her bed. "Come here, baby brat, and tell me all about it."

The sweet sympathy in her voice was just enough to burst the dam of tears I'd barely restrained all evening. I blurted out the entire story beginning with the party to which I was not invited and ending with the "brassiere game," for which I was not prepared. "Let's face it, Cece. I'm just an ugly, four-eyed, flat-chested dog!"

Cece crossed over to our study desk, where she withdrew a portfolio of sketches. "I've been waiting for the right time to show you this." She thumbed through a stack of colored charcoal works and handed me a sketch she'd never shared before.

"Who is she?" I wondered aloud as I stared at a picture of a pretty, young girl.

Cece smirked. "Why, it's you, of course! I'm not that bad of an artist!"

I studied the sketch more closely. Something was missing. "But where are my glasses? That's why I didn't recognize myself."

"I know, but I wanted to depict you the way I see you. You have the softest, shiniest hair and the greenest green eyes. I didn't want the glasses to obscure those emerald eyes. That's how I see you. And of course, those precious dimples. Boys just love dimples."

"They do?" I asked in amazement.

Cece leaned down to kiss me on either cheek. "You know what Diddy told me once about your dimples? He said they were where the angels kissed you."

The next day when Cece came home from work at the Paris Shoppe, she tossed a pink bag on my bed. "I bought you a little something," she winked.

Inside was a brassiere, size 28 AA. I was delighted. "I didn't know they made brassieres this small!" When I tried on my new lingerie, it was the perfect fit.

As I hugged my big sister, she offered a stern warning. "The next time that pudgy Buddy Harlowe tries to pop your strap, you tell him he's a pig and your big sister knows his big brother James would not tolerate such crude, rude behavior."

We giggled. Once again my sweet Cece worked her magic; all my insecurities simply evaporated.

As Aunt Bird and I gathered up items for the rummage sale, she dug through one of her bureau drawers until she located a small pink box. "What's that, Aunt Bird? Is it going to the sale?" I opened the box's lid. Inside was a small pink electric razor.

Aunt Bird brushed away a stray curl. "Well, I'll be. I meant to put this in your Christmas stocking this year. Before long you may want to shave your legs and under your arms. Why don't you just keep it?"

I sensed Cece had shared my troubles with Aunt Bird but declined from asking. "I saw the cutest two piece swimsuit in your sister's *Seventeen* this month," she continued. "I cut it out and sent it to Mimi to see if she could make one like it for you. I also sent her some padding for the top."

"Padding?" I wasn't certain what Aunt Bird meant.

Aunt Bird sat down on the floor beside me. "Amanda in Tennessee Williams' *Glass Menagerie* stuffs her daughter's brassiere with what she refers to as 'gay deceivers.' We'll have Mimi add just enough padding to give you a perfect look." She showed me the foam padding, which was shaped exactly like a woman's breast. I'd always called it a "falsie," but since I'd be wearing them, I preferred Aunt Bird's terminology.

I was glad at the moment there were no men living in our house. Somehow I think the entire hoopla about my agonizingly slow journey into puberty would have made Diddy blush.

Some months earlier Uncle Hoyt had returned Diddy's jacket, the one hanging on his coat rack with my Valentine in its pocket. Although I'd long since secured the Valentine in the box under my bed, I held his jacket close to my face in hopes of catching one last whiff of chewing gum and printer's ink. As I did so, I searched for something else that should be hidden in the pockets of this jacket.

My aunt stopped her folding and packing to watch me. "Allie? Are you missing something?"

I was puzzled. "This is the jacket Diddy had on the day he died, and something should be in his pocket." Aunt Bird raised her eyebrows at me. "You know that little black monogrammed case that held his insulin and syringe. It's not there. I was thinking Cece might like to have it."

"That's a thoughtful idea, Allie. Maybe Hoyt put the case in your daddy's desk at the office. Or maybe Miss Opal found it and put it in a safe place." Aunt Bird promised to check with them about the missing case.

Josie and I were the only two scouts to work the rummage sale from mid-afternoon until closing, and Mrs. Edwards awarded us a "good citizenship" badge. Rachel's party was a great big flop. Her mother wouldn't allow any rock and roll; instead she insisted on a Lawrence Welk album. The girls danced with each other while the boys had a cupcake food fight. So much for maturity!

No one at the newspaper office found Diddy's black case. Since I knew he always kept it with him in case of an emergency, this disturbed me for a few days. But by the last day of school, my mind drifted toward summer and ultimately my final days as a tomboy.

Chapter 20

By the spring of seventh grade, I fell under puberty's plague. During bathroom breaks when girl talk turned to "monthly" cramps, I commiserated and shared my Midol. But contrary to Cece's predictions, my chest continued to resemble that of an ironing board. Luckily, poor Josie shared in my dilemma, and together we set about in search of a remedy for our non-existent boobs.

I began a daily regimen of lying on my back with outspread arms while lifting the two fattest encyclopedias in the set. Cece said the high school's new, young P.E. teacher, a size 36 DD herself, had recommended this radical exercise to the less-endowed girls in health class. Although after six months of training, I still barely filled up my AA cups, my biceps were more defined than any girl's or boy's in the entire seventh grade.

Josie chose another route altogether. When her cousin swore that soaping her boobs regularly would result in a busty figure, Josie went to work right away. However, after Lorna complained that Josie was running through four cakes of Ivory in a week, her mom put an end to the experiment. Josie's soaping activity resulted in absolutely no mammary growth but did earn her the nickname of "Sudsy," which stayed with her throughout her high school career.

Josie and I retired our skateboards and reclaimed our bicycles when we discovered three boys riding their bikes down Avalon Road one April afternoon. Although they'd always lived in our neighborhood, Josie and I had never, until now, been interested in them. The trio included Stuart Sims and David Banks, who were both eighth graders but would be repeating with us again next year. They weren't failing students, just promising football stars who needed another year of growth before they were ready for the high school team. "Holding a student back," as it was called, was a tradition with boys whose parents wanted them to have four full years on the high school squad. Aunt Bird, a true academician, detested the "held back" policy, but Flintville was a football town where everything else took a back seat.

The third member of the bike brigade, Tyrone Hastings, was our age. Ty would only spend one year in eighth grade since he was the biggest boy in the entire junior high and outweighed every player on the freshman team. I figured Ty's size was the result of all the free ice cream he had at his disposal since his father owned Hastings Pharmacy.

Stuart, whose father was Flint County's Farm Bureau insurance agent, was taller than Josie although she outweighed him by a good twenty pounds. "The coach told me to drink banana milkshakes every night before I go to bed, and my dad's ordered me some special formula called *Mighty Mo*. It's supposed to build muscles overnight," Stuart explained.

David was not quite as tall as Stuart, but much more muscular. I assumed he was already on the *Mighty Mo* regimen. Unlike most seventh grade boys whose voices croaked, David spoke in a rich, deep voice. Like me, he wore glasses, and he never once referred to me as "four eyes."

The five of us became bicycling buddies over those warm spring months. If we weren't biking, we were playing "roll the bat" in Josie's front yard.

Though Josie and I had no love connection with any of our new friends, there was romance in the air for another Sinclair. Cece fell head over heels for Bradley Hamilton Royal, a descendant of the Hamiltons who owned all the textile mills in Flintville. Tall, dark, and handsome, Bradley was a senior who would attend West Point Academy after graduation.

Bradley and Cece became inseparable. I rarely entered our living room without finding them listening to the weekly *Parade's Hit List* on the hi-fi and staring goo-goo eyed at one another.

Calling these session "study dates," they kept their notebooks open in case Aunt Bird checked in on them. Fortunately for them, Aunt Bird could not have been more pleased with the match since she knew Bradley had the highest grade point average at Flintville High and impeccable manners, the result of a proper Southern upbringing, according to her.

Since Bradley was a Methodist, we knew little about his family. I did know that his mother, the former Meredith Hamilton, had died the year before from brain cancer. Bradley's father, John Bradley Royal, served as payroll manager for every Hamilton Mill in Flintville. While Aunt Bird considered Bradley the perfect fit for Cece, I wasn't as easy to convince. He reminded me too much of that slick Eddie Haskell from *Leave It To Beaver*.

Although a perfect gentleman in Aunt Bird's presence, in her absence, Bradley smirked at me and dismissed me as though I was a gnat. "Why don't you go play with paper dolls or something?" he'd admonish in a condescending tone. Instead of taking up for me as she usually did, Cece would giggle and ignore me. While Cece's attitude hurt my feelings, Bradley's behavior made my entire butthole draw up, a description Josie and I'd adopted for the grossest occurrences we could imagine.

Just before graduation, Cece began to wear a gold chain sporting Bradley's class ring. Aunt Bird had always frowned on the idea of teenagers going steady; nevertheless, she agreed to allow the arrangement as long as Cece maintained her grades. Although she never brought home any grade lower than a B+ in Algebra II, how Cece was able to pull it off was a mystery to me.

When she and Bradley were not parked on our living room couch or off for a drive in his new Mustang, she was glued to the Princess phone. One night as I tried to complete an essay for Georgia history, Cece lay in her bed with the phone cradled to her while she and Bradley listened to one another breathe. It was so disgusting that I retreated to the side porch where Aunt Bird was grading papers.

She looked up from the essay she was reading. "Do you need some help with that history report?"

"No, Aunt Bird, I just need some space. I'm surprised the windows in our bedroom are not fogged over with all the cooing going on in there. They're sickening!" I flopped down on the settee.

Aunt Bird smiled. "Oh, young love, first love. It can be all consuming," she sighed as she continued marking papers.

Although I'd begun to find the opposite sex tolerable, I could not imagine ever behaving like Cece. I was secretly relieved that Bradley would leave soon for West Point and would not return until Christmas. I figured she'd moon over his absence for a week and then find another boyfriend.

The final day of school coincided with graduation day at Flintville High School. Aunt Bird excused me from the boring ceremony and agreed that I could accompany Josie to Weaver Park for summer's first softball game. Stuart, David, and Ty, all playing for the Flint Dairy Tigers, had invited us. I was delighted. I'd spent more than my share of time at dull commencements forced to listen to boring speeches by honor graduates and an epic oration from Superintendent Hartman.

Aunt Bird was required to sit on the field with the rest of the faculty. Needless to say, Cece would be there not only to see her darling Bradley but also to serve as a graduation marshal, an honor bestowed upon junior members of the National Honor Society. The boys served as ushers while the girls dressed in pastel semi-formals and stood at designated points on either side of the fifty-yard line between the seated rows of graduates and faculty. As graduates were called, they'd walk through the aisle created by the junior females arrayed in soft shades of blue, pink, yellow, and green.

While Cece put the finishing touches on her makeup for the big event, I sat on my bed and listened to Pete Potter, WSFT's afternoon deejay, sign off the air. Cece turned from the mirror and smiled. "Well, do I look like an honor student?"

She was wearing a mint green dotted-swiss dress, compliments of our Mimi, of course. Tiny daisy flower appliqués were sewn to the garment's spaghetti straps. Cece had painstakingly glued the extra flowers to a headband adorning her gold spun hair, which hung softly across her olive-skinned shoulders.

"You're too pretty to be an egg-head!" I exclaimed. "You'd better carry your report card as evidence."

Cece giggled as she pushed my glasses up on my nose and kissed me atop my head. She smelled divine with just the perfect amount of *Heaven Sent* perfume. For a brief moment, I had my big sister all to myself.

Then I heard Aunt Bird's high heels tapping down the hall. "Cece, if you're riding to the stadium with me, we need to go. Now, Allie, you're to ride home from the game with the McClendons, and I'll pick you up there."

"Aw, Aunt Bird, Josie wants to sleep over here tonight. It's our first night of summer vacation, and she leaves in a week for horse camp."

In a rush, Aunt Bird gave in easily. "Okay, that's fine, but I have a hair appointment at 8:30 in the morning, so I'll probably be gone before you girls get up. That means you'll have to make your own breakfast. Now you behave yourself at the game." With her final instructions, Aunt Bird was down the hall and out the door with Cece scurrying to catch up with her.

The Tigers slaughtered the Presbyterian Pirates in a 10 to 2 victory. Ty hit a homerun in the fifth inning while David had two singles and a double. Stuart stole second base in the sixth and third base in the ninth. He was skinny, but he was fast. Maybe that *Mighty Mo* was starting to work.

By the time Josie and I got home, Aunt Bird was clad in her bathrobe and was warming some milk on the stove. As I chattered about the game, I realized she wasn't listening as intently as usual.

I saw her massaging her temples. "Are you okay, Aunt Bird?"

She swallowed a pill with her milk. "I'm coming down with one of my migraines. I just took one of those knockout pills that Dr. Justice gave me. I think if I can settle down before the pain intensifies, I can sleep it off."

Helping Aunt Bird back to her room, I reassured her we'd be just fine, and that I'd remind Cece to lock up when she got home.

By 10:00 P.M., Josie and I were digging into our third bowl of ice cream while we watched *The Twilight Zone*. Afterwards, we watched the news and even waited for the Atlanta station to sign off the air. I knew Cece would show up at the door any minute.

"Let's turn out the living room lights. Maybe we'll see them smooching underneath the porch light when Bradley brings Cece home," Josie suggested.

"I'd hate to have his big, sweaty lips on mine," I grimaced in disgust. We waited in the dark until 11:45. "Woo woo, if Aunt Bird was awake, she'd be pacing the floor. How lucky can Cece get! The one night she's late, we'd have an easier time waking the dead than Aunt Bird." By midnight I began to worry. Cece had never, ever been this late without calling.

Josie and I amused ourselves for a while with a game of Canasta, which the McClendons had taught us to play last Christmas. It wasn't as much fun with just the two of us, though. Then we entertained ourselves by practicing the boogaloo and the jerk, the latest dances on *American Bandstand*.

We wore out quickly and lounged on the sofa. I'd just dozed off as the phone began to ring. Jumping up with my heart in my throat, I grabbed the receiver and prayed Aunt Bird was too far gone from her migraine pill to have heard it. "Hello?"

At first all I could hear was the blaring voice of Elvis Presley singing "Return to Sender," and what sounded like grown men laughing. Then someone yelled, "Hey, Blanche, how 'bout another Pabst Blue Ribbon?"

This time I yelled into the receiver, "Hello?"

Above the hubbub, a woman's drawl, somehow familiar, came across the line, "Is this the Sinclair residence?"

"Yes, it is. Who are you calling?" I inquired in my best telephone manners.

"Well, this is Blanche Bledsoe. Is this Allie I'm speaking at?" she yelled over the music, *Wild thing! You make my heart sing!*

Blanche Bledsoe, I remembered now, the waitress who used to flirt with Diddy when he went in for coffee. "Yes ma'am. Are you at the Blue Goose Café this late?"

Miss Bledsoe laughed. "No sugah, that's my day job. I'm at the River Ranch, you know, down on Old River Road. Your sister's out here and needs a ride home. I'd bring her myself, but my shift ain't over for another hour. There's a lot of fellers who've been out frog giggin' and done come in here to get drunk. Can you get your aunt to come out here and pick Miss Cece up, honey?"

I hesitated. What was Cece doing at the River Ranch? Where was Bradley? I decided not to bother Miss Bledsoe with these concerns. I had to get Cece home before Aunt Bird came out of her migraine stupor. "Umm, yes ma'am, my aunt and I will be to get her right away."

"Okay then, sugah. I gotta hang up now. I've got some thirsty boys to serve," and then she hung up.

Josie, wide-eyed with curiosity, waited for me by the phone. "Who in the world is calling this time of night? Where are you and your Aunt Bird going? It's 1:00 in the morning, for gosh sakes!"

She followed me into my bedroom where I threw on some clothes. "I'll explain on the way, Josie, but right now I need your help. My sister's in trouble. So just get dressed." Obediently, Josie changed into her clothes and laced up her tennis shoes.

In the meantime, I dug out the extra set of car keys to the Studebaker from our nightstand table and grabbed the two biggest encyclopedias, still resting underneath my bed from my bust enhancement exercises. "We've got to drive to the River Ranch and pick up Cece before Aunt Bird wakes up."

Josie gulped. "The River Ranch? That honky-tonk down on Old River Road? My mama will tan my backside, and my daddy will ground me until I'm twenty!"

I grabbed Josie by her skinny arms and shook her. "I'm not kidding! I need you to help me. Are you in or not?" I pleaded in desperation.

"Okay, okay," Josie responded in a calmer tone. "You know I'm not going to let you go out there by yourself."

I tiptoed down the hall and peeked in on Aunt Bird. Satisfied she was in an unconscious state, I motioned Josie out the kitchen's back door. At the last minute, I scurried back to our bedroom and grabbed Cece's frilly hair bonnet she wore over her curlers at night and her bathrobe hanging inside our closet door.

We didn't utter a sound until we reached the Studebaker, which was parked on the curb by our driveway. Even though I wasn't certain if He approved of what I was about to do, I breathed a quick "Thank you, Lord" for that small miracle. Cece had been parking by the curb since one cold February morning when the old "blue bullet" wouldn't crank. Uncle Hoyt had taught Cece to crank the Studebaker by giving it a rolling start down the street until she could pop the clutch and jumpstart the engine.

As I stacked the encyclopedias in the driver's seat, Josie climbed into the passenger's side. "Are you sure you know how to drive this thing?"

"Of course! Uncle Hoyt taught me when he was teaching Cece. Don't worry; I've done this plenty of times." I failed to mention that I'd never cranked the car from a rolling start, which would allow us to be far enough away from the house so the roar of the motor wouldn't awaken Aunt Bird. I breathed another prayer, put my foot on the clutch, released the emergency brake, and allowed the vehicle to glide down the hill. Holding my breath as I waited for the perfect moment, I popped the clutch. Miraculously, the motor began to hum. "See," I smirked at Josie, "there's nothing to it."

Although I'd never been to the River Ranch, I'd ridden by it when Uncle Hoyt and I went fishing. Josie and I drove in silence for the next five miles, and I was thankful that she didn't ask a zillion questions about what Cece was doing at such a forbidden den of iniquity. As we pulled off the paved Crest Highway onto the bumpy, dirt Old River Road, I eased the car over and put it in neutral.

The ride had given me time to devise a plan. "Josie, I'll go in to get Cece while you sit in the car. Miss Bledsoe is going to ask about Aunt Bird, so here's what we're going to do." I retrieved Cece's bathrobe and hair net from the back seat. "Here, put these things on. You've got to be Aunt Bird."

Josie protested, "Me? I don't look a thing like your Aunt Bird. That's just plain stupid, Allie."

"It may be stupid, but it's the only plan we've got. And if I don't get my sister away from that hell hole and back home before daylight, all three of us may never see daylight again!" The tone of my voice frightened Josie; she pulled the housecoat over her clothes. I waited as she adjusted the hairnet. "All you have to do is sit in the car. I'll park as far away from the front as I can, and if Miss Bledsoe comes out, you just wave at her and nod."

Luckily, there were a number of vehicles parked under the lights, so I had no alternative but to park under a tree, which protected us from the glare of the establishment's neon sign. Cece kept some loose change in the glove compartment for emergencies. I opened it and pulled out two nickels. "Josie, count to 500, and if I'm not back, you hightail it to that phone booth and call your parents."

Josie turned pale. "My parents? Dear God, just get back here before I finish." As I exited the car, Josie chanted "One, two, three," and I was gone.

Although it was almost 2:00 A.M., the River Ranch was hopping. As I opened the door, my nostrils were attacked by the odor of cigarette smoke mingled with the sour smell of spilled beer. I prayed that Miss Bledsoe would be looking out for me because I felt a bolt of lightning would strike me if I crossed the threshold. I stood just inside the doorway until my eyes adjusted.

In one corner of the room, four rough looking characters in sleeveless undershirts stood around a pool table while a fifth fellow lined up the eight ball. I swallowed and took a step in the other direction towards the bar where I hoped to encounter Miss Bledsoe. Instead, I found a burly man with a five o-clock shadow. He was drying beer mugs on his apron as a cigarette dangled from his mouth. When he saw me approach the bar, he raised his eyebrows and hollered, "Hey, Blanche, I think that visitor you've been waiting on is here."

Miss Bledsoe peeked over two swinging doors. She rushed out and grabbed me. "Allie Sinclair, what in the world are you doing in here by yourself? Where's your aunt?" She didn't look like the Blanche Bledsoe from the Blue Goose Café where she always wore a shirtwaist dress and a starched apron. Her hair was teased into a tremendous beehive, and she was wearing a skintight skirt and an even tighter sweater barely stretched across her ample bosom.

94

Recovering from the shock of her appearance, I tried to answer nonchalantly. "Uh, she's in the car, Miss Bledsoe. She didn't want to come in because she's in her housecoat. That's why she sent me." I rattled off as quickly as possible. "Is Cece still here?"

"Why of course, sugah. She's in the back room. I had her lie down on the cot for a while. She was a sight when she come in earlier, but she seems a might better now. Come on through the kitchen, sugah." She grabbed my arm and pulled me through the double doors. I followed her through the reek of putrid chicken grease and into a smaller storage area with shelves holding tremendous cans of lard.

Cece sat on a cot in the corner. I surveyed my sister quickly. Thank the Lord, she was all in one piece. "Where is Aunt Bird?" were the first words out of her mouth.

"She's in the car because she wasn't dressed to come in. Um, Miss Bledsoe, is it all right if we go out this back door instead of through the front?

"Why of course, Sug. I'll go speak to Miss Sinclair." She pulled a cigarette pack from her cleavage and lit up a Marlboro.

While I pulled Cece along with me, I protested as politely as possible. "Oh, that's okay, Miss Bledsoe. My aunt's real embarrassed about letting anybody see her with her hair in rollers and no makeup on. Why don't you just wave to her from the front."

"Well, okay. I need to get back inside anyway before those fellers get thirsty again," she agreed as we rounded the corner and approached the front of the building. From the shadows where the car was parked, we could only make out the silhouette of Josie, clad in the ridiculous getup and sitting behind the wheel of the car; thank God she'd had the sense to move over to that side. Josie waved her hand out the window at Miss Bledsoe and Miss Bledsoe waved back. "Now, you be careful going home. And, Miss Cece, don't you worry about what happened tonight. It won't take you long to figure out that all men are pigs every now and then."

Cece, still shaken from whatever had happened to her, came to her senses enough to respond. "Thanks so much for your kindness, Miss Bledsoe."

"Don't you think nothing about it. I've never known a finer gentleman than your daddy; too bad there ain't more men like him 'cause if I ever find one, I'd be sinking my claws into him and hanging on for dear life." Then, Miss Blanche Bledsoe, my sister's savior, headed back into the River Ranch.

As we approached the car, Cece got her first good look at Josie. "Josie, what are you doing in my bathrobe? Allie, where's Aunt Bird? How in the world did you get out here?"

I pushed my glasses back up on my sweaty nose. "Aunt Bird had one of her migraines and took a knockout pill. She doesn't have a clue about all of this mess, and I'd prefer to keep her clueless, if you don't mind."

"You mean you and Josie came out here by yourselves? You could have been stopped by the police! Allie, what were you thinking?" She grabbed me by my arm. I smelled beer on her breath.

Just then two drunk guys stumbled toward the pickup beside us. I opened the door and pushed Cece into the back seat. "Shut up, Cece," I whispered. "I'll explain it all when we get home."

Cece was too shocked or too tired to argue with me when I slid behind the wheel. She sat mute in the back seat. It was 3:15 A.M. when I parked the car alongside our curb. Shedding her "disguise," Josie headed straight for our sleeping bags on the porch without changing back into her pajamas.

I followed Cece into our bathroom where she was surveying herself in the mirror. She had yet to offer an explanation. "What in hell's name were you doing in a place like that?" I began through clenched teeth.

Cece turned on the faucet to wash her face. "Allie, don't cuss. It's not ladylike."

"Oh, but hanging out in a riverside honky-tonk with a bunch of drunks is okay." I couldn't hide the anger and fear in my voice. In the brightness of the bathroom light, I examined my sister more closely. Her mascara was smeared as though she had been crying. Her dress was all rumpled, two daisy appliqués were missing from one of the spaghetti straps, which was torn away from the back of her dress. "What happened to you, Cece?"

She sat down on the side of the tub and began to cry. Clutched between her fingers was the gold chain that held Bradley's class ring, but the ring was gone. "I don't know what happened," she sobbed softly.

I was not only exhausted but also exasperated. "What do you mean, you don't know? You were there, weren't you? Or maybe you entered the Twilight Zone."

Cece ignored my sarcasm and continued. "After graduation we went to a party out at Joe Nix's cabin on Crystal Hill," she began. "All the guys had beer. I drank two, and I guess Bradley had three. When things got rowdy at the cabin, we left. Bradley drove us back to his house on the bluff overlooking the river. He wanted to take me on a canoe ride so we could see the moon better. So I sat on his dock and put my feet in the water while Bradley went back to the garage to get canoe paddles. The sky was absolutely magnificent, and I remember wishing I had a canvas and my paints with me. And then," Cece hesitated as she twisted the broken chain around and around her fingers.

"And then what?" I demanded.

Tears streamed down her cheeks. "I don't know what. The next thing I remember, I was at the River Ranch. Miss Bledsoe gave me a glass of water, but I was trembling so I couldn't hold it in my hands."

I was furious. "Bradley's not just a jerk; he's a son of a bitch! I'm calling Uncle Hoyt right now! He'll go out to their fancy house on the Bluff and whip Bradley Hamilton Royal's ass!" I stormed out the bathroom towards the telephone.

Cece was right behind me. "Stop it, Allie! Stop it right now! How do you know Bradley did anything wrong? Maybe I was drunk out of mind. Maybe I embarrassed him. What you did tonight was stupid but brave, and I can never repay you for rescuing me. I'm okay now, and I can take care of myself. As far as Bradley is concerned, it's over between us, and I don't ever want to discuss him or this night again. Do you hear me?"

I was too tuckered to argue. "Yes, I hear you." As I headed to the side porch, I looked back at Cece still dangling the chain in disbelief. My heart ached for her. "I'm sorry, Cece. I know you thought you loved him. I was scared for you tonight, Cece, and I'd kill anybody who ever tried to hurt you."

She looked at me with tear-filled eyes. "I know you would, Allie, I know you would. I'm okay now, so get some sleep."

Seconds later, it seemed, a horn blew in front of our house. "Oh no, Josie, it's your mom!" I groaned. Josie scrambled out of her sleeping bag and headed for the door. Her mom was taking her to buy a new riding habit for horse camp. "I'm sorry about last night, Josie."

She rubbed the sleep from her eyes. "What are friends for? Anyway, that was the most fun I've had in a long time. Too bad I can't tell anybody about it!" Only a best friend would understand the night's activities were sworn to secrecy.

When I stumbled into the kitchen, Aunt Bird was long gone. I assumed the medicine had done its job, and her migraine had dissipated. I doubted that death itself could prevent my aunt from making her hair appointment.

Cece was already dressed and picking through a bowl of corn flakes. She had to be at the Paris Shoppe at 10:00 A.M. on Saturdays. There were no outward signs of the night's trauma save dark circles beneath her eyes.

"Aunt Bird said to remind you to start cleaning out the garage," Cece remarked in a normal tone.

"I guess that 'knockout' pill took care of her migraine. It was easy to sneak out last night. Aunt Bird was so dead to the world I could've tap-danced on her forehead!"

Cece smiled, and I was relieved to see she still had her sense of humor. After she left, I discovered her lovely dotted-swiss dress, neatly ironed, hanging from a padded hangar in our bedroom. She'd removed two daisy appliqués from her headband and sewn them on the now mended dress strap.

I'd never truly hated someone before, but I hated Bradley Hamilton Royal for the rest of the day as I cleaned out the garage. By the time Cece arrived home from work, I was worn out from all that hating. I decided my energy would be better spent loving her.

Chapter 21

All summer Cece remained true to her promise. She never once mentioned Bradley's name. The jerk's absence from our living room suited me just fine. I enjoyed the peace of sitting on the sofa without his haughty stare dismissing my existence.

I often heard Cece crying in bed when she thought I was asleep. One night as I retrieved a magazine from the living room, I overheard Cece sniffling on the porch while Aunt Bird consoled her.

"I know it hurts now." I stood motionless in the hallway as Cece blew her nose. Aunt Bird continued, "Honey, if I made a list of every young man who broke my heart along the way, I could wrap it around this porch. Consider every little heartache inflicted by some boorish male as one more attribute to add to the 'don't' column of what you want in a partner. I always think of those lines from Tennyson: 'It's better to have loved and lost than never to have loved at all.'"

Cece sniffled again. "If men are all boors, I'd just as soon lose them instead of love them. It's too painful."

I felt the warmth in Aunt Bird's reply. "Don't you worry, there are a few good fellows left in this world. You'll find your knight one day."

"But how will I know he's the right one?" Cece challenged.

The rocker squeaked as Aunt Bird swayed in it. "The first time I met Hoyt, I felt my heart in my throat. And to this day, every time I see him, my heart skips a beat. That's how you'll know."

Cece's giggle was a relief to me. "Well, you'd better marry that man who makes your heart skip before he skips out on you."

"Now, Cece," my aunt retorted, "that is not our topic of discussion tonight!"

I silently scurried down the hall before they discovered me.

While Cece swore off the male population, I began to collect friends of the opposite sex. Without Josie for the summer, I became desperate for companions my own age. My fragile relationship with the girls in my class had soured even more since Josie and I were snubbed from Rachel Fountain's party. There was not a single thirteen-year-old female other than Josie that I could tolerate. The rest of them were too "goody-goody" or too worried they'd mess up their hair to ride a bicycle.

That left Stuart, David, and Ty, who appeared most willing to include me in their daily football game. I wasn't certain if it was because my front yard boasted the most level playing field, or if they needed one more player nimble enough to catch a pass. I later learned that Teddy Gaddis had fallen off a moped and broken his arm.

Nevertheless, late afternoons, the bike brigade arrived with football in tow. Stu suggested a tackle game was too physical for a girl. I figured he was more concerned about his wellbeing than mine. Even after months of the *Mighty Mo*, Stu's arms still hung like toothpicks from his t-shirt. I rummaged around in the garage until I found a roll of masking tape. Each player wore a six-inch strip of tape on his back. Snatching the tape from a runner's back was the equivalent of a tackle. Although I couldn't run as fast or throw as hard, they were impressed with my knowledge of the game. I had Uncle Hoyt to thank for that.

One evening as the four of us sat in pools of sweat on the front steps, Cece, carrying a tray of lemonade, sashayed out the screen door. Dressed in madras shorts and a sleeveless pink blouse with her blonde hair pulled back in a ponytail, she looked like she'd walked off a page of **_Seventeen_**. "Aunt Bird said ya'll should take a break. It's still too hot out here." She set the tray on the step beside me, retreated into our screened porch, and sat down to polish her nails.

I poured myself a generous cup first. "Ya'll help yourselves. Aunt Bird makes the best fresh lemonade, not that frozen kind." I rattled on until I realized I had no audience. All three boys, mouths agape and eyes wide, were following Cece's every move. As I readied to tell them their behavior made me want to puke, the phone rang, and Cece left to retrieve it.

Ty regained consciousness first. "Geez, your sister is one knockout! If I was older, I'd be on her like white on rice."

Stu laughed. "You're wolfin' yourself if you think Cece Sinclair would ever give the likes of you the time of day."

David, trying to defog his sweaty glasses with an even sweatier shirt, emitted a low whistle. "Only in your dreams, guys. Only in your dreams!"

I began to boil from the inside out. "Well, if ya'll wanna just sit here and moon over my sister all afternoon, I guess you can go on home!"

"Gosh, Allie, I forgot you were sitting here. Sometimes, it's hard to remember you're not a boy," Stu offered. As my head drooped and my eyes settled on my boy-like chest, I could understand their infatuation with my sister.

Throughout the remainder of the evening, I silently cursed my sister for being so pretty. Why had God blessed her and not me? When she turned out our bedside lamp and whispered her usual "Good night, sleep tight, don't let the bugs bite," I pretended to be asleep. After all, in one brief moment, she'd destroyed my summer friendship with three relatively cute boys.

I was still despising Cece as I stumbled into the bathroom the following morning. I caught her sitting on the edge of the tub where she was about to inject herself with insulin. She looked up and smiled at me. How could she possess such stunning outward perfection but be imperfect inside? I'd read enough about her disease to know that over time, diabetes ravaged a person's body. Before she could say anything, I kissed her atop her blonde head. "Morning, Cece, I love you." She grinned and jabbed herself with the needle.

With Cece and Aunt Bird at work, I found myself alone for the better part of each day. After my chores, I'd take a late morning bike ride and occasionally stop by to visit with Miz Gertie. We'd sit on her back patio in view of a tiny plot of ground she'd converted into a vegetable garden.

One pleasantly cool morning as I pedaled by her house, Miz Gertie, clad in a straw hat and gardening gloves, called out for me to stop. She handed me a basketful of fat red juicy tomatoes. Miz Gertie grinned. "For once I listened to Clara Davis and bought the *Big Boy* plants. I've never had so many nice sized tomatoes before! Now, you take these home to your Aunt Bird."

I was thrilled to oblige Miz Gertie. "You sure you left enough for yourself?" I objected half-heartedly.

"Don't you worry about me. Now if Roscoe Ray were here, I couldn't have enough tomatoes. That boy does love a juicy tomato sandwich with lots of mayonnaise." I caught the slightest choke to her voice.

"You miss him, don't you, Miz Gertie?"

She paused to readjust her straw hat. "He loves his job. He's building me a bookcase, and they're shipping it down here all the way from Martin's Furniture in North Carolina. Mr. Martin is the one who hired Roscoe Ray, and Roscoe Ray has his own apartment over the workshop, right behind the Martins' house. The Martins just love Roscoe Ray and have asked him to stay on after his apprenticeship. I'm so proud he's made a life for himself. I was just getting too old to care for him myself."

"You're not old, Miz Gertie. At least you don't act old," I interjected.

She smiled. "Well, thank you, Allie. But you see, Roscoe Ray needs to make his way in this world, to have a life of his own, and I couldn't give him that here. Now, when the Lord gets ready to take me, I can go with peace of mind that Roscoe Ray will always have someone to love and care for him."

As I tucked the tomatoes into my bicycle basket, I added another definition of love to my ever-growing list. There was the totally devoted love that Mama and Diddy had shared; there was the protective sisterly love that Cece and I felt for each other; there was selfless love that prevented Aunt Bird from leaving us; there was patient love, the kind that kept Uncle Hoyt and Aunt Bird together, and then there was a mother's love. Because she loved him as though he was her very own son, Miz Gertie had made the ultimate sacrifice for her step-son Roscoe Ray. She let him go.

Since most stores closed at noon on Wednesdays, Cece and Margaret spent those afternoons at Parker's Pool, and I usually tagged along. One August afternoon, I sat in the back seat of the blue bullet as we traveled along Crest Highway with the windows rolled down. I would have preferred to enjoy my grape snow cone in silence while the wind dried my wet hair.

Silence, however, was not to be had with Margaret, who kept up a constant chatter. "Mother's taking me to Atlanta tomorrow to buy my school wardrobe." Margaret, the only child of one of Flintville's three doctors, didn't have a summer job.

"I wish you'd take the day off and come with us, Cece," Margaret prattled. "We're going to have lunch at the Magnolia Room in Rich's." I groaned; I could think of nothing more miserable than wearing Sunday clothes in this heat and eating itty bitty sandwiches with a bunch of overdressed ladies. I'd rather watch pigs wallow in mud than be subjected to another Magnolia Room luncheon.

"Thursday is my day to change the window displays, and Mrs. Mason wants to start ticketing the new fall lineup," Cece explained.

Margaret sighed. "What are you wearing to the dance Friday night?" When Cece didn't reply, Margaret continued, "You're going, aren't you? I saw David Estes talking to you on the sun deck today. He's really gotten cute since he went off to college. I think he's still got a crush on you."

"I wish he still worked the soda fountain at Hastings Pharmacy," I remarked. "I could just mention Cece's name to get an extra scoop of fudge ripple!"

Cece laughed. "Shame on you, Allie! I'm not going Friday night," she added hurriedly.

Margaret gasped. "Not going? Cece, enough is enough! You need to let everyone know you're eligible again, and the dance is the perfect place to start."

Cece pulled into Margaret's driveway. "No, I've already made plans to go out to the river with Uncle Hoyt and work on one of my watercolors while he fishes. I need a good sunset for my portfolio."

When not working, Cece was chin deep in chalk or paint or charcoal. Mrs. Watson, her art teacher, thought an extensive portfolio could be Cece's ticket to a college scholarship. Cece often took a newly completed work by the library for Miss Benton, still mean as ever, to critique. Cece was the only student I'd ever seen enter that witch's glass domain of her own accord.

That Cece was tagging along on a fishing expedition we'd planned weeks ago was news to me. A girl unaccompanied on the river at night was still a "no-no" in Flintville etiquette. So, I guess Uncle Hoyt and I were stuck with her.

Before exiting the car, Margaret lowered her sunglasses. "Cecile Sinclair, I refuse to allow my best friend to spend the most exciting year of high school like she's taken a vow of celibacy! Besides, a convent wouldn't accept a Southern Baptist. Before August is over, you'll go to a dance if I have to drag you by your blonde ponytail!" We rode home in silence.

Aunt Bird came home without Cece for lunch on Friday. "She's working through lunch to get off early to go fishing with you and Hoyt," she explained.

I took a swig of iced tea. "Aunt Bird, what does being a nun have to do with celibacy?"

Aunt Bird ceased chewing. "Whatever sparked your interest in this topic?"

I shrugged my shoulders. "Margaret said since Cece was a Southern Baptist, she might as well stop acting like a nun. She was trying to get Cece to go out with David Estes. Do you think Cece wants to be a nun?"

Aunt Bird almost choked on a potato chip. "Don't worry, hon. Cece's not contemplating a life in a nunnery. Everyone, including Margaret, needs to give Cece some time. The waters run deep in Cece's heart; she just needs a season to heal before she's ready to date again."

I didn't understand how her heart could still be hurting over that stupid Bradley. "Is there anything I could do to help Cece?" I implored.

Aunt Bird pushed my glasses back up on my nose and gave me a big hug. "Just keep doing what you're doing, my little one."

I looked up at her. "What have I been doing?"

"Loving her like you always do."

When I walked through the newspaper's press room later that afternoon, the roar of the presses mingled with the aroma of printer's ink filled me with comfort. While Aunt Bird dragged me to Pleasant View Park each season to place a floral arrangement at Mama and Diddy's graves, I never felt Diddy's presence when I stared at the cold marble with his name etched upon it. The moment I entered the pressroom, however, the essence of his spirit enveloped me.

I waved at Mr. Beasley and Mr. Pittman running the presses and headed to the front offices. As I looked into the glass room that'd once been Diddy's, I found Uncle Hoyt, reading glasses settled on his nose and chomping on a piece of gum, as he leaned back in Diddy's chair. Only a hint of pain crossed my heart; time, as Miz Gertie once told me, was the greatest healer.

I tapped on the glass. "Hey, Uncle Hoyt. You ready to head to the river?" Uncle Hoyt looked up, grinned, and motioned me inside.

"Almost, Allie. Why don't you run up to the Blue Goose and pick up the sandwiches I ordered for supper. By the time you return, Cece should be here, and we'll be on our way. Pick me out something for dessert and something for yourself, too." Uncle Hoyt knew Cece avoided sweets except on special occasions. I often wondered if I would've had the will power to forego desserts.

Just my luck Miss Blanche Bledsoe was working the counter at the café. Instead of her tightly fitting River Ranch waitress outfit, Miss Bledsoe was clad in a modest black shirtwaist and white apron. I wondered how she found time to change before her night shift at the honky-tonk.

"Well, hello Miss Allie. Long time, no see! You here to pick up Mr. Hoyt's order?" She reached underneath the counter and withdrew a paper bag with a ticket stapled to it. "Let's see. That's three ham and cheese sandwiches, three bags of chips, and some coleslaw. Will there be anything else, hon?"

I spied a cake plate displaying chocolate iced brownies. "Uh, yes ma'am. Two of those, please." I did my best to behave politely without looking her straight in the eye in fear she'd remember our last meeting, one I'd tried to forget.

She rang up my order. "So, Mr. Hoyt is taking you and your sister fishing, I hear."

"Umm, yes ma'am. My sister wants to sketch the sunset while we fish," I explained as I accepted my change.

"That sounds nice. I bet she'll have the perfect night for a sunset on the river. Ya'll put plenty of bug repellent on 'cause the skeeters are fierce out there by the water. And you tell your sweet aunt I said hello."

I gathered up my order. "Yes ma'am, I'll do that."

Just as I reached the door, Miss Bledsoe added. "And say hello to your little friend Josie. You know the one who likes to wear hairnets!" She winked at me, waved, and went back to pouring coffee.

So she had known all along. What was I to make of this woman, who played respectable waitress by day and honky-tonk queen by night? There was one thing for certain about Miss Blanche Bledsoe. She hadn't told on us. Maybe she figured her second job, as well as that terrible evening's events, were nobody's business.

I entered the alley where Cece and Uncle Hoyt were loading her easel and supplies into the pickup. "WSFT's fishing report said sunset is at 7:23 this evening, Cece. I hope that gives you enough time to get what you need," Uncle Hoyt remarked as we piled into the truck's cab.

Cece gingerly balanced a canvas wrapped in paper on her lap. "That'll give me plenty of time," she assured him. "This canvas is complete with the exception of the sky. I want to catch all the colors as the sun goes down behind Riverview Estates on Spruell Bluff."

Uncle Hoyt eased his old pickup onto West Main Street. "I know the perfect spot."

Ten minutes later as Uncle Hoyt turned onto Old River Road, my stomach flip-flopped. The last time I'd traveled this path, I was illegally driving the Studebaker as Josie, disguised as my aunt, sat beside me. Uncle Hoyt slowed and pulled onto the gravel parking lot of the River Ranch. Now, both my stomach and my heart turned cartwheels.

He climbed out of the truck. "I need some fresh bait if Allie and I intend to catch anything. You girls wait in the car; this is no place for a lady." He slammed the truck door and ambled toward the same entrance through which I'd once traveled alone.

The color drained from Cece's face, and her hands shook. I grabbed the hand nearest me and patted it. "Nobody's going to recognize you; you don't look anything like you did that night." Clad in a t-shirt and bermudas, Cece bore no resemblance to the shattered, disoriented figure huddled in the bar's back room on that horrible night.

As I prayed and Cece trembled, Uncle Hoyt reappeared with his bait. "I hope those fish are hungry." He whistled as we bumped the final few miles to the river.

By the time he pulled over in a small clearing, color had returned to Cece's complexion, and her hands appeared steady enough to hold a paintbrush. We gathered our fishing gear as Uncle Hoyt pointed toward a path up an incline. "Now, Cece, at the top of that hill, you'll have the perfect vantage point for the sunset."

Uncle Hoyt was right. As we reached the summit after a short hike, the river in all its majesty came into sight. Just beyond the other side of the river sat Spruell Bluff. Atop the bluff stood three of the biggest mansions in Riverview Estates. Cece gasped in approval. "I've never seen the bluff from this side of the river. It's magnificent." Uncle Hoyt helped Cece set up her easel before we headed down to his favorite fishing hole.

Within a half hour, I'd hooked three small bream, and Uncle Hoyt had reeled in a nice sized bass. I grew restless as my feet smoldered in my canvas Keds, and my hands reeked of worms. "Allie, why don't you take off your shoes and walk along the edge of the water. Just around that bend, there's a little wading pool." He pointed a few yards downriver, and I took off.

I hadn't walked far before I came to a clear pool where the water was trapped by rocks. As I eased my bare feet into the river's coolness and felt the smooth river rocks on my toes, my eye caught an unusual looking object glinting in the last rays of sunlight. It was attached to the riverbank about ten feet downriver

I squished through the mud as the shimmering object drew me closer. Once upon the unnatural apparition, I discovered it was a two-foot wooden crucifix painted white. It was engraved in small block lettering: "Rest in Peace, Macy Dunn."

My heart pounded in my chest, and an old drowning sensation returned to me. I turned around to run back but instead ran smack into Uncle Hoyt's stomach. "Allie, what's wrong? You look like you've seen a ghost!"

I pointed to the crucifix. "It's got Macy Dunn's name on it. Is she buried here, Uncle Hoyt?"

He kneeled and studied the painted object. When he straightened up, he wrapped his arm around my shoulder. I was shivering despite the heat. "No, honey, she's not buried there. If my recollection is correct, this is about the location her body was recovered. I guess someone placed the crucifix there in Macy's memory. Come on, let's have some supper."

Arriving at the clearing, we found Cece enjoying a ham and cheese sandwich. "Cece, you won't believe what I found—a crucifix, and..."

She interrupted. "It has Macy Dunn's name on it. The high school's band officers placed it there shortly after she drowned. I can't believe it's still standing. That was three years ago."

Had it been that long, I thought as I unwrapped my sandwich. I wondered if time, which had softened the absence of Diddy, had lessened Essie Dunn's grief.

Cece stood up and brushed off the seat of her shorts. "I think my canvas should be dry by now. Can I get some help carrying my supplies back to the truck?"

Uncle Hoyt gathered our gear. "I can handle the fishing equipment, so why don't you help your sister, Allie?

I scrambled up the hill ahead of Cece. When I reached the summit, I stopped to study her painting, still resting on its easel. Cece had so captured the stunning colors of a perfect sunset that it took my breath. My eyes slowly shifted to the rest of the painting. The scene included a dock with the silhouette of young lovers, their hands intertwined, their feet dangling in the water. Although the shadows on the dock hid their identities, I recognized the couple as Bradley and my sister. I wondered if the image was drawn from her memory of their final night together.

Cece reached the summit and stood behind me. "I call it 'A Modern Grecian Urn,'" she breathed softy.

"It's amazing, Cece! Your best ever, and I'm not wolfin'!" She smiled amusedly. "But what does that title mean? Isn't an urn a big container ?" I studied the painting again. "There's no urn in this picture."

Cece smiled. "No, you're right. The only thing hidden is the meaning of the painting's title, and you'd have to know the poet John Keats to understand."

My Lord! If getting a literature lesson from Aunt Bird wasn't enough! Now I had to endure Cece's, too. But I was curious. "What did this Keats poet write about?"

Cece carefully lifted the canvas from its easel. "A poem about an urn that contained etchings of the perfect moment."

"A perfect moment? Like what?"

Cece handed me her easel. "Well, there are several moments depicted on the urn, but my favorite is of two young lovers captured for eternity in the brief instant just before they kiss."

"Sounds kinda stupid to me. Why didn't the artist draw them kissing? That would make a better picture."

Cece sighed. "It's not the kiss itself but the longing for that kiss which offers ultimate perfection."

I pushed my glasses back up. "Huh?"

Cece stared at her painting and traced her fingers over the silhouette of the two lovers. Then she began to recite from the poem.

> Bold lover, never, never canst thou kiss,
> Though winning near the goal—yet, do not grieve;
> She cannot fade, though thou hast not thy bliss,
> Forever will thou love, and she be fair!

"Perfection to Keats is not in the moment of consummation but in its anticipation," she explained.

Since Uncle Hoyt cleared the hill at that moment, I didn't ask for a definition of *consummation*. The ride home was a quiet one, giving me an opportunity to consider the poem. Although I'd never been kissed by a boy, I had thought about it. Mr. Keats seemed to be saying that the thought was much more satisfying than the kiss itself. If that was the case, I guess I wasn't missing anything.

When we pulled into the alley behind the newspaper office, it was dark. "How about a treat from Dairy Queen, ladies?" Uncle Hoyt suggested. "I thought I'd pick up a strawberry sundae for Bird."

Cece climbed out of the truck. "Not for me, Uncle Hoyt. I have to open up the Paris Shoppe tomorrow. Thanks so much for including me tonight. I could have never found a better view of the sunset."

Having no reason to refuse a free ice cream, I accompanied Uncle Hoyt. We sat at a picnic table and enjoyed our treats.

We were quiet for a while until I ventured a thought. "Uncle Hoyt, have you ever had your heart broken?"

He rubbed his lame leg. "Well, I guess I had it broken a time or two. But it mended after a while, so I reckon it was never permanently damaged. Why do you ask, Allie?"

I considered whether I should be sharing such intimate details of my sister's love life, but I figured Aunt Bird had already confided in Uncle Hoyt. "I think Cece's heart is truly broken, and I don't think she'll ever get over Bradley."

He handed me a napkin for my sticky fingers. "Give her time, Allie, give her time."

"That's exactly what Aunt Bird says. Aunt Bird's heart skips a beat every time she sees you," I added as we climbed into the truck.

The back of Uncle Hoyt's neck reddened. He cleared his throat. "Is that a fact? That's certainly good to know about the woman who's held my heart for all these years."

That night as I struggled to fall asleep, my head spun. Maybe Macy Dunn jumped into the river on purpose because she'd been jilted by her boyfriend like Cece had. Would Cece ever consider doing such a thing?

I hoped Aunt Bird was right; maybe Cece was satisfied to have "loved and lost than never to have loved at all." She and Bradley must have experienced that perfect moment on the dock, the one Cece captured in her painting. I drifted off praying that the Lord would send Cece someone worthy of her love.

Chapter 22

Josie and I barely had time to share the highlights of our summers before school began. We were thrilled to find ourselves, along with Stu, David, and Teddy Gaddis, fully recovered from his broken arm and now a member of our football games, in Mrs. Stratton's eighth grade homeroom. Mrs. Stratton, the prettiest and youngest teacher in Flintville Elementary, wore bright red lipstick and high heels. The girls admired her dark hair, styled in a modern Jackie Kennedy flip, while the boys stared at her long, shapely legs whenever she stood to write on the board. One day as Mrs. Stratton bent over to retrieve some chalk, Teddy, the worst ogler of them all, quipped under his breath. "That dame's a real looker."

By winter, Mrs. Stratton's belly resembled a watermelon. Although the boys were mortified over her pregnancy, I was too busy having my own metamorphosis. Finally fitted for contact lenses, I welcomed the temporary discomfort of growing accustomed to foreign objects floating around my eyes in exchange for no glasses. David, who'd also started wearing contacts, joked that our "four eyes" labels were a thing of the past.

Teddy stopped staring at Mrs. Stratton's legs, which were swollen and not half as attractive now that she was wearing comfortable flats instead of her high heels. Nor did he acknowledge Rachel Fountain's constant advances in the hall and at lunch. Instead he flirted with me.

"Gosh, Allie, I never knew how green your eyes were," Teddy admitted as he sat on my front porch one rainy Sunday afternoon when our game had been scratched. In a habitual move, my hand reached to push up my now non-existent spectacles as Teddy continued. "And you've got the cutest dimples, did you know that?"

My heart did a cartwheel as I stared back into the bluest eyes with the darkest lashes I'd ever seen. By week's end, Teddy Gaddis and I were going steady. That meant wearing his "Midget League" gold football on a chain around my neck and passing notes to one another during class.

Our romance was short-lived. Within two weeks Teddy dumped me and my ironing-board chest for Rachel Fountain, who grew boobs overnight. Our nubile classmate enticed my boyfriend by offering to teach him the art of French kissing. Not ready to have any tongue in my mouth besides my own, I bowed to the inevitable.

That evening Cece caught me striking a match behind the garage. "Allison Sinclair, if you're smoking, I'll tan your hide before I turn you over to Aunt Bird!"

I was about to throw the match into a trashcan containing two weeks' worth of Teddy's notes and his class photos from second through eighth grade. "I'm not smoking, Cece. I'm ridding myself of one big jerk." I proceeded to recount the day's trauma of losing my boyfriend to my well-endowed nemesis. I ended with "and I hope Miss Rachel Fountain's butt grows to be ten times the size of her boobs!"

"That's a really hateful thing to wish upon any girl," she admonished me half-heartedly and then burst into laughter. She retrieved Teddy's class photos. "Are you certain you want to destroy these? Look how cute he was in second grade all snaggle-toothed."

"Yeah, and if I could, I'd knock out those two front teeth all over again. Maybe we Sinclair girls just aren't meant to have boyfriends."

Cece had maintained her "nun-like" status thus far in her senior year. She seemed content to pour her energy into preparing her portfolio and completing college applications to the best art schools in the country. I figured she'd end up at the University of Georgia. Uncle Hoyt and I were already anticipating football games "between the hedges," as fans called Sanford Stadium where the Georgia Bulldogs battled each autumn.

Cece smiled wistfully as I threw a burning match into the pile of notes. "Maybe it's just not time for us to meet our knights in shining armor. But one day, they'll come riding down Kingston Road and sweep us off our feet."

She ran her finger across the bridge of my nose, still sporting an indentation from years of wearing eyeglasses. "Girls like Rachel Fountain are all used up and worn out before they finish high school. You just wait; those green eyes and dimples of yours are going to break some hearts in the next few years." Cece had become quite adept at saying just what I needed to hear.

Teddy and I decided to be friends again, our reconciliation spurred on by the rest of our football gang who wanted to renew our Sunday games. Although no longer interested in Teddy, I delighted in seeing Rachel Fountain dump him for some pimple-faced tenth grade boy.

By late spring, however, the boys started football training at the high school. Josie groaned as we tossed the football on my porch steps. "I bet you and I could make the football team easily."

"Shoot, Josie, your mama and Aunt Bird would have a duck fit! Maybe we could go out for managers and carry the coach's clipboard or hand water to the players."

Josie sighed. "Coach Brewster saves those slots for the boys too puny to play. Besides, the managers have to wash the team's dirty uniforms and jock straps."

"What's a jock strap, anyway?" I pondered.

"I don't know for sure, but I heard Stu say that some of those defensive linemen hit so hard it almost knocked his jock strap off."

A chortle came from behind us where Cece sat on the porch swing.

"What are you laughing at, Miss Priss?" I quipped indignantly.

"The proper name for a jock strap is an athletic supporter," Cece explained.

Josie was wide-eyed. "Well, what does it support?"

We both turned to face my sister. "Boys wear them to protect their private parts down there. Haven't you ever seen a boy get kneed or kicked below the belt? It's very painful. Kind of like if a baseball hit you right in your chest."

"Ohhhh!" Josie and I replied simultaneously. We both protectively folded our arms across our small, sensitive chests.

I considered other alternatives. "We have to figure out a way to get as close to the field as possible."

"What about joining the high school band?" Josie suggested.

"That's ridiculous! Josie, you can't even carry a tune in chorus, and I despised the year of piano lessons Aunt Bird made me take."

We heard the porch swing squeak as Cece got up and stretched. "If you two really want to be a part of the football scene, go out for cheerleading."

We stared open-mouthed at one another. "All those girls are more coordinated. Josie and I could never learn all those cheers and stunts," I complained.

Cece danced down the steps between us. "I've watched you two climb the highest mimosa in Miz Gertie's backyard, plummet down Avalon Road on your bicycles without even touching your handlebars, and catch a twenty yard football pass from Stu. If you can do that, making the cheerleading squad will be a cinch."

For the next three weeks, Cece taught us every cheerleading move in her repertoire. I was able to master each skill with the exception of a cartwheel. While Josie's long legs created the perfect execution, my short, stubby ones gave me the appearance of a frog.

Cece assured me. "What you lack in cartwheel execution, you make up for in pep and personality."

Cece was right. Josie's graceful, lithe gymnastics and my spirited enthusiasm landed us on the 1965 Flintville Raiders Cheerleading Squad. Uncle Hoyt took the family to the Blue Goose Café for supper.

As I dug into a celebratory brownie a la mode, Cece cleared her throat. "I have an announcement myself," she began as she opened a letter. "It came through, Aunt Bird. The scholarship that Miss Benton recommended to me. I got it!"

Aunt Bird stammered, "Oh, Cece, I'm so proud of you!"

"Uncle Hoyt!" I interjected. "We'll have football with the Raiders on Friday nights and with the Dawgs in Athens on Saturdays. Who could ask for more?" I attacked my brownie while everyone else remained mute.

Cece broke the silence. "Allie, I'm not going to the University of Georgia."

I held my fork in mid-air. "What do you mean? I saw your acceptance letter from UGA weeks ago."

Aunt Bird intervened. "Cece's received a number of acceptance letters. She's just been waiting for the best opportunity for her art studies."

"Okay, so where's the best opportunity? Certainly you're not going to Georgia Tech?" My entire family stared at me. A sudden queasy sensation shook the pit of my stomach.

Cece gently placed her arm around my shoulder. "I'm going to New York University." Her soft tone did nothing to cushion the pain of her news.

New York City? That was an eternity away from Flintville. There would be no monthly trips home for Cece, no weekend visits to her dorm for me. She might as well move to Egypt. Tears pooling in my eyes, I wriggled out from under Cece's embrace, and muttered, "I'll meet ya'll at the car."

Even though a new episode of *The Fugitive* aired that night, I went straight to my room. Cece slipped in and sat on the edge of my bed where I thumbed through the latest issue of *Seventeen*.

"Come on, Allie, at least discuss this."

Pretending to be engrossed in an article about cleansing pores, I mumbled, "What's there to talk about?"

"Do you know how many renowned artists have studied at NYU? And with a full scholarship, I can go without putting a burden on Aunt Bird. If it hadn't been for Miss Benton, I wouldn't have even applied."

"I wish that hateful old bat would mind her own business," I seethed as I flipped the page.

"That's cruel, Allie. She's been a wonderful mentor to me. If Mama were here, she'd be so excited for me, and so would Diddy," Cece added.

My anger hit its boiling point. "Yeah, well Mama and Diddy are both dead and gone. And now my sister's leaving me, too. You promised you'd never, ever leave me. You lied, Cece, you lied to me!"

She tried to protest, but I wouldn't allow her. "No, I don't want to talk about it anymore! Just leave me alone! Since you're going to be leaving me for good in a few months, I might as well get used to it!" I threw the magazine across the room, pulled the bed sheet up to my chin, and turned toward the wall. I was too proud to let her see the tears streaming down my cheeks.

An uneasy peace reigned in the Sinclair household that week. The three of us ate dinner in strained silence. To my surprise, Aunt Bird didn't lecture me about my behavior towards Cece. I guess she figured we were old enough to battle our differences without her intervention.

The fact that Aunt Bird was waging her own battle never occurred to me until Miz Gertie called that Saturday. "If I drive you by Hastings Pharmacy, will you run in the drugstore and pay for my prescription? I'll spring for a milkshake."

As I tried to enjoy my milkshake on our drive home, Miz Gertie attempted to engage me in conversation. "I hear your sister is going to school in New York!"

I stared out the window. "Yeah, I guess."

Miz Gertie patted my leg. "You sound about as enthusiastic as your aunt does."

"What do you mean?"

"She's just trying to adjust to Cece's news. Letting her go so far away isn't easy for your aunt, but she'd never tell Cece that."

"Why not? I told Cece just what I feel about it." My face grew warm as my anger bubbled up once again.

Miz Gertie pulled into her driveway. "And how do you feel, Allie?"

Her question unraveled the few threads holding my emotions intact. "I, I feel betrayed!" Tears stung my cheeks. "She's all I have, Miz Gertie. She always knows what I'm feeling, when I'm hurting, and she fixes the hurt. I'm afraid to be without her, Miz Gertie. I just can't lose her, too!"

Miz Gertie pulled a tissue from her purse. "There, there, Allie. First of all, Cece is not all you have. Your Aunt Bird would lay down her life for you, and Hoyt thinks you hung the moon. And by the way, I'm quite fond of you myself." She handed me another tissue. "Secondly, Cece is not leaving you; she's just beginning a new chapter in her life, and to do that, she has to make a change. We human beings are creatures of habit. We feel threatened by anything that reshapes our world. Did you consider that Cece is just as frightened as you? You'll still be here in your comfortable little existence where everyone knows you and loves you while Cece embarks on a journey into the unknown all by herself."

"If it's going to be so frightening and lonely, why does Cece want to go?" I asked.

Miz Gertie smiled. "Well, because she's a Sinclair."

"What does that mean?"

She settled her hands in her lap. "I've had the delight of watching you and Cece grow up. In your few years, you two have weathered more change than most people do in a century of living. I believe your ability to endure and to adapt is the result of the stock from which you're made. I never saw your daddy run from a fight or compromise his principles, and he wasn't afraid to push for change in our community when needed. When your sweet mama went to her untimely death, your daddy made the changes necessary to care for you girls. That's the legacy he instilled in the two of you. Neither one of you is a quitter, nor have you ever shrunk from a challenge. You Sinclairs always find the courage and faith to move forward. That's why Cece is going to New York, and that's why you'll let her go."

As I contemplated Miz Gertie's explanation, I realized I wasn't angry at Cece; I was afraid. I breathed a silent prayer: "Dear God, help me find the courage Miz Gertie says we Sinclairs have, and God, please send Mama or Diddy to be Cece's guardian angel in New York. I guess I can take care of myself since I still have Aunt Bird and Uncle Hoyt."

Aunt Bird was sprawled on her bedroom floor, which was littered with family photos. "Allie, will you help me clean this up before Cece gets home?"

Each photo included Cece in various stages of her life. "What are you doing, Aunt Bird?"

"I'm making Cece a memory book to take with her to NYU. Maybe some pages from her life will keep her from growing homesick. Oh my, look at this one!" She picked up a photo. "That was Cece's fifth birthday. Look at you in the high chair, Allie! You've got more icing on your little face than the cake does! And there's your mama." I peered over Aunt Bird's shoulder. My mama, handing Cece a birthday gift, looked so young, so beautiful, so happy. "I believe this may be the last photograph made of your mama. I think Cece should have this one, don't you?"

"Aunt Bird, how do you feel about Cece going so far away?"

Aunt Bird's emerald eyes, brimming with tears, met mine. "I'll miss her more than words can convey. I'm afraid for her, if you must know. And it's not her diabetes that frightens me."

I added photos to a stack. "Then what worries you?"

She groped for words to explain. "Allie, your sister is not like you, at least not in the emotional sense."

"What do you mean?"

"Well, emotionally, you're an open book, Allie. I know when you're upset because you wear your heart on your sleeve. When you reach a boiling point and those feelings start to bubble, everything spills out of you."

I grimaced. "In other words, I'm a big cry baby!"

She wrapped an arm around my shoulder. "Not at all! You're one tough cookie, but even cookies crumble. And once you've fallen apart, you pick up the pieces and rebuild. Cece, on the other hand, never cracks. She keeps all of her emotions intact. She rarely allows anyone to penetrate her armor, and I worry that the wall she's built around herself may come tumbling down some day."

My mind returned to the disastrous night at the River Ranch. "And we won't be there to protect her," I added.

Aunt Bird hugged me closer. "You're exactly right. And that's why letting Cece go scares me."

"Then maybe we should convince her not to go," I suggested.

Aunt Bird shook her head. "Is that fair for Cece? She's been given a full scholarship to one of the most prestigious universities in our country because she's truly talented. I love her too much to snatch this opportunity away from her. So, I have to let her go. We'll be all right, Allie. I promise."

I sensed she needed reassuring. "I know we'll be all right. We're Sinclairs."

Aunt Bird looked puzzled. "Whatever do you mean, Allie?"

I proceeded to explain Miz Gertie's interpretation of the Sinclair women. "I'm certain you're included in her definition since you're a Sinclair, too."

My aunt grinned. "I feel honored to be a member of such company. I agree with Miss Gertie. We Sinclair women are indomitable!"

Cece and I had the house to ourselves that night. I found her on the side porch reading the autograph section of her yearbook. "Cece, do you think I could come to New York one Thanksgiving for the Macy's Parade? I've always wanted to see if that Bullwinkle balloon looks as big in real life as it does on television."

Cece smiled at me. "So, squirt, have you decided to keep me after all? I figured you were in the market for a new sister."

I sighed. "No, it'd take too long to break in a new model." I lay my head on her shoulder, and we sat silently as the dusky sky became a velvet backdrop for the night's first stars. "It's just that New York is so far away. What if you get lonely? Worse than that, what if I get lonely for you?"

Cece ran her fingers through my hair. "We'll still share the same sky, Allie."

Her comment struck an almost forgotten chord. "Do you believe in guardian angels, Cece? One time Roscoe Ray pointed out the two brightest stars in the sky to me. He told me the two stars were Mama and Diddy, and they were watching over me." I tugged at Cece's hand and led her out the screen door into our side yard.

The night was still as my sister and I stood hand in hand and gazed at the heavens. Just overhead two spectacular diamond-like bodies twinkled in a brilliance that outdid all the others. "See. That's got to be Mama and Diddy, don't you think?"

Cece squeezed my hand tightly. "I do believe they're sharing the same sky that we share, Allie. I think they're telling us that no matter how far apart we are, our hearts will always be intertwined."

We kept our eyes heavenward for the longest time. Finally, when our necks grew stiff and the night air grew cool, we retreated to the warmth inside.

The summer of 1965 seemed shorter than usual. I spent almost every weekday either at cheerleading practice or at Parker's Pool where Josie and I flirted with Jimmy Bolton, the pool's lifeguard and quarterback for the Flintville Raiders. Jimmy, who'd be a senior, had his pick of any girl at Flintville High School, and neither Josie nor I could outshine Rachel Fountain as she pranced around in her two-piece with a DD bust line.

The weekend before our first football game, Uncle Hoyt loaded up his pickup with all of Cece's belongings. Since Aunt Bird and I had already started school, he volunteered to make the three-day trip to New York with Cece. He planned to stop in Washington, D.C. on his return to visit an old army buddy.

On Saturday night we held a small going away party for Cece. Although Aunt Bird suggested we invite her closest friends, Cece declined the offer. "I think I'd rather spend my last night with you and Allie, if that's okay."

After a meal with Cece's favorites, we retired to the side porch for dessert. I was surprised when Cece asked Aunt Bird for a second piece of pecan pie, still warm from the oven.

Cece savored each bite. "Do you know how much I'm going to miss your cooking, Aunt Bird? Not to mention this old house. I bet it's already too cold in New York to enjoy a fall evening on a screened porch."

Aunt Bird, her freckled face still flushed from an afternoon in the kitchen, sat down with a glass of iced tea in one hand and a package in the other. "If I could, I'd send the Georgia weather and a daily home-cooked meal with you. I guess this will have to suffice when you need a little taste of Flintville." She handed Cece the package containing the memory book. In addition to the photographs, there were mementos from her school years—each report card from first through twelfth grade, programs from all the football games, ribbons from every corsage she'd ever worn, and two pages of funny family anecdotes penned by Aunt Bird herself.

We spent the remainder of the evening in reverie of our life together on Kingston Road. With each remembered story, we giggled like little girls at a slumber party. It was almost midnight before Aunt Bird insisted that we get to bed.

I waited until we were alone in our bedroom to present my going away gift to Cece. After our night of star gazing a few months earlier, the idea had struck me. I'd never shared with anyone Roscoe Ray's gift, the two carved stars of black flint rock, until I took them along with Mama's sapphire and diamond bracelet to Peavy's Jewelry Store a month earlier. Spending every dime of my summer allowance, I had Mr. Peavy remove two tiny diamonds from a link in my mother's bracelet, drill holes in the middle of each flint star, and implant the sparkling diamonds. He then added a loop so each star could hang from sterling silver chains, one for Cece and one for me.

As Cece unwrapped the tiny velvet jewelry box, her eyes grew wide. "Allie Sinclair, what have you gone and done?" She opened the lid of the box and gazed upon its contents. "Why this is the most exquisite necklace I've ever seen! Where in the world did you get it?"

I revealed my identical necklace, which I was wearing beneath my shirt. "Roscoe Ray carved the stars from some flint rocks we found at the river. So, now you can actually take a piece of Flintville with you."

"Roscoe Ray carved these? He is talented. But, how could you afford the diamonds, Allie?"

"Don't worry, I already had the diamonds. Mr. Peavy took a link I didn't need from Mama's bracelet. The diamonds represent our guardian angels. You know, Mama and Diddy, the brightest stars in the sky. I figure anytime I'm lonely for you or worried about you, I can touch my star of flint, and I'll know Mama and Diddy are watching over you. And you can do the same for me."

There was a slight crack in Cece's armor as her eyes welled with tears. She stood in front of the bureau's mirror with her back to me as she fastened the chain around her neck. When she turned around, her eyes were once again dry. "I'll never remove it, Allie, not as long as we're apart."

Too early the next morning, Aunt Bird and I stood in the driveway and waved goodbye to my sister. As I watched the tail lights on Uncle Hoyt's pickup fade into the distance, I wondered what the future held for the Sinclair sisters. I fingered the star of flint dangling from its chain and prayed that Mama and Diddy would watch over us. Little did I know how much we'd need God Himself in the coming seasons of our lives.

Part III
1965-1975

Chapter 23

Though intending to mourn Cece's absence every moment, I was quickly distracted by the hardships of high school. The routine of maneuvering a crowded hall to a different class each hour came easy, perhaps because I'd roamed the high school since I was a six-year-old waiting on Aunt Bird to finish her day. Nor did I feel threatened by any of my teachers, all of whom I'd known my entire life.

My intimidation came in the form of a five-foot-tall fireball, Flintville High's cheerleading captain Cassie Sue Causey. Cassie, a senior who'd cheered her entire high school career, loved that she was finally in charge. "Allie Sinclair, you need to clap with more spirit, and Josie, hold your shoulders up!" The squad's only freshmen, Josie and I became the victims of Cassie's instruction. After Cassie insisted a cheerleader couldn't promote spirit without showing her teeth at all times, we nicknamed her Captain Smiley. When the team stampeded onto the field each Friday night, sharing in Flintville's football fever was worth enduring the edicts of Captain Smiley.

Though our front yard football buddies Teddy, Ty, Stu, and David dressed out with the varsity, they rode the bench until the season's final game. By third quarter and a formidable lead against Pike County, Coach Brewster emptied the freshmen bench. When Stu Sims dove over the goal line for a touchdown with one second on the clock, Flintville fans went wild. As the cheerleaders rushed the field, Dave grabbed me and picked me up above his shoulders. From my higher vantage point, I saw Stu, still lying across the goal line, surrounded by coaches and Dr. Justice. Our hero's chin had been the first thing to hit the ground, and his jaw was broken.

For six weeks we suffered with poor Stu; his jaw wired practically shut, he sipped liquid meals through a straw. Even so, Stu participated in our conversations although we often couldn't understand him through his clenched teeth.

Shortly before Christmas, Stu was released from his wire prison. He started devouring everything in sight and gained ten pounds in two weeks!

"The doc says I can lay off the *Mighty Mo* shakes," he announced on my porch as the six of us wrapped Christmas toys for the needy. As members of the *Raider's Club*, we freshmen had been delegated the wrapping committee while the seniors, led by its president Cassie Sue, would have the honor of delivering the packages.

Josie stretched. "I guess this'll be the last time I see ya'll until after the holidays. We're heading to LaGrange tomorrow."

"I'll be around if you fellas want to watch some of the bowl games here," I suggested.

Ty perked up. "When does your sister get home?"

Ty's interest in Cece usually irked me, but I was too excited about her visit to care. "In two days. Put those tongues up, boys. Aunt Bird doesn't want your drool all over her floor. Besides, Cece has a boyfriend."

Stu moaned. "If only she'd waited a little longer now that I'm filling out."

"You fools might as well forget my sister. She's a New York ingénue—refined, cosmopolitan, sophisticated. What could she possibly see in bumpkins like ya'll?"

Two days later as Uncle Hoyt drove us to the Atlanta Airport, I wondered if I would recognize my sister. Had New York City changed her? Did she speak with a Yankee accent? Would she find her small-town, unpolished sister boring? In her letters, Cece sounded like the sister she'd always been, but I had no living proof yet.

When Cece walked through the gate, her beauty took my breath. Clad in a royal blue wool cape with fringe and a matching blue beret, her eyes gleamed like sapphires. "Cece, Cece! Over here!" The next moment her arms enveloped me, her soft scent surrounded me, and her sweet, Southern voice assured me that my big sister was still the same. Well, at least for the most part.

After hugs all around, Aunt Bird remarked, "Let's have a good look at you, New York lady!" Cece twirled around as my aunt took inspection. "Where in the world is the hemline of that skirt?" I hadn't noticed Cece's tall boots and short, short skirt.

"It's the latest style in New York. It's called a mini-skirt."

I thought Aunt Bird would have a conniption, but instead, she just shook her head in surrender. "I do hope you have something a little more conservative for church on Sunday."

I changed the subject. "I love your cape, Cece. Where'd you buy it? At Macy's?"

Cece put her hand in mine. "Actually, it's called a poncho. It's all the rave in the village!"

"What village?"

"Greenwich Village," she explained. "NYU is smack dab in the middle of the village with coffee shops and art studios everywhere."

Uncle Hoyt chuckled as he headed the car downtown. "How about some Varsity hamburgers for supper? I bet you can't get that in New York now, can you?"

Cece giggled. "That's for sure, Uncle Hoyt. They serve something called hash browns with their eggs. I've yet to find a good, warm bowl of grits," she complained as we pulled into the Varsity.

"We'll remedy that problem while you're home," Aunt Bird assured Cece. "How did you fare with your exams?"

"Three A's and one B in Algebra, the only math I have to take. I loved my Still Life art class. Next semester I'm taking Pottery. The department has its own kiln, and I'll learn to throw pots," Cece bubbled in excitement.

As I sipped my milkshake, I delighted in Cece's enthusiastic babbling. "Why would you want to know how to throw a pot?"

"Throwing pots is art terminology for spinning clay on a special wheel to make a pot," Cece explained patiently.

There was much for me to learn about the life of an artist. Over the holidays, I received quite an education.

The following morning, I was helping Aunt Bird make fudge before Cece emerged from our bedroom. Still in her pajamas, she shuffled to the refrigerator and poured herself some orange juice.

"Aunt Bird, is there any fresh coffee?"

Aunt Bird raised her eyebrows. "And since when did you start drinking coffee?"

Cece found a mug and poured herself a cup from the percolator. "Everybody in the village drinks coffee. It gets your motor running. Phoebe and I have our own coffee pot."

Phoebe Libowitz, a native New Yorker, was Cece's roommate. Cece had sent me a photograph of them standing in front of the Empire State Building.

"Well, what shall we do today?" Aunt Bird handed me a spatula with remnants of warm fudge. "Cece, I thought you might want to check out the winter styles at the Paris Shoppe."

Cece poured herself a bowl of cornflakes. "The styles at the Paris Shoppe are last year's runway headlines. New York fashion is much more with it! Besides, Phoebe, Marcus, and I invested in a sewing machine so we can keep up with the latest looks without destroying our budgets. I actually made my poncho, but Marcus found the beret in a thrift shop."

"Marcus sews?" Cece'd shown me a picture of Marcus standing with her outside an art gallery. He was tall, dark, and handsome, and had played point guard on his Minnesota high school basketball team. I couldn't imagine him threading a needle. I laughed out loud at the thought.

Cece glowered at me. "Don't make fun of Marcus!"

I licked the last sliver of fudge off the spatula. "I'm just not used to a boy partaking in feminine activities."

Cece rolled her eyes. "Some of the world's most prominent fashion designers are men! Haven't you ever heard of Oscar de la Renta or Pierre Cardin?"

"Good grief, Cece. I won't make fun of your boyfriend anymore."

Her voice rose. "And that's another thing. Marcus is just a friend, not my boyfriend."

Aunt Bird tried to defuse the situation. "Cece, hon, even I assumed that Marcus was your boyfriend. You talk about him so much in your letters."

"Well, he's not. He doesn't even like girls. He's, he's, you know, different."
Cece hesitated.

"You mean he's a queer?" The words toppled from my mouth.

Aunt Bird dropped a cup of chopped pecans on the floor. "Allison Sinclair, where did you hear that term?"

"All the fellas talk about Bennie Jordan that runs his mama's flower shop. They say he's queer as a three dollar bill."

Aunt Bird sighed. "If you must refer to a person of such a, hrmm, persuasion, you will use the proper term—homosexual."

I was surprised my aunt knew such an individual existed; she'd probably read about sissy men in some of her novels. I was curious with questions for Cece. "Does Marcus have a boyfriend? Do they kiss? Does he like to wear dresses?"

Cece rolled her eyes again. "Allie, you're so naïve. Marcus is just coming to terms with his sexuality. Why do you think he moved to New York? For the very reason poor Bennie Jordan should have left Flintville years ago. Small town people tend to have small minds and big prejudices." She stomped out of the kitchen.

"I don't think everybody in this town has a small mind, do you?" I complained to Aunt Bird.

"No, Allie, there are many open-minded people in our community, and Cece knows that."

"Then why'd she get her panties in a wad about Marcus? She acts like New York is the only place where people are civilized. What's wrong with her, Aunt Bird?"

"Panties in a wad? Allie, where *do* you come up with these vulgar phrases? Cece's just facing her rite of passage and growing up, that's all."

"I don't think Cece's acting very grown up right now."

Aunt Bird began chopping more pecans. "That's because she's just embarked on her journey. She's questioning the value system on which she was raised and wondering if everything she was taught to believe was wrong. Her struggle can be painful for her and for those who love her, but when she reaches the other side, she'll have her answer. I wager she'll discover people, no matter where they live, are basically the same. "

"Well, how long will this rite of passage thing take?"

Aunt Bird chuckled. "I'm not certain, but I promise the sister you love will come back to you. Give her time."

As soon as Cece was dressed, she fired up the Studebaker and drove over to Margaret's house. In such a hurry, she even failed to make her bed.

Having our bedroom to myself, I decided to wrap my few Christmas presents. I studied the leather-bound manicure kit and six variety bottles of nail polish for Cece; I doubted she'd be impressed. The colors were probably "has-beens" in New York circles.

Just as I began to believe a stranger wearing my sister's body had come for a visit, the Cece I knew returned. On Christmas Eve, she sat down at the kitchen table where Aunt Bird was chopping celery and onions for the cornbread dressing. "I'm so glad you're making turkey and dressing tonight," she gushed. "I can't wait to eat real cornbread dressing. Some New Yorkers stuff their turkeys with oysters."

Pleased Cece had discovered something wrong with New Yorkers, I interjected. "Eww, oysters look like snot!"

Aunt Bird paused from her chopping to admonish me. "Allison Sinclair, what have I told you about using such vulgar phrases? You've never even tried an oyster. Your daddy absolutely adored your Mimi's oyster stew."

I shuddered. "Gross! The thought of those slimy little creatures sliding down my throat makes me want to puke!" Aunt Bird gave me another stern look.

"Allie, wanna open a present early?" Cece asked. "I've been dying to give it to you."

Cece and I darted to the Christmas tree. We returned to the kitchen with my gift so Aunt Bird could watch me unwrap it. Folded amidst pink tissue lay a pair of nylon stockings. When I withdrew them from the box, I discovered that the stockings didn't stop at the thigh but had a trunk attached.

Cece explained. "They're called pantyhose. They eliminate the need for a garter belt or a panty girdle. Aren't they fantastic?!"

Aunt Bird recovered before me. "Stockings that don't require a girdle? How can that be?"

Cece laughed. "Aunt Bird, look at Allie. Her stomach is flat as a washboard. Does she really need a girdle? "

I agreed. "I love them Cece. I can't wait to show the cheerleaders."

The remainder of the afternoon was spent singing Christmas carols and helping Aunt Bird with dinner preparations. As I finished setting the table, Uncle Hoyt arrived for our Christmas Eve feast. Except for the painful twinge I felt as I remembered Diddy and Mama, it was a perfect celebration. I figured they were celebrating with us, anyway.

The following morning after a lavish breakfast, we adjourned to the Christmas tree. Cece appeared thrilled over the manicure set as well as the polish. After brushing a tad of "Wild Strawberry" on her toenail, she exclaimed, "This will be the perfect color to go with my NYU sweatshirt!"

Uncle Hoyt presented me a heavy box containing Diddy's old Underwood typewriter. "I don't use it, and it's just gathering dust. I oiled the keys and replaced the ribbon. Bird said it'd fit perfectly on your study desk." Too choked up to respond, I gave Uncle Hoyt a bear hug.

My gifts from Cece were the best. In one large box lay a dark green wool poncho, identical to her blue one. "That color's so good with your green eyes," she said. "Marcus and I searched four fabric shops to find the right shade."

"Aunt Bird, don't come unglued before I explain," Cece pleaded as I tore into the final package. It was the cutest tartan plaid mini-skirt! Cece beamed, "Allie, with your little figure in that outfit, you'll be Flintville High's Fashion Plate."

I held the tiny skirt against my waist. Aunt Bird shook her head. "Over my dead body, Allison Sinclair. You'll be sent home if you wear that to school."

Cece went to bat for me. "By next fall, all the girls in Flintville will be wearing these. Besides, I added a pair of navy tights for Allie to wear underneath!" Cece turned her attention to me. "All she needs is some stylish boots. Maybe we can find some on sale if you'll visit me this summer."

Cece's final statement shattered me. "Aren't you coming home for the summer, Cece?"

Aunt Bird's face wore the same surprise as mine. "Cece, there's been no discussion of your spending the summer in New York," she issued in her authoritative tone. "I thought we'd agreed you'd work at the Paris Shoppe this summer."

"Oh, Aunt Bird, how can I work there after I've experienced true fashion? Phoebe and I have been offered jobs in an art shop in the village. The owner will be in Europe all summer and needs someone to keep the store running. She's even offered us her rent-free apartment over the shop. Phoebe's parents have already agreed. By alternating our hours at the shop, we can each take a class or two," Cece delivered her prepared argument without taking a breath.

Staring at the ceiling, Aunt Bird called out in a somewhat desperate voice, "Heavenly Father above!"

Uncle Hoyt, mumbling something about more coffee, retreated to the kitchen. When Aunt Bird resumed speaking, it was a tone of quiet defeat. "Cece Sinclair, I should have never taught you the art of persuasion when you were dueling with your daddy a few years ago. I'll have to talk to Phoebe's parents and this art store owner before making a decision."

Cece ecstatically hugged my aunt; I knew the decision was made. Once again I'd be without my sister, who was changing by leaps and bounds while I stood still.

That night after Cece and Aunt Bird were asleep, I slipped out the front door and sat on our porch steps. Darkness enveloped our neighborhood as I looked up at the cloudless, starry sky. I'd become quite adept at surrendering my worries to the stars.

As I'd done many times before, I addressed my stars of Flint as though their twinkling points were actually ears. "Hey, Diddy. Hey, Mama. I guess you heard Cece's not coming home this summer. So, it'll just be me and ya'll again. Well, and Aunt Bird, too. Please watch over Cece. And don't let her forget the people who love her best are right here in Flintville, not in New York City." Clad only in my pajamas, I sensed the night air's chill. I began to shiver.

The screen door squeaked. Cece, carrying a tattered afghan knitted by our Mimi long ago, sat down beside me. She wrapped the blanket around our shoulders and took my cold hand in her warm one.

Looking up at the sky, she whispered into my hair. "I won't forget, Allie. I promise."

Chapter 24

In August of 1969, I gazed out the window of Delta Flight 208 as it taxied the runway for takeoff. After three years of making promises and juggling impossible schedules, I was on my way to visit Cece in New York.

Josie sat in the aisle seat beside me. A seasoned flier, she'd generously allowed me the window seat. Josie sensed my apprehension when the aircraft's engines roared. "The takeoff is the worst part. Once we're in the air, it'll be smooth sailing, I promise." She held my hand as our plane gathered speed.

Reaching a higher altitude, the roar eased into a soft, low hum. Yawning and rubbing her bloodshot eyes, Josie announced, "I'm going to sleep. Enjoy the view." She adjusted her seat, closed her lids, and was completely out before I lost sight of Atlanta.

My best friend was suffering a hangover. Last night we'd attended a farewell celebration for the *B&B Brigade*, a nickname for our group of pals, including Josie and me, Ty, Teddy, Stu, and David. Only the six of us knew that *B&B* stood for *bicycles* and *ballfields*.

I took delight in others, like Luke Madison, who tried to decipher the abbreviation. Luke was a flirtatious junior who claimed to adore older women. Sidling up at my locker one day, Luke whispered, "*B&B* stands for *Beauties and Bozos*, and I know you're not a bozo. If you want a bad boy, go out with me." Unimpressed, I giggled at Luke and headed to class.

Josie and I dated our share of guys who'd ultimately disappointed us. Our sophomore year was the "season of the dumb jocks." I opted for senior tight end Dwayne Jackson. We carried on a torrid relationship during football season, probably because we had something to talk about. At the sock hops after each game, Dwayne grasped me tightly, my head on his shoulder, as our local band's tenor belted out "Unchained Melody." By basketball season, however, when I caught Dwayne flirting with Denise Ware, a busty freshman, it was over. I was no competition for big boobs.

My junior year, I shunned jocks for the James Dean type. Rusty Donovan met all the requirements. But by spring, I grew tired of Rusty cancelling dates so he could work on his car and waiting on him during lunch while he puffed on a cigarette at the smoking wall.

The fellows in our brigade fared about the same in romances. Each had their share of girlfriends, but by summer before our senior year, they too were footloose and free. In the humid evenings of that unforgettable summer, we spent every free moment with one another. After work, we'd meet at the Dairy Queen, park our cars, purchase the flavor of the week milkshake, and pile into my Studebaker since it could accommodate all six of us. We'd drive up to Crystal Hill, sit atop the car, stargaze, and talk. Although Josie had several dates with Ty, and I went out with Stu a few times, we never considered ourselves real couples. When Josie and I discussed our less than steamy make-out sessions, we came to the same conclusion: kissing Ty or Stu was like kissing a brother.

Since all four boys would be gone before Josie and I returned from New York, we held our farewell to Flintville the night before we left. Ty was headed to Livingston State in Alabama with a scholarship as a field goal kicker. "Ty the Toe" had proved worthy of his name when he kicked a 54-yard field goal against Valdosta in the state championship even though we lost by a touchdown.

Stu was following Ty to Livingston State as a "walk on." Stu's physique had metamorphosed over the past two years. He'd added pounds to his once skinny frame, and his regimen of daily weight training had rewarded him rippling muscles.

Teddy and David would soon be en route to Ft. Benning for Army Basic Training. "The recruiter told us if we volunteered for the draft, we'd only have to serve two years. Then we're eligible for the GI Bill," David explained. We avoided a discussion of where they'd end up after training, but we knew they were headed for Vietnam.

Last night, there'd been no mention of going to war or being cut from a college football team. By the time we arrived at the Hastings fishing cabin on the river, Ty had located his uncle's beer stash and iced it down in a metal washtub on the screened porch. Ty held up his Budweiser. "Here, here! Let the festivities begin!" With his announcement, the boys chugged simultaneously.

"Hey, don't leave me out!" Josie dug below the ice for the coldest can. Unlike Josie, the smell of beer made me nauseous. I credited this aversion to my sojourn into the belly of the River Ranch where I'd once retrieved Cece.

David moved over on the old, ragged sofa and patted a spot for me. "Allie, we didn't forget about you." He pulled a bottle from his cooler. "I found this in my dad's refrigerator in the garage. He'll never miss it. It's a sissy drink called Champale, a poor man's champagne." He popped the cap and handed it to me.

I pretended indignation. "David Banks, you know I'm no sissy. Who was the first one of us to swing out on that rope over the river last year? Just tell me that!"

Stu snickered. "Yeah, but the only reason we had you go first is that you're a runt, and we figured the rope wouldn't break with you."

David apologized. "Oh, come on, Allie. We know you're not a sissy. Just try the drink."

The concoction tasted nothing like beer but had a bubbly quality, and after finishing it, my nose was tingling. Luckily, David had only brought me two bottles, or I couldn't have driven home. The boys didn't even have a car. Mr. Hastings, probably suspecting what they were up to, had driven them out.

We played cards a while, and then sat on the dock until the mosquitoes ran us back inside. Josie suggested a game. "Let's play ten years from now. When it's your turn, tell us where you'll be in ten years."

"Ten years! We'll be in a nursing home by then," Teddy joked.

Josie glared at him. "You won't even be thirty in ten years. Okay, if you're going to act silly, I'll start. I'll have my degree in elementary education, and I'll be teaching kindergarten in the morning and running my own riding school in the afternoon. I'll call the school 'Horse Feathers,' I think." A vision of Josie ten years from now tumbled across my mind's eye. I could see her and some handsome cowboy atop two fine horses as they rode off into the sunset. "Okay, Stu, it's your turn," Josie announced.

Stu leaned over the washtub for another beer. I could see the outline of his muscular back through his t-shirt. "After I win the Heisman, I'll go on to play professional ball. Then I'll come back to Flintville to coach the Raiders to state championships every year."

Ty slapped Stu on the back. "That's perfect, Stu. But, what if Coach Brewster's not ready to retire when you return to Flintville, which will probably be sooner than later?" All the boys chortled.

Stu flexed the muscles in his arms. "I'll become a professional body builder, or maybe I'll come back to Flintville and sell insurance at my dad's company." Stu was a pragmatic dreamer; I knew he'd give football his all but was relieved to learn he had a backup plan.

Next was Teddy, our happy-go-lucky, womanizing class clown. He took a swig from his Budweiser. "After I win two purple hearts and a bronze star in Nam, I'm moving to Atlanta. I'll be a bartender at a go-go bar, you know, where I can pick up hot foxes and have lots of one-night-stands." Josie and I moaned in disgust while Teddy chugged his beer. "Then I'd like to come back to Flintville and develop some of this river property. Don't ya'll know we're sitting on a goldmine? I bet in ten years, there'll be houses all along the river and not just those mansions on the Bluff." Summertimes, Teddy assisted his dad, a carpenter who worked with the major builders for Riverview Estates.

We all turned our gazes on David. "Come on, Dave!" I prodded. "Tell us."

"I want to study medicine. I figure after my Army stint, I'll start undergraduate school. Eight years after that, I'll be a full-fledged doctor."

"Good God!" Teddy gasped. "You really will be over thirty by then!"

"Shut up, Teddy!" I snapped. "It's a grand dream, David, and you'd make a super Dr. Kildare type." Of all the four boys, David was the most special to me. Maybe it was because we'd both suffered the taunts of being called "four eyes" before getting contacts.

Everyone admired Dave's fearlessness. Once when we sat eating sandwiches outside Porky's BBQ Shack, a car with a Pike County license plate skidded into the parking lot while one of its passengers jumped out and heaved a beer bottle at Porky's storefront window, shattering it. David chased the boy down, tackled him, and held him in a headlock while Mr. "Porky" Traylor called the police.

Though his selfless courage made David a hero to many, it was something else that won my devotion. Our junior year, integration arrived at Flintville High School. Lincoln Village High School sent their best and finest, including Harold Atwell, Bertha's nephew. Harold demonstrated his incredible athletic qualities, and

Coach Brewster rewarded him with a middle linebacker position. David, the other middle linebacker, took Harold under his wing and taught him all the plays after practice each day. Midway through the season, we played our archrival Griffin High School. During a timeout, David asked Coach Brewster if he and Harold could swap sides. "I'm having a hard time with that blocker on my side, and Harold's a little quicker than I am," David explained sincerely enough that the coach agreed.

Afterwards, Ty gave Josie and me the real story. "That Griffin offensive lineman facing off with Harold kept mumbling 'nigger boy.' Harold ignored it; I guess he's heard worse, but David was fuming. When they changed sides, David almost tore that lineman's head off. I bet that fella's bell is still ringing." David never mentioned the episode to us. By the end of that football season, Chuck Purdy had christened David and Harold "the gruesome twosome." Harold was slated to play at Morehouse College in Atlanta, and I wondered if he would become a preacher like his uncle.

David's protective attitude toward Harold Atwell continued after football season. More than once, I observed him smack some white boy against the back of his head for making a racist remark about Harold or his beautiful, intelligent girlfriend Juanita, who'd received a scholarship to Spelman.

The Saturday before school ended, Parker's Pool opened up for the senior class's annual picnic. Josie and I were sitting on the edge of the deep end watching Teddy and Stu do cannonballs off the high dive. Harold and Juanita, dressed in swimsuits, maintained a cautious distance from the water. Buddy Harlowe, still the class bully even at the age of eighteen, kept threatening to throw Harold in. Of course, Buddy was nothing but talk especially since Harold outweighed him by a good fifty pounds.

"Hey, bathing beauties. Whaddya doing?" David stood outside the chain link fence behind us. He was dressed in a new pair of yellow Bermuda shorts, a madras shirt, and a pair of Weejuns without socks.

"Finally got a date with Lindy McMichael, I see. When did she turn fifteen? Yesterday?" I kidded. David had kept Lindy in his sights all year, but her parents insisted that she had to be fifteen before she could date.

David just grinned. "Actually, her birthday was two days ago. I'm picking her up in an hour. I figured I'd be safer on this side of the fence, or one of those fools will try to splash…" David stopped mid-sentence as his eyes left mine and darted toward the pool's deep-end. Suddenly, he scaled the fence and dove in the pool. Seconds later David popped to the surface holding Harold Atwell in one arm. Buddy, unaware Harold couldn't swim, had playfully pushed Harold in.

David glared at Buddy and then gave Harold a friendly punch in his shoulder. "You all right, buddy?" Poor Harold offered David an appreciative nod. "Well, I'm out of here then. I need to go change my clothes." With that David strolled off to his car.

"Allie? Come back from the Twilight Zone. It's your turn." David's voice pulled me from my reverie.

Ty laughed. "Hell, we all know you'll win a Pulitzer in journalism before another decade passes." Ty's comment made me blush.

"Yeah Allie," Ted interrupted. "Why don't you become a war journalist and follow us into combat! Your butt would look great in a pair of fatigues."

Ever since Honor's Night when I'd received the *Atlanta Journal Cup* scholarship, the brigade had given me grief. "When I'm at Georgia next fall, I'll become the first female sportswriter for the Bulldogs. Ten years from now, I'll be going in locker rooms to interview the winning quarterback."

Teddy whistled. "Cover your jock straps, fellas!" He fell over laughing.

I fumed for a moment. "Say what you like, Teddy Gaddis. But 'the times, they are a-changin'.'"

Josie, slurring every syllable, began singing, "We shall overcome!"

Ty handed Josie another beer to shut her up. "You two read too much of that Helen Gurley Brown stuff. Anyway, it's my turn." I was grateful for Ty's interruption. Musing upon my own future frightened me somewhat.

"Well, after I beat Stu out for the Heisman, I'll come back to Flintville and open a second Hastings Drugs. Before long I'll have a chain of Hastings Drugstores all over the Southeast, just like A&P grocery stores. Then I'll set Dave up in his own practice, and he'll send all his patients with prescriptions to me."

"I hope Dave becomes a gynecologist," Teddy interrupted. All the boys laughed.

Josie rolled her drunken head to one side. "Stop grossing me out, ya'll! I already feel like I'm about to ..." Josie's face turned to chalk. In one quick swoop, David carried her to the bathroom where she puked her guts out.

Stu and Ty helped her out to the Blue Bullet. There were hugs all around, but I hung onto Dave just a second or two longer. "Until next time, *B & B's*! Love you all!" I waved out the window and put the Studebaker in gear. I'd have gladly broken my curfew if I'd realized the next time we were together, one of our brigade would no longer be with us.

As the rattle of the beverage cart jolted me into the present, Josie returned from the depths of unconsciousness. "Finally! My throat feels like a cotton ball." She asked for a Coke as the stewardess handed us a tray that resembled a TV dinner.

Josie took one look at the food and turned up her nose. "Airplane food is nasty! If I eat, I'll barf all over again! Let's focus on something, anything but food for the time being," she begged.

"Okay. I can't believe my aunt and your parents allowed us to take this trip on our own, can you?"

Josie whistled softly through her teeth. "Just think, an entire week in the Big Apple without parental supervision! It beats restocking the underwear display at my dad's store."

While Josie despised her summer job at McClendon's Dry Goods, I fell into the perfect part-time employment. Since my sophomore year, I'd spent every free afternoon working at the newspaper.

Uncle Hoyt determined I should learn the newspaper business from the ground up. That meant spending most of my time in the back room with the big presses. Mr. Barton, a deaf-mute who operated the linotype machine, taught me how to work the machine's oversized typewriter. I loved the hum of the presses, the aroma of the melted lead, the tapping of the linotype, the crunch of crisp paper being fed into the printing machines.

One July afternoon before my senior year, I leaned against the drink box and enjoyed a cold Strawberry Nehi. Uncle Hoyt scurried out the back door of his glass office. "Allie, could you come out front and help Miz Opal for a while?" He handed me his handkerchief and pointed to a smudge of ink on my chin. "You'd better clean up a little first." Reluctantly I wiped away the ink, swigged down my remaining Nehi, and followed Uncle Hoyt.

Miz Opal appeared harried. "Oh, thank goodness, Allie. Charlene had to leave; her grandmother broke her hip. Poor thing! I'm up to my eyeballs with these stories for tomorrow's society page. Can you help?"

What did I know about garden club meetings or wedding receptions? Miz Opal sensed my anxiety. "Don't worry, honey. All the information is on the form. You just have to convert it into a readable article." For the next three hours, I waded through details about Miss Turnipseed's kitchen shower, where she wore a lovely pink linen coatdress accompanied by stylish, white patent leather pumps. Did anybody actually read this stuff?

Contrary to my belief, Flintville's female population devoured the society page. "I see your byline on the society page. Aren't you proud?" Aunt Bird smiled at me over the paper the following evening.

"I wish they'd just put Miz Charlene's name on the byline as usual. Mrs. Agnes Jefferson called the office after lunch all upset because I'd omitted one dessert served at the Methodist luncheon. Who cares that Miss Ada Oliver brought her famous fresh coconut cake? How does that little tidbit really matter in the scope of things?"

Aunt Bird patted my arm. "Miss Ada Oliver is the oldest living member of Flintville Methodist. I think your first articles in print are quite impressive even if it's not your kind of journalism. Your daddy used to say a good community newspaper should represent all the people in the community."

"I'd prefer to represent those interested in football scores and police chases, not tea parties."

Little did I know that I would soon have the opportunity to try my hand at much more important journalism.

Once again I was jarred into reality as our plane bumped across some clouds: I instinctively fingered the star of flint on the chain around my neck. Two rows up was a young man in a military uniform. I prayed he wasn't headed to Vietnam. I closed my eyes and saw the flag-draped coffin that provided me the journalistic opportunity for which I had wished.

Unable to fit journalism into my senior schedule, Mrs. Woodall, the sponsor, suggested I serve as a guest writer for the *Raider Review*. The paper's pompous editor, Chester Montgomery, a studious senior with a bad complexion, doled out assignments, and I usually ended up with the leftover articles no one wanted.

In early February, Chester caught me at my locker. "I really need you to write this article for next week's edition. Can you help me out?"

I expected some inane Valentine feature. "I don't know, Chester. My term paper's due at the end of the week, and I have to cheer at the basketball games."

Chester picked at a pimple on his chin. "This one's really important. It's about a soldier from Flintville; his family just got word that he was killed."

My heart sank, but my ears perked up. "Who is it? Somebody that graduated from Flintville High?"

"He graduated five or six years ago, I think. His last name is Copeland. His family lives in Milltown. Are you interested? It doesn't have to be a long article since most of the student body won't really know who he is."

Something about Chester's nonchalant attitude about the death of a young man irked me. "Yeah, I'll do it."

He handed me an index card with the family's address. "Just a paragraph or two 'cause we've got a lot of Valentine copy for this issue," he added as he started down the hall. After school, I headed my old Studebaker toward the mill village. As I followed the directions, I soon realized that I'd traveled this route before, but last time, I'd been a passenger and the Studebaker had belonged to Diddy.

The Copelands lived on L Street, exactly three doors down from where I'd played jacks on the sidewalk with Essie Dunn...and then a few months later sat on her porch swing after her sister died. There were children playing in the Dunn's old yard, and I wondered if they knew where Essie lived now.

Several cars were parked along the sidewalk in front of the Copeland's house. People were already paying their respects although I'd learned that their son's body wouldn't arrive for several days. As I knocked on the screen door, I heard a woman weeping. Feeling like an intruder, I turned to leave when a girl of perhaps thirteen opened the door. "Can I help you?" she asked. She was a skinny, gangly thing with straight dark hair and soft brown eyes.

I cleared my throat. "I'm... um...Allison Sinclair from the Flintville High School *Raider Review*. I was hoping to speak to a member of the Copeland family. We'd like to write an article about um ...about their loss." The girl stared at me as I listened to voices comforting the sobbing woman inside. I turned to go. "Maybe it would be better for me to come back later."

The girl suddenly found her voice and started down the porch steps towards me. "You can talk to me. Larry's my big brother." She hesitated a moment, swallowed hard. "I mean he *was* my big brother. My name's Louise, but everybody calls me Lulu." Her shoulders flinched as the sobs of her mother's grief permeated the air.

"Why don't we sit in my car? Maybe that would be a good place for us to talk," I suggested. We spent the next hour talking about Larry Copeland, who'd joined the Army after high school. He was smart enough to be sent to NCO school. "That's Non-commissioned Officer School," his sister explained. "We went to his graduation at Fort Bragg when he earned his sergeant's stripes. I remember the battalion singing when they marched on the field at graduation: 'I want to be an Airborne Ranger, live a life of death and danger!' He'd just gone back for his second tour in Vietnam six weeks ago." Her voice faltered, and I felt my own heart in my throat.

"I'm so sorry, Louise," I began.

"Call me Lulu. My brother gave me my nickname. He called me his 'little Lulu,' like the girl in the comic strip." She paused, and I watched her eyes as she tried to swim away from the pain just as I had once. "Are you going to write about my brother?"

I closed my notepad. "I certainly am. I'll send you a copy if you'd like one."

She shook my hand. "Thanks, I'd like that. One day I can show it to my children so they'll know about the uncle who nicknamed their mama 'Lulu.'"

As she opened the car door, I grabbed her hand. "The pain, Lulu, it gets better. I promise you. It just takes time."

I wrote my article from the perspective of Larry Copeland's sister. I thought students could better relate to Louise's grief. Mrs. Woodall overruled Chester's front page layout to make room for my article. Two days later, Uncle Hoyt ran it in the *Star*.

The following week Josie and I met Stu and David at a library table as far away from Miss Benton's cage as possible. The boys were falling all over the latest edition of **Seventeen**, featuring summer's two-piece swimsuits, while Josie and I rolled our eyes and snickered.

So involved in our own world, we were oblivious that Miss Benton had emerged from her lair and was making her slow journey toward our table until we heard the undeniable "pink, pink, pink" of her rubber-tipped crutches.

"Allison Sinclair, follow me to my office this moment!" she snarled, and my heart sank. I'd been snared after surviving three and a half years without invoking her wrath. Moments later, I emerged from her glass prison bearing a smile of relief on my face and a journalism scholarship application in my hand. "She liked my article," I whispered. "She said she thought I had a real future in writing, just like my daddy."

Once again I was jarred into reality as our plane hit what the captain called "a little turbulence." I couldn't wait to tell Cece firsthand about my trip to the glass cage.

The plane's wheels screeched down the runway as the captain brought his big bird to a halt. "We invite you to fly Delta again in the future."

Future? What did it hold for me? As I grasped Josie's fingers in one hand while my free hand twirled the tiny flint star dangling from its chain, I knew I'd figure it out.

Chapter 25

Cece was waiting at the gate. Her blonde hair, several inches longer, was styled straight and parted down the middle. She was clad in a long, billowy cotton skirt printed with tiny sunflowers and a pale blue blouse gathered softly around her shoulders. My heart melted when I noticed her tiny star of flint hanging from the silver chain around her neck.

Cece exclaimed. "Well, I see the mini-skirt has arrived in Flintville." Our short coatdresses seemed sadly outdated against Cece's wardrobe. "It's the new peasant look. It's all the rage in the Village," Cece explained in the taxi.

This would be her last summer in the Village. Clementine, the proprietor of the art supply shop where Cece worked each summer, was moving to San Francisco. "Actually, she's already moved; Marcus and I have to pack and ship her supplies to her Haight-Ashbury store."

Our cab stopped in front of a small shop with a tattered yellow awning. *Clementine's Art Goods* appeared in bold letters across the store's front window. A *Going Out of Business* sign hung from the door.

The door swung open and out burst a tall, swaggering man clad in bellbottom jeans, white t-shirt, and green Nehru jacket. He was astonishingly handsome with dark hair hanging below his ears and gorgeous white teeth. Most girls would have swooned at the sight of him, but I knew better. Marcus, Cece's best friend in New York City, was a flaming queer.

I'd been warned by Cece to be polite, but I was speechless. Luckily, Marcus broke the ice and gave me little need or opportunity to say anything.

"Oh God, you're here!" He grabbed me by both hands and spun me around. "You divine, petite Southern belle! Cece told me your green eyes were like emeralds. Just magnificent! And this must be Josie!" He released my hands to grab Josie, who stood wide-eyed and speechless. "This elegant swan could be the next Twiggy!" Josie blushed.

My sister rescued us. "Marcus, give them a minute to get their bags off the sidewalk before someone steals them!"

Marcus gallantly retrieved our suitcases. "Now, ladies, while you're here, you'll be under my watch and care. When Cece's working or whatever, I'll show you this glorious city." Josie and I fell in behind Marcus as he led us down an aisle displaying artists' brushes, through a back room cluttered with packing boxes, and up a narrow staircase to the loft where Cece lived.

"Here we are!" Marcus exclaimed cheerily as we reached the top. The loft was basically one gigantic room with a tiny bathroom enclosed in one corner.

"This is where Cece lives? This one room?" Josie gasped in disbelief.

Marcus set our suitcases down. "Oh, honey, she's lucky to get this place with real estate at a premium in the Village. It's the perfect location for a budding artist like Cece, and now that Phoebe's in Israel living in a kibbutz, Cece has the place all to herself."

"What's a kibbutz?" Josie questioned.

Marcus smirked. "The perfect place for an American Jewish girl to find a husband."

Cece emerged at the top of the staircase. "A kibbutz is a communal farm where young Israelis often live for a period of time. Phoebe's parents gave her the trip as a graduation gift."

"And it's the opportune time for her to find a good Jewish man to marry," Marcus interjected as he sat down on a dilapidated sofa surrounded by studio chairs. "All the women I love have no sense about the opposite sex. First, Phoebe leaves in search of her Israeli prince, and now Clementine is traipsing across the country after some long-haired folk singer who'll dump her when he depletes her trust fund!" As Marcus lit up a cigarette, Josie and I exchanged incredulous glances.

"Marcus, no smoking while the girls are here." He dutifully snubbed out his freshly lit Marlboro as Cece continued, "And don't be so cynical; Clementine and Frankie are in love."

Marcus turned towards Josie and me. "See, Clementine inherited this chunk of money from her grandfather. Frankie's going to suck poor Clementine dry. He's twenty-four, and Clementine's almost thirty, not to mention she has a big ass. She'll be back with her tail between her fat thighs before Christmas."

Josie and I burst into hysterics. "Marcus, please watch your language!" Cece steamed.

"Oh hon, relax. These young ladies are about to become real women." Marcus grinned at us, and I liked him in spite of myself. "I'm meeting Roland at the Stonewall Inn. But you girls are all mine tomorrow. We're going to give you delectable darlings a new look for college." He leaned over and cupped my chin in his hands. "You dear, have the perfect face for a Judy Carne cut."

He dropped my face and pointed toward Josie. "And I can't wait to see this long-legged philly in some chunky heels. Now, be ready at ten o'clock tomorrow. We'll let Cece tend to her love affair," he gave her a disapproving look, "while the three of us spend a divine day on Broadway!" Marcus sashayed out the door.

Cece offered us cold drinks, and as we sipped them, Josie, who been silent thus far, came to life. "I've never met anyone like him! What's the Stonewall Inn? And who's Roland?"

"The Stonewall Inn is a gay bar two streets over, and Roland is Marcus' latest friend," Cece explained.

Josie guffawed. "You mean, like boyfriend?"

"Yes, Josie, that's what I mean. Marcus is a wonderfully talented designer who will one day have his own fashion studio. I hope you can see him for all of his gifts and not for his sexuality."

Josie seemed embarrassed. "Oh, I'm sorry, Cece. I really like him. He's so honest...and so good-looking. What a waste that he prefers men."

"I know; it takes some getting used to, but if you give him a chance, you'll adore him in no time. He has an entire itinerary for ya'll tomorrow. He has all these friends in the beauty business. You'll get a complete makeover free of charge."

"Good, I'm ready for a new look. Are we going to get some supper before long, Cece? I'm starved," Josie admitted.

As we headed down the street towards *Schwartz's Deli*, Cece wrapped an arm around my shoulder. "You're awfully quiet, baby sister. Cat got your tongue?"

"No, I'm just tired from the plane trip," I lied. I felt betrayed that I had to learn from Marcus about Cece's boyfriend.

After Josie devoured a pastrami sandwich and some cheesecake, she was ready for bed. She insisted on taking the sofa so Cece and I could have the two twin beds. She was in Never Never Land before I'd brushed my teeth.

Cece had already changed into pajamas and was sitting on her bed when I returned. "So, did you get the graduation gift I sent you?"

"Oh yeah, thanks. I love the leather-bound journal." I pulled down the covers and climbed in.

"I thought you could start writing down all your thoughts. It could become fodder for your first novel," she teased. "I figure you'll have a couple of bestsellers before I sell my first painting." When I barely responded, she continued. "What's wrong, Allie?"

"Dammit, Cece, I resent learning about your 'love affair' from Marcus! Once again I'm the last one to know!"

"I didn't want to tell you in a letter. This is too important...I wanted to tell you face to face. Marcus doesn't know when to shut up!"

When I saw the flush in her cheeks and the sparkle in her eyes, my anger dissolved. I plumped up my pillow. "Okay, we're alone now, so spill the beans."

"Well, about two weeks into winter semester, we had a big snowstorm, and NYU cancelled classes for two days. A bunch of us took the subway to Central Park. We were all goofing off, throwing snowballs at each other. I sat down on a bench to drink some hot chocolate. That's when I heard him call my name." Cece stopped to catch her breath.

"Who?" I interrupted.

Cece smiled mysteriously. "I looked up and saw this gorgeous army officer standing before me. He had on his uniform and an overcoat, but I knew him immediately. He leaned down, brushed the snow from my cheeks and said, 'You don't know how many times I've dreamed of looking into your eyes again.'"

"Again?" I was confused. "When was the last time he'd seen you? Who is he?"

My sister's eyes shone. "It's Brad, Brad Royal. He's back in my life, Allie. Can you believe it?"

I was stunned and furious. "That sonnabitch who left you out at the *River Ranch* that night? Please tell me this is a joke, Cece!"

Tears filled my sister's eyes. "Allie, you don't know the truth about that night. See, it was all a big mistake. Brad thought I'd broken up with him, and I thought he'd broken up with me. He was too proud to call me, and I was too ashamed to face him."

I was livid. "Ashamed? What did you have to be ashamed of? It was the strap of *your* dress that was torn. *You* were the one cowering in the back room of that seedy bar. Brad was nowhere to be found!"

Cece shushed me. "Calm down, you'll wake Josie."

"She knows all about that night. She was with me! Don't you remember?"

"No, Allie, I don't remember. I know I had some beer that night, and I think I did something terribly foolish, something that embarrassed Brad. Thank God, he's enough of a gentleman not to rehash the events of that night," she sighed. "Now we have a second chance, but we don't have long to work things out."

"What's to work out other than admitting he's a jerk?!"

I regretted my words when I saw the anguish in Cece's eyes. "Brad ships out for Vietnam right after Christmas. He's a second lieutenant in the First Air Cavalry, and he'll finish his flight training in November."

I pretended to be interested. "What kind of plane does he fly?"

"He's training to be a helicopter pilot, and he'll be flying a Huey."

I thought of Louise Copeland's brother who was buried only months ago. I shivered. "That sounds pretty dangerous."

"Yes, it is." She faltered for a moment. "But he's getting the best training available at Fort Rucker in Alabama."

I couldn't help but relish the thought that Brad was in Alabama while my sister was here in New York. "What was he doing in New York?"

My sister regained that dreamy look in her eyes. "He'd flown up to attend a friend's wedding at West Point but got stuck in the city because of the storm. He took a stroll through the park while he waited on the roads to clear. I believe my guardian angels were looking after me." Cece gazed out her tiny bedroom window, which offered a pie slice view of the night's sky.

I groaned. "Don't drag Mama and Diddy into this. Maybe the stars got all crossed up like they did in *Romeo and Juliet*."

Cece turned towards me. "No, Allie, the stars were lined up just right that day. You remember Aunt Bird telling us that her heart still skips a beat every time she sees Uncle Hoyt? My heart is like an acrobat turning somersaults every time I think of him. I love him, Allie, and he loves me. Please try to understand."

I began to relent. Hadn't I prayed the Lord would send her someone to love? "Well, if I ever see Mr. Bradley Royal again, he'd better have learned some manners. I refuse to be dismissed from his presence as though I'm nothing more than a gnat!"

Cece threw her arms around me. "He goes by Brad now. Lieutenant Brad Royal—doesn't that sound so debonair? And by the way, you were a little spy back then."

"He always looked down his nose at me. Now that I'm older, I think I could hold my own with your lieutenant. That is, if I ever see him again."

Cece cut her eyes shyly at me. "Well, you'll get your chance. Brad has a three-day pass, and I'm meeting him at the airport tomorrow. That's what Marcus was talking about."

I gulped. "Tomorrow? I thought this was our week together!"

Cece climbed into bed. "He'll only be in the city for one night, and then he's meeting some West Point friends for a reunion. They'll be shipping out all over the world in the next few months. It's the perfect time for the two of you to get to know one another. Go to sleep, baby brat; we both have a big day tomorrow."

Cece hadn't called me "baby brat" in years, but at the moment, I felt as though I were a kid again and my opinion didn't count at all. Before long, I could hear her rhythmic breathing as she slept.

Sleep didn't come as easily for me. In my restless dreams, I kept seeing my sister's lovely dotted swiss dress with its torn strap.

If Josie had heard my bedtime conversation with Cece, she didn't mention it. Besides, with Marcus on his quest to transform us, there was no time for discussion.

His friend Eleanor was a makeup artist at the cosmetic counter in *Bloomingdales*. She worked on my makeup with effortless ease as Marcus occasionally made suggestions.

"I think Allie needs a little more of that green shadow on her lids, don't you, Eleanor? It really brings out her eyes, don't you think?" Marcus offered.

Eleanor retorted in the thickest Bronx accent I'd ever heard. "You gay guys think you know everything about color. Stick to fashion and leave the face to me, will ya'!" Throughout her tirade, Eleanor plucked my eyebrows with such a vengeance that tears ran down my newly "frosted pink" cheeks.

Marcus replied apologetically. "You're right; I'll stick to fashion. Speaking of which, I see you located a bra you didn't burn."

Josie stole a wide-eyed glance at me. "I didn't burn any of my bras. I've just been making a statement about women's rights. Why should we have to suffer with these tit-slingers when you male chauvinist pigs don't? My manager insists I wear one when I'm working the counter."

Marcus grinned and pecked Eleanor on the cheek. "You women and your movements—I'm all for them. But those boobs of yours need to be harnessed." Before Eleanor could lash out in rebuttal, Marcus continued. "You've got fabulous ta-tas, dearie, when they're corralled properly. I saw a pink sweater on sale in *Saks* yesterday and thought of you. I'll pick it up for you the next time I'm over there."

Eleanor smiled, and I assumed all was forgiven. Before we left, she filled two shopping bags with enough makeup samples to last our college career.

Josie and I exploded with curiosity. "Did she really burn her bras? Was it at a women's rights protest? Does she really go out in public without one on?"

Marcus held up both hands as if deflecting our barrage of questions. "Whoa now, you two curious kitties. Eleanor's a big follower of Gloria Steinem and that cult of men haters. Suits me just fine, though! It makes more men for me!" He giggled at the shock on our faces. "Oh, get a clue, ladies. The only thing I've seen being burned on a street corner was a draft card. Some of those braless libbers were around for the protest, but I didn't see any lingerie thrown into the fire."

Marcus continued. "Ladies, this world is changing, and you either change with it, or get crushed along the way. Anyway, the two of you both have such pert, little ta-tas that you could get away with going braless."

I gulped. "Not me! I've no intention of giving up my falsies!" Marcus howled with laughter. I couldn't believe I'd made such a pronouncement to a man, but Marcus was more at ease talking about brassieres than Aunt Bird.

Next we headed to a little hair salon on the corner of Broadway and Seventy-Fifth Street. As we walked, Marcus explained that Leo, the proprietor and premier stylist, was once his lover.

After some convincing, I allowed Leo to highlight my hair with a sprinkling of blonde and cut it almost Twiggy short. When I viewed my new style in the mirror, Marcus sensed my doubts. "Oh—My—God! Allie, it's perfect on you! Not many women can wear their hair so short, but those little fringy blonde bangs make your eyes ten times bigger. Those college guys will go gah-gah!" My misgivings faded, especially when I realized there'd be no more sleeping in painful rollers.

Leo chopped four inches off Josie's shoulder-length flip and sculpted it into something he called Vidal Sassoon's geometric bob. Once free from Dippity-do and layers of Aqua Net, her chestnut locks took on a natural sheen.

From the salon, Marcus marched us straight over to *Macy's*. Josie, her billfold laden with graduation cash, took our makeover master's advice and purchased two pairs of chunky heels.

Marcus convinced me I should have a pair of the shiny vinyl knee boots although I said they were too expensive. "Oh, never fear, ma cherie, your sister gave me a little spending money to blow on you."

I felt guilty taking Cece's hard-earned dollars when I knew she lived on a tight budget, but the boots felt terrific and made me two inches taller. I spent some of my graduation cash on a trendy vinyl coat to match my boots. Josie bought a peasant skirt and blouse, and Marcus insisted I buy a paisley skirt that was so short I wouldn't be able to bend over in it.

We returned to *Schwartz's Deli* for lunch, compliments of Marcus as a graduation gift. When we objected that he'd already done enough, he laughed. "I loved watching two gorgeous butterflies emerge from their hometown cocoons. You'll be all the talk when you get home to Flintville. Although, Allie, I wouldn't recommend modeling that mini-skirt for your aunt."

"You must have heard about our Aunt Bird's tendency to suffer conniptions."

Marcus chuckled. "That she's conservative and a dyed in the wool Southern Baptist? But Cece says your aunt is educated and keeps an open mind."

"I just wonder how open her mind is going to be when she finds out about Brad Hamilton Royal," I mused.

Josie sighed. "I overheard your sister last night. How could she fall for that stupid jerk after what he did to her in high school?"

I shook my head in disgust. "I don't have a clue, but that guy has some kind of hold on my sister. I hope four years at West Point really changed him." I picked dismally at the crust of my cheesecake.

"Whatever are you talking about? I've met Brad, and he seems totally devoted to Cece. What did he do to her in high school?" Marcus lit a cigarette and sat back in anticipation.

He listened raptly as Josie and I shared every detail of our harrowing drive to the *River Ranch* to rescue my sister. When we finished our tale, Marcus sat quietly blowing smoke rings in the air. I felt sure he'd help me convince Cece that she was making the biggest mistake of her life.

He stubbed out his cigarette. "Allie, I can understand your concern, but people can change. When I was seventeen, I played on the basketball team, hung out with the guys at our local hamburger joint, and even dated a cheerleader."

Josie whistled. "You went out with girls? But I thought you were qu—, I mean I thought you were, you know..."

"We prefer the term 'gay' these days, but yes I was queer—queer as a football bat!" Marcus laughed sarcastically. "But no red-blooded American boy from the Midwest was going to admit such a thing in 1963. My father is a burly man with tattoos from his stint in the Navy. Every time I showed an interest in fashion or art, he'd slap me on the back of my head, and tell me such stuff was for pussies. My mom tried to intervene, but she was as distressed over my behavior as my father. When she caught me going through a women's dress pattern book in her sewing room one day, she just turned around and closed the door behind her."

Marcus lit another cigarette. "I learned to pretend for the sake of my parents. As soon as I graduated, I high-tailed it to New York and haven't been home since." He took another drag of his Marlboro before looking up with sad eyes. "People can change. Maybe Brad had a pretty fucked up childhood. Didn't he lose his mother when he was a teenager? "

"Yeah, I think so." I realized Marcus sat squarely in my sister's camp and had no intentions of changing her mind about Brad.

Marcus lifted my chin. "Oh, come on now, you precious little vixen. Let's give Brad a chance, for Cece's sake. One thing I know for certain, honey. You can't mess with love, and your big sister's got a bad case of it. You might as well resign yourself to having Lieutenant Royal in your life, at least until he flies off into the wild blue yonder."

As soon as we made it inside *Clementine's* with our packages, Marcus ushered Josie back out the front door. "We won't take time to go upstairs. I'm taking your friend to Little Italy. You do like pizza, don't you Josie?" Obviously, Cece had arranged for Marcus to entertain Josie while I got reacquainted with Brad. "Say hello to the lieutenant for me."

Loaded down with shopping bags, I trudged up to Cece's loft. I could hear my sister's easy laughter coming from the apartment. Unable to open the door, I bumped on it with the toe of my shoe.

Cece opened the door almost instantly. "Allie, you're back. Look at your hair! I love it! It's so chic. My Lord, did ya'll buy out Macy's?" She relieved me of several bags.

"Yeah, well Marcus isn't just a fashion expert. He's also quite persuasive when it comes to spending money..."

I stopped mid-sentence as my eyes fell upon a tall stranger clad in a khaki uniform leaning against the kitchen sink with a bottle of beer in his hand. Brad looked nothing like I remembered him. His shoulders were broader and more muscular, his dark, wavy hair was cropped short, and his face had matured. His eyes locked on mine, and he gave me a genuine smile, devoid of any haughtiness.

Cece broke the awkward moment. "Allie, do you remember Brad?"

I feigned a ladylike demeanor for her sake. "How are you Brad?"

He kept grinning. "My, my, my!" were his first words. "Cece told me you'd grown up, but I wasn't ready for such a transformation. You're as pretty as your sister." He smiled once more. "So, Miss Allison Sinclair, I believe I owe you several apologies for my ungentlemanlike behavior."

I was so taken aback by the humility in his voice that words failed me. "Huh?"

Brad continued. "You know, for running you out of your own living room. I was such a pompous little ass back then. Can you ever forgive me?" He and Cece gazed at me with anxious eyes.

"Sure," I responded. Of course, there was no mention of the night he deserted my sister. Somehow, though, as I watched Cece with her head resting contentedly on Brad's shoulder, I wondered if his past transgressions were important after all.

Brad insisted on taking us to dinner. We went to Chinatown where I sampled my first Chinese food. After a few bites of undercooked fish and mushy rice, I decided I would've preferred pizza in Little Italy. During the meal, Brad regaled us with flying stories. He appeared to take a sincere interest in my journalistic ambitions and listened intently as I discussed print journalism as opposed to broadcast journalism. I caught a spark of relief in Cece's eyes.

Marcus and Josie were waiting on us when we returned. "Anybody up for late night dessert?" Marcus suggested. "I hear the deli is having a run on pie a la mode tonight." I was certainly game after my disappointment with Chinese cuisine. We left Cece and Brad to say their goodbyes in private.

"So, what do you think of him?" Marcus ventured through his cigarette smoke. He'd allowed me to finish a ham and cheese on rye before beginning the inquisition.

I eyed the half-eaten brownie on Josie's plate. She slid it over with expectant eyes. "He's all right, I guess. I mean he was really nice to me and actually seemed interested in my future. And there's no doubt he adores Cece. Maybe you're right, Marcus. Maybe people can change."

That night, however, as I climbed in the bed across from my sister, I wondered if Brad was the "real McCoy" or if I'd been hoodwinked.

Cece devoted the remainder of our visit to entertaining Josie and me. We took the ferry to Ellis Island, climbed to the top of the Statue of Liberty, viewed

Central Park from the back of a horse-drawn carriage, watched the Rockettes kick across Radio City Music Hall, and blew the rest of our graduation money on lunch at Tavern on the Green.

Early Sunday morning when we headed to the airport for our trip home, Marcus was standing at the front door of the store. His hair was a mess, and his clothes looked like he'd slept in them.

"Marcus, you look wretched." Cece remarked.

Marcus lit up a cigarette. "Oh, my God, dear. It's Sunday morning, the only time this city sleeps. I didn't get home from the Stonewall Inn until 4:00, and then Roland pitched a little shit fit because I spent too much time talking to Leo and his friends. My God, sometimes he's so irrational." He blew smoke rings in the morning air as Josie and I exchanged glances and giggled.

Both Marcus and Cece cried as we said our goodbyes at the departure gate. "Christmas is just a few months away, Cece. I'll write you every day from college," I promised.

Marcus sniffed. "Oh, get a clue, little Southern belle. You'll be way too busy fighting off the boys to write!"

As I waved to Cece, I could see her star of flint glinting on the chain around her neck, and it comforted me. No one, not even Brad Royal, could sever the bond between my sister and me.

While Josie dosed on the flight home, my thoughts returned to Brad. If Cece's lieutenant had truly experienced a change of heart, could I? Each time I tried to convince myself to accept the man of my sister's dreams, a nagging doubt crept down my spine.

Chapter 26

In September, I moved into University of Georgia's Creswell Hall, a monstrous nine-story brick structure unlovingly called "Cres-Hell" by its inmates. The dormitory housed 1,000 freshman females. My tiny room consisted of two twin beds, two minuscule closets, and two miniature dressers, which also served as desks.

My roommate Teresa Carson, a perky blonde from Decatur, was an early riser. She'd hop out of bed at the crack of dawn, open the blinds to our postage stamp window, and cheerily skip to the hall's communal bathroom. Returning from her sunrise shower and reeking of *Jean Nate* body splash, she'd burst through the door in song. My only solace was that Teresa, a music major, possessed a melodic voice.

I lived for the weekends when I had my pathetic dwelling to myself. Teresa went home each Friday to her boyfriend, a buck-toothed saxophonist attending seminary school.

Georgia's football games offered me a release from my boring core classes and miserable housing. I'd manage to get a date with an eligible freshman for most home games, unless Uncle Hoyt drove up. For away games, my friends and I usually ended up at some fraternity house on Milledge Avenue where we'd drink beer (or sweet wine, in my case) and listen to Larry Munson, the "voice of the Dawgs," announce the game on the radio.

The one freshman course that challenged me was English 201, where one comma splice or run-on sentence would earn your weekly paper an immediate *F*. After my third *A* paper, Dr. Ferrell called me into his office. I told him I planned to major in journalism, and he handed me an application for a staff position with the **Red and Black**, the university's newspaper.

The following Monday, I approached a tired-looking brick structure tucked within an alley in the middle of downtown Athens and climbed a set of rickety wooden stairs to the **Red and Black's** offices. At the top of the stairs, I could hear the unmistakable pecking of a manual typewriter, and the sound made my heart quicken. A scrapbook of articles I'd written for my high school paper and the **Flintville Star** tucked under my arm, I sailed through the door of the sports department with an air of confidence.

Mason Sorrells, sports editor, fraternity president, and male chauvinist asshole, wasted no time in squelching my burning ambitions. After thumbing through my scrapbook, Mason explained that he wasn't certain there'd ever been a female byline on the sports page.

When I spouted off statistics from every Georgia football game for the last decade, Mason appeared shocked and indignant. "Football is for senior staffers only," he replied in a patronizing tone. "Sorry, but I have a deadline to meet." He returned to his typing.

I held my ground. "Just give me a chance to prove myself. You won't be sorry even if I am a girl."

Whether I wore him down or he just wanted to be rid of me, he relented. "If you really want to get your feet wet, I need someone to cover an intramural sports event on Wednesday."

Mason smirked as he handed me the assignment, a women's softball tournament sponsored by the Baptist Student Union. After spending hours on the piece, I turned it in ahead of deadline. Mason cut the entire article save a small score box at the bottom corner of the sports page.

As promised, I found time to write Cece. I always looked forward to her chatter about the new loft she shared with her high school pal Margaret Justice, who was now attending NYU's medical school.

Cece was juggling a part-time job as a tour guide at the Metropolitan Museum of Art with NYU graduate classes in painting. She never failed to mention something funny Brad had written in his latest letter or offer the exact number of days until they'd meet again. Brad was to attend another wedding at West Point in November, and Cece's calendar countdown was as meticulous as a rocket launch. It made me sick to my stomach.

For the first time in five years, both Cece and I would be home for Thanksgiving. Cece and Margaret flew home together, and I volunteered to pick them up at the airport. Josie, feeling "totally smothered" by her mother, jumped at the chance to accompany me.

"I can't believe this old Studebaker has withstood time so well," Josie said as we headed up the Atlanta Highway. She whistled through her teeth, and it was like sweet music to my ears.

"Uncle Hoyt tunes it up every time I come home," I explained. "Your mom said you haven't been home since September. I told her you're definitely in love with college life!" I chortled knowing full well that it wasn't college life keeping Josie in LaGrange. "So, tell me about your cowboy."

Josie's face took on a glow I'd never seen. Still sporting the hairstyle Leo had given her in New York, her dark locks gleamed in the autumn sunlight. But there was something else—a sophistication that erased her tomboy naiveté. I wondered about the change in her as she rattled on about Zeke Tyson, the boy who'd stolen her heart.

"He's twenty-one. Mom and Dad would die if they knew that. But he's such a gentleman and so good with horses." Josie's letters to me had focused solely on Zeke, who worked part-time at her uncle's stable. "He's going to veterinary school at the University next year. You'd like him, Allie. He's funny and handsome, and-and, well, sexy." Josie's cheeks flushed

I had to ask. "Josie, have ya'll gone all the way?" I saw the skin on her neck grow splotchy the way it did when she was nervous. "Oh come on, Josie, it's me. I'm not going to tell anybody!" Josie sighed as her faced colored. "So, you've done it, haven't you? Oh—My—God!"

Josie covered her face with her hands and giggled. "Just once! I swear on my grandmama's grave!"

"Well, what was it like? Did it hurt?"

Josie giggled again. "Not really, but by the time we did it, he was so excited, he couldn't get his rubber on. I had to put it on for him."

"Ewww, gross!" The thought made my skin crawl.

"Well, it beats getting pregnant!" Josie insisted, and I agreed. "Anyway, he was gentle and loving, and it was so beautiful, Allie. I never thought I could feel this way about a boy!"

"Boy, my ass! That's a man messing with my best friend. He better treat you right, or I'll personally whoop up on him!" I threatened.

Josie asked about my first quarter at Georgia, but there was no way to top her news. Josie was in love and Cece was in love and I was shit out of luck.

An unexpected snowstorm delayed Cece's flight, so Josie and I roamed the terminal where an endless number of young military men were returning for the holidays or leaving for parts unknown. I could tell which soldiers were headed for Nam by the swarm of family flocked around them—fathers with stoic expressions, mothers with worried smiles, and girlfriends shamelessly shedding tears.

I suggested we find a snack bar. While I smothered a hot dog in mustard and sauerkraut, Josie sipped a Coke. "Do you think David and Teddy will have to go to Vietnam?" she asked.

"Probably," I admitted. The tone of David's recent letters had me preparing for the worst. "David says Teddy's got a girlfriend in Columbus now. He met her when they had a weekend off."

Josie hooted. "I guess that explains why Teddy's letters have been non-existent. I haven't written either of them since I met Zeke," she admitted.

"I hear from David regularly. They're supposed to be home for Christmas before they start their AIT—that's Advanced Individual Training. David's hoping to get in the medical corps. He thinks he and Teddy will be able to stay together; at least that's their plan. He says if he's got to go, he wants to be with somebody who'll always have his back." My heart ached at the thought of my friends going away to fight a war that no one seemed to understand.

"Hey look, there are people coming out of Gate 41," Josie interrupted. "Isn't that Cece's gate?"

We reached the gate just as Margaret and my sister emerged from the hallway. Cece, elegantly dressed in a pink mohair sweater and a gray kilt, practically pushed Margaret down as she ran to hug me. "Allie, I'm back in God's country!"

I caught a whiff of her *Heaven Sent* perfume, a fragrance that always carried me home to the bedroom we'd shared for so many years.

"I've missed you so much," I mumbled into her soft, glossy hair.

We hugged until Margaret cleared her throat. "Enough! People will think you're lesbians!"

Josie laughed. "Sounds like you've met Marcus!"

"Isn't he a scream?" Margaret retorted as we headed to baggage claim. "I've got the best wardrobe in med school. He's a miracle worker with my shoestring budget." Studying her trendy suede skirt, I noticed Margaret's continual nudging of my sister. "Tell them, Cece, or I will!" she uttered in exasperation.

Blushing with excitement, Cece grabbed my hands in hers. "I've got a surprise. Are you ready?" She held up her left hand. "I'm engaged!" And there it was—the inevitable moment I'd been dreading. On her left ring finger shone a solitaire diamond resting in an elegant platinum band. The only thing sparkling more than its brilliance was my sister's eyes.

I had nothing to say, but my silence didn't seem to matter. The entire ride home, Cece and Margaret talked non-stop about wedding dates and bridesmaids' dresses and color schemes until my head ached. When Cece flashed her hand before Aunt Bird, my aunt reverted into a giddy teenager with squeals and tears.

Cece and Aunt Bird spent the remainder of the week plotting and scheming. Thanksgiving morning, as I helped cut onions and celery for Aunt Bird's cornbread dressing, I'd finally had enough. "Good Lord, can't we talk about something besides this damn wedding!" I'd never cursed in front of my aunt, who raised her eyebrows but said nothing. "You've got months to plan this stupid affair. Give it a break for a while!" I stormed out of the kitchen and into the living room where I turned on the Macy's Thanksgiving Day Parade.

Before too long, Aunt Bird joined me as she carried a dessert plate in one hand and a glass of milk in the other. "I thought you might want to sample my chocolate cake since you didn't eat much breakfast." I couldn't pass up my aunt's peace offering.

As I savored the rich chocolate, she started in on me. "Allie, your sister deserves to be excited. This is the happiest time of a young woman's life, don't you understand?"

"I guess," I muttered half-heartedly.

Aunt Bird patted my hand lovingly. "Don't worry, Allie, your day will come soon enough."

"My day?" I was stunned. "You think I'm jealous of Cece? Believe me, that's not my problem!"

"Then what's wrong, Allie? You haven't been yourself all week. You've been moody and quiet..."

"Who can get a word in edge-wise with all this talk about invitation lists and receptions and all that shit!"

"Allie Sinclair, you may talk like that at college, but I shall not have such crudity in my house!" She was on the edge of a conniption, which sent me over the edge and into tears. Aunt Bird's anger melted into concern. "What's wrong, Allie?"

I tried to explain. "I don't know, Aunt Bird. There are just too many changes in my life at once. And now Cece's going to marry Brad! What if he's the wrong one, Aunt Bird? What if Cece's making the biggest mistake of her life? What if he gets stationed in some foreign country and drags Cece with him?"

Aunt Bird spoke soothingly. "Let's not borrow any trouble. Life is a series of changes, my dear, and how we deal with those changes makes us who we are. Just remember that the Lord never gives us more than we can bear, and He'll either see us through to the other side of our troubles or intervene on our behalf."

I couldn't help but hope the Lord would intervene before my sister became Mrs. Bradley Royal. "How can Cece be absolutely certain she wants to spend the rest of her life with Brad?"

My aunt smiled. "Love's not an exact science like algebra or physics. We can't analyze love because it's not something we think; it's something we feel. Just look at Cece. Have you ever seen her so completely alive? When your daddy died, the candle seemed to go out for her, but now that light inside her has life again. Only love can do that, I believe."

The rattle of Uncle Hoyt's pickup in our driveway brought me to my senses. "Now go wash your face before Hoyt sees you this way," she advised.

Life might be a series of changes, but I could always depend on my Aunt Bird. Like my two favorite stars in the night sky, she would remain a constant for me.

The table overflowed with a bounty of the best food in the world, but before we could dig in, I knew we'd be subjected to a Sinclair tradition. Each of us must offer something for which we were grateful. Since my belly had been growling for hours, I came armed with a prepared statement. "After suffering through cafeteria food for three months, I'm most thankful to sit at Aunt Bird's table and know she'll send leftovers back to school with me!"

Cece was next. "I'm most thankful that all my family can share in my engagement and wedding plans." She grabbed my hand and squeezed it. "And I'm so blessed I have Allie to serve as my maid of honor." This was the first I'd heard of her plans to bestow me with such an honor, one that I felt dubious about accepting. I feigned a weak smile.

Aunt Bird's face appeared flushed. "Well, I'm thankful I'll marry before either of my young nieces do!" she pronounced.

For a moment Cece and I remained speechless. Then our words tumbled out simultaneously. "You're getting married? Really? When? Where?"

Uncle Hoyt held up his hand. "Hold on! I've not been allowed my turn." He cleared his throat. "I'm thankful that the most beautiful redhead in the world will be my wife come this Valentine's! Now let's say the blessing so we can eat before this glorious meal gets cold."

I spent the remainder of my holiday helping Aunt Bird and Cece address invitations for Cece and Brad's engagement party. The event would be held during the Christmas holidays, when Brad would have two weeks' leave before he shipped out for Vietnam. The "happy couple" had agreed on a June wedding after his return from Vietnam.

Although Cece and I appealed for a joint engagement party, Aunt Bird wouldn't hear of it. "There will be no such thing!" she insisted. "Hoyt and I have been engaged for years."

"Let's at least schedule your ceremony on the church calendar before someone else steals that date," Cece suggested.

"Whoa now, Miss Nellie Belle!" Aunt Bird interrupted. "There will be no elaborate ceremony. Hoyt and I have decided to marry here in our living room with the two of you and Frannie and her husband as our witnesses."

"But, Aunt Bird, you've waited so long for this day! Don't you want a wedding with all the frills?" Cece implored.

"Oh, Cece, I'm too old for all that hoopdedo! Hoyt and I shall be just as married, I assure you." Though Cece needled her all evening, Aunt Bird held firm. I agreed with my aunt. Cece's "hoopdedo" of a wedding would be more than enough for me.

I was thrilled at the thought of finally having Hoyt as my real uncle. Though he'd never tried to take Diddy's place, Uncle Hoyt filled my need for a fatherly figure. I still missed Diddy and knew I always would, but Uncle Hoyt had become such a fixture in my life that I could not imagine our family without him.

The following day, Cece and I took off in the Studebaker to Atlanta for a visit with Mimi. "You drive," Cece insisted. "It's been too long since I've changed gears."

"City girl," I snickered. "You never were any good with a clutch."

Cece giggled. "Uncle Hoyt truly had the patience of Job with me that summer. I'm so happy for him and Aunt Bird. Just think, Allie. Soon, there'll only be one single Sinclair female."

I fumed. "And I plan to keep it that way for quite some time!"

"Oh, your knight will show up before you're an old maid." I shot her a bird with my gear-changing hand as she continued. "In the meantime, your duty is to serve as my maid of honor, which means you're responsible for tending to the bride's every need."

"Does that mean I have to wipe you after you pee?"

Cece playfully slapped me on the leg. "Marcus insists on designing the bridesmaids' dresses. I just need to settle on a color. What do you think?"

I hated to spoil her exuberant mood. "Any color but yellow. Yellow makes me look like a mummy."

By the time we reached Mimi's in Virginia Highlands, Cece had debated every tint in a 100 pack Crayola box. My head pounded, and I needed to use the bathroom.

Our grandmother met us at the front door. A diminutive woman who'd once been my height, Mimi's osteoporosis had caused her to shrink over the years. Although her head barely reached my shoulder, she squeezed me so hard I could hardly breathe. "Oh, I just can't get enough 'sugah' from my two girls when they come for a visit! Now, Cece, tell me all about this beau of yours. I understand his mother was a Hamilton?"

"His name is Bradley Hamilton Royal. His mother was Meredith Hamilton," Cece explained knowing that our grandmother would be concerned about what kind of family my sister was marrying into.

Mimi nodded in approval. "Her daddy was Marvin Hamilton, wasn't he? I recall he'd always come in our store when he left the mill in the afternoon. I remember Meredith vaguely; she was just a couple of years older than your mama but attended boarding school in Atlanta."

Cece nodded. "Meredith passed away several years ago from cancer. Brad's daddy still manages payrolls for Hamilton Mills."

"I remember reading about her untimely death," Mimi interjected. "I don't really know her husband, though. John Royal, is that his name?"

"Yes ma'am. He met Brad's mother in Atlanta at the close of World War II, but he grew up in Pennsylvania," Cece explained.

Mimi grinned. "At least he had sense enough to marry a Southern woman! Now let me have a look at that engagement ring." Cece willingly displayed her left hand. "Why that's lovely. I think platinum is just so refined and will endure with time. Have you set the date?"

I wondered why I'd even taken the trouble to come. I resurfaced from my miserable pit of pity in time to hear a discussion of the ever-important bridesmaid's dress.

"No really, Mimi, I know you're overwhelmed with clients in the spring with all the proms and summer weddings. I have a friend who's volunteered to make the bridesmaids' dresses if I can just decide on a color," Cece explained.

"What does your friend know about fashion?" Mimi queried. "Has she had any training?"

"Oh, *she* just graduated with a degree in fashion design at NYU." Cece shot me a "keep your mouth shut" glance. I guess we could never get Mimi to understand why a man would want to sew clothes for women. "Now, if I can just find the right wedding gown. I want something sophisticated, traditional, and unique all wrapped into one. I haven't seen a single gown like that in the bridal magazines."

Mimi's eyes took on a new sparkle. "Maybe I can help. You girls follow me; I have something to show you."

We filed in behind Mimi down the basement stairs into her seamstress shop. One corner of the room had been converted into three changing cubicles hidden by dressing curtains. Inside one of the cubicles stood a wardrobe mannequin dressed in the most elegant wedding gown I'd ever seen.

Cece gasped. "It's absolutely stunning, Mimi. I mean it's everything I envisioned! When did you have time to make this? "

Mimi smiled. "I made this dress quite some time ago. It belonged to your mama." I realized I'd seen the dress before—in Mama and Diddy's wedding photo, which still sat on our mantle at home. Mimi continued, "I had it sealed and stored until the first of this week. When you called with your news, I thought the time was right for me to see if the years had damaged it."

"It's in perfect condition. It's just what I've dreamed of having!" Cece's excitement spilled out of her.

"We'll need to make a few alterations, but nothing that a nip and a tuck can't fix. Would you like to try it on?"

Cece retreated behind the curtain with Mimi while I thumbed through a pattern book with new spring fashions. I was wondering if Mimi could make me a pair of mini-culottes in tie-dyed material when my sister emerged from behind the curtain.

"What do you think, Allie? Is this the dress for me?" Cece twirled around once to give me the entire view. "What's wrong, Allie? Cat got your tongue?"

It was as though my mama had stepped out of the photo on our living room mantle and into my life. I gazed once more at my sister. "You are the most stunning creature I've ever seen except maybe for our mama. Yes, Cece. It's the dress for you!"

"So, I guess you've resigned yourself to serve as my maid of honor," Cece asked as we drove home.

"Since I'm the only sister you have, I don't have much of a choice, do I? Just make sure Marcus knows I need some padding in the bust line of my dress."

Cece roared. "Aqua, that's it, aqua. It will be perfect with your green eyes."

Chapter 27

Friday evening before Christmas I was clad in my best Sunday dress, pantyhose, and heels; I would've preferred jeans and my favorite sweatshirt. I stood in the kitchen placing my aunt's homemade cheese straws on a silver tray.

Cece chatted excitedly about the guests who'd soon arrive for her engagement party. "I can't believe all the cheerleaders RSVP'd. I figured some of them wouldn't be home."

Though Cece had arrived this morning, there'd been absolutely no time for us to visit. She and Brad had been disgustingly glued to each other ever since. When he left to prepare for the party, they stood on the front porch as though an hour's separation was sheer torment.

Aunt Bird pulled the final batch of cheese straws from the oven. "Be careful, Cece! Don't get any grease on your dress; it will ruin that velvet," Aunt Bird warned as my sister filled a platter with sandwiches.

"I just hope my hair doesn't flop before everyone's here. I thought about having Miss Thelma put it up in a French twist, but Brad begged me to wear it down." Although I hated to admit my sister's fiancé was right, her satiny blonde locks hanging loosely around her shoulders framed her face perfectly. Cece's eyes sparkled like sapphires against the blue velvet dress, a simple sleeveless A-line adorned with our mama's string of pearls.

The dress had been a parting gift from Marcus who'd declined to travel to Flintville for the gala. I guess he sensed our small Southern town would be a bit provincial. Though Aunt Bird had offered him an invitation, I could just see her trying to explain a flaming queer houseguest to her Sunday school friends.

A tap at the kitchen's back door startled me. Behind it stood Bradley carrying two dozen red roses and wearing a toothy, shit-eating grin. He smiled down at me. "Hey, little sis. I figured since I'm almost family, I could come in the back door," he explained as he sailed into the room.

I fumed. "No, you pompous son of a bitch," I wanted to scream. "You're not a member of this family yet, and I'll never be your little sister or your little anything, for that matter!" Instead, I smiled and silently wished for a strong drink.

By the time Cece oohed and aahhed over the flowers, guests began arriving. Although Josie was invited, she and her parents had driven to LaGrange to meet Zeke and his family for dinner. I hated Josie for deserting me.

Trying to escape the festivities, I volunteered to replenish the food table and punch bowl when needed. Aunt Bird was so appreciative of what she thought was a selfless act, I felt ashamed. "That will give Hoyt and me time to chat with Bradley's father." Mr. Royal was the only other adult invited to this evening's grand affair.

Uncle Hoyt, serving as official greeter, popped in a few moments later. "Whew!" he whistled. "I've never seen so many folks so gussied up in my life!" he laughed as he drew a glass of water from the kitchen sink and eased into a chair. "I'd forgotten how a bunch of women can talk especially when they haven't seen each other in a while."

I welcomed his company. As I transferred a fresh batch of cookies to a Christmas platter, I decided to see what he thought of Brad.

"Uncle Hoyt, do you think this engagement can last while Brad's in Vietnam?" I began.

Uncle Hoyt sampled one of the cookies. "What do you mean, Allie?"

"Well, a year's a long time to be separated. Who knows? Maybe Cece will find someone she likes better once Brad is gone. She's so young and pretty and..."

"And very much in love with Brad," Uncle Hoyt interjected. "No, I think it's the real thing with those two." He eyed me curiously. "Don't you approve of their plans?"

I hesitated before continuing. "I just think Brad's a little too pushy." Uncle Hoyt's bemused expression told me he was clueless. "I mean they're not even married yet, but he already thinks he's family," I protested.

Uncle Hoyt chuckled. "Your aunt and I aren't married, but you treat me like a family member."

"That's different. You've been around long enough that I can trust you. I know your intentions with Aunt Bird are completely honorable."

"And you don't think Brad's intentions are honorable? I mean, he does want to marry your sister, but he's willing to serve his country, and that's a damn honorable thing as far as I'm concerned." I could see I was getting nowhere.

Aunt Bird pushed through the swinging door with a dignified gentleman in tow. "Hoyt, you know John Royal, don't you?" The two men shook hands. Since the Royals attended the Methodist church, I'd grilled Josie for information about them. She knew very little, though. Although Mr. Royal attended church services, Josie said he didn't socialize much with the church folks since his wife's death.

"Well, well! You're Allie, aren't you?" Mr. Royal spoke through the same toothy grin as Brad. "I think you know my niece Juliet. She went to boarding school, but her mother tells me you attended Juliet's birthday parties in the summer."

"Um, yessir, I remember Juliet." I thought of her massive canopy bed, which always reminded me of the Dunn sisters and the tiny bed they slept in together before Macy died. "Where's Juliet now?"

"She's a freshman at Agnes Scott University. And I understand you're a journalism major at the University of Georgia?" He smiled again, and I realized he'd done his homework.

Aunt Bird smiled. "Yes, I believe this one will follow in her father's footsteps. You do remember my brother, don't you, John?"

He flashed that gigantic grin again. "Why, of course. A.L. and I were in the Kiwanis together. A fine man, yes, a fine man."

As the conversation ebbed, Aunt Bird suggested I say hello to Cece's guests. "I'll man the kitchen for a while."

The first person I bumped into was none other than Cassie Sue Causey, the cheerleading captain who'd made my freshman year a living hell. "Allie Sinclair, you haven't changed one little bit!" she exclaimed in her peppy, high-pitched voice.

"Hi, Cassie Sue. What's going on in your life these days?" I asked with as much interest as I could muster.

"I graduated last year from Auburn, and now I'm traveling with the National Cheerleading Association. We conduct cheer camps for high school squads all over the Southeast. I just love it! "

Just when I expected Cassie Sue to turn a cartwheel in our dining room, Aunt Bird rescued me. "Could you replenish the punch bowl? I think it's almost empty."

When I wriggled away from Cassie Sue's spirited grip and returned to the kitchen, I discovered Donna Sims washing out punch cups. Donna was a Milltown girl who'd served on student council with Cece. "Hi, Allie. I offered to give your aunt a hand. I'm the only guest without a date since my boyfriend's working an extra shift at the mill tonight." She was a pretty girl with short, stocky legs, a tiny waist, and a big bust line. She wore her dark curly hair in a short style, accentuating her tremendous brown eyes.

As we washed out cups and replenished the dining room table, we made small talk. Donna attended Tift College about thirty miles south of Flintville. "It's taking me longer because I'm on the Work/Study scholarship plan," she explained.

Each year, Hamilton Mills awarded Work/Study scholarships to a half-dozen students whose parents worked in the mills. The scholarship paid for tuition and expenses if, in return, the recipient agreed to alternate a quarter of college with a quarter of employment in one of the mills.

Balancing a tray of punch cups in one hand and a pitcher of punch in the other, I pushed open the swinging door with my backside. Before I could return to the kitchen, Cassie Sue cornered me again. "I want you to meet my boyfriend Chip Larson." Then she plunged into an excited discussion about their plans to marry and start their own nationwide cheerleading clinic.

After a ten-minute monologue, Cassie Sue was just warming up. Fortunately, she spotted Betsy Meeks heading our way. "Oh, Chip, you just have to meet Betsy. She was my co-captain at Flintville High!"

Seizing the moment, I made a fast retreat to the kitchen. Donna wasn't at the sink where I'd left her. Instead, I heard two male voices, in what sounded like an argument, coming from our slightly opened pantry door. "You better think about what you say to me, or I'll make your life miserable!" a deep, vaguely familiar voice warned.

Mystified, I called out. "Donna? Are you in the pantry? Is everything all right?"

To my utter bewilderment, Mr. John Royal, straightening his tie, emerged from behind the pantry door. Behind him stood a red-faced Brad, eyes filled with embarrassment at the sight of me.

Mr. Royal cleared his throat. "Oh, hi Allie. I was just telling Donna here about a new secretarial position at the mill. Isn't that right, Donna?"

Donna cowered in the back corner of the pantry. Her cheeks flushed and eyes turned down, she nodded timidly. "Um, your aunt said there were more cocktail napkins in the pantry, Allie. I found them." She handed me a package of red napkins monogrammed with "Brad & Cece" in gold. "I think I'll head home. My boyfriend gets off in an hour." She darted out the swinging door without looking back.

"Don't you think you should get back to your guests and your lovely bride-to-be?" Mr. Royal guided Brad toward the dining room, and I watched as my sister's humiliated fiancé obeyed his father's command without even a whimper.

Alone in the kitchen, Mr. Royal smiled at me with that same condescending look Brad had often given me years ago. "Donna's quite smart for a mill girl, don't you think?"

I despised his tone and expression. "She's smart enough to get an education that will get her out of the mills," I replied as I stared Mr. Royal straight in the eye.

Before he could respond, Aunt Bird rushed into the kitchen. "Allie, we want to get some photos of the entire family. Oh, there you are, John. We need you, too."

Mr. Royal made certain to stand at the opposite end of the table from me while Margaret took pictures. Shortly thereafter, I heard him apologize for leaving so early. "Thanks so much, Miss Ophelia," he began in a gracious voice as he shook my aunt's hand. "I hope this is just the beginning of many Sinclair/Royal celebrations."

The following day when I stopped by Josie's to pick her up for lunch, she was in the shower. Lorna, still the McClendons' maid after all these years, kept me company while she folded laundry on the kitchen table.

Cece and Brad's engagement was already the talk out in Lincoln Village, according to Lorna. "I'se know all about the Royals," she explained. "My sister-in-law Juanita worked for Mr. Marvin Hamilton and helped raise Miz Meredith, and she sez Miz Meredith's folks was most upset when she married Mr. John Royal cause he from up north. But when's they marry, Mr. Hamilton gives Meredith's husband a job in the mills, and that Mr. Royal clumb up the ladder to a big position out there." Lorna took a breath as she set up the ironing board.

"How does your sister-in-law know Bradley?" I inquired.

"Wells, when Miz Meredith had her son, she wanted some help, so Mr. Marvin sent Juanita to works for the Royals. How Juanita did love Miz Meredith and her chile little Bradley! She don't care too much for Mr. John Royal. He never wanted no noise from that baby when he get home from work, and he'd pitch a fit if little Bradley had any of his'n toys strung on the floor. Then when Miz Meredith tooks sick with the cancer, Juanita sez Mr. John would come home later and later from work, so Juanita gots to staying overnight to take care of Miz Meredith. It wuz a sad day when Miz Meredith passed on. Juanita sez she'd cooks for Bradley and Mr. John, but Mr. John wuz so tore up, he didn't come home 'til late at night after poor Bradley done got his homework all did and gone on to bed. Juanita sez Miz Daphne Hamilton, Miz Meredith's sister-in-law, watched over Bradley and saw to it that he gots some lovin, 'cause that boy did miss his mama, and his daddy just didn't seem to have no love in him at that time." Lorna turned back to her ironing just as Josie entered the kitchen.

"Ready for lunch?" she asked.

Sitting in my Studebaker outside Porky's BBQ Shack, I recanted the events of the party to Josie. She whistled through her teeth. "Good Lord! What do you think was going on in the pantry? Do you think Mr. Royal caught Bradley flirting with Donna?"

I sipped on my Cherry Sprite. "I can't be sure. Who knows? Maybe Mr. Royal made a pass at Donna, and Brad interrupted it!"

Josie almost choked on her barbeque sandwich. "Oh, that's just too gross! Mr. Royal's old enough to be Donna's daddy, maybe even her granddaddy!"

I sighed. "Donna does work in the mill office every other quarter. Maybe Mr. Royal offered her the secretarial position to buy her silence about whatever was going on in our kitchen. What bothers me the most was the way Mr. Royal talked about Donna after she left. I mean, his tone was so demeaning."

"That's disgusting!" Josie popped a French fry. "Are you going to tell your sister?"

I shrugged. "What's to tell? Nothing really happened, I guess. Maybe I can use Brad's weird behavior as leverage against him if I ever need it. I mean, if I ever suspect he's cheating on Cece."

Josie whistled again. "Why would Brad want to cheat on your sister? She's the prettiest, most sophisticated girl in all of Flintville!"

"God if I know! Brad is about all the Royal blood I can bear! He's a jerk, but his daddy's a major asshole!"

"Maybe you should mention the pantry episode to your aunt," Josie suggested.

I shook my head. "I've already bad-mouthed Brad so much Aunt Bird's lectured me about needing an 'attitude adjustment.'"

"I know what you mean. My folks are furious I'm driving back to LaGrange tonight to be with Zeke. God, can't they understand that watching *Hee Haw* on Saturday night with them isn't my idea of fun?!"

I actually understood how Josie's folks felt, but I didn't say anything. They were afraid of losing Josie just like I was.

After I dropped Josie off, I drove out to the river. The time alone gave me the opportunity to digest Lorna's information about the Royals. I almost felt sorry for Bradley. When Brad's mother died, Mr. Royal didn't offer Brad the comfort that my family gave me after we lost Diddy. Brad seemed to have no one except for his Aunt Daphne, whom I vaguely remembered from her daughter's birthday parties. Miz Daphne was married to Oscar Hamilton, the son and sole heir to the Hamilton Mills. She was tall and slender with perfectly coiffed hair, and always walked and talked with a princess-like gracefulness. From my stint working the society page at the paper, I knew she devoted her time to charity work. Perhaps she'd once considered Brad, her own nephew, a charity case. Whatever the case, the more I learned about that pompous John Royal, the more I detested him. I could only pray that Brad and Cece's children would take after the Hamiltons, or better yet, the Sinclairs.

I began my bumpy descent down Old River Road past the *River Ranch*. I considered stopping to see if Miss Blanche Bledsoe was serving beer to drunk patrons. Not ready to head home where I'd be subjected to more wedding details, I drove out to Ty's family cabin. I knew nobody would be there this time of year. I could sit on the dock in peace and watch the sun set over the river. I was surprised, however, to see David Banks' Camaro in the grass beside the dock. Dave's last letter had said he wouldn't get leave until Christmas Eve. Maybe David's father had come out to fish, I surmised, until I heard "Come on baby, light my fire!" blaring. I couldn't envision Mr. Banks as a fan of The Doors.

Dressed in civilian clothes but sporting a military haircut, he was perched atop the hood of his car where he swayed and drummed the beat on his thighs. He was so oblivious to the world around him that I climbed on the hood before he saw me.

"Allie! Oh my God! How'd you sneak up on me?" He slid off the hood pulling me with him, grabbed me up in his arms, and practically swung me around his head. "God, it's great to see a foxy lady after all that hard tail I've been putting up with for weeks!"

I giggled. "Well, if it's not my soldier boy!" I rubbed the top of his closely cropped head. "Fuzzy Wuzzy wasn't fuzzy, was he?!"

"Ah hell! This is a month's growth. After my first shearing session, I was practically bald! At least I have a round head. Teddy's looked kind of like an inverted ice cream cone. He wouldn't take off his hat for two weeks!" Dave chortled.

"Where is Teddy? And what are you doing home? I thought the Army was keeping you until Christmas Eve."

Dave gave me a boost back on top of the car and climbed up beside me. "Hell, the Army's always changing its mind. After graduation yesterday, our drill sergeant announced we had leave until January 3rd! Teddy's dating this older chick, Trixie, who has her own apartment near the base in Columbus. He's shacking up with her this weekend and not coming home until Monday."

"Same old Teddy, I see. How are you? How's Army life? Did you get your orders for AIT yet?"

"I'm great, Army life sucks, and yes! How about a drink? I found Ty's uncle's stash a little while ago. Want a *Southern Comfort* and Coke?" I followed him down to the dock where he pulled cups and ice from a cooler and mixed the concoction before I could object. Handing me a cup and raising his in the air, Dave made a toast: "Here's to the fucking Army and how it can fuck up your life!"

Dave had never uttered such profanity in front of me. I realized he was already drunk.

He guzzled half his drink while I stared in astonishment. "What's wrong, Dave? Your letters sounded like Army life was tough but nothing you and Teddy couldn't handle."

He sank down on the edge of the dock with his bare feet touching the water. I sat cross-legged beside him and waited quietly for his explanation. The late afternoon sun grew into a ball of orange and hovered just above Spruell Bluff on the other side of the lake. I sipped my Coke and *Southern Comfort*, the first whiskey I'd ever tasted. It burned as it slid down my throat, but after several sips, I had a warm, fuzzy sensation. The sun slipped behind the bluff just as the first frogs began to chirp.

Dave refilled his cup. "I got the AIT I wanted," he began. "I'll get training as a medic at Fort Sam Houston in San Antonio. I'm on my way to Texas right after New Year's."

"But that's great, Dave! When you get out, you'll already have some medical training. That should count for something when you apply to medical schools." He stared out at a lone duck settled on the riverbank a few yards away. "And Texas isn't bad. You and Teddy could have ended up in some God-awful place like New Jersey!"

Dave laughed sarcastically. "It won't be me and Ted. So much for the fucking 'buddy system' that sonnabitch recruiter sold us on! Ted's going to Fort Polk, Lousiana for infantry training."

"Oh, God. I bet he's furious. Wasn't Teddy interested in medical training, too?"

Dave drained his drink. "The Army doesn't work that way. They give you a battery of tests and determine where you'll best perform."

"I'm really sorry, Dave. How's Teddy taking all of this?"

Dave shrugged. "That's what really bothers me. He's fine with it. Says he'll be close enough at Fort Polk to go to New Orleans on leave. All he talks about is all the topless bars on Bourbon Street. It hasn't dawned on him that after AIT, he'll be shipping out to Nam."

My heart sank. "What about you, Dave? Maybe they'll send you to Germany instead."

"You sweet, innocent little Allie Cat." He stared down at me. "God, I'd forgotten how beautiful your green eyes are!" He brushed my bangs away from my forehead, and for a brief moment, I thought he would kiss me. I waited with my chin upturned and worried he could hear the thunder of my heart.

The lone duck decided at that moment to squawk and take flight. Dave turned his gaze from me and stared at the river. "No, we're both headed to Nam, just in different companies. Odds are, I'll never even see Teddy once we get over there. How can we watch each other's back that way? Damn, I'm so pissed!"

As a chill permeated the twilight's air, Dave pulled a blanket from the trunk of his car and wrapped it around us. We sat on the dock in total silence until the cloudless sky glittered with stars.

In the wee hours of the morning, I eased the Studebaker into our driveway. Luckily, the porch light was burning, or I would have stumbled all the way up the back porch steps. I'd stayed with Dave until we sobered up enough to drive. We'd stopped at the *River Ranch*, where I waited in the car until he returned with black coffee and a couple of burgers. I dreaded coming up with an explanation for Aunt Bird.

I tiptoed down the hall into my room. Remembering Cece would be asleep, I fumbled in the dark for my pajamas and banged my knee on some unknown object. "Crap!" I seethed under my breath.

"Stop trying to be quiet," came a voice from the dark. "I'm not asleep." Cece switched on the lamp between our beds. "Where have you been, Miss Priss?"

"I ran into Dave, and we pitched a little party on the Hastings' dock," I explained.

Cece smirked. "A party, huh? Until 2:00 in the morning? Must have been a humdinger of one!"

"I had no idea how late it was! How long did Aunt Bird wait up for me? I bet she's pissed, isn't she?"

Cece giggled. "You should be happy she didn't have Sheriff Brady and his posse out looking for you!"

I stumbled toward the bathroom to brush my teeth.

"Are you okay?" Cece eyed me suspiciously. "Allison Sinclair, you're drunk, aren't you?"

"Not as drunk as I was a couple of hours ago," I admitted. I figured there was no sense in lying to Cece who followed me into the bathroom. I studied my bloodshot eyes in the mirror. "Have you ever had *Southern Comfort*? After you get used to the burn, it really gives you a nice feeling."

"I wonder how nice you'll be feeling when you have to accompany Aunt Bird to church in just a few hours," Cece surveyed my disheveled hair and smeared mascara. "You look like warmed over Jell-O!"

"Oh crap! Church? In the morning?" I moaned as a wave of nausea swept over me. "Aunt Bird's going to kill me," I moaned again. Cece lifted the toilet seat just in time.

A few minutes later my big sister applied a cool, moist cloth to my forehead and offered me two aspirin. "Here, take these and this," she insisted as she placed a fizzing glass of water in my hand. "Marcus swears two aspirin and an Alka-Seltzer will take the edge off a hangover. I wouldn't know myself since I've never had any *Southern Comfort*. Allie, that's just pure whiskey."

"Damnit, Cece! Stop your preaching! I'm sure I'll get plenty of that from Aunt Bird in the morning." I crawled under the covers and prayed the bed would stop spinning.

"I told Aunt Bird that you called while she was in the shower and you were spending the night with Josie, so you're in the clear." Cece turned off the bedside lamp.

"Thanks for covering for me, Cece, but didn't you wonder where I was? Or maybe you were glad to be rid of me for a while!"

Cece sighed. "Actually, Dave called looking for you just after you left to have lunch with Josie. I figured he caught up with ya'll at *Porky's*. Just before sunset,

Brad and I rode out to his house on the bluff, and I spotted your and Dave's cars on the other side of the river."

"And you weren't concerned that a young Southern lady like myself was all alone down at the river with a red-blooded American soldier home on leave?" The bed's spinning had slowed as the aspirin took effect.

"I figure you're old enough to make those decisions for yourself. However, if that soldier breaks my baby sister's heart, he'll have me to reckon with!" Cece said something else, but I was too far gone to hear her.

Moments later, I nursed the throb behind my eyeballs during Preacher Clayton's sermon. I wondered if Cece thought Dave and I were an item. He did almost kiss me. Could David Banks actually be my very own knight in shining armor? The thunder of "Standing on the Promises" and the pounding in my head drowned out whatever my heart tried to tell me.

Two days after Christmas amid hugs and tears, we said goodbye to Cece. Since Brad reported to base the same day as Cece's flight to New York, Mr. Royal volunteered to drive them both to the airport. I could tell Cece was disappointed with this arrangement. Once Brad landed in California, he'd process out to Vietnam. I guess my sister wanted Brad to herself for those final hours before he went away to war.

Brad, dressed in his uniform, waited with Mr. Royal in the car as Cece clung to Aunt Bird and me on our front porch. "I'll be home two days before your wedding so I can help with all the last minute details," she promised my aunt.

Then she held me so tightly I floated in her *Heaven Scent* perfume. "And you watch that soldier boy of yours," she whispered softly in my ear. "There's something about a fella in uniform that can really pull at a girl's heartstrings. Then he flies away to fight a war in another world."

The slight quiver in her voice made my heart ache for Cece. In just hours she would bid farewell to her fiancé, and although the verdict was still out on my opinion of Brad, I couldn't bear to see her suffering.

"Don't worry, Cece," I whispered as I straightened the star of flint dangling from the chain around her neck. "Our stars shine down on that other world, too. They'll protect him."

With the exception of Stu Sims, who went skiing in Colorado, the entire *B&B Brigade* was in town for New Year's Eve. Ty graciously hosted a celebration at the lake cabin.

Even Josie made an appearance with Zeke. I took to Zeke Tyson immediately. He was tall and slender but well-sculpted, from hours of handling horses and shoveling hay. His voice was slow, low, and easy; his laid-back disposition earned him quick acceptance into our circle.

Not calling it a date, Dave offered to drive me out to the lake. "There's no reason for all of us to have a car out there," he'd explained.

Flintville had yet to experience any true winter weather, and with the fire Ty erected in a clearing by the lake, I was quite comfortable in my jeans and soft green pullover.

There was enough beer for everyone thanks to Teddy. The case of beer had been a parting gift from Trixie, who'd lied about being divorced. While Trixie and Teddy shacked up in her apartment, Trixie's truck driver husband showed up two days earlier than expected. Teddy's basic training skills served him well at that desperate moment. He bolted out the bedroom window, swung down a fire escape, and raced away to freedom. The following night, Trixie met him in the alley behind the bar where she worked and loaded his trunk down with a variety of alcohol including three bottles of *Cold Duck.*

"Damn, Teddy! I hope she didn't steal all this stuff for you!" Ty exclaimed as he opened another bottle of Budweiser.

"Well hell! What if she did?" Teddy argued. "She owed me after lying to me! Let's change the subject." Teddy and Ty's dates, who'd gone to "powder their noses," were approaching the campfire.

"Leave it to Teddy to have an extra female waiting on the sidelines," Ty muttered as he elbowed Dave. The "other" female was my junior high rival, the big-breasted Rachel Fountain. Her pink alpaca sweater stretched across her double-D boobs, and I was disappointed to discover that my prayer for her rear end to grow the size of an elephant's had fallen on deaf ears.

Ty's date was Pammie Reese, my baptismal buddy from years earlier. I giggled to myself when Ty invited Pammie to take a moonlit paddle down the lake in an old canoe, and she insisted on a life jacket.

As midnight neared, Josie and Zeke took off. Zeke had to feed the horses at daybreak. Shortly thereafter, Pammie made some excuse about having a curfew. Exasperated, Ty shrugged his shoulders and escorted her to his car.

Rachel and Teddy excused themselves to the back seat of Teddy's car. Every once in a while, we'd hear Rachel giggle. "Shit, Teddy is such a cock hound!" Dave sniggered. "Look at the steam on his windows. If they get that vehicle rocking anymore, it's going to roll into the lake."

"At least he's on the rebound after his heartbreak over Trixie." I stood up and stretched my legs.

"Heartbreak, my ass! As long as Teddy's got some sweet little thing to screw, his heart's just fine. Let's walk out on the dock. Maybe somebody on the river will be shooting some fireworks." He grabbed my hand and a bottle of unopened *Cold Duck.*

Except for a swig of Dave's beer, I chose to remain sober. My body was still recovering from my *Southern Comfort* binge a week earlier. Besides, I wanted to know exactly what I felt about Dave if the opportunity arose for him to kiss me.

We heard Teddy moan and Rachel giggle once again. Dave shook his head. "What will all the loose women do without Teddy around for the next year? They'll probably go into mourning."

I decided to take matters in my own hands. "I guess Teddy's probably got a dozen girls lined up to write him when he goes overseas. How many do you have?"

He looked at me and brushed my bangs aside just as he had done a few nights earlier. "Just you, Allie. God, your eyes are as green as a cat's. That's why I call you Allie Cat, you know. Damn, I'm not good at saying what I want to say. All I can think about lately is...is..."

"Is what, Dave, what?" I pleaded as I turned my face towards his.

He gave me the answer I wanted when he took me in his arms. As a new decade dawned, we made fireworks of our own.

Chapter 28

The last Saturday in February, Cece and I were together in Flintville to serve as the maids of honor for Aunt Bird's wedding.

Cece, as lovely as ever although she appeared thinner, wore her blue velvet engagement party dress. I wore an identical dress in green velvet designed by Marcus. Mrs. Frannie Parker, Aunt Bird's best friend and matron of honor, was clad in a red velvet dress.

The three of us waited tensely in the church vestibule as Miss Ethel Crumpton played the final notes of "Whither Thou Goest." The following number was "Pachelbel's Canon," which served as the bridesmaids' cue to begin our slow trek down the aisle. Uncle Hoyt, his best man Ellis Parks, and Preacher Clayton would be making their entrance to the altar in just moments. There was just one minor problem: Aunt Bird, a stickler for promptness, was late to her own wedding.

Just as Miss Ethel pumped out the initial notes of the bridesmaids' march, the vestibule's outside door swung open. Aunt Bird, panting and trembling, scurried into the waiting area with us. "Merciful Father above!" she whispered. "I almost missed my own wedding after all these years! Thelma had a time with this curly bush of mine. I thought she'd never get it all on top of my head!"

Miss Frannie attended to my aunt, whose cheeks, flushed from the February air, needed a tad of powder. Grasping her bridal bouquet in trembling hands, Aunt Bird took a deep breath to compose herself. "If we'd done this thing at the house like I'd wanted, I would not be such a nervous wreck."

The matron of honor, without a pregnant belly for the first time in a while, shushed my aunt. "Ophelia Sinclair, don't you dare have a hissy fit right before you walk down the aisle. There was absolutely no way to accommodate the Baptist choir and the school's faculty in your living room!"

Miss Frannie gave me a gentle push. "Go Allie, you're first down the aisle." I had no time to give Aunt Bird a final hug.

It wasn't until Miss Ethel pounded a thunderous transition into the wedding march that I truly got a look at my aunt. She wore a demur ivory wool suit with tiny pearl buttons. Her copper red hair, swept up in curls atop her head, was adorned with a few sprigs of baby's breath. No lace, no tulle, no sequins, the simplicity of her dress allowed her pure beauty to radiate throughout the entire room. Her emerald green eyes were not the only ones to tear up as she held Hoyt's hand and listened to the reading of the "Love Chapter" from First Corinthians: "Love beareth all things, believeth all things, hopeth all things, endureth all things."

When Preacher Clayton presented "Mr. and Mrs. Hoyt Lloyd" to the congregation, the entire choir as well as the English department stood up and cheered. My dear sweet aunt finally had her knight in shining armor.

Chuck Purdy donned a coat and tie to serve as wedding photographer. By the time we arrived at Miz Gertie's house where the reception was being held, the celebration was already in high gear. The newlyweds rushed to cut the cake while Mr. Purdy ducked under the crowd to capture a shot of Uncle Hoyt playfully feeding a bite to Aunt Bird.

I headed straight for the groom's table where the newspaper's secretaries were serving a three layered tower covered in chocolate frosting. Miz Opal cut me a generous slice while Miz Charlene chatted. "Oh, Allie, I wish you had time before you go back to school to write up this wedding. I hope I can do it justice on the society page."

I smiled politely. "I'm certain your article will be fine, Miz Charlene. Besides, I'm into sports journalism these days."

"Humpph!" I heard a disgruntled voice behind me. "And why would you waste your talent writing about ballgames?" Over the din of all the well-wishers, I'd missed the distinctive "pink-pink-pink" of Miss Benton's crutches. I found myself face to face with the crotchety old librarian. She pointed an arthritic finger at me. "You should set your goals higher, young lady! I expect to see you working as an investigative reporter for the *Atlanta Journal* before I die, you hear me?"

She hobbled away before I had to think of an appropriate answer. I watched as she made her slow journey to where Cece was sitting near the punch table. A half hour later as the guests gathered outside with packets of rice, Miss Benton and Cece were still engaged in conversation.

"Excuse me, Cece, but if you want to say goodbye to Aunt Bird before they leave, you'd better do it now." The old bat, obviously irritated I'd disturbed them, eyed me with disapproval.

Cece made a graceful apology to Miss Benton and followed me to Miz Gertie's guest bedroom where Aunt Bird was closing a small overnight case. The newlyweds would spend one night at Callaway Gardens. By the time they returned, Cece and I would be gone.

"Oh girls, I've hardly seen you this trip. Give me a hug!" She squeezed us both against her ample bosom. "There's plenty of food at home, and I left a number where we can be reached." My Aunt Bird—looking after us, even on her wedding day.

As I helped Miz Gertie box up leftovers, she rattled on proudly about Roscoe Ray's woodworking business and his "family" in North Carolina. "Roscoe says he's 'adopted' the Martins since they have no children of their own. They're driving him down here for a visit this spring. He's making me a rocking chair. I guess he thinks I'm getting old!"

"Miz Gertie, you haven't aged one bit. You've got more life left in you than most ladies half your age."

She handed me a box of leftovers to take home. "I've weathered many challenges over the years, but I can still plant a heckuva garden and play a mean hand of bridge." She hugged me as I headed out the door.

When I arrived home, Cece, already dressed for bed, was lying on the couch. She looked pale, and her eyes were red and puffy. I plopped down in the easy chair. "You look like crap!"

She sat up and sipped on a glass of water. "I've been a little queasy all weekend." She looked like she might burst into tears. "Thank God Aunt Bird's gone. I have to tell you; I have to tell someone. I can't stand this anymore!" Her voice was filled with anguish, and her eyes were strained with pain.

"Stand what, Cece? What's wrong? Is it your diabetes? Is it Brad?" I asked, frightened.

Cece dropped her head into her hands. "I'm pregnant."

"You're what?"

Cece's eyes appeared vacant, her face drawn and taut. "You heard me the first time. Don't make me repeat it," she added in a voice devoid of any emotion.

I wanted to slap her. "How in the world could you allow this to happen? Lord, you're a grown woman, not a teenager. Don't you and Brad know anything about protection? I mean, you've heard of a condom, haven't you? Or how about birth control pills? Ya'll can't be this stupid!"

"I can't take birth control pills because of my diabetes," she explained in the same toneless voice.

I was ready to kill Bradley Hamilton Royal. "Well, then your stupid fiancé should have taken care of things. Damn, is he too good to wear a rubber?"

"Stop it, Allie! You don't have to be so crude. It's so unbecoming."

I began to seethe. "You can cool your holier than thou attitude, big sister! At least I'm enough of a lady not to get myself knocked up!"

Cece grimaced. My comment had hit its target. I felt no remorse; I was too pissed at her stupidity. "So, what are you and Brad gonna do? I guess Mimi could fashion a papoose that matches Mama's wedding dress, or will the baby be walking by then?"

My sister collapsed on the couch as though she had no energy to sit up, much less argue. I studied her sunken cheeks and the circles underlining her eyes. Aunt Bird and I had been too busy with the wedding to notice Cece's appearance before. She was far too pale and thin; she looked like she hadn't slept or eaten in days.

Cece appeared so lifeless that I thought she had fallen into a coma, or worse. Memories of finding her unconscious in our bathroom years ago flooded back to me as my throat constricted in fear.

When I found my voice, I spoke gently. "Cece, I'm really sorry for what I just said. It was a stupid, gut reaction. Okay, so you're pregnant. I mean, you and Brad are going to be married in June. Maybe you could move the wedding up? Doesn't he have an R&R scheduled in April? So, you could meet him in Hawaii and elope. That would be pretty romantic, don't you think? You know guys; they don't care anything about a big wedding."

Cece looked up at me. Her blank, lifeless stare was replaced with a look of determination. "Brad doesn't know. And I'm not going to tell him."

"What?" I realized I was almost screaming and tried to regain some control. "Cece! You gotta tell him! He's fathered a child. He needs to take responsibility!"

159

"No, I'm not telling him. He's got enough to worry about right now. I'd rather he concentrate on staying alive."

I felt the fury take over my body. "He's just as guilty as you are in this situation. He's going to have a baby, for God's sake!"

Cece's expression turned to stone. "He's not having a baby, and neither am I. I'm having an abortion, and there's nothing you can say to stop me."

I went berserk. "An abortion? Have you lost your mind? First of all, you're refusing to tell the man you love you're carrying his child. Then, you're going to kill it? My God, Cece, what's happened to you?"

Though her pale face was streaked with tears, Cece's voice was steady and unyielding. "Okay, Allie, I need your help. So, I guess you deserve the truth."

"What do you mean?"

Cece sighed deeply, but seemed in total control of her emotions. "It's not Brad's baby."

"Sweet Jesus!" I moaned. "Then who in the hell is the father?"

My sister stared straight ahead. "I'm not certain," were her almost inaudible words. Stunned into silence, I waited for her to continue. "New Year's Eve I went out with Marcus and some of his friends. We started at a straight bar in the Village. There was this really cute guy named Jeff, who kept flirting with me. It seemed quite harmless, but after a few drinks, I decided not to wait out the New Year. Jeff walked me out and hailed me a cab."

When she paused, I finished the scenario for her. "And he came home with you and made passionate love to you."

"I don't know!" Her answer swept me back to another time, a time that seemed centuries ago although it'd only been five or six years. The night I'd rescued her from the *River Ranch*, she'd worn the same disoriented, vacant expression as she did now. I watched her dig for the memory of what happened. "The next thing I remember it was morning, and I was naked and alone in my bed."

My stomach began to churn. "You were too drunk to remember if this Jeff guy even got in the cab with you, so how can you be sure ya'll had sex?"

My sister flinched. "There was blood on the sheets, and I knew someone had been with me."

"Blood?" I asked incredulously. "Whose blood?"

"My blood. It was my first time," she admitted.

"Oh crap, Cece! You mean you and Brad have never done it? What a mess!" I began to pace the living room.

"We wanted to wait," she was sobbing now. "We wanted it to be perfect." She grew silent, and I could see her hands were trembling.

I was exasperated by her behavior. "Get ahold of yourself, Cece. It's not the end of the world."

She ignored me as she dug in her purse and retrieved a candy bar, which she quickly devoured. As the sugar did its job, the trembling in her hands subsided. "I've been having insulin reactions ever since I realized I was pregnant. I don't know if it's physiological or psychological," she explained.

I felt foolish for not realizing she was having a reaction, but all I could manage as an apology was to put my arm around her and draw her close. "Cece, are you okay?"

"I'm fine for now, but I do need your help, Allie." She stared at me from her gaunt face. "The only other people who know are Marcus and Margaret. We've found a doctor Margaret says is reputable—abortion is legal in New York. I've scraped together every cent I can, but I'm still short."

"How much more do you need?" I couldn't believe my own voice. Was I really going to help my sister have an abortion?

"I need $300 by the middle of March. After that, the procedure becomes more dangerous especially with my diabetes."

I looked into her pitifully weak eyes. Despite the anguish, despite the shame, despite the confusion, those blue eyes spoke my sister's resolve. "Don't worry, Cece. I'll figure something out. Now, let's get you to bed."

Exhausted from the torture of her secret, Cece drifted off to sleep quickly. Once her breathing fell into a rhythmic pattern, I eased out of the room. Dragging the worn afghan knitted by Mimi long ago, I wandered out to the side porch. I'd never been good at keeping secrets, and I longed for Josie or Dave to serve as my sounding board. Maybe I should phone Aunt Bird. Although she'd be devastated, she'd talk some sense into my sister. But I couldn't stand the thought of ruining my aunt's honeymoon. Anyway, did I really want to violate my sister's trust?

I fingered the chain around my neck as I searched my heart for the answer. Suddenly, I realized there was someone I could trust with my secret. Wrapping the afghan snugly around my shoulders, I pushed open the screen door and sat down on the top porch step. The night was so clear that I found my stars in no time. "Tell me what to do, tell me what to do. Dear God, I need your help," I prayed softly. By the time I climbed into bed, I had a plan.

As I drove Cece to the airport the following morning, I chose not to berate her about her decision. She seemed so fragile, so vulnerable. "I'll have the cash when I fly to New York the third Friday in March," I explained. Cece gazed suspiciously at me through sunken eyes. "You have scheduled the procedure for that day, haven't you?"

"Yes, but it's not necessary for you to be there, Allie. Margaret and Marcus will take me to the clinic. Just wire me the money."

"The hell you say! No sister of mine is going through this alone."

Cece grinned weakly. "Thanks, Allie. Thanks for everything."

After dropping Cece off, I returned to Flintville instead of heading to Athens as planned. Fortunately, the newlyweds were still gone when I arrived.

I waited and watched from our front porch until I saw Miz Gertie pull in her driveway. She always came straight home from church on Sundays. What better time to ask a person a favor than when she'd just returned from the Lord's house.

Giving her time to remove her hat and gloves, I hurried up the street, darted into her carport, and tapped on her kitchen door.

"Allie, what a surprise! I thought you had to drive Cece to the airport. You haven't had car trouble, have you?" she queried as she ushered me to her kitchen table.

"Um, no ma'am. I got Cece to the airport in plenty of time. I, uh, I left a textbook that I really need for a test I have this week, so I came back to get it."

"Well, you're in luck, then!" she exclaimed. "I have enough chicken salad to feed my bridge club! Will you join me for lunch?"

I couldn't take advantage of her hospitality. "Um, no thanks. I'm not hungry," I lied. "Actually, there's something I need to ask you..."

Miz Gertie sat down beside me. "What is it, dear?"

Even though I'd rehearsed my spiel on the way home from Atlanta, my tongue felt like cotton. Miz Gertie sensed my discomfort. She placed her hand atop mine. "What is it, Allie? Whatever you have to tell me can't be that terrible."

I took a deep breath and spilled my guts. "Miz Gertie, I need to borrow $300. I can't ask my aunt or Uncle Hoyt. They would want an explanation—an explanation I can't offer because I'm sworn to secrecy. I've worked out a payment schedule so I can repay every dime to you." I pulled a sheet of notebook paper from my jeans pocket. "It may take me a while, but I promise you'll get all of the $300 plus interest back before I graduate from Georgia." I delivered my speech swiftly so she wouldn't interrupt me before I finished.

Miz Gertie studied my payment plan, folded the paper, and returned it to me. "Allie, I won't loan you any money." My heart sank. "However, I shall be happy to give you the $300." She went to a desk, withdrew her checkbook, and began writing. When she handed it to me, I was speechless.

Guilt crept into my heart. "It's—it's for a friend, a friend in trouble," I began.

"I see," was Miz Gertie's reply.

Although she didn't pry, I couldn't help myself. "She's got a problem that her family won't understand. She's a good person. She just made a really stupid mistake."

Miz Gertie covered my hand with hers. "Allie, it's not necessary to explain to me. But my dear, I hope you'll be more careful next time."

She thought the money was for me. "No, Miz Gertie, you don't understand, I-I-I..."

She patted my hand again. "Don't worry, Allie. I do understand. It's for a friend. Your secret is safe with me."

The drive back to Athens seemed interminable. I hated that Miz Gertie thought I was the one in trouble. And yet, I could not divulge the truth. I knew she would honor her promise. Aunt Bird would never find out about Miz Gertie's gift, and though I felt ashamed for lying, I must protect Cece at all costs.

The mere thought of shielding my "big sister" made me laugh out loud. Cece had always been the one to protect me, the one to keep me centered, the one with the level head. Suddenly our roles had changed—but I did not feel level-headed or in control. I had a pregnant sister engaged to someone who did not father her child. I had taken money from a sweet, old lady under false pretenses. And I was about to become a co-conspirator in the annihilation of a precious little soul. As I entered my dormitory, I wondered if I'd condemned my own soul to hell.

Winter made its final curtain call on a dreary March afternoon as I boarded a flight to New York. Before leaving Athens, I'd worked the combination to my mementos box of dearest treasures. The box held Mama's bracelet, Essie Dunn's letter, the Valentine I'd given Diddy the day he died, a rabbit's foot from Josie, a peach crate label with Mimi's picture on it, and finally, a tiny picture frame lined in blue velvet. Against the velvet lay two locks of hair, one a soft brown belonging to me when I was a little girl, the other a corn silk blonde, a tiny remnant from my sister's beautiful head. The only item I'd removed, however, was an envelope containing $300.

As we taxied down the runway, tiny droplets of rain splashed against my window. I stared at a dismal gray sky and tried to ignore the voice gnawing at my heart. Although the same voice had echoed within me for the past month, disregarding it had been easy when I was taking notes in class or typing up an article for the **Red and Black**.

Now, as I sat thousands of feet above the earth, the song of guilt held me captive. I closed my eyes in hopes of a respite from the incessant banter that had taken up residence within me. Instead, I envisioned those tiny locks of hair encased in the velvet frame. What color was the hair of my sister's unborn child, a child who would never climb a tree or ride a bike or throw a football?

I'd never considered myself a religious person. Perhaps Christian values took like a vaccination, or maybe Cece had been correct years ago about her theory of osmosis. I'd simply absorbed these principles from being exposed to them so many times just as I'd learned the rules of the comma from sitting in Aunt Bird's English class when I was a kid.

As I wrestled with the guilt of this conspiracy, I couldn't help but wonder what Cece was feeling. Regardless of the father, this baby was half my sister, half Sinclair, half the natural beauty and creative spirit possessed by its mother. I kept remembering some words from Diddy: "Babies are God's precious gifts to us, and we take God's gifts when He gives them even if it's not convenient."

As the plane began its descent and the bright lights of the city came into view, I prayed I could change my sister's mind—or better yet, that Cece would change her mind on her own.

I was surprised to see Marcus instead of Cece at my arrival gate. "Come here, you sexy coed, and give me a hug!" He swept me up in his arms. "Oh, baby, I'm so sorry I have to be the bearer of some unexpected news," he continued in a voice struggling to free itself of emotion.

"What's wrong? Where's Cece?"

"Calm down, baby cakes." He collected my one bag and hailed the next cab. "I'll explain everything. Let's get out of this weather first!"

My stomach churned with too much anxiety to notice that what had been rain in Georgia was snow in New York. Marcus pulled a Marlboro from his pocket and lit it, patted me on the leg, and sighed. "Cece's just fine. She had a little procedure two days ago, however, and the doctor instructed her to stay off of her feet."

My heart pounded in my throat as I realized Cece hadn't waited for me to arrive. There would be no opportunity to dissuade her, no chance to remind her of the reasons I'd enumerated in my head and heart, reasons that seemed senseless now. I remarked sardonically, "So, the deed is done?"

Marcus, flicking an ash out the window, eyed me skeptically. "The deed? What deed?" His matter of factness about the entire business stung my heart. Despite my best intentions to remain stalwart, tears trickled down my cheeks. "My God, Allie, are you crying? Don't worry, honey, she's going to be all right. Women have miscarriages every day, and according to Margaret, doctors perform a simple surgical procedure so that nothing's left to infect the uterus."

I eyed him incredulously. "Cece had a miscarriage? You mean she didn't have an—an—." I could not bring myself to say the word.

Marcus finished for me. "An abortion? No, baby, she didn't do that. She started bleeding Tuesday morning. By the time Margaret got her to the emergency room, it was too late." He blew smoke circles in the cab. "Thank God for the grace of Mother Nature. I doubt she'd have gone through with the abortion anyway."

Cece had been so adamant about terminating her pregnancy when she asked for my help. Had she experienced a change of heart? Before I could ask Marcus, the taxi stopped in front of an old brick apartment building.

Cece and Margaret's apartment was on the third floor. "My God!" Marcus panted as we climbed the stairs. "Maybe one day we'll all be rich enough to afford a penthouse with an elevator."

Margaret, raincoat on and book bag across her shoulder, greeted us at the door. She gave me a quick hug. "I'm sorry I have to rush out, but my chemistry study group meets in ten minutes. Since I missed the lecture yesterday, I need to copy some notes from my lab partner." It dawned on me that Margaret had missed class to take care of my sister. "Cece's asleep right now. Wake her up in an hour for her antibiotic. And try to get her to eat something. There's soup on the stove and clean sheets if you want to make up the sofa bed."

She headed for the stairs before I had time to thank her. Two steps down, she turned and pointed a finger at Marcus. "No smoking inside the apartment! Use the fire escape landing to light up your cancer sticks," she admonished.

Marcus laid his hand across his heart. "I'll follow your instructions, Doctor Justice!"

My sister's apartment was larger than the tiny loft over Clementine's art supply store. There was a living area that spilled into a small kitchen. Each girl had her own bedroom separated by a single bathroom. The door to one of the bedrooms, obviously Margaret's, was opened. I peered inside at an unmade bed cluttered with notebooks and a huge textbook entitled *The Human Anatomy*.

The door to Cece's room was shut. I wanted to burst in and announce my arrival, but Marcus discouraged me. "She hasn't slept much since we brought her home from the hospital. We'll wake her up when it's time for her medicine."

I followed him into the kitchen where he offered me a *Coke*. "Unless you want something a little stronger, say like *Southern Comfort*?" he teased, and I realized Cece had been sharing my sins with him.

I moaned. "Damn, is nothing sacred these days?"

Marcus cackled. "Oh, honey, don't be mad! Your sister said you were such a darling little drunk. And I hear you have a boyfriend to boot! Ooh, I bet he's cute. Cece told me he was a star football player in high school. Tell me about your lover boy."

I'd forgotten how absolutely irreverent Marcus could be. "He's not my 'lover boy'!"

"You know you've let him cop a feel. I mean the poor man's in the Army. Don't send him off to war with blue balls!"

My neck reddened. "Shut up, Marcus! We've only made out once before he left for AIT training. He's supposed to be home this month before he ships out."

"Well, don't waste any time when he's home, dearie. That man needs to go into battle feeling satiated! I've got a friend in the lingerie business if you need some sexy stuff to turn your man on."

I giggled shyly as I thought of my frayed Carter's cotton bikini panties and my padded bra. "I'll think about it."

I followed him out to the fire escape landing where he lit up another Marlboro. Big, soft snowflakes fell from the sky. "Wow, it's beautiful!"

Marcus exhaled smoke into the cold air. "Yep, you know, snow is kinda like life can be. It starts off so soft and lovely, but it can turn into one frozen shit sandwich!"

"It looks like my sister took a whopping bite out of that sandwich. She's really screwed things up, hasn't she?"

Marcus flipped his cigarette into the night air and ushered me back inside. "Cut her some slack. Believe me, she doesn't deserve your punishment. She's become quite an expert at self-flagellation."

I plopped down on the tattered sofa. "Maybe she needed to suffer and do a little soul searching."

"What do you mean by that?" Marcus queried.

Marcus made the perfect confidant. He never appeared shocked or became judgmental, perhaps because he'd been judged by others his entire life. "I just expected more from my sister than her decision to kill her baby."

"And you should have," came a reply from behind me. It was Cece, clad in a soft blue robe, pale and fragile, her blue eyes brimming with tears.

We fell into each other's arms. She felt so weak, so frail as she gasped for air between sobs. "I wasn't going to do it. I'd decided I couldn't go through with it. I'm sorry I made you a part of this sordid mess. I'm so sorry, Allie. Can you ever forgive me?"

At that moment as I bolstered my sister, too weak to support herself, I wondered what would she do in my place. What had she always done? She had loved me completely and unconditionally. "Everything's going to be all right, Cece. I'm here now."

Two boxes of tissues later, my sister and I shared a bowl of tomato soup and a grilled cheese sandwich, my favorite comfort food since Miz Gertie had served it to me the day of Diddy's funeral. Marcus had slipped out long before our tears stopped.

"I guess Marcus is totally male in at least one way," Cece commented between bites of sandwich. "He can't stand to see women cry." As I watched my sister smile, the faint gnawing sensation lost its grip on my heart.

Instead of the sofa bed, I opted for a pallet on Cece's bedroom floor. If she needed anything, I'd be certain to hear her. I slept soundly, the voice of guilt vanquished.

When I awakened, I heard water running in the bathroom. Cece's bed was empty, and I assumed she was in the shower. With the morning's light peeking through the blinds, I surveyed her living quarters. Her tiny study desk held several art books, and there was a small nook at the window where she'd set up an easel. A covered canvas rested on the easel, and as I contemplated taking a peek, Cece appeared rubbing her wet hair in a towel.

The color had returned to her cheeks, and her eyes had regained their shine. She sat down on her bed and combed the tangles from her hair.

As I folded my pallet, I noticed two unopened envelopes, the telltale blue and red edges indicating airmail deliveries, resting atop Cece's Bible on her nightstand. Cece caught me as I studied Brad's military APO return address.

"They came earlier in the week, but I didn't want to read them until I'd decided what to do about the baby," she explained.

I sat down beside her. I had to know. "Last night, Cece, you told me you'd decided not to have the abortion. What made you change your mind?"

She picked up the old leather Bible with her name monogrammed on the front. "Aunt Bird gave me this for my tenth birthday. At the time, I was more interested in my new Barbie doll. It's funny; I have no clue what happened to that Barbie doll."

"I think it may have been one of those Barbies whose hair I sheared so that Josie and I could play army with them," I admitted.

"Aunt Bird worried you'd never grow out of your tomboy phase," Cece remarked as she thumbed to a verse in the Old Testament. "Something led me to this passage; I guess my guardian angel." She touched the tiny diamond star around her neck.

Then she pointed to the words: "I knew you even before you were in the womb."

Cece picked up the two unopened letters. "I guess once I made my decision, God took over." Her voice quivered. "The doctor said I might never be able to carry a baby to full term because of my diabetes. It would break Brad's heart if we couldn't have children. I guess remaining childless would be just punishment for what I almost did."

I slid my arm around her. "*Almost* did—that's just it, Cece. You made the right decision, and now you have to let go of it. What is that saying of Aunt Bird's? 'Sometimes you have to tie your regrets to a balloon and send them heavenward!' You have a life to live, a wedding to plan. Crap, I can't believe I brought that up. I've heard enough about aqua bridesmaids' dresses to last me a lifetime!"

She slapped me lightly on the back. I caught her hands in mine. "Let go of it, Cece. We'll never talk about it again, I promise."

It was time to change subjects. "What's on that canvas? Can I take a peek?"

She paused. "It's the first of a series I'm working on for a class project. I haven't shown it to anyone."

"Well, who better than your sister, and best critic I might add, to be the first to view it?" I reasoned. "Does your series have a title?"

Cece moved reluctantly toward the covered canvas, but I knew I was wearing her down. "I'm calling this one *A Georgia Summer*. It's the first of a series depicting all four seasons." She pulled the cover away, and there was Kingston Road, our little white clapboard house, the front porch swing.

I felt as though I'd stepped into Flintville, as if through some unseen dimension, I could have walked into the painting. A little girl, barefooted, freckled, and bespeckled, glided down the street on a blue bicycle.

I gulped. "Cece, it's me! It's my bike! Oh my God, did I really look like that?"

"Yep, it's when you were almost ten, the summer before we lost Diddy. It was the perfect Georgia summer, wasn't it?"

I studied the painting for a long moment. "You're right, Cece. It was the perfect Georgia summer. It was the summer before we lost our innocence."

The following week, I sent Miz Gertie a check for the $300 with a note explaining that my friend hadn't needed it after all. I knew she'd assumed I was actually the "friend," and perhaps in some ways, she was right. The entire ordeal drowned any naïveté remaining within me. I was joining the sea of adults whether I wanted to or not. I wondered if I would sink or swim.

Chapter 29

As I sipped a milkshake at the Varsity in Atlanta on a Friday afternoon, I trembled with second thoughts. While I'd toiled over winter quarter exams, Dave arrived in Flintville. He'd be in town for a week before shipping out for a year-long tour in Vietnam. Our plan was to meet at the Varsity and drive to the nearby *Holiday Inn* for our furtive rendezvous.

While patrons carrying trays of chili dogs and onion rings floated by, I wondered if my life was about to change forever. I tugged at the strap of my French bra, compliments of Marcus, who'd tucked a small package in my bag before I left New York two weeks ago.

"Now, darling, don't get upset with me," he'd explained as he hugged me goodbye. "I found the perfect lingerie for your 'coming out' party with your soldier boy. When he sees you in this, he'll have a boner for a month!"

I'd felt my ears coloring in embarrassment. "Oh Marcus! You don't even know my sizes."

He'd grinned with assurance. "Size 5 in bikini panties and a 34B bra! Honey, I can read a woman's bust size like an architect reads blueprints. This French bra will lift those tiny 'ta-tas' of yours and spill them out into a cleavage you never knew existed."

I'd turned crimson again. "Marcus, I don't know whether to thank you or slap you!" He'd smirked as he dragged on his ever-present Marlboro.

Now, my stomach churned as I thought of the mint green lace bikinis and matching French bra hidden beneath my short denim skirt and tie-dyed t-shirt. I'd managed to shave my legs without a single nick and, remembering Cece's old advice, applied just a tad of my *Tojours Moi* perfume to every pulse point on my body.

Just as I took a stealthy sniff of my wrist to see if the scent was still working, I saw Dave enter the room. He was clad in his military uniform, and my heart beat so loud I could hear it.

He smiled easily when he saw me, but I coaxed myself to stay seated and allow him to approach me. Once he was in reach, I jumped up and encircled his neck with my arms.

He smelled like *Jade East* cologne as he pulled me to his chest. "My Allie Cat," he whispered in my hair. "God, I've dreamed about staring into those sea green eyes!"

We stayed wrapped in an embrace until we felt the eyes of fellow diners upon us. Dave cleared his throat. "I think we'd better get out of here!"

My knees weak, I put my hand in Dave's. "Lead the way, soldier!"

The cool March air brought us to our senses as we stumbled through the parking lot. "Your car or mine?" I queried as Dave kept his arm tightly around my waist.

"It'll have to be your car," he admitted in a dispirited tone. "I got here in a taxi."

Dave pinned me against the hood of the Studebaker and kissed me until neither of us had any air left in our lungs. "Hold on, cowboy!" I playfully pushed him away. "We've got all night!" The frown on his face and pain in his eyes took my breath for a moment. "What's wrong, Dave?"

He held my face, hands trembling. "Allie, we don't have all night. As a matter of fact, we don't even have an hour."

My heart did a belly flop. "What do you mean, Dave?"

He pulled my face to his chest. "I got a call from my platoon sergeant about an hour before I left Flintville. They're desperate for medics, and my orders have been changed to travel with an advance crew. I've got less than thirty minutes to get back to the airport."

My knees grew so weak that I was glad Dave had hold of me. My throat burned as I tried to hold back my tears. "But what about our night together?"

He ran his fingers through my hair as he held me close. "I'll dream of it until I'm home, Allie."

By the time we made it to Dave's departure gate, passengers were already boarding. We waited until final call before disentangling from our embrace. "I know we haven't made any kind of commitment, Allie. That wouldn't be fair to you while I'm thousands of miles away."

I would have been willing to make any promise his heart desired, but he stopped me when I began to speak. "Don't obligate yourself to anything, Allie. Just write me often so I can know what life is like in the real world."

"I'll write you every day," I promised as I choked back tears, "as long as you promise to come home."

He cupped my face in his hands. "Let me have one last look at those green eyes of yours. I think I'm in love with you, Allie Cat."

Before I had enough sense to respond, Dave kissed me on my forehead, picked up his duffel bag, and headed toward the plane, never once turning around.

It was dark when I pulled into my dorm's parking lot. Thank God, Teresa had already left for the weekend. I should have driven straight to Flintville, but I couldn't stand having to make small talk with Aunt Bird and Uncle Hoyt. I'd drive home tomorrow.

With the utmost care, I used some liquid detergent along with the last drops of my perfume to wash out my lingerie and hang it over the radiator to dry. The dripping "pitter patter" of drops from my unseen undies made perfect harmony with my own tears.

For the next nine months, I devoted most of my free time to letter writing. As promised, I mailed a letter a day to Dave, trying to keep the conversation upbeat. I filled pages of airmail stationery with every statistic about Saturday's football game, and complained I knew more about the Bulldog's defense than that chauvinistic Mason Sorrells, who relegated me to covering the women's swim team for the **Red and Black**.

"When 'Mason the asshole' graduates in June, I'll battle for the right to cover football next season," I wrote.

Dave's letters arrived sporadically. Sometimes, I'd dejectedly discover an empty mailbox while on other days, two or three airmail envelopes awaited me. I'd arrange them in order of the date written before devouring every word. Dave wrote about Vietnam's weather, the difficult language, his platoon buddies, and his sergeant. "He's a black dude, but he has the coldest, bluest eyes I've ever seen. His eyes could drill a hole through a person. This is his third tour of duty over here; I guess that's why he has such a mean stare, kinda like he's seen everything evil there is to see."

Dave's description of his sergeant was the closest he ever came to writing about the war itself. I sometimes wondered if he used his letters to escape the gruesome reality of what he faced every day. Other times I thought Dave wanted to protect me from the horror, the death. His attempt to shield me from the truth was futile since the evening news offered a daily body count.

I also corresponded with Cece. Her responses, always cheerful, gave me hope that she'd conquered her demons. Like Dave, Cece chose not to talk about the body count or the war itself. Instead, she kept her vision on the future—upcoming bridal showers, a honeymoon in Bermuda, the promise of Brad's next military assignment being a location where Cece could accompany him.

My sister battled the loneliness of their separation by diving into her art. Her two paintings *A Georgia Summer* and *A Georgia Autumn* won all kinds of awards at NYU. Her professor even offered hope that a gallery would sponsor her first exhibition.

For my birthday, Cece sent me a framed sketch of the first painting from the series, the one of me on my bicycle. It hung over my dorm room desk. On gloomy, desolate days, I'd study the little girl as she pedaled down the road, the wind billowing her shirt. I could lose myself in a time when life had been so simple, so innocent, so unencumbered with worry or sorrow or regret. If I stared at the sketch long enough, I could almost hear the murmur of the gentle wind, a wind carrying Diddy's voice whispering the same promise: "Everything's going to be all right."

Christmas came early for Cece when Captain Bradley Hamilton Royal appeared at her front door with December's first snow. Brad sported the bars of his recent combat promotion as well as new orders. He and Cece would report to the Philippines the first of February.

The blissful couple flew home to be feted as the guests of honor at a whirlwind of parties, all moved up to accommodate their rescheduled wedding plans. While Aunt Bird fretted over moving a June wedding to January, Cece suggested they have a small affair in New York. Brad made a few phone calls, and before Aunt Bird dissolved into a complete conniption, the cadet chapel at West Point was reserved for the second Saturday in January.

It was a glorious January day. Snow fell early that morning, thankfully after the out-of-town guests had arrived. Besides Aunt Bird, Uncle Hoyt, and me, Brad's father and Margaret's parents flew up for the event. There were also a dozen or so of Cece's New York friends and one of her graduate professors sprinkled among Brad's uniformed military buddies. Noticeably absent was Cece's dear, queer friend Marcus Owens. The day before, he'd made last-minute fitting nips and tucks to my bridesmaid's dress, a soft satin in deep aqua.

Although I'd begged him to come, Marcus wouldn't budge. "Honey, I'd just turn too many heads and spoil Cece's special day," he'd explained through teeth holding a half-dozen straight pins.

A winter sun glistened across the Hudson River as Uncle Hoyt and Aunt Bird sang a harmonious rendition of the Carpenters' "We've Only Just Begun." Uncle Hoyt then escorted my aunt to her special seat and returned to the back of the church where Cece and I were waiting. He beamed with pride to serve, at Cece's request, as her "father of the bride."

Sliding Cece's arm in his, Uncle Hoyt whispered, "I hope I'll do your daddy proud." Cece, our mama's wedding gown adorning her gloriously, squeezed Uncle Hoyt's hand and kissed him on the cheek.

Without an inkling of second thoughts or last minute jitters, Cece appeared calmer than Uncle Hoyt or I. Mimi's alterations had transformed Mama's dress into a perfect fit for my sister. A wreath of tiny, pink sweetheart roses adorned her head. Her corn silk golden hair hung softly around her creamy, bare shoulders just the way Brad liked it.

Making my way down the aisle, I studied my soon to be brother-in-law, standing proudly next to his best man, his roommate from West Point. I'd noticed some subtle changes in Brad since he'd come home from war.

His cocky demeanor had evolved into a quiet self-assurance that suited him. I noticed the slightest hint of graying around his temples and some new lines in his face, which gave him a sensitive maturity, a confident manliness. His serious countenance sprang into a joyous grin when Cece made her way down the aisle.

As Cece and Brad repeated their vows, a sense of peace and certainty filled my heart. Their year apart seemed to solidify their commitment, a commitment I finally understood and appreciated.

Tomorrow the newlyweds left for a week in Bermuda. Then they'd return to New York where Cece would pack up her belongings and move to the Philippines. The final two unfinished canvases from Cece's *Seasons of Georgia* series were crated in storage.

Uncle Hoyt offered the first toast at the reception. "To Brad and Cece, may you always be one another's best friend, may you build your commitment on Christ the Solid Rock, and may you be blessed with many little Royals for Bird and me to spoil!"

There was no toast from the groom's father, who was conspicuously missing from the circle of well-wishers. Earlier I'd observed him smiling at a young female server as she offered him a glass of champagne and wondered if he'd cornered the poor girl as he'd done Donna Sims in my aunt's kitchen months earlier.

By the time the newlyweds danced to "Blue Velvet" and prepared to cut the wedding cake, Mr. Royal reemerged from the direction of the men's rooms. Maybe he had the shits, I hoped.

Aunt Bird and I accompanied Cece to the bride's room where she changed into a gorgeous two-piece Jackie Kennedy style suit in sapphire blue, the color of her eyes. The cashmere outfit was a wedding gift from Marcus, who had designed it himself.

While Cece brushed her hair, Aunt Bird laid a small package on the dressing table. "A little something you can tuck in your suitcase when you and Brad head for the Philippines."

"Oh, Aunt Bird! You and Uncle Hoyt have already done so much for us!" Cece protested as she pulled the pink ribbons from the tiny white package. Inside lay a small, silver two-sided frame. One side of the frame was pictureless, but the other side had a small copy of Mama and Diddy's wedding photograph.

"Once you get your own wedding pictures back, you can see you and your mama side by side in that same dress. When you walked down that aisle today, I thought I was seeing your mama again. You're just as beautiful as she was," Aunt Bird choked back tears. "Now, I'm going to leave you two alone to say your goodbyes."

I attempted some humor. "Two years?" I began. "By the time you're back, the Bulldogs will have a national championship, and I'll be covering college football for *Sports Illustrated*!"

Cece's tear-filled blue eyes started my own waterworks.

Tears spilled on my lovely aqua bridesmaid's dress. "Crap! Marcus will kill me if I spot this satin. Plus, I'm ruining my mascara!" I grabbed a tissue from the dressing table and blew my nose.

Cece pulled me close to her. I held on tightly and breathed her in. I wanted to remember everything about my big sister. Today, I was little "baby brat" once again, and she was the sister I worshipped and adored.

My cheek brushed against the chain on her neck, and I looked up questioningly. "You're still wearing your star of flint, aren't you?"

She smiled as she wiped the tears from my cheek. "Just because I'm married doesn't mean I'm no longer your sister." She pulled the chain out from beneath her suit jacket. "We'll always be Sinclairs first, no matter what. I promise, Allie."

I smiled lamely. "I know, Cece, I know. They have stars in the Philippines, too, or so I hear."

Within the hour, Cece and Brad were swept away to the airport and their tropical honeymoon. Within twenty-four hours, I sat at my study desk finishing the last few pages of John Milton for my British lit test.

Instead of concentrating, I found myself studying Cece's sketch of the little girl on the bicycle. In my mind's eye, I caught a glimpse of Cece when she was about fifteen, sitting on the front porch of the house in the sketch. She was painting her toenails in some luscious Cutex shade.

When I awakened, daylight peeked through the shades. My neck was stiff, my head throbbed, and I had drooled all over the last two pages of *Paradise Lost*.

Weeks later, I returned to the dorm around midnight after a grueling evening in the library. Teresa sat straight up. "Call your aunt. She's called twice; she said to return her call no matter how late…"

I was at the pay phones before Teresa finished. Aunt Bird picked up on the first ring.

"What is it? Has something happened to Cece? Please tell me she's okay," not even giving my aunt an opportunity to respond.

"Hold on, sweet baby, Cece's okay. It's not that, but Allie honey, it is bad news. Dave's mama called, and…"

"No! No! No!" I wailed. I felt that horrible sinking sensation like my head was underwater and I couldn't come up for air.

Shirley Crews, the hall's resident advisor, rushed out of her room. "Allie, what's wrong?" She grabbed me as my knees buckled and the receiver fell from my hand. She took the phone and spoke to Aunt Bird. "Yes ma'am, I can tell her that. Yes, she'll call back as soon as she calms down."

Shirley placed the receiver in its cradle. "Your aunt said to tell you it's not Dave. It's Teddy. She said you'd understand."

Dear, sweet, lovable Teddy Gaddis. He'd played football in my front yard. He'd given me my first kiss. He'd flirted with everything in a skirt, including my big sister. I thought of his lopsided grin and the way he could snow a girl into believing she was his one and only.

The whack of a rifle as the honor guard began its salute snatched the precious image from me. Josie, standing beside me at the graveside service, squeezed my hand with each report of the rifle. Behind us stood Stu Sims and Ty Hastings, still stunned and heartbroken. The entire *B&B Brigade* had come home for the funeral of Corporal Theodore Gaddis.

Even Sergeant David Banks had returned from the jungles of Vietnam. When Teddy's parents learned of his death, Mr. Gaddis remembered a letter in which Teddy requested that if he was killed, David should accompany his body home.

Teddy's request took some finagling as well as some calls from Congressman Jack Flynt, who grew up in Griffin with Coach Brewster. David, wearing his dress greens, sat with Teddy's family in chairs under a tent. He'd arrived with the body just yesterday. When the honor guard handed Mrs. Gaddis a folded flag from Teddy's casket, I saw the poor woman's shoulders crumple. Dave helped her back to the limousine while the crowd of mourners began to break up.

Dave made his way toward me and our closely-knit group, one less now. His progress was impeded by members of the current Flintville Raider football team, many of whom had played with Teddy. Several Flintville cheerleaders also gathered around Dave. I recognized Lindy McMichael, the pretty freshman redhead Dave briefly dated our senior year. It dawned on me that Lindy would soon finish her junior year at Flintville High.

When he finally reached us, the guys shook hands silently. As Dave and I embraced, I sobbed against his shoulder. When I looked up, his eyes seemed vacant, as cold as stone.

"Let's get out of here. I have to be back at the airport before daybreak tomorrow." He walked to my Studebaker and climbed in beside me. Josie, Stu, and Ty followed in her Volkswagen. Dave issued a request. "Let's drive out to the river. There's something I gotta do."

We rode in silence. When I reached Old River Road, I instinctively headed toward Ty's cabin. Ty was out of Josie's car first. He unlocked the cabin and went straight to his uncle's stash, a full bottle of *Jim Beam.*

The five of us walked out on the dock. Dave became talkative. "All through basic training, Teddy talked about coming back to Flintville one day and developing this river property." He laughed. "I asked him if he planned to put a whore house out here!"

His humor relaxed us. "At least Teddy got his share of snatch before he left this earth!" Stu mused.

"I bet all the loose women in three counties will be without any for months!" Ty added.

Josie exploded. "Shut up! Our best friend is dead, and all you can talk about is how much pussy he got! That's disgusting!"

All three guys turned surprised gazes towards Josie. "Geez, Josie! I can't believe a little Southern belle like yourself would utter the 'p' word in mixed company," Stu kidded and handed her his handkerchief to blow her nose.

"Teddy did do more than chase skirt!" I interjected. "I always wanted him on my team when we played touch football. He could outrun the rest of ya'll."

"He was a helluva running back." Ty fiddled with the seal on the whiskey bottle. "Coach Brewster used to say if you needed someone to run straight up the middle, send in Gaddis. He'd charge like a bull!"

Ty twisted the cap off the pilfered bottle, raised it high in the air, and announced, "Here's to Teddy Gaddis, a cockhound, a hustler, a Raider, a fine friend!" He drank from the bottle and handed it to Stu.

We passed the bottle around our precious circle, a circle grown smaller in such a short time. As the sun sank behind the bluff, our grief-stricken "brigade" bid farewell to our fallen brother.

With twilight approaching, Josie offered Stu and Ty a ride into town. I stayed behind with Dave, who sat with his feet dangling over the water. I could tell he didn't want to talk, so we sat side by side and listened to the frogs begin their evening song.

"He was less than ninety kilometers from me when he stepped on the land mine," Dave began in a soft voice. "They said he bled to death before they reached the helicopter. If I'd been there, maybe I could have saved him."

I saw the tears gather in the corner of Dave's eyes. His face, drawn and thin, seemed too worn for someone barely twenty. I wondered what horrors he'd seen in the past months. I put my hand in his and waited for him to continue.

"When we were in fourth grade, I got my first pair of glasses, and the lenses were thick as the bottom of a *Coca Cola* bottle. Do you remember Buddy Harlowe? He was such an obnoxious fat ass. As soon as I walked into class, Buddy started in on me. He called me 'four eyes' and 'Mr. Magoo' over and over. I ignored him, but Teddy finally had enough. At recess, Teddy bet his prized cat's eye marble against anybody who thought they were man enough to win it. You remember that big oak on the corner of the playground where all the boys would shoot marbles?"

I nodded. "Yeah, it was strictly off limits to us girls. What did ya'll do out there?" There were rumors that boys peed behind the tree, which served as a screen from teachers and tattletales.

"You'd be surprised. When fat Buddy got on his all fours to take his shot, Teddy jumped on his back and rode him like a bucking bronco. A couple of good kicks in Buddy's ribs, and Teddy had him splayed out in the dirt like a busted watermelon. Teddy got Buddy in a headlock and had him whimpering. When I pulled Teddy off, I heard him whisper into Buddy's ear, 'You make fun of my best friend's glasses one more time, and you won't have any eyes at all. You hear me, you big blubbering baby?' Buddy limped away and never said another word to me."

Dave wiped the tears from his face as I pretended not to notice. "After that, Teddy and I were inseparable. No matter what, we had each other's back. Teddy didn't need me too much. If he couldn't fight his way out of a situation, he'd talk his way out of it." Dave chugged the final bit of *Jim Beam*. "The one time he needed me, I wasn't there to help him. Damn, how screwed up is that?"

There was absolutely nothing I could say to make Dave feel better, so I just listened. "And you know what's weird? Even though he's gone, Teddy's still looking after me."

"What do you mean, Dave? Like a guardian angel?"

He stood and pulled me up beside him. "You might say that. I got a call from my C.O. this morning before the funeral. They're not shipping me back to Nam."

For the first time all day, a cloud lifted inside me. "Thank God! But what did Teddy have to do with it?"

"The Army's doing some research on better treatments for the wounded in the field. They want a medic with recent experience in Nam, and I'm their man. I head for Washington, D.C. tomorrow. I'll spend the rest of my tour at Walter Reed Army Hospital."

Dave pulled a set of dog tags from his pocket. He rubbed them between his fingers. "Teddy loved this river. He'd always dreamed of building out here." He looked down at Teddy's dog tags. "Thanks for saving my ass one last time, buddy. I'll see you on the other side someday." He tossed the tags into the dark water.

Dave had promised to stop by and see Teddy's parents before leaving for the airport, so I dropped him off at the Gaddis house. He pulled me to him and held me tightly. "Our day will come soon, Allie Cat. I promise." He handed me a copy of his new address in D.C. "Don't stop writing, okay?"

I held back my tears. There'd been enough sorrow for one day. He kissed me on the cheek, and then he was gone. I watched him straighten his tie, square his shoulders, and walk up the drive to Teddy's front door.

As dogwoods budded and azaleas burst into color across campus, I felt renewed in spirit. With just weeks before Dave would be home, I grew hopeful that love would finally blossom.

I continued my letter campaign to Dave including every detail of my life— what I wore to class, how disgusting the cafeteria food was, which of my professors challenged me and which bored me beyond tears. I also included a few intimate details. In one particularly erotic passage, I described my mint green lingerie, still waiting amidst scented tissue in a box on my tiny closet shelf.

Dave's correspondence, however, grew more sporadic with each week. When I'd receive a letter, it was filled with his excitement over the new "trauma techniques" the Army was studying. "Before long there'll be trauma units in every hospital in the United States, even trauma ambulances to treat victims at accident scenes," he explained.

Although he rarely wrote about our future together, I was happy he was moving forward. As weeks fell away, fond and funny memories of Teddy replaced his longing for what could never be.

In late April, the tone of David's letters changed. He seemed more distant, more remote than ever. I rationalized that he had jitters about returning to civilian life until one letter put things in perspective for me. His final paragraph hit like a heart punch:

> *Allie,*
> *I'm glad we never made a serious commitment to one another. I hope you're dating other people because I need to "play the field" a while when I return to the real world. Let's just plan to take things slow and easy at first. Don't you agree?*

I spent my laundry quarters on a long distance call to Josie. "Relax, Allie! Don't read something into his words that's not really there. Remember, he signed away his life to the Army for two years. Maybe he's wary of another commitment right away. Wait 'til he gets you in bed for the first time. All that big talk and resolve will melt away."

I prayed Josie knew what she was talking about, and in my next letter I tried to sound as though I agreed with Dave.

You're right, Dave. Promises are hard to keep when two people are living on separate continents or even in separate states, for that matter. We'll take things one day at a time when you get home.
See ya soon,
Allie

One day at the **Red and Black**, Mason asked if I'd cover the men's tennis team. When I jumped at the opportunity, he replied, "Actually, you'll follow one player, Harrison Dix. They think he's Wimbledon material. We'll do a series of feature articles, 'A day in the life of a tennis champion,' that kind of thing."

Mason refrained from sharing that this tennis champion was one pompous prick. I showed up to watch practice and spent some time with a team trainer checking for dead tennis balls in a metal ball basket. "What can you tell me about Harry, um, Harrison Dix?" I asked casually.

The trainer eyed me suspiciously. "If you're one of Harrison's groupies, the coach banned them from watching practice. It messes up Harrison's concentration."

"No," I held up my staff badge in defense, "I'm here to write a feature series on him. Is it Harrison or Harry, anyway?"

The trainer smirked. "Don't refer to him as 'Harry' or he'll go ape shit on you."

"I see." What parents in their right minds would plague their son with a name like Harry Dix, I wondered.

At that moment, Harrison Dix, UGA's hopes for a Wimbledon contender, growled up at the trainer. "Randy, get me some more damn water. Can't you see I'm dying out here? And some more dry towels." Then Harrison returned to his volley practice with another player.

I followed Randy to the water cooler, "What can you tell me about UGA's newest champion?"

"He's a champion asshole," he muttered. "But don't quote me on that. I need this job," he added. "Sorry, I have to get some towels from the locker room," and he vanished.

Needing ammunition before a face off with Harrison, I decided to do a little research. Through some news articles in the library, I learned he'd grown up in Buckhead, a posh neighborhood for the wealthiest of the wealthy in Atlanta. His father owned Dix Realty, which sold the wealthy their mansions in Buckhead. Harrison's mother was an Atlanta debutante in the 1950's; her maiden name was Harrison, and her father and grandfather had been in the construction business.

Young Harrison was probably a disappointment to his father and grandfather, who'd both attended Ivy League colleges. He graduated with a marginal grade point average from Lovett, one of Atlanta's most exclusive private schools. His athletic ability, however, had earned him a UGA scholarship on the tennis team. It was a shame some spoiled, wealthy kid was using up one of our scholarships. I bet poor Randy the trainer could have benefited from that money.

Teresa caught me reading a society page article from an old Sunday edition of the Atlanta paper. "Aren't you a little behind in your reading, girl? And since when did you give a rat's behind about Atlanta society?" Teresa, over the course of two years, had grown on me.

"Just doing some research. You ever heard of Harrison Dix, the tennis star?"

"Have I ever! He went out with Suzanne Talbot for about a week until he got into her britches. Then he dropped her."

"Hmm, interesting." I decided to watch my step with Harrison Dix.

My first interview took place after Harrison waxed his Tech opponent in an easy two set singles match. He was barely sweating as he swaggered by the bleachers where his adoring groupies giggled and clapped.

I caught up with him in front of the locker room. "Excuse me, Harrison? I'm Allison Sinclair from the **Red and Black**." I pointed to my staff badge.

He smiled leeringly. "I know who you are. I've seen you watching me at practice. So, you want an interview?" He leaned in towards my face, "It's gonna cost you, sweetheart," and then he winked at me.

I took one step backwards and held my ground. "I'm sorry to inform you, Mr. Dix, but the **Red and Black** does not pay for interviews. I'll see if I can get the information I need from Coach Bailey." I turned on my heels to leave.

He laughed uncomfortably. "I'm just kidding. How about tomorrow after practice? I'll meet you in the bleachers where I saw you last week. Weren't you wearing a green t-shirt and white hip huggers?"

"My, you're observant," I quipped. "Maybe you should give up tennis for journalism. I'll be here." I took off before he could respond.

One May morning, I dragged myself back to the dorm after my final chemistry lab. I'd pulled an all-nighter to prepare for it. I checked my mailbox—empty once again. I hadn't heard from Dave in a week.

I shed my clothes and threw on my favorite old t-shirt. Pulling the blinds tight to shut out the sun, I crawled under my covers and set my alarm clock for 1:30. Maybe the mail hadn't come yet, I consoled myself as I drifted off to sleep.

Seconds later, the intercom box in my room squawked my name. "Allison Sinclair, are you there? Allison, you have a visitor."

"Okay! Okay! I'll be there in a minute!" I groaned as I checked my alarm clock. It wasn't quite noon. Who the hell would bother me in the middle of the day?

I grabbed my glasses instead of putting my contacts back in my tired eyes. I wriggled into a pair of cutoffs spilling out of my dirty clothes bag and stumbled down the hall.

Sandra Armstrong was manning the check-in desk. "It's some guy I didn't recognize. He said he'd wait out front in the sun."

Some guy she didn't recognize? I dashed to the front door. Dave was standing under one of the huge oak trees with his back to me. He had on yellow Bermuda shorts, a plaid shirt, and Weejuns. He looked like he was eighteen and here to take me to a dance at Parker's Pool.

"Crap!" I thought. "Look at yourself, Allie. You're an absolute mess!" I reversed my steps. Maybe I could rush back upstairs and put on my contact lens, but it was too late. He turned around, caught sight of me, and rushed up the stairs.

The next moment he was swinging me in the air, just like all the times he'd swung me over his head after Flintville football games. When he set me down, my heart was racing wildly. "I guess this forgives you for not writing me in a week."

"Yeah," he grinned slyly. "I wanted to surprise you." He looked good. He'd put on some much needed weight. His hair was longer, and his relaxed, confident demeanor had returned.

Dave waited in the lobby while I rushed back to my room. I quickly brushed my hair, popped in my contacts, and took a fast "whore bath" of mouthwash, deodorant, and perfume. I changed into my white hip huggers and a tie-dyed shirt and smeared on some lipstick.

Thirty minutes later we were having burgers at *The Grill* downtown. Dave explained that he'd been in Flintville since Monday.

I pretended to be indignant. "You've been back for four days and are just getting around to seeing me?"

Dave seemed embarrassed. "I'm sorry, Allie. I had some other people to see first like family and..." He fiddled with the saltshaker. He couldn't look me in the eye.

My stomach turned to jelly. "And?" I mouthed almost inaudibly.

Dave looked at me with tender eyes. "Allie, I didn't want to tell you in a letter. I couldn't do that to you. Remember Lindy McMichael?"

The pretty little freshman cheerleader, who was all grown up now. I nodded as I fought back the tears.

"That night after you dropped me off at Teddy's house... Well, Lindy's mom and Mrs. Gaddis are good friends. Lindy and Mrs. McMichael were putting food away in the kitchen. When they offered me a plate, I accepted."

I could imagine her long red hair and big brown eyes and her petite, athletic figure.

"Anyway," David continued. "We talked. She asked if she could write me while I was at Walter Reed. She's really matured since I dated her in high school." He smiled to himself. "I stopped going out with her because she was too young. But that night in Teddy's kitchen, I realized I'd never gotten over her."

I will not cry, I will not cry. There was no way I'd allow Dave to pity me. Somehow, I found my voice. "That's great, Dave! I've been thinking about us anyway. I mean, we've been friends for so long; I couldn't really picture us as a couple," I lied with my best theatrics. "Besides, you kept the only promise you made to me. You came home safely."

I saw relief in his eyes as he took my hand in his. "I knew you'd understand, Allie. I'll always love you as a dear friend, Allie Cat; you know that."

We said goodbye in the lobby of my dorm. He hugged me tightly. "Take care of yourself, Allie." I watched as my knight in shining armor drove off into the sunset without me.

For the next twenty-four hours, I stayed in bed except for an occasional trip to the bathroom and once to buy a *Coke* from the vending machine. I'd rummaged through Teresa's records until I found Janis Joplin's "Piece of My Heart," which I played over and over.

Late Saturday afternoon, Shirley Crews knocked on my door. "Allie, you have a phone call." When I dragged myself to the door, Shirley was waiting on me. "And Allie, people are complaining about that music. Give Janis a break for a while, will you?"

I made my way to the pay phones. "Hello?" I said in a despondent tone.

It was Josie. "I'm in Flintville for Daddy's birthday. I ran into Dave on the square a little while ago. Allie? Allie, say something!"

When my answer was a woeful sob, Josie proceeded to call Dave every profane word in the English language. She ended with, "I'd like to wring the sonnabitch's neck!"

The image of Josie's skinny fingers throttling Dave's muscular neck tickled me. "He'd swat you down like a mosquito!"

"Not if I kicked him in the nuts first!" she insisted and then burst into tears herself. "Oh Allie, I'm so sorry. Is there anything I can do?"

She didn't realize she'd already done exactly what I needed. My dear, sweet Josie.

Before we hung up, she offered one word of advice: "You need to wash that man right out of your hair, you hear me!"

Sunday morning I decided to take Josie's advice. I crawled out of bed to take a shower and wash my greasy hair. Retrieving the one clean towel from my closet's shelf, my hand brushed against the box holding my unseen, unappreciated lingerie. The sight of the lacy bikinis and the provocative French bra inspired me.

I headed to the shower dressed in my fancy underwear and carrying my trashcan. I threw a lit match in the can, stuffed with every letter I'd received from Dave in the past two years. Still wearing my panties and bra, I climbed into the shower. I shed the two items in a sort of private striptease act and tossed them into the flaming trashcan. The thin, airmail paper blazed quickly. I watched as my beautiful lingerie shriveled and curled in the fire.

After final exams, I helped Teresa pack up our room. Since I didn't start my summer job at the **Star** for a week, I saw no rush in returning home where I'd risk running into Dave. With our last few dollars, Teresa and I splurged on a farewell supper at *Allen's*, a local burger and beer joint.

Allen's, usually overrun with frat boys, was unusually quiet. A couple of guys in Kappa Sigma jerseys competed for highest score on a pinball machine while their brothers fought over the last of a pitcher of beer.

As I studied the dessert choices, Teresa, eyebrows raised, turned her attention to the front door. "Crap, Allie! You'll never guess who just strutted in."

More interested in a hot fudge cake than a riddle, I barely acknowledged her. "Oh my Lord, be cool, honey. He's coming over here!" Teresa tucked her head back in her menu.

When I looked up, Harrison Dix stood over our table. He wore a white polo-style shirt and white tennis shorts. I wondered if he owned any other clothes. His shorts accentuated his tan, muscular legs. His brown hair, streaked blonde by the sun, was styled in a surfer's cut with long bangs swept to the side.

"**Red and Black's** star reporter—Miss Allie Sinclair in the flesh! I've missed having you as my shadow. Mind if I sit down?" He sat before I could object. "Who's your gorgeous friend?" He smiled charmingly at Teresa.

"My roommate Teresa, and we're about to pay our check, aren't we, Teresa?" I softly kicked her leg under the table.

"Didn't you want to split some dessert with me?" she smiled innocently.

"I've changed my mind." I kicked her a little harder this time. While my roommate ordered ice cream and Harrison asked for a beer, I drummed my fingers impatiently on the table.

When the waitress returned with Harrison's second beer, I asked for our check. Teresa, however, chatted on. "That frosty mug looks great. I love beer on a hot day, don't you?"

I'd never seen my roommate drink anything alcoholic. Teresa prattled on. "Now Allie here. She won't touch beer."

Harrison turned to me and winked. "Really now? I'd never suspect you to be a teetotaler!"

"Oh she's not!" Teresa interjected. "Allie likes wine when she can get it. Don't you, Allie?" I kicked her harder this time.

Harrison put his arm around me. "I happen to have a bottle of *Cold Duck* in the refrigerator at my apartment. What say you and I crack it open in celebration of your article about me? I mean if it's not unethical to fraternize with someone you've interviewed."

He smelled good. Was it *Canoe* or *English Leather* cologne? I wasn't certain, but when he grinned at me again, my brain's common sense wiring shorted out. "Sure, why not?" I heard myself saying.

After insisting on paying our check, Harrison walked Teresa to her car. "I'll be home in a while," I insisted as Teresa started the ignition.

She grinned. "I won't wait up for you!"

Shirley Crews had dorm lobby duty on Wednesdays. As she was locking the front door for the night, Shirley saw me racing up the steps and kindly waited. "What happened, Allie? Did you lose track of the time?" She held the door opened for me.

"It wasn't the time I just lost," I muttered as I trudged up three flights of stairs to my room.

Two glasses of *Cold Duck*, and I'd fallen straight into bed with Harrison Dix. There'd been no coaxing, no manipulating on his part. I was totally aware of what was happening, and I allowed it to happen.

There wasn't a single awkward moment, even when he casually reached into his nightstand drawer for a condom. And for that sweet brief moment of ecstasy, I forgot my shattered heart. I gave myself totally and completely to Harrison Dix, a real dick, who could chalk up one more conquest to his list of foolish, foolish girls.

When Teresa left on Friday, I sat at my study desk feeling as hollow as our now empty dorm room. I pulled a legal pad from the last box I had to pack in my car and wrote the whole sad business in a letter to Cece. My final paragraph recapped why 1971 was my year of hell:

> *Let's see now. In January, I lost my sister to the whim of Army orders. In February, I lost one of my best friends to a war no one seems to understand. In May, I lost the man of my dreams to a younger, prettier woman. Two nights ago, I lost my virginity to a shallow, undeserving cad. I guess there's not much else to lose.*

I made one stop before heading home. As I entered the sports department of the **Red and Black**, there sat Mason Sorrells cleaning out his desk. Freshly graduated, Mason was headed to the sports department at *The Atlanta Journal* where he'd be under the tutelage of Furman Bisher, a staple for Georgia sports enthusiasts. I figured Mr. Bisher would take Mason down a notch or two.

"Allie! I'm glad you stopped by. I'm recommending that our advisor make you co-editor of the sports page. You might even get to cover the less important football games."

There was no fight left in me this day. And in that moment, I realized I didn't give a damn about reporting sports. Crotchety old Miss Benton was right. It was time to set my goals higher.

I dumped all the junk from my desk into a nearby trashcan. "Thanks, but no thanks, Mason. I'm joining the news department next fall. I've decided sportswriting is the same ol' song, just another verse over and over. I need more challenge than reporting some jock's latest feat."

He was speechless. Just as I reached the door, I turned around. "Oh, by the way, Mason, best of luck with your future. I think sportswriting suits you perfectly."

Chapter 30

In September 1971, I loaded up the Studebaker for my sojourn back to University of Georgia. Uncle Hoyt insisted on checking my oil before I pulled out of the driveway.

"Keep her under sixty miles per hour, or she'll run hot," he reminded as he closed the hood. During the summer, he'd tinkered with every detail of the old Blue Bullet and had it running in tip-top condition.

Aunt Bird rubbed an oily smudge off his cheek. "I guess Hoyt will have to find himself another love now that you're taking away his precious automobile."

"I've already found her!" Uncle Hoyt teased as he sweetly brushed a curly tendril from my aunt's forehead. I watched them wave from the driveway until they were out of my sight. Although anxious to begin my senior year at UGA, I'd miss them. The drive to Athens provided me a chance to reflect upon the past three months.

Initially, I'd worried that spending the summer with newlyweds would fester the wound in my jilted heart. In truth, watching their longtime commitment mature into a loving marriage had a curative effect. As they bade me goodnight each evening and closed their bedroom door, I realized their love was built on devotion and sacrifice long before sex came into play.

Catching Uncle Hoyt playfully pat my aunt's behind or her steal a kiss on the back of his neck, I knew physical intimacy played a vital role in their marriage. Sex, nonetheless, was only one ingredient in a fulfilling relationship. This newfound awareness set me to wondering about David. Had we actually done the "dirty deed," would there have been anything else to share? I'd been confusing love with lust.

As summer progressed, my heart struggled to relinquish its hold on a romance that would never be. I also grappled with guilt over my foolish transgression with Harrison Dix. Only Cece knew about my tragic night of indiscretion. Cece, above all others, understood.

Dear Allie,

You write about your losses—my leaving, Teddy's death, David's rejection—as though you blame yourself. Remember that none of those events could be controlled by you.

Okay, so your final loss occurred because of a poor decision on your part. Yes, you'll have to live with that decision, one made when you were hurt and vulnerable. Are you going to be crippled by a single mistake? Not if you're still a Sinclair!

Diddy once told me that his work and his children provided the therapy he needed after Mama died. On days when I'm so homesick I can barely breathe, I pull out my easel and go to work. You can do the same. Take solace in your talent, Allie. You're a damn good writer, so dive into it and get on with your life.

Send all that sorrowful baggage straight to our stars. They'll dispense of it for you.

I Love You,
Cece

I sat on the side porch steps and took Cece's advice. As I peered at our special orbs glittering against a cloudless sky, a sense of renewal enveloped me. Cece was right; we Sinclairs had better things to do than feel sorry for ourselves.

Now rolling down the Atlanta Highway towards Athens, I patted the scrapbook of articles I'd written for the **Star** during my three month tenure. The scrapbook would serve as my introduction to the **Red and Black's** news department.

The first few weeks of summer, I'd retreated to the pressroom where the roar of the presses drowned out the sound of David's voice and the constant whisper of guilt over my encounter with Harrison. In mid-June, as I rode home with Uncle Hoyt for lunch, he grumbled about being short of help and long on news. "I could use somebody to pick up the slack, Allie, unless you intend to hide out back all summer."

By summer's end, I'd run the gamut of small town newspaper reporting. I traveled to Pine Mountain to report on the Girl Scout Jamboree. I'd climbed out of bed in the middle of the night to witness an overturned peach truck that scattered hundreds of peaches across the Crest Highway. There was an account of Miz Minnie Farnsworth, who ran her new Buick through *Charm's Beauty Shoppe* when she hit the accelerator instead of her brake. Thankfully, the shop was back in business by Aunt Bird's next appointment with Miss Thelma.

Chuck Purdy taught me to paste-up a full-page advertisement for the new *Big Star* grocery. I even tried my hand at writing obituaries. But I just couldn't get the hang of making someone like Mr. Otto Earls, a notorious drunk, appear to be "a fine, upstanding gentleman who went to his everlasting rest after many good years on earth." The obits seemed to be the one newspaper section that offered less than the truth.

Despite my journalistic success at the **Flintville Star** and the loving attention of Aunt Bird and Uncle Hoyt, my summer had been a solitary one with Cece so far away and Josie in LaGrange for summer school. I was looking forward to seeing Teresa, who'd written to announce her engagement to her bucktoothed boyfriend.

As I toted the last box into my dorm room, Teresa appeared sporting a marquis diamond on her ring finger. "Isn't it gorgeous, Allie?!" Feigning excitement, I silently prayed she wouldn't ask me to be a bridesmaid.

In its waning months, 1971 redeemed itself somewhat. My beloved Georgia Bulldogs racked up a stellar season. Their one loss to Auburn spoiled our perfect record, but it didn't matter when the Dawgs went on to defeat North Carolina in the Gator Bowl.

Sharing football season with Uncle Hoyt softened the emptiness of Thanksgiving and Christmas without Cece. Nevertheless, my sister sent us authentic Filipino Christmas gifts.

Uncle Hoyt and I received yo-yos with an historic account of how the toy had been invented by Filipino hunters in the sixteenth century. Aunt Bird's package contained linen Christmas napkins, hand-embroidered by a Filipino artist my sister had befriended.

Our best gifts, original artwork by my sister, arrived in special freight two days before Christmas. Uncle Hoyt had a framed ink drawing of a Jeepney, the Filipino version of a World War II Army jeep. Aunt Bird's lifelike watercolor depicted a classroom filled with precious Filipino children with dark, shining eyes.

My gift was an almost surreal watercolor of Christmas lanterns lining a city street in San Fernanda, Pampanga. "I hope it will light the way for you, Allie," Cece wrote, "but if the lanterns are not enough, note the night's sky."

Even though the lanterns blazed in brilliant glory, Cece had managed to include a starry night sky. As I located our special Sinclair stars, Christmas felt complete.

By late winter, Cece and Brad were making plans to return to the states. My sister wrote that they'd be home by March, and Brad would have a month's leave before his next orders began. Cece was praying he'd land a teaching stint at West Point so she'd be close enough to NYU to complete her graduate studies.

In mid-January, cold, hungry, and exhausted, I trudged back from the **Red and Black** to my room. Teresa huddled over the latest issue of **Brides** magazine.

"Your aunt just called. She said she'd be up until 11:00." She tacked another bridal gown choice to her bulletin board.

"Oh crap, I forgot to call her again!" For the past two weeks, I'd been absorbed in a story for the paper. Last week I'd covered a "peace sit-in" war protest held underneath the school's famous arch, where a thousand protestors sat for ten hours despite the freezing temperatures.

Joe Riley, our news editor, had been impressed with my coverage. "This is good stuff, Allie. You really remain neutral and give an honest picture of what was happening."

I didn't tell Joe my neutrality resulted from a conflicted heart. How could I champion peaceniks when my dear Teddy gave his life for the very cause they were protesting? Yes, the day had been cold, and the protestors suffered some discomfort, but then they returned to warm, safe dormitories without fear of stepping on a land mine.

I convinced Joe that a second story from the viewpoint of a newly returned veteran would show our impartiality. When he gave me the green light, I found several veterans attending UGA on the G.I. Bill, but only one, a young man named Bobby Tilton, was willing to discuss his experiences in Nam. He told me about how someone spat on him outside the San Francisco airport when he returned to the States and how bitter he felt after serving his country and coming home to watch "pampered, self-serving coeds prance around with peace signs when they had not a clue what sacrifice meant." So wrapped up in the article, I'd totally forgotten my weekly call home.

Aunt Bird picked up on the first ring. "She's coming home! Cece's coming home!" she sang out before I had to apologize for not calling.

Although Brad would stay behind until March, Cece had an opportunity to head back early. While I believed the days would drag interminably as we awaited Cece's arrival, I was too busy to notice.

Shortly after my second story entitled "The Other View" came out, the **Athens Daily News** picked it up. Then an editor from *The Atlanta Journal* requested permission and offered a small fee to print my piece. The "small fee" turned out to be the equivalent of my entire allowance for winter quarter.

Before the New Year barely had time to blink, my little world underwent a complete turnaround. In just two weeks' time, I'd become an authentic journalist, and soon I'd have my sister home to celebrate with me. Life was good.

Nothing could've prepared me for the storm about to break.

Chapter 31

The following Friday, I submitted my final research project, cut all my classes, fired up the Studebaker, and headed for Flintville. I'd barely pulled in the driveway before Cece bolted out the back door and had me in a bear hug. She wore a pair of faded blue jeans with an old NYU sweatshirt, and her hair, pulled away from her freshly washed face, flowed like an unleashed skein of silk halfway down her back. "I couldn't find anybody to cut it right over there," she explained. "But I've already made an appointment with Miss Thelma to get rid of this stringy mess." I marveled at the easiness of her beauty.

As we sat around the kitchen table and enjoyed Aunt Bird's homemade pecan pie that night, I felt the years melt away. Cece, sporting a ponytail and the barest of makeup, could've been in high school again. She wasn't really married nor was I about to graduate from college. I looked at the head of the table and spied Diddy stirring his coffee...no, that wasn't Diddy; it was Uncle Hoyt.

"Allie? Did you hear me?" Aunt Bird stood over me as she offered me a scoop of ice cream for my pie. "You always did love your ice cream, didn't you?" I wasn't the only one feeling nostalgic.

Late into the night, Cece and I sat on our twin beds sharing the highlights of our months apart. Reliving the heartbreak of Teddy's death and the disappointment of Dave's rejection offered me the catharsis I needed. Now that Cece could wrap her arms around me and share my suffering, I no longer felt alone.

"Okay, that's it!" I proclaimed as I blew my nose. "I'm putting the pathetic mess to rest," and I meant it. "Now, show me your art so I can see what this island of yours really looks like!" I pointed to the long cylindrical tube resting against our closet door.

"You may be disappointed." She withdrew several layers of drawings separated by thin tissue sheets. "The islands are breathtaking, but it's the Filipino children who stole my heart."

Each unrolled sheet contained a charcoal sketch of a child or a group of children, each with the brightest, darkest, most innocent eyes peering out at me. "They're such precious little urchins."

"Aren't they?" she mused as she studied one portrait. "Maybe before long Brad and I will have our own little urchin."

I gasped in astonishment. "Cece, are you..."

"No, no, no," she sighed. "At least not yet, but we're trying," she whispered as she climbed under the covers. "Don't say anything to Aunt Bird. She'd just worry."

As she switched off our lamp, I began to worry myself. Drifting off to sleep, I remembered what the doctor in New York had said about Cece's chances of carrying a baby to full-term.

With a promise from Cece that she'd visit me in Athens the next weekend and a care package of Aunt Bird's leftovers on the car seat beside me, I headed back to school on Sunday. By Thursday, I was planning Cece's tour of the campus when someone yelled that I had a phone call.

"Allie, hi honey. How are you?" I could feel Aunt Bird's feigned calmness even over the telephone. Bradley had suffered a jeep accident on an unpaved road in the Philippines. The windshield had shattered, and fragments of the glass did some damage to one of his eyes. The Army was sending him to see a specialist at Walter Reed in D.C., and Cece was on her way to meet him.

Leave it to Brad to screw up my weekend with Cece, I couldn't help but think. But as Brad's recovery turned into weeks, I felt ashamed of myself. Finally, in early May as I mailed the last of my resumes to perspective newspapers, Cece and Brad returned to Flintville. After a barrage of tests, Brad received the final prognosis. There was permanent damage to his right eye—his days as an Army pilot were over.

Less than a month later, the entire family attended my graduation. Uncle Hoyt snapped photos of me in my cap and gown while Cece oohed and aahed over my *Magna Cum Laude* diploma. Aunt Bird, tears spilling from her green eyes, patted my arm with pride. "I always knew you were a smart little thing!"

Brad, a black patch covering his right eye, remained withdrawn until I caught my sister elbowing him. "Snap out of it!" she whispered. "Today is Allie's day!"

Brad sauntered over and smiled for the first time all day. "Congratulations, Allie!" was all he could muster. As I watched him struggle to remain festive during our celebratory lunch at *Allen's*, I felt somewhat sorry for my brother-in-law. Just as I readied to begin a promising career in journalism, Brad's life as an aviator had been snatched away from him.

A few days later, suffering from a hellacious hangover and carrying the last box to tuck in the only space left in my Studebaker, I took my final journey down the steps of Creswell Hall. "We can meet at *Rich's* when the bridesmaids' dresses come in. I'll treat you to lunch at the Magnolia Room!" Teresa suggested as she waved goodbye to me.

I wondered if I must don a hat and gloves for the occasion now that I was a grown woman? My stomach churned at the thought of the Magnolia Room's little chicken salad sandwiches, but my head throbbed too much to object.

My hangover was the result of a farewell celebration thrown for Joe Riley and me by the **Red and Black's** news department. I'd lost three times to Joe in a game of "Thumper," as our fellow staff members chanted for me to "Drink, chugalug, drink, chugalug, drink!"

Mercifully, my nausea subsided before I reached Flintville, and I began to ponder my future. As I wrestled between my two best offers, my dearest friends were plunging easily into their careers.

Teresa had accepted a position as a music teacher in an elementary school in DeKalb County and would begin her duties shortly after her honeymoon. Josie would be teaching second grade in LaGrange where she could be near her beloved horses while Zeke finished up veterinary school at UGA.

I'd received a number of offers from small papers all over the Southeast, but I'd narrowed my choices to a position with the **Flintville Star**, offered by Uncle Hoyt of course, and one with the **Savannah Times**.

Uncle Hoyt, bless his heart, refrained from making me feel guilty. "There's always a place for you here, Allie. My Lord, your daddy built this paper, but the **Savannah Times** would be a great opportunity for a talented reporter. You'd probably get to do some investigative work, like you've always wanted. I guess in a town the size of Flintville where everybody knows everything about everybody else, there's not much room for investigating."

Since the **Savannah Times** job didn't begin until autumn, I had a few months to make up my mind. In the meantime, I'd spend the summer working at the Flintville paper. After my first week back, my job description was about to be upgraded. Instead of working in the safety of my uncle's shadow, I would serve as editor for the next three weeks so he and Aunt Bird could finally take a honeymoon to France.

"You cut your teeth on this newspaper, Allie; it'll be a cinch," Uncle Hoyt offered with confidence. When I stammered with insecurity, he reassured me. "Relax, Allie. It's not the **Savannah Times**. The biggest story we've had all year was a knife fight out at the *River Ranch* back in April," he laughed. "Buford Cole cut his own brother Rayford for cussing in front of Miss Blanche Bledsoe. That's as dramatic as it ever gets in Flintville."

Though we now resided in the same town, I hadn't seen much of Cece. She and Brad were living temporarily with Mr. Royal in his big mansion in Riverview Estates. The first Sunday I was home, she came to church without Brad and sat with me.

Cece politely declined Aunt Bird's dinner invitation. "Brad wasn't feeling well this morning. I need to get back and check on him. Maybe another Sunday, okay? Ya'll have a wonderful time and take some photos of the Louvre!"

With Aunt Bird and Uncle Hoyt headed to France, my reign as editor-in-chief officially began. During my first two weeks, the most exciting event occurred at 2:00 A.M. on a Thursday. I was summoned from a deep sleep by Flintville's fire chief after the city's street sweeper backed into a fire hydrant on Main Street. After getting a couple of shots with the newspaper's camera and a quote from Chief McEachern, I stumbled home for a few hours' sleep before my real day began.

By the beginning of my third and final week as editor, I'd found my stride. Uncle Hoyt was right, I thought. This job is a cinch. Just as I put the finishing touches on my makeup that Tuesday morning, Cece called. "Hi. Miss Editor-in-chief," she began. "Great story about the fire hydrant last week," she giggled. "Did you wear your pajamas to the scene?"

"I got the story, didn't I? Who cares what I looked like?" I chose not to tell her that I'd been sleeping in my clothes in case a story broke in the wee hours. I glanced at my watch and realized I was about to be late. "What's up, Cece?"

"Could you give me a ride back out to the Bluff at lunch?" she asked. "Brad's dropping me off to run some errands in town before he heads to Atlanta to see another eye specialist." The only car they had was Brad's old Mustang from his high school years.

"I thought there's nothing they can do for Brad's eye." Then I realized how insensitive I sounded. "I'm sorry, Cece. I didn't mean that."

"It's okay, Allie. He just wants one more opinion." She quickly changed the subject. "I thought we could have lunch together, and then you could run me home. Would that work for you?"

I was delighted. I'd have Cece all to myself for an hour. When she showed up at the newspaper just before noon, I was proofing an editorial I'd written about Flintville's lack of cultural experiences. Writing an editorial for Wednesday's edition was a highlight of my temporary position.

In this week's editorial, I challenged Flintville's citizens to consider a community arts center, a venue for concerts and plays and art shows. I'd heard both Aunt Bird and Uncle Hoyt bemoan having to travel to Atlanta for any kind of cultural event.

As we drove to the house, I filled my sister in on my editorial. "What do you think, Cece?"

"I think you're right on target. You'll need people to contribute money for such an endeavor. I don't know if there are enough folks who care that much about hearing a symphony or seeing a Shakespearean performance," she added.

"Yeah, I know money would be the big problem, but at least I can get the community thinking about it." I pulled into our driveway. "I figure you and Brad may end up here, and you'll need somewhere to showcase your art. Aunt Bird told me that Mr. Royal finagled Brad a job in the mill's office."

From the look on Cece's face, I realized I'd butted too far into her and Brad's personal business. "I'm sorry, Cece. I guess I'm being presumptuous."

Cece sighed. "Everybody presumes we'll be staying now that Brad's been grounded. The mill job isn't Brad's only offer. Can you keep a secret better these days than you did as a little twerp?" She eyed me cautiously.

I stopped at the back door to draw an "X" over my chest. "Cross my heart and hope to die. Look the devil in the eye!"

Cece hesitated as I ached with curiosity. "I don't want to find this revelation on the society page of the *Star*!"

I grew indignant. "Come on, Cece! I will not tell a living, breathing soul!" I begged as I held the screen door open for her.

She leaned against the kitchen sink and regarded me with shining eyes. "The commander at West Point called last week. They have a position for an experienced pilot to instruct trainees on a simulator, and they've offered the post to Brad."

"Is he going to take it? Will you get to finish your graduate work at NYU? When will Brad have to report?" I pummeled my sister with questions.

"Whoa! Hold on, Miss Reporter! You're not at a press conference!" She turned around to wash her hands at the sink. "No matter what happens, living in Flintville is our last choice. The sooner we get out of Mr. Royal's house, the better!"

she muttered as though she hadn't meant for me to hear it. Then she turned around and smiled. "Let's get some lunch; I'm famished!"

There'd been a basket of Miz Gertie's tomatoes on the front doorstep when I'd arrived home last night. We listened to the radio while I fried bacon and Cece sliced two ripe, juicy tomatoes and slathered mayonnaise on slices of white bread.

Cece laughed out loud. "Oh my Lord, can you believe *WSFT* still broadcasts that *Swap Shop* segment?" We both hooted as we listened to a caller trying to swap a litter of kittens for an outboard motor. After a commercial, the station began its daily broadcast of *Ebony Bulletin Board* with the baritone voice of its black host, the Reverend Elijah Atwell, son of Moses and Berthie Atwell.

"When Elijah delivered some church announcements for the paper, he brought some plum jam from Berthie." I crunched into a dill pickle. "Don't let me forget to give you a jar to take home."

Cece grimaced. "It's not my home, Allie. It's just a place we're staying right now." She surveyed the kitchen. "Now this feels more like home," she smiled, "and I think I'll have another sandwich now that I'm eating for two."

I almost choked on my pickle. "Two? What the hell? Cece Sinclair Royal, are you pregnant?" When she just grinned and nodded, I began to jump up and down. "Oh, my God! I'm going to be an aunt! Oh—my—God! Why didn't you tell me?"

Cece beamed. "I did just tell you. You're the first person to know besides Doctor Justice. That was my errand in town this morning. Brad doesn't even know yet. I couldn't stand to disappoint him if it was a false alarm. He's had enough disappointment lately. This news will turn things around for him, for us!"

A tiny voice in my head whispered its reservations, but I didn't dare spoil my sister's mood. "Oh Cece, I can't believe it! When are you going to tell Brad?"

That same tiny voice had obviously spoken to her. "I'll wait a few weeks. You know, to make certain everything's all right. Brad hasn't been himself since the accident. He says his flying days had just begun, and he wanted us to see the world before we settled down anywhere. But with this offer from West Point and the promise of a baby, I think he'll see things differently. We can buy a little house near the school's grounds; they have some really reasonable deals for officers. And it would be *our* house, not his father's. Brad hates being beholden to his father! Mr. Royal's so controlling—he and Brad begin and end every day with some kind of argument."

I listened intently as my sister unloaded, but for the first time in my life, I withheld any comment. To hear my kind-hearted, non-judgmental sister say anything derogatory about anybody, much less her own father-in-law, confirmed what I'd known all along. Mr. John Royal was one "royal" ass!

After lunch Cece asked me to drop her off at Mrs. Daphne Hamilton's house, the nearest residence to Mr. Royal's house. Each estate on the Bluff included a sizeable amount of property, and all the houses were at least a mile apart.

Cece, her dark moment subsided, rattled on about Miz Daphne. "Aunt Daphne and I have become good friends. She's redecorating her living room and asked if I'd look at some fabric swatches. She's such a lovely lady, so elegant and graceful! Do you remember her?"

I nodded as I geared down for the incline to the top of the Bluff. "Yes, I used to go to Juliet's birthday parties each summer."

"That's right! Juliet's in Europe for the summer. Daphne was very close with her sister-in-law Meredith, Brad's mother. With Juliet away and both Meredith and Mr. Hamilton dead, Aunt Daphne seems quite lonely. We've been good for each other these past weeks. Since Brad's gone so much, and I don't have a car, it's a nice walk over to her house. She was actually majoring in art at Agnes Scott when she and Mr. Hamilton got married. She never finished her degree, but she has quite a collection hanging in her house."

I pulled into the circular drive at the front of the Hamilton home, a stately brick mansion with white columns. Cece kissed me on the cheek. "Hey, baby brat, thanks for lunch and the ride. And remember, mum's the word!" She held her finger to her lips as she shut the car door.

Driving back to town, my head teemed with questions. Cece's revelations had overwhelmed me. I knew she'd be happier if she and Brad returned to New York. Flintville didn't offer what my sister needed, I had to admit. I wondered why she was so adamant about having a baby right now, though. And why did Brad leave Cece alone so much? He wasn't working. Where did he go when he left her? What did Brad and his father argue about each day?

Just as my curiosity began to spin out of control, I pulled into the alley behind the newspaper office. Mr. Barton stood in the doorway of the pressroom. "Allie, we gotta problem. One of the presses just blew. I think I can fix it, but I'm going to need your help on the linotype if we want tomorrow's edition out on time."

Mr. Barton and I didn't leave the pressroom until midnight, but we had both presses up and running to print the next day's edition.

Much too early, I stood yawning behind the ad counter in our outer office as I finished a paste-up for a *Hastings Drug Store* advertisement. Miz Charlene and Miz Opal, both at their desks, were busily typing articles for the society page when Brad's father stormed in through the newspaper's front door.

I hadn't seen Mr. John Royal since the wedding, and I was not prepared for his distraught appearance. He had a disheveled look, as though he'd slept in the clothes he was wearing. I realized something was wrong.

"Mr. Royal? Hi, I'm Allie, you know, Cece's sister. Can I help you?" I began as I wiped rubber cement from my hands.

He appeared distracted. "Oh yes, Allie. I remember now. Where's your uncle? I need to speak to him at once!" he demanded in a voice both stern and condescending.

I suppressed my loathing toward the man, whose entire presence reeked of a crude superiority. "I'm sorry, Mr. Royal. My uncle and aunt are out of town until this weekend. They've been in Europe for two weeks now. Didn't Cece or Brad tell you?"

He sighed impatiently. "I guess I'll have to talk to you since no one else seems to be in charge." I cringed to think that Cece had to put up with this man's haughty attitude day after day. The pecking of both Miz Opal and Miz Charlene's typewriters ceased, and I knew they were listening. Chuck Purdy had just left to interview the new football coach, and I felt a strange vulnerability, an uncomfortableness I'd never felt around a male before.

The bell on the front door jingled, and I turned around to see Elijah Atwell's warm, friendly grin. His appearance gave me a moment to regroup and center myself. "Hi, Elijah!" I greeted him. "Aren't you a little early this week? We don't run church announcements until Friday's edition."

"Howdy do, Miss Allie. I don't have my announcements yet, but I promised my mama I'd bring you these fresh-baked muffins. She was out picking blueberries at daybreak. She said she knew you weren't eating a good breakfast while your aunt was out of town. She's so proud of what you've been doing with the paper in your uncle's absence."

"Well, wasn't that sweet of Berthie!" I exclaimed. "Oh, forgive my manners. Mr. Royal, do you know Reverend Elijah Atwell? He does the *Ebony Bulletin Board* on the radio."

Mr. Royal barely acknowledged him, but Elijah, ever the gentleman, nodded to Mr. Royal. "Howdy do, sir." Then he turned to me. "Now you make certain you have one of those muffins while they're still hot. Good day to all of you!" He nodded again as he made his exit.

I returned my attention to Mr. Royal, by now drumming his fingers on the front counter. "Mr. Royal, since I'm in charge this week, how can I help you?" I spoke in a strong, firm voice so there'd be no doubt I was up to the task, whatever the task might be.

He cleared his throat. "Hrrm, it's a personal matter. It would be better if we spoke in private." He eyed Miz Charlene and Miz Opal, who simultaneously ducked their heads and began typing furiously.

I led Mr. Royal to Uncle Hoyt's office. I offered him a seat, but I remained standing. I crossed my arms and leaned against the old mahogany desk where Diddy once sat. "Now what is this personal matter, Mr. Royal?" I inquired with as much authority as I could muster.

He removed a handkerchief from his back pocket. He blotted at sweat beads forming on his brow. "Neither Bradley nor I got home until late last night. I had a dinner engagement with a client, and Bradley was in Atlanta."

I wondered how the comings and goings of the Royal men had anything to do with me, but I held my tongue and allowed Mr. Royal to continue. "Cece wasn't there when we got home, and we figured she spent the night at your aunt's house. Did she?"

My heart leapt into my throat. "No, she didn't." I willed myself to breathe normally. "I bet she spent the night with Mrs. Hamilton. I dropped her off there after lunch yesterday."

Mr. Royal shook his head. "I called Daphne first thing this morning. She drove Cece home around dinnertime."

I began to grasp at straws. I thought of Uncle Hoyt's favorite fishing spot and the time Cece went with us so she could paint. "Maybe she went across the river to paint the sunset. She could've had an insulin reaction and blacked out or something."

Mr. Royal shook his head. "I took the boat out at first light to look for her. I'm on my way to the sheriff's office now, but I wanted to make certain she wasn't with you or your family."

The palms of my hands began to sweat, and my knees felt weak. "Where's Brad? Maybe he's found her."

"I'm not certain where Brad is. I'm, uh, sure he's out looking for Cece, though."

I forced myself not to panic. "Okay, then. You alert the sheriff, and I'll start calling anybody who might have seen her. Maybe Margaret's in town."

Mr. Royal rose stiffly. "I'm sure she's okay. She just forgot to leave Brad a note. I'll speak with the sheriff and drive back to the house. Maybe she's shown up."

As soon as Mr. Royal left, my knees buckled. I felt myself sinking to the floor as though some uncontrollable force was pulling me underwater. "I will not fall apart—Cece needs me. I have to think...I have to act!" I lectured myself as I clung to the edge of the desk for support.

Slowly, I pulled myself up from the floor and found my eyes level with a green, glittery soup can, the can I'd painted Diddy for Christmas so many years ago. Uncle Hoyt still kept it stocked with chewing gum. "Okay, what would Uncle Hoyt do? What would Diddy do? Think, Allie, think."

I sat down at the desk and began making a list of places Cece might have gone. Having a plan of action calmed me. I started with Dr. Justice's office. Maybe Cece had gotten sick, or worse yet, maybe she'd had another miscarriage. The receptionist said they hadn't heard from my sister since her appointment yesterday. I began calling Cece's high school friends who still lived in town. I even called Miz Thelma at the beauty shop. No one had seen my sister in the last twenty-four hours.

I sank into Uncle Hoyt's swivel chair and closed my eyes. I felt dizzy, and it dawned on me that I'd left home this morning without any breakfast. As a matter of fact, I'd been so tired last night I'd eaten no supper. I glanced at the basket of muffins Elijah had delivered and unfolded the red-checkered napkin.

Just as I removed a still-warm muffin, I spied an envelope tucked between the napkin's folds. I guess Berthie had sent me a card, but as I removed it, I could see the back of the envelope was marked with small, block lettering: "Urgent Information for Allie Sinclair."

My hands shaking, I tore open the envelope to discover Berthie's message: "Come to the Atwell's house. Your sister needs you. DO NOT TELL ANYONE WHERE YOU ARE GOING. You'll understand when you get here." It was signed "Berthie Atwell."

Something was terribly wrong. Why was Cece with Berthie? Was my sister sick? Was she hiding from Brad? What did it matter, I told myself. Cece's okay; she's safe, and I knew Moses and Berthie would guard my sister with their lives if necessary.

As I reentered the outer office, Mr. Purdy had returned and was busily typing up his interview for today's sports page. Miz Charlene was helping a customer with a birth announcement, and Miz Opal was proofreading some copy.

"Miz Opal, if ya'll can handle things for a couple of hours, I think I'm going to take an early lunch. I didn't get much sleep last night, and my head is killing me. I'll be back before today's edition is printed."

Miz Opal eyed me suspiciously. "Are you sure you're okay, Allie?"

"Oh, I'll be fine. I'll be back in a while." I waved and headed out to my car in the alley.

The only time I'd traveled to the Atwell's home had been that long ago summer day with Josie on our bicycles. Though some of the shacks along the route had been replaced by small brick structures, little else had changed. Black children, playing hopscotch in the dirt, stopped to wave as I drove by.

Old Moses greeted me at the end of their gravel driveway. "Miss Allie, I think it'd be wise if you'se pulls your car around back." I did as instructed.

Moses escorted me through the back door straight into the kitchen. Berthie, a little grayer and a few pounds heavier, stood at the stove. "Lawdy, Lawdy! Look how's you'se growed up, Miss Allie Sinclair! Come here and give your Berthie a hug!" She enveloped me with her fat arms before I could ask about Cece. "Now, don't you worry that pretty little head of yours, sweet chile. We gots your sister, and we's takin' good care of her, bless her little heart!"

"Where is she? What happened to her? Why did she come way out here?" I asked.

"You'se sit down here and have some of my vegetable soup, and I'se tell you all about it. I'se finally gots Miss Cece to drink some warm milk, and she's done drifted off to sleep. She's wore out, that chile is. She's wore out," Berthie repeated as she ladled soup into a bowl for me. "Now's you'se gonna eat before we's gonna talk. I knows you'se been tore up with worry about Miss Cece, and I bet you'se ain't had a bit of lunch." She pulled a pan from her oven. "Here's some warm cornbread to go with your soup, and I bet you'se could drink a glass of sweet tea, now couldn't you?"

I nodded like an obedient child. The tension that had been building in my neck since Mr. Royal had entered the office suddenly eased. Berthie's soup soothed my hunger as well as my worry. When I'd finished two bowls and some warm peach cobbler, Berthie was satisfied.

"What happened, Berthie? Why is Cece here? Can I take her home with me?"

Berthie settled herself in a large rocker in the kitchen corner by a window fan. "Wells, chile, it's a sad tale, but I'se gonna tell you what I knows, and then Miss Cece, bless her heart, gonna have to tell you the rest."

She drank some iced tea from a fruit jar. Although aching for information, I realized Berthie Atwell wouldn't be rushed.

"Do you knows Juanita Wilson, Mr. Royal's maid? She nursed Miz Meredith on her deathbed, and she tooks care of Bradley Royal from the time he be just a baby. And now she cleans Mr. Royal's house and do all his laundry and cooks when he asks her to."

"Yes ma'am," I replied. "I know who she is. Lorna, the McClendon's maid, told me about Juanita."

"That's right, chile. Juanita kin to Lorna through marriage, and Lorna akin to the Atwells way on down the line. Course, we just one big family out here in the Village."

"Yes, ma'am," I answered succinctly in hopes Berthie would continue.

"Well, long's about seven o'clock this morning, Moses done gone out to check on his corn, and I hears a car coming up the drive, and it was Juanita's. She was dressed in her uniform, and I'se know it was her day to be at Mr. Royal's house. She was all distracted looking and a-wringing her hands. She say, 'Oh Berthie, it's Miss Cece. She's done begged me to get her away from there, and I'se don't know nowheres else to bring her.'

"I looks in the backseat and sees Miss Cece lying there all pale and pitiful looking, and Juanita helps me get Miss Cece in the house. All the time Miss Cece just a-cryin and a-beggin for us'n not to take her back there. And when' I asks her if'n she wants me to call her husband, she just pitch a fit and sez, 'Don't let him find me; please don't let him find me!' I calms her down enough to get her to talk some sense, and she says to get you, but she's so afeared of somethin', and she don't want nobody else to knows. That's why I sent Elijah with the muffins. I knows you'se find my note before long.

"So once I gets Miss Cece in the bed and puts a cold rag on her head, I asks Juanita what be going on at the Royal house. She tell me that Mr. John Royal tore out of there early this morning saying he's alookin for his daughter-in-law."

"Was Brad with Mr. Royal?" I interrupted.

Berthie shook her head sadly. "No, chile. Juanita sez she ain't seen hide nor hair of Mr. Bradley today. He's usually there in the mornins nursing his hangover."

I was confused. "Hangover? What do you mean?"

"I'se sorry to be the one to tells you. Mr. Bradley done tooks to the bottle since he finds out he can't fly no more. Juanita sez Miss Cece try to hide it from everybody. Juanita sez Miss Cece done had it rough between tryin' to sober up Mr. Bradley and tryin' to referee his'n and Mr. John's arguments."

I thought of Cece's comments at lunch just yesterday. Had her remarks about Mr. Royal been a cry for help, one I'd completely missed?

Berthie sipped on her iced tea. "Wells, when Mr. John left this morning, Juanita wents out to the garden house 'cause the garage on the bottom be where she stores mops and things. She sez she heared someone overhead crying real soft like. Juanita ain't got no key to the upstairs part of the garden house. She says that's where all Miz Meredith's special things be stored, and Mr. John keep it all locked up. She sez for a minute she be afeered it be Miss Meredith's ghost, but then she hears Miss Cece a-sayin, 'Help me, help me.'

"Juanita go up the stairs and see the door ain't locked, and she find Miss Cece a-lyin on the floor and a-whimperin like a puppy. She knowed Miss Cece need her insulin, and she fetch it from the big house and give Miss Cece a shot, 'cause she used to give Miz Meredith her pain shots. Miss Cece kinda comes around aftern that, and she begs Juanita to take her where Mr. John Royal and Mr. Brad Royal won'ts find her.

"Juanita wanted to drive her over to your aunt's house, but Miss Cece kept beggin, 'No, no! They'll find me there' All's the time, Juanita sez, Miss Cece clutching this red velvet bag, and she won'ts let go of it for her dear life. That's how Miss Cece wind up out here. Then when Juanita left, Miss Cece she begs me to get you. I promise, and I finally gets that bag out'n her clutches, and gets her to fall asleep."

"What's in the bag? Where is it?" Certainly the velvet bag held the answer to Cece's behavior.

Berthie walked out on the back porch to an old wringer washer. "I'se put it in here for safekeeping. I'se don't thinks nobody be lookin' in this old washer. It ain't worked for twenty years now."

She handed me a red velvet bag, a lady's lingerie bag, I thought. The bag's drawstring ribbon was tied tightly in a knot. "Me and Moses decided not to looks inside 'cause it must be something terrible that got Miss Cece so distracted. I knows you can figure out what to do with it."

The journalist in me knew I had to look. I opened the bag and found three items wrapped separately in velvet and tied with thin satin ribbons.

I tugged lightly at the first ribbon and unfolded the covering. Resting on the soft cloth was a collar off a woman's blouse. The collar, frayed and faded pink cotton, was shaped in the Peter Pan style popular when Cece was in high school. Attached to one side of the collar was a tiny silver flute, similar to the jewelry girls wore in the sixties.

The second package felt so weightless, I wondered if it held anything. When I unrolled the velvet, my heart stopped. It was the strap to a lady's sundress. The strap had a daisy appliqué. I recognized the pattern—it belonged to Cece's lovely dotted swiss sundress, the dress she'd worn the night I'd retrieved her, disoriented and heartbroken, from the *River Ranch*.

What did it all mean? Although Cece'd never revealed the details of their argument so many years ago, I wondered if Brad, in a drunken stupor, had torn my sister's strap and kept it as a souvenir. My theory made little sense now that Cece and Brad had reunited and buried the past.

It was the final item that offered some clarity to the situation. Within the remaining square of velvet lay something so familiar to me, so dear to me, so forgotten to me for so many years.

"What the hell? What the hell?" I didn't realize I'd uttered the words aloud until Berthie rushed to my side.

"Lands sake, chile! What is it?" She eyed the precious item as I turned it in my hands. "Some kind of case, ain't it?"

"My daddy's syringe case. His initials are right here on the front. It's been missing since the day he died." My voice quivered in fear, in rage, in a sudden, horrible realization. "Don't you see, Berthie? He didn't die from a heart attack. He was murdered. They killed him!"

"Oh chile, you'se must be mistakin. Nobody's in they rights mind woulda want to hurt Mr. A.L.!"

"Somebody did! He killed Diddy! Oh my God, he killed Diddy!" I began to sob against Berthie's big heaving chest.

She held me. "Now chile, I thinks your imagination done got the better of you. There ain't nobody that evil here in Flintville, I just don't think so, honey chile."

"Yes there is!" The answer came from my sister, who stood pale and shaking in the doorway. "Oh God, Allie, what have I done? How could I have been such a fool?" She began to sway, and I caught her just before she hit the floor.

"Sweet Jesus, help us!" Berthie sprang into action. Together we got Cece back in bed. "Now, you'se two needs to talk about all this. But, Miss Cece, if'n you'se try to get outta that bed by yoself again, I'se gonna have to tie you down. You'se sick, sweet baby, you'se sick! Now I'se gonna call Doc Justice."

As Berthie headed towards the kitchen, Cece cried in protest. "Don't call the doctor. He'll tell them, and they'll find me! Please, Berthie, don't"

Berthie, her hands on her hips, spoke in a soothing voice. "No need to worry yo purty little head about that, chile. Doc Justice come out here every month to gives Moses his B-12 shot. I'se gonna call him and tell him Moses been feelin real poorly and I done baked a fresh peach cobbler. Doc Justice can't resist my desserts. He won't know that you'se here 'til he gets here." She closed the door behind her.

I took my sister's soft, weak hand in mine. Her eyes were vacant like she'd traveled to another world and couldn't see me. "Cece, can you tell me what happened?" I wasn't certain she'd even heard me. I sat quietly beside her and stroked her beautiful hair, all matted and wet with sweat now.

Suddenly, she came back to me and began to talk. I felt like I did that day on the front porch of Essie Dunn's house, when we sat on her swing in silence until Essie was ready to spill the sorrow in her heart. I did not push; I did not question. I just listened.

"Yesterday after you dropped me off at Aunt Daphne's, she asked me to join her on the patio for some lemonade. She said, 'You have a secret, don't you?' I couldn't lie to her. I told her about the pregnancy, and she was thrilled for Brad and me. She understood my reluctance to tell Brad right away because of my diabetes. Then she started talking about what a precious baby Brad had been and how much he looked like his mother. I wanted to see some photographs, and she suggested I look upstairs in the garden house for some old scrapbooks. When I told her Mr. Royal kept the upstairs locked, Aunt Daphne laughed and said, 'Oh, John Royal is such a pain in the derriere! Don't worry, honey, I have a key to that room.' Apparently, Meredith gave Aunt Daphne a key before she died. Aunt Daphne lent me the key and drove me back to the house on her way to her bridge club."

Cece hesitated, and I wondered if she'd drift away again. "Can you get me something to drink, Allie?"

As I headed out the bedroom door, Berthie greeted me with a tray. "Here's some refreshments for your sister. Now you tries to get her to eat some of this soup, you hear me?" She waddled back towards the kitchen.

Cece drank some tea and ate two spoonfuls of soup. "Remember, you're eating for two now!" I encouraged her.

My sister burst into tears. "Oh, Allie, how could I have been so stupid? Why couldn't I remember? Why?"

I tried to remain calm even while I watched her eyes glaze over. She left me again, off to her own secret place. I squeezed her hand tightly. "Remember what, Cece? Cece? Try, please try!"

A moment later, her eyes focused on me. "Have you looked inside the velvet bag?" she asked. I nodded. "When I unfolded the strap to my dress, it came flooding back. I remembered what happened that night when you found me at the *River Ranch*. Oh God, Allie, why couldn't I remember then?"

I patted her soothingly. "Maybe you were in shock. Maybe it was God's way of protecting you. Can you tell me what happened?"

She stared out the window. "We were sitting on the dock at Brad's house. There was a full moon, and Brad suggested we take the canoe and paddle downriver. He realized the paddles were up in the garage. So, I waited on the dock while Brad went to get them. Then...he touched me on my shoulder; he'd been so quiet I hadn't heard him walk up. He said he needed to talk to me about something." She stopped, closed her eyes, and rubbed her forehead as if she could conjure up the memory.

I tried to help her. "So, what did Brad want to talk about?"

She peered out the window again. "It wasn't Brad who tapped me on my shoulder. Brad went to get the paddles, but he never came back."

Tears splashed on her blouse. "It was his father. Mr. Royal said that since Brad had broken curfew and been drinking, he wouldn't be returning. Then he told me that Brad had a message for me. Mr. Royal said the relationship had been a mistake from the beginning, and that I should return Brad's class ring. He put me in his car to drive me home. I was too hurt and humiliated to question him. He turned the opposite way on River Road and pulled off on an old dirt road. When I asked him why we'd stopped, he said he'd help me get Brad's class ring off the chain around my neck."

Cece put her hands around her neck for a moment, closed her eyes, and went on in a trembling voice. "I remember he was pawing at me and pulling at my dress. I guess that's how he tore my strap. Then, a car's headlights rounded the corner, and I jumped out. When Mr. Royal saw the car, he drove off and left me standing in the middle of the road. Some old man and his grandson pulled over in a pickup truck. The old man said, 'Honey, looks like you done had a fight with your boyfriend.' He said they were headed to the *River Ranch* for some bait and offered me a ride."

I began to seethe. "I'm going to kill that sonnabitch if it's the last thing I ever do!" My outburst sent Cece back to her other world, obviously a world free from the truth and the pain.

There was a tapping on the door, and I looked up as Doctor Justice entered. "Don't worry about me, Allie," he said. "Berthie told me enough to know this is the safest place for Cece right now. Give me a few minutes to examine her."

I left the room and telephoned the newspaper. It was after 5:00, and Miz Opal answered. "Allie, is everything okay? We called the house, but you didn't answer."

I faked a laugh. "Goodness, Miz Opal, I fell asleep. I guess that late night in the pressroom just did me in. Have I missed anything?"

"Not a thing. You just rest, Allie. The paper's out, and we're closing shop for the night."

I exhaled in relief. "That's good news. I'll see ya'll in the morning." Just as I hung up, Doctor Justice strolled into the kitchen. "How's she doing? Is she going to be okay?"

He washed his hands in Berthie's sink. "The baby's fine, and your sister's fine physically, considering what she's obviously been through today. I'm more concerned about her mental and emotional state." Hearing Doctor Justice speak to me as an adult unnerved me.

I struggled to sound as grownup as he was treating me. "I'm concerned, too, Doc. One minute she's making sense, and the next minute she's off in the Twilight Zone." I cringed, realizing that didn't sound very adult.

Doctor Justice sat at the table beside me as Berthie busied herself with some peach cobbler for him to take home. "Allie, your sister has suffered some emotional trauma too painful for her to bear right now. She drifts off into the 'Twilight Zone' because it's her escape when things get too scary for her. It's called post-traumatic stress syndrome. Soldiers often experience something like this after battle. The Army's conducting a new study on how to treat the disorder, but the findings aren't out yet."

"Well, what can I do to help her?"

"Just be patient, Allie. When she's ready to talk, she'll talk. Don't push her."

Berthie handed him a foiled wrapped container. "I believe what Doc Justice be saying is that's we's gotta give that chile all the love we can if'n we's wanna nurse her back to health. Lawd, I didn't knows the chile be pregnant!"

The doctor gave Cece a sedative to help her rest. I seized the opportunity to hurry home and pack a few things. When I returned, Berthie had made a pallet on the floor beside Cece's bed and brought the kitchen fan into the room.

Around 4:00 A.M., Cece began to thrash about in the bed. "I need some water!" she moaned. I offered her a glass, and once she had her fill, she was wide-awake.

"Do you know where you are, Cece?" I began softly as Doc Justice had instructed me.

Her sapphire eyes, focused and alert, gazed directly at me. "Yes, Allie, I'm okay. We're with Berthie, aren't we? I remember telling you about the night on River Road. I remember finding the velvet bag in the garden house." Her eyes filled with tears.

I kept my voice low and controlled. "How'd you find the bag?"

She wiped the tears from her cheeks. "It was in the wedding gown box. There was this tremendous cedar chest–that's where Aunt Daphne told me I could find the scrapbooks. At the bottom of the chest was a big cardboard container that held Mrs. Royal's wedding gown. The box had a clear top so I could see the bodice of the dress. I carried it over to the window so I could get a better view, and I realized the seal was broken. I thought that was odd because Aunt Daphne said the dress had been sealed up just before Mrs. Royal died. I decided I'd take the box to her in the morning, and she could take it to the cleaners and have it resealed so the dress wouldn't yellow. If I'd just left the dress in the box..." She began to sob, and I feared she'd stop talking.

"I lifted the dress out of the box, and the velvet bag fell on the floor. At first I thought it probably held mementos from Mrs. Royal's wedding. So, I opened the bag and looked inside. Oh God, why did I do that? Why?" Tears streamed down her face.

I bathed her with a cool cloth as I murmured, "It's okay, Cece."

"No! It's not okay! I have to tell you before I forget again. Don't let me forget again," she begged.

I ached for her. I wanted to protect her from her torment, but I couldn't.

"After I found my dress strap, I was so confused. Then I unfolded the second bundle, and everything made absolute sense to me. Oh God, oh God, why didn't I remember when it happened?"

I assumed Cece was talking about Diddy's syringe kit. "How could you remember about the kit?" I offered. "You weren't there when the kit was stolen."

Cece stared at me. "What kit?"

I realized such a revelation could push Cece over the edge. I answered softly. "Oh, I really don't know what it was. It probably belonged to one of the Royals," I lied. "So, what did you find in the second package?"

She clinched her fists open and shut a few times. "I rewrapped the package containing my dress strap and returned it to the bag. Just as I unfolded the second velvet package, I heard Mr. Royal's car pull in the driveway. I turned off the lights in the garden house. I lay on the floor and barely breathed. He stood on the patio and lit up one of his cigars." She stopped.

"Were you afraid he'd be angry at you for being in the garden house?" I tried to keep Cece's thought on track.

She began to shiver although the bedroom was hot and sticky. She spoke in a whisper. "I was afraid he'd do it again."

"Do what again, Cece?"

She shivered and shook, and I drew the covers around her. Then she began to sob. "What did he do, Cece?"

Her words came slowly as though each syllable pained her. "The last time I wore my blue beret was on New Year's Eve when Brad was still in Vietnam. It was the night I went bar-hopping with Marcus and his friends in the Village." She hesitated as a tremor shook her body. "It was the night I lost my virginity."

"I remember, Cece. But that's all in the past now," I assured her, but she began shivering again. "What is it, Cece? Did Mr. Royal find out about that night? Are you afraid he's going to tell Bradley?"

She returned to her narrative as if she hadn't heard me. "His cigar smoke drifted up through the garden house windows, and the smell, along with the contents of the second package...it all came flooding back to me."

An overpowering sense of dread seeped into me. "What came flooding back to you, Cece? What was in the second package?" I didn't understand what Diddy's syringe kit or a Peter Pan collar had to do with that New Year's Eve and Mr. Royal's cigar.

"I didn't put it back in the red velvet bag. I left the other three packages in the bag; I promise I did. But this one was mine. He had no right to take it. Why did he take it from me?"

The velvet bag must have contained a fourth package Cece had chosen to keep. "Where is it, Cece? What did he take from you?" I begged with as much control as I had left.

She reached under the covers and pulled out her blue beret. "That Jeff guy at the bar didn't come home with me on New Year's Eve," she began. "He hailed me a cab and then went back to the bar–I remember now. That night, I'd worn my beret and my wool cape, the one Marcus made for me. But the next day, I couldn't find my beret."

She closed her eyes and laid her head on my shoulder. "Yesterday, when I opened that second package and smelled his cigar, I remembered his breath on me that night in New York. He'd been waiting by my door when I got home. He said he had some business in the city the next day and had decided to fly up early with the hopes he could take me out for dinner. I invited him in. When I excused myself to hang my cape up in my room, I turned around, and he was right behind me. He had a pistol: he stuck it in my mouth. He told me he'd ruin Brad and me if I ever told anyone. He took it, Allie; he took it from me. Why did he have to take it?" She searched my eyes for an answer.

"I don't know why he took the beret, Cece. Some sick perversion, I guess."

"No, I'm not talking about the beret. Why did he have to take me?" The agony in her voice sickened me. "Please don't let him hurt me again. He tried to hurt me that night on River Road, but I got away. Then he stole my virginity. Don't let him take my baby, too. He'll try; I know he will. Don't let him, Allie. Promise me!" She held onto me as I cradled and rocked her.

Cece fell into a listless sleep. Exhausted from the stress, I slept, too. As the first streak of dawn peeked through the window, I jerked awake. When Cece didn't stir, I eased quietly from the old iron bed we were sharing. I tiptoed to the bathroom at the opposite end of the hall.

Berthie was already dressed and in the kitchen mixing dough in a wooden bread bowl. "I'se making biscuits for you two. Coffee's still hot, too. Moses done gone out to picks his corn before this heat burns it all up."

I tried to smooth out the wrinkled skirt and blouse I'd been wearing since yesterday morning. My head ached and my eyes burned. "Berthie, can you watch over Cece while I drive into town? I have to talk to the sheriff about a crime that's been committed."

"Honey, be careful what you'se say to that new sheriff." She handed me a plate of bacon and eggs, the sight of which turned my stomach.

"What do you mean, Berthie?" I'd heard Sheriff Hill had met with some opposition by the older people in our community when he beat out Sheriff Brady last election. I knew Uncle Hoyt and Aunt Bird supported Sheriff Brady, who'd been the law in this county my entire life. It'd been a hard-fought campaign with Clarence Hill and his supporters insisting that Flintville needed newer, younger leaders.

Berthie set some warm biscuits on the table. "When Sheriff Brady be's the sheriff, he hads a black deputy to handle problems out here in the Village. Deputy Maurice Johnson is a fine young black man and a deacon in the church out here. He kepts the few troublemakers in the Village in line, and he'd arrest 'em when need be."

"Maybe I could talk to Deputy Johnson instead of the sheriff."

Berthie shook her head. "Maurice ain't deputy no mo'. Soon's Sheriff Hill tooks over, he fired our deputy. He says he was cuttin' back on the overhead, and since Deputy Johnson be the last one hired, he be the first one fired."

"Sounds like the sheriff's a bigot, but that doesn't mean he wouldn't be fair if the crime involved white people, does it?" I could have kicked myself for asking this sweet black woman such an insensitive question.

Berthie didn't seem to mind. "Well, you see, the sheriff's top supporter be Mr. John Royal. My sister's son-in-law Henry, he works out at the country club and he see Mr. Royal and the sheriff all the time. Henry sez those two be thick as thieves. You know, just before Mr. Hamilton passed, he been talking to Moses and Elijah about hiring black folk to work in the mills. But that all falls through now that Mr. Royal done tooks over. I guess Mr. Royal and Sheriff Hill be's cut from the same cloth."

I sighed. "Yeah, the white cloth they make robes and hoods out of, I guess."

"Lawd chile, there ain't been no Klan in Flintville since Moses be a little boy. Course they be other ways to keep us black folk down."

It dawned on me that hiding out here could bring trouble to the Atwells. "Berthie, maybe I should move Cece someplace else. I don't want to cause you and Moses any harm for helping us."

"I won't hear no such talk. You and Miss Cece be welcome here for as long as you'se need to stay. Everybody in the Village knows the Sinclairs be good people. Ain't nobody gonna give Miss Cece's hiding place away, so you'se just stop your frettin. Here come Elijah right now. I bets he can tells you what to do."

Elijah suggested we drive out to Sheriff Brady's cabin on the river. Since he'd lost the election and then his wife to cancer, Sheriff Brady had sold his house in town and moved there. The cabin was miles up river and hard to find, and Elijah insisted on guiding me.

"I go out there to work on the sheriff's old truck every now and then. He doesn't have a phone, and he only comes to town about twice a month for groceries." Elijah understood I needed to talk to him immediately.

Elijah agreed we shouldn't be seen leaving town together, or someone might become suspicious. Instead, I'd drive out the Crest Highway about ten miles. "There's an old well in the middle of Mr. Blackwell's peach orchard. There's a road that runs through the orchard, and I'll be parked there. One of us can leave our car, and we'll go the rest of the way together."

We decided to meet at the orchard around 2:00 P.M. That would give Elijah time to finish his *Ebony Bulletin Board* spot on the radio.

I had to take care of some details of my own. I needed to shower and change my clothes before I stopped by the newspaper. I also needed a reasonable alibi for Mr. Royal and Brad. I used Berthie's telephone to call Dr. and Mrs. Justice, who agreed to participate in my ruse. If they were asked, the Justices would say I'd been so upset about Cece's disappearance that they'd insisted I spend the night with them in Margaret's old room.

Before leaving, I checked on Cece. Berthie was sitting in a rocker by her side and seeing that Cece ate a little breakfast. Though frail and exhausted, Cece managed a weak smile. "Berthie says I'm as finicky an eater as our mama used to be."

Berthie laughed. "Lawd chiles, when yo mama be a little girl, she just hated turnip greens tils I mixed 'em with a little cornbread and makes her turnip green houses." She pulled herself up from the chair. "I'se start boiling my chicken for some stew." She waddled out and left us alone.

Cece held her arms out to me as tears welled in her eyes. "What are we going to do, Allie?"

I hugged her closely. "Don't worry, Cece. We're Sinclairs, and we'll think of something. Berthie and Moses are going to watch over you for a few hours while I take care of some business in town. Will you be okay until I can get back?"

She nodded, but as I tried to release myself from her, she held on tightly. "There's something else I didn't tell you...something you need to know in case you talk to Brad."

The little color she had regained once again drained from her face, but she didn't give into her fear. She stayed with me as her eyes filled with dread. "A few minutes after Mr. Royal lit his cigar, I heard Brad's Mustang pull in the garage. He obviously went in the house, but when he discovered I wasn't there, he stumbled out on the patio. He was drunk, I could tell. He and his father began to argue; they're always bickering, but this argument was different."

"How was it different?" I sat down beside her so I could hear her words, which grew weaker with her fear.

"Brad accused Mr. Royal of knowing where I'd gone, why I wasn't home. Mr. Royal told Brad to shut up, that he was drunk and acting stupid. Then Brad said he'd kill Mr. Royal if he ever hurt me."

Cece began to tremble again, so I wrapped my arms around her.

Where she found the courage was beyond me, but she steadied herself and continued. "Then Mr. Royal said, 'I don't know why you're so protective of that slut. Her grandparents were lintheads, and I wouldn't even wrap a dead fish in her daddy's paper. It's a good thing your mother died so she didn't have to suffer the humiliation of seeing her son marry some lowly tramp.'

"Brad was furious, but I was so afraid, I couldn't move a muscle. I just lay on the garden house floor and listened. I think Brad pushed his father into one of the patio chairs, and then he screamed, 'Don't you ever call my wife a slut again, you sonnabitch!' I heard the patio door slam. A few seconds later, I heard the Mustang crank up again, and I knew he'd taken off."

Cece relaxed in my arms as a tiny baby does when she gives up the fight to stay awake. I knew she'd told me the worst. By the time Berthie returned to take up her watch, Cece was sleeping soundly.

Heading home, I regretted not asking Cece where Brad went to do his drinking, but I doubted she knew. Certainly, Brad had enough discretion not to pitch a drunk somewhere like the *River Ranch* where people might recognize him. There were several new honky-tonks out the Atlanta Highway on the other side of Griffin. Maybe I'd drive out and look for him. Perhaps I could talk some sense into him.

At the moment, I had enough worries. After a quick shower and a fresh change of clothes, I headed to the newspaper. The office was abuzz with the news of Cece's disappearance. Chuck Purdy met me as I came in through the pressroom. "We can take care of things here if you need to help with the search. I've written a story about your sister's disappearance to run in tomorrow's edition, but I'll leave it open-ended in case the situation changes."

Appearing distraught and exhausted came easy, even though I knew Cece's whereabouts. I thanked Chuck, waved at the ladies in the front, and retreated to Uncle Hoyt's glass office where I closed the door.

I picked up the phone and dialed Mr. Royal's home number. To my surprise a woman's voice answered. "Hi, this is Allie Sinclair. I was hoping to speak with either Brad or Mr. Royal."

"Oh, Allison, yes! This is Daphne Hamilton. I'm manning the phones while John works with the sheriff. I don't know where Bradley is at the moment. I'm certain, though, he's out searching for your sister."

Or out getting soused again, I thought. "Yes ma'am. I hoped Brad might have some news." We promised one another to call with any news. I was relieved I didn't have to talk with Mr. Royal; I doubted I could have controlled my utter revulsion.

Because Cece had hidden her blue beret beneath her pillow and I didn't want to disturb her, I opted to bring the red velvet bag containing the other three pieces of evidence. I could account for Cece's dress strap as well as Diddy's insulin kit, although I had no way of knowing how the kit came into John Royal's possession. It was the other item, the piece of collar with the little flute pin that bothered me.

By the time I reached Elijah's car in a grove of peach trees, I had a theory. I doubted we'd be able to get John Royal on a rape charge; it would be his word against Cece's. I figured he could even wriggle his way out of any charge for having Diddy's insulin case. There was nothing inside the case, and Mr. Royal would argue that there could be thousands of identical cases with the same initials. However, if my hunch proved correct, we could still entangle John Royal in his own web. The Macy Dunn case had never been closed.

The trip to Sheriff Brady's house took almost an hour. I was thankful to have Elijah as a guide through the desolate dirt roads on the furthest outskirts of Flint County. Elijah finally pulled onto an even narrower, bumpier road, which was Sheriff Brady's driveway. A battered pickup was parked in front of a homey-looking cabin with a wrap-around porch.

"Good, he's here!" Elijah assured me as he stopped the car. "Why don't you let me go in first and prepare Sheriff Brady for company. He's grown right ornery since his wife died. He doesn't take much to people showing up uninvited."

Elijah pounded on the cabin's door for a couple of minutes and then walked around the porch to the backside of the cabin. When he returned, Sheriff Brady, a shotgun lying over one arm, was following him. He laid the shotgun against the door and nodded at Elijah, who in turn waved a "come on" signal to me.

Sheriff Brady smiled as he shifted a wad of chewing tobacco to one side of his jaw. "Allison Sinclair! I've enjoyed reading the paper these last few weeks with you serving as editor. You're a chip off the old block, I believe!" He stopped to spit tobacco juice into the yard.

"Thank you, Sheriff Brady," I answered modestly.

His grin vanished. "Just call me Hilton, please ma'am. I'm no longer the sheriff. Now what brings you way out here on this hot day? You need a quote for an article you're writing?" His smile returned as he offered me one of the rockers on the front porch.

"Well, something like that," I began. "Sheriff, Mr. Hilton, do you remember the Macy Dunn case?"

He chuckled. "Hell yes! It's the unsolved ones I remember best. Even though that fool coroner said Macy drowned accidentally, both me and A.L. thought something didn't make sense. We just never had any evidence to pin it on our one suspect."

I withdrew a package from the red velvet bag. "Maybe I can help you with that." I handed the sheriff the packages and watched as his big fingers struggled with the tiny satin ribbon.

"My God! Where'd you get this? It looks like—it could be—I'm not sure, but I think!" He pulled a pair of reading glasses from his shirt pocket to study the tiny flute pin. "Why don't we go inside and let me check something in my file cabinet."

Elijah opted to stay outside. "I'll check and see if that carburetor's still breathing all right." The sheriff nodded, and I followed him inside.

The cabin's interior was neat and clean. There was a nice living area with a large leather sofa and a recliner. The windows had bright chintz curtains; the cabin had obviously benefited from Mrs. Brady's touch before she died.

We passed through the kitchen onto a screened-in porch with an oak desk, swivel chair, and a large file cabinet. "I took all the inactive files when I left office." He opened a drawer labeled "Unsolved Cases" and retrieved a file thick with documents. Stapled on the inside cover was a yearbook photo of Macy Dunn wearing a pink blouse with a Peter Pan collar. Attached to the collar was a tiny flute pin identical to the one in the velvet package. "My God, where in the hell did you find this, Allie?"

"It's a long story, Sheriff." I couldn't help addressing him by the title he'd had my entire life, but he didn't seem to notice this time. As I told him everything from beginning to end, he sat in rapt attention without interrupting.

When I finished, his eyes lit up and he smiled kindly. "Don't you worry, Allie Sinclair! I do believe we've got the sonnabitch now! I always knew John Royal was somehow responsible for Macy's death, but I *never* suspected foul play with your daddy's death." He scratched the stubble on his chin. "Hold on a minute; let me check something." He opened another file drawer and removed a second file, the edge of which had my daddy's name printed on it. "I knew it! That has to be the connection. The same sorry coroner filed both of these reports. He must have messed with the findings, somehow."

A sense of relief flowed through my veins. Finally, I had a confidant, someone who knew what needed to be done. "So, Sheriff, what's our next move?"

He stood up and squared his broad shoulders. "I think it's time we have a talk with Mr. John Royal, a talk I've been waiting to have for over ten years now!"

I rode with Sheriff Brady in his pickup while Elijah followed. We stopped at Mr. Blackwell's orchard to get my car. "I'll say my goodbyes, now, Miss Allie. My wife likes me home on time for supper. I'll let Mama know you'll be a little while."

I shook Elijah Atwell's hand. "My daddy told me long ago that the Atwells were fine people. Thank you, Elijah!"

"God bless you, Miss Allie!" He smiled and waved to Sheriff Brady.

"I doubt Royal's still at the mill. Let's go out to the house in Riverview Estates. Now, Allie, you park on the curb and wait on me. Let me do the talking, you hear!"

"Yessir!" I agreed. Sheriff Brady had no inkling how comforted I was to have someone else in charge.

The sheriff had been correct. We found Brad and Mr. Royal's cars parked in the circular drive. I assumed they were plotting their next move in their search for Cece, but I was wrong.

As we walked up the drive to the front door, we heard raised voices coming from the back patio. The two men were arguing, and Bradley, his speech slurred, was obviously drunk. The sheriff put his finger to his lips in a "shushing" sign, and I felt as though I were ten again and playing a spy game with Josie.

I followed the sheriff as he crept slowly around to the side of the house. He stopped behind a large crepe myrtle, the perfect vantage point. Although we were well-hidden, we could easily see the patio.

What I saw took my breath. Mr. Royal, sitting in a patio chair, gazed with sheer terror at Brad, who held a bottle of Jim Beam in one hand while he waved his service revolver in the other. Sitting on the wrought iron patio table was the laundry box my sister had so vividly described. Mrs. Royal's wedding gown lay in a heap at Mr. Royal's feet, and I realized he'd been in the garden house and discovered his precious red velvet bag missing.

I glanced at the sheriff. He shook his head in disgust while miming to me that he didn't have his gun. Then he whispered, "Stay put. If Brad starts firing, run like hell to your car and get help."

The sheriff, obviously confident that he could defuse the situation, strolled out into the open so that both Royals could see him. I cowered behind the tree as sweat trickled down the sides of my face. "What's going on here?" I heard Sheriff Brady ask in the tone of a teacher interrupting two little boys engaged in horseplay.

The sheriff's casual greeting caught both men off-guard. I saw Mr. Royal relax his shoulders and exhale. "He's drunk, Hilton. Why don't you take him down to Sheriff Hill and tell him to lock Bradley up. He needs to sleep it off."

The sheriff held his arms out as if in supplication. "Whaddaya think, Bradley? That sounds like a good idea to me."

Bradley suddenly pointed the gun at the sheriff. "Don't come any closer! I mean it, Sheriff Brady!" The sheriff froze in his tracks as Brad continued. "Actually, I'm glad you stopped by. I think my father has something he needs to confess. Don't you, dear old Dad?" He turned the gun back on Mr. Royal.

With the sheriff's appearance, the cocky Mr. Royal, the one I knew and hated, returned. "The only thing I need to confess is the obvious fact that my son is a drunk!"

His remark infuriated Brad. "You sonnabitch! Then I'll confess for you. I saw you that night on the dock with that mill girl. You thought I was asleep, but I wasn't. I sat on the back porch and watched you."

Mr. Royal was indignant. "Shut up, you drunken fool. You don't know what you're talking about!"

The sheriff took this opportunity to move closer to Brad, but Brad was younger and quicker. "Sheriff, I don't want to shoot you, but I will if you move again."

This time Sheriff Brady stayed put. "Okay, Brad, we can work this out. I believe what you're saying, and I may even have the evidence to prove it."

The news encouraged Brad, and he turned the gun back on his father. "Tell him, you perverted bastard! Tell him! If you don't, I will!" For once Mr. Royal had no condescending comeback.

Brad continued. "I watched you with her. I heard you tell her if she didn't cooperate, you'd see to it she lost her job at the mill. You filled her with beer, but she still wouldn't give in, would she?"

I saw the fear in Mr. Royal's eyes. "Shut up, Brad. You're hallucinating! It's that liquor talking, you drunken imbecile."

"I'm no imbecile. I saw you slap her and then pull her into the water and hold her down until she stopped fighting. God knows why I didn't say anything to anybody. I thought I wanted to protect you. Mother hadn't been dead but a year. What would I do without a mother or a father?" Brad began to cry. "So, I kept my mouth shut. And now look what you've done. You ran my wife off. Why'd you do that, you selfish bastard, why?"

"I'm not responsible for that slut wife of yours!" Mr. Royal had rediscovered his courage now. He knew exactly which buttons to push on Bradley. He was a pro at controlling his son, or at least he thought he was.

"She's no slut!" Brad screamed as he waved the gun in Mr. Royal's face.

Mr. Royal smirked. "Oh, I beg to differ, my dear son. I had a piece of her before you did!"

He'd gone too far. Brad's tears turned into a drunken rage. Sheriff Brady lunged for the gun, but Brad was too agile. He fired right at his father's face. I almost vomited as pieces of Mr. Royal's brain splattered on his dead wife's wedding gown.

In what felt like an underwater scene, I watched as Brad sank to his knees and guided the barrel of the gun towards his mouth. I began screaming as I ran toward him. "Stop, Brad! Stop! We know what your father did! It'll be all right! Cece's all right, I promise!"

"She's better off without me, Allie. Tell her I'm sorry."

"No!" I heard Sheriff Brady scream as he lunged again, but again he was too late. My brother-in-law, my sister's beloved husband, the father of her child lay crumpled over his mother's wedding gown.

Chapter 32

Chuck Purdy covered the tragic event for Friday's edition of the ***Flintville Star***:

> *In what law enforcement officials are calling a murder/suicide, Mr. John Royal, Vice President of Hamilton Mills, was shot by his son, Captain Bradley Royal of the U.S. Army, at approximately 5:15 P.M. yesterday at 302 Riverview Estates in Flintville. Captain Royal then turned the weapon on himself. Dr. Nathan Garmon of the Flint County Hospital pronounced both men dead from single gunshot wounds to the head.*
>
> *According to the eyewitness account of Mr. Hilton Brady, former Flint County sheriff, the two Royal men had been arguing on the patio of Mr. John Royal's home. Mr. Brady had accompanied Allison Sinclair, sister-in-law of Captain Royal, to the house to inform the family that her sister, Mrs. Cecile Sinclair Royal, was not missing, as previously believed, but had gone into seclusion to protect herself from the ongoing argument, which had escalated between the two Royal men over the past few days.*
>
> *Captain and Mrs. Royal had been living with Mr. John Royal for the past six weeks as Captain Royal recovered from an eye injury suffered in the Philippines, where he served on active duty in the Army. Mrs. Cecile Royal, who remains in seclusion at an undisclosed location, was unavailable for comment. According to Miss Allison Sinclair, Mrs. Cecile Royal's sister, a statement from the family is forthcoming.*
>
> *Funeral services for the two men will be announced within the week, pending the completion of autopsies by the State Crime Lab.*

Late Thursday night, Dr. Justice had accompanied Sheriff Brady and me back to the Atwells' home to tell Cece. When Cece saw the three of us standing on Berthie's front porch, she somehow already knew.

"Brad's dead, isn't he?" she asked in an amazingly strong voice. When I just nodded, she collapsed in my arms. Sheriff Brady gathered up her frail body and carried her back into the house. Dr. Justice shooed us all out of the bedroom while he attended to my sister.

Berthie had a full meal awaiting us at her table, and she insisted we sit down and eat. While I gingerly pushed my food around my plate, the sheriff devoured his. "I'd forgotten what a woman could do to fresh vegetables, Berthie. I haven't tasted a meal this good since my sweet Aileen's been gone."

"Now's whose fault that be?" Berthie kidded as she ladled more potato salad onto the sheriff's uplifted plate. "I'se done told you'se a dozen times that you'se always welcome at this here table, Sheriff! All's you'se gots to do is comes in from them woods ever now and then!"

The sheriff ducked his head in shame. "Aw, Berthie, I guess I've gotten too set in my ways. The woods and the river are about all I need these days. If I could just get a little of your home cooking every now and then, I'd be in hog heaven!"

Berthie was quite pleased. "Well, for now's on, when's Elijah be coming out to the river, I'se send you'se a little care package."

Their chatter comforted me. After I was interrogated for two hours by Sheriff Hill and his deputies, I had no desire to rehash the horror of the scene on Mr. Royal's patio.

Just as Sheriff Brady thanked Berthie for the meal and said his goodbyes to me, Dr. Justice reemerged. "I've made certain Cece won't wake up for the next eight hours or so." He pulled up a chair and sat down in front of me. "Allie, let me check your vital signs, how about it?"

"I'm fine, Doc Justice!" I protested as he wrapped a blood pressure cuff around my arm and took my pulse.

"I guess you are fine!" He smiled as he removed the cuff. "You Sinclairs are made of some sturdy stock." He cleared his throat. "I suspect it'd be better to wait on your aunt and uncle to return before making Brad's funeral arrangements. That will give your sister some time to adjust to the reality."

"I pick them up at the airport late tomorrow. Do you think Cece will be okay here until I get back from Atlanta?"

"I think your sister could be in no better hands," he nodded at Berthie who smiled as she placed a container of leftover bread pudding beside his medical bag.

"Berthie Atwell, I'm going to have to buy a bigger belt if you're not careful!" Doctor Justice leaned over and tousled my hair. I almost expected him to offer me a post-examination lollipop as he had so many times over the years. Instead, he lifted my chin in his oversized hand and smiled down at me. "Allison Sinclair, your daddy would be mighty proud of the way you've handled all of this. It's over now, honey, it's over."

Doc Justice was wrong about one thing. It wasn't over yet. I had to uncover all the answers to the sinister mystery of Mr. John Royal before I would truly have closure.

I dreaded the reunion with Aunt Bird and Uncle Hoyt the following day. How could I explain the tragic horror my sister had suffered while they'd been too far away to protect her? Fortunately, we'd planned for me to pick them up outside baggage claim, so they'd be in the privacy of Aunt Bird's car before I broke the news.

Aunt Bird took one look at my face and sensed some powerful trouble. As soon as she wrapped her arms around me, I broke down into a torrent of sobs. Now that she could shoulder some of the responsibility, I finally let my tears flow.

Once inside the car, I shared the events of the past few days. Aunt Bird trembled all over as she bowed her head in a private prayer. The car was tensely quiet for a few moments until she looked up and took my hand in hers. "Sweet baby, we'll be all right, I promise you that. The Lord will get us through to the other side of this pain."

"I'd like to give that sonnabitch Royal some pain! I always knew there was something too slick about that crafty bastard!" I'd never heard Uncle Hoyt curse before. He gripped the steering wheel so tightly the knuckles of his fingers were white. "If I'd had an inkling he was hurting one of my girls, I'd have throttled his throat as sure as black powder burns."

His outburst complete, Uncle Hoyt said nothing more as he started the engine for the drive home. I'd opted to sit in the front seat between Aunt Bird and Uncle Hoyt, whose jaw tensed as he silently worked through the devastating reality he would face when we reached Flintville.

Two days after everyone had time to digest the horrors of the previous week, we gathered at Flintville Memorial Gardens for Brad's graveside service. Although too weak to stand on her own, Cece insisted on being there in a wheelchair for the ceremony.

As requested by my sister, an American flag draped Brad's casket. Reverend Huff from the Methodist Church read *Psalms 32*, and Uncle Hoyt played a subdued rendition of *Just As I Am* on the guitar. Aunt Bird and I stood on either side of Cece's wheelchair clenching her hands in ours.

The only other person in attendance was Mrs. Daphne Hamilton, elegantly attired in a black suit and a big-brimmed black hat. She dabbed at her eyes with a lace handkerchief. At her own expense, she'd had John Royal's body shipped north to Chicago where Mr. Royal's younger sister lived. Mrs. Hamilton simply refused to bury him next to his wife in the Hamilton family plot.

I was glad that John Royal's remains would not be allowed to decompose in Flint County soil. The mere thought of his dust mixing with the dust of my loved ones nauseated me.

Barely a month later, Cece, with a clean bill of health from Doctor Justice, announced she was ready to travel. She was going back to New York where Margaret and Marcus awaited her return.

No amount of pleading on the part of Aunt Bird or me could convince my sister to remain in Flintville. Cece said she couldn't spend another day surrounded by the curious stares of Flintville residents.

Doctor Justice, taking Cece's side, persuaded Aunt Bird to relent to my sister's wishes. "She needs to escape from the sorrow of this town before it smothers her, Ophelia," he reasoned with my aunt. "Let her go somewhere she feels safe, where she can lick her emotional wounds."

Our aunt had hovered over and coddled my sister until Cece, determined to regain her independence, willed herself back to health. Aunt Bird insisted on accompanying my sister back to the New York apartment Cece would once again share with Margaret, who was finishing her internship in obstetrics.

"If Doctor Justice hadn't assured me that Margaret knows more than he does about caring for a high-risk pregnancy, you'd be staying put, Cece!" Aunt Bird told her.

Although Cece's color had returned and she'd started to regain weight, the emotional scars, the ones hidden from the naked eye, would take much longer to heal. Dr. Justice had given Cece the name of a therapist who dealt with the type of nightmare she'd suffered.

"Are you certain you have enough insulin to last until you see your doctor in New York?" Aunt Bird queried with worry as Uncle Hoyt loaded the last bag into the car.

"Oh, quit fussing over me, Aunt Bird! You know, I've taken care of myself for a while now. I am quite capable!"

"That was before you were with child. Since I expect my great niece to be absolutely perfect when she enters this world, it's my duty to watch over her mama!" Aunt Bird insisted that Cece was carrying a girl. I prayed her prediction came true. I couldn't stand the thought of Cece's child being a little boy who might remind her of Brad.

Cece threw her arms up in surrender. Uncle Hoyt, his eyes glistening with tears, gave my sister one last hug. "You know there's always a place here for you, sweetheart, if you ever get tired of big city life." He opened the back door for Aunt Bird.

"And please don't let Bird spend all her clothing allowance at *Macy's* up there. She'll come home looking so gorgeous I'll have to fight all the coaches at the high school!" he kidded as he kissed my aunt goodbye.

Backing my aunt's car down the driveway, I yelled to Uncle Hoyt. "Don't forget to send someone to get a shot of the *Raiders* at summer training camp. Mr. Purdy won't be back from his fishing trip until the weekend, and I want it to run in tomorrow's paper."

My uncle grinned from ear to ear. "How did I ever manage the **Star** without my efficient assistant editor? See you Sunday night!" He waved one last time.

Our farewells at the airport took a little longer. I wasn't certain when I'd see my sister again. We held onto each other at their departure gate until Aunt Bird insisted she and Cece must board. "I'll be there when the baby comes, I promise! Oh Cece..." There was so much more I wanted to say, but the lump in my throat prevented me.

She reached up and adjusted the tiny diamond star around my neck. Then she pointed to hers, still dangling from the silver chain, the very one I'd given her when she went away to New York the first time. "You know what a safe harbor is, Allie?"

"I think so. It's someplace where a person feels totally safe from any harm. Is that what New York is for you? A safe harbor?"

She smiled for the first time in weeks. "Well, I think New York is where I need to be. But that's not what I mean. You're my safe harbor, Allie. You saved my life, Allie. You saved my baby's life. You're my safe harbor." She kissed me gently on the cheek, and then my sister was gone.

When I pulled into the Virginia Highlands neighborhood where Mimi still lived, I did my best to refocus on the other reason for my trip to Atlanta. The Monday after Brad and Mr. Royal's deaths, the **Flintville Star** had issued a statement from the Sinclair family:

> *The tragic deaths of Captain Brad Royal and Mr. John Royal have shaken Flintville's community. Mrs. Cecile Sinclair Royal and the entire Sinclair family appreciate the outpouring of love and concern during this time of grief. At Mrs. Royal's request, a private burial service will be held on Tuesday. As the facts concerning this tragedy unfold, a more detailed account of the event will be printed.*

Two days after Brad Royal was laid to rest, Uncle Hoyt pulled me into his office. "Okay, Allie, the statement printed in Monday's **Star** bought us a little time. But it won't be long before every citizen in Flintville starts clamoring for more information. If we don't give it to them, the rumor mills will begin to churn." He handed me the police and autopsy reports. "I know this isn't exactly the investigative reporting you'd dreamed of, but we rarely get to choose the news in our line of work. We just get to report it. Are you up to the task?"

I'd been waiting for this moment. "Uncle Hoyt, that day Brad shot his daddy and then himself, Doc Justice told me this was over, but he was wrong."

"What do you mean, Allie?" Uncle Hoyt stared at me intently.

I picked up the green soup can of chewing gum to examine my handiwork from so long ago. "Diddy used to tell me that a good reporter always finds the truth even if it is an ugly truth."

"I agree with your daddy, Allie. But this time that ugly truth could hurt you and your family. Are you willing to take that chance?"

I returned the soup can to its resting place and studied my hands. Tiny bits of glitter like little stars sparkled on my palms. I had my answer. "Yes, Uncle Hoyt, I'm willing. I have to do this for Cece to heal, and I have to do this for Diddy to rest in peace." Most of all, I knew I had to find the truth for myself.

Mimi waited on the front porch as I climbed the steps with my overnight bag in tow. "You get prettier and more grown up every time I see you. Come give your Mimi some sugah!" She grabbed me in a warm, loving embrace.

Aunt Bird had given Mimi the short version about Brad's death. We'd agreed to spare the gory details from my grandmother, who was approaching her seventy-fifth birthday. I knew she had a subscription to the **Star**, which she devoured from cover to cover, and I assumed she'd spoken with a couple of her friends still living in Flintville.

However, Mimi seemed to take all of the news, and the gossip, in stride. I guess the years had taught her to weather times of trouble. Despite her tiny, withered frame, she still had a sparkle to her eyes. "Come on back to the kitchen and let's fix us a sandwich. You can say hello to Cora Lou. She's down in her back and sitting on her heating pad." I smiled to myself as I wondered if Mimi's cousin was ever up in her back.

After my usual conversation with Miss Cora Lou, who filled me in on all her ailments, Mimi showed me the beginnings of a pink and blue blanket she was crocheting. "I wanted to get started while my arthritis is behaving. Since I don't know the sex of Cece's baby, I thought I'd cover both bases." If my Mimi could move forward at a time like this, I figured I could, too.

Mid-afternoon found me standing outside the emergency entrance to *Grady Memorial Hospital*. A week earlier, when I'd told Doctor Justice I was doing some investigative research and needed his help, he'd shown me an article about post-traumatic stress syndrome. However, he admitted it was outdated. "Allie, if you want the most recent findings, you should talk to David Banks. Do you remember him? He spent some time at *Walter Reed Army Hospital* after his tour in Vietnam. They studied how the stress of battle can make some soldiers block out certain memories. David might be able to shed some light."

I hadn't laid eyes on David Banks in over a year. Josie, who'd spent the past weekend by my side, told me David still worked as an orderly in the emergency room at *Grady* and he got off work at 3:00 every afternoon.

As I leaned against a brick retaining wall near the entrance, my palms began to sweat, and I wondered how I'd react to seeing him. Would my heart skip a beat? Would I have a sudden spasm of loathing?

A stream of personnel, dressed in hospital greens, trickled out the door. I caught Dave's easy gait before I even saw his face. So involved in conversation with another young man, Dave almost tripped over my feet. "Oh, excuse me!" He looked up. "Allie? I'll be damned!" He grabbed me and swung me around just like he'd done after our high school football games.

My heart skipped not a single beat, and my stomach churned not a single revolution. I smiled. "Hi David. It's been a while, hasn't it?"

"Damn! I'd say! I've wondered if I'd ever see you again. I've missed you, Allie Sinclair!" I knew he meant he'd missed our friendship, a friendship that perhaps could be mended after all. And right now I needed a friend, one I could trust.

"I thought I'd buy you supper," I began. "That is if you don't have any other plans." I'd done my homework and knew David was still dating Lindy McMichael, who was taking summer classes at West Georgia College fifty miles away.

"I'm meeting a friend at a local joint around 5:00, but I've gotta be back at the hospital tonight. I'm taking the second half of a buddy's graveyard shift," he explained.

I was disappointed. "Oh then, I won't mess up your plans. I just had some questions Doctor Justice said you might be able to answer."

All of a sudden, Dave looked embarrassed. "Gosh, Allie. Doc Justice? I'm a fool! How's your sister? Ty called and filled me in on what happened." He hesitated for a moment. "I thought about calling to check up on you, but I didn't know if you'd talk to me."

Our conversation, one I had dreaded, was so comfortable. I felt like we'd picked up where we left off in high school, before we'd tried and failed at romance. "My sister is okay physically," I began. "Actually, that's why I'm here. I want to pick your brain about post-traumatic stress syndrome. It's for a story I'm working on, a story about what happened to Cece and Brad and Mr. Royal. Maybe I'll come back tomorrow when you have more time."

"No way!" Dave insisted. "I've got the time! Well, I have a couple of hours. You know where *Manuel's Tavern* is in the Highlands? That's where I'm meeting my buddy. You can follow me, we'll have an early supper, and then when I have to leave, my buddy won't be disappointed."

"What do you mean?"

Dave grinned. "How could he be disappointed with a green-eyed babe like you to keep him company?"

Dave ushered me into *Manuel's Tavern*, a local watering hole. The front room sported a long, mahogany bar with three burly bartenders, all of whom waved and called Dave by name.

"So, you're a regular here, I see." I slid into a booth and Dave took the other side of the table.

"It's good food, great pinball machines, and cheap beer. And you never know who you might see. Last week the mayor popped in for lunch, and I've seen a pitcher for the *Braves* in here a couple of times."

One of the bartenders, a hefty fellow with a well-trimmed sandy beard, stopped to take our orders. Dave ordered a steak sandwich and explaining he had to work, opted for a Coke to drink.

For the next hour, Dave gave me the latest information available on post-traumatic stress syndrome while I took some notes on a legal pad. Although he didn't ask why I wanted to know, I felt I owed him an explanation.

"My sister began remembering some things that happened to her a while back. Bad things. They involve Bradley's father. We found some evidence at the Royal house, some evidence that may confirm Cece's memories." With the exception of Diddy's syringe case, I described the items we'd discovered in the velvet bag and the effect they'd had on Cece.

"That makes sense," Dave concurred. "The sight of something, sometimes even the scent or taste of something, can trigger a memory. That sonnabitch Royal! May he rot in hell!"

"My sentiments exactly," I added. "But can you keep all this a secret? I've got some more investigating to do before I write the story."

"Allie, you know this stuff is safe with me. I just wish there was something else I could do to help."

I laughed sarcastically. "Only if you could link me up with a criminal investigator!"

Dave gave me a strange look.

"I need to track down a person who's disappeared from the face of the earth...somebody who might be able to shed some light on our investigation." I paused as our waiter arrived.

"Thanks, McAfee!" Dave nodded to our bartender, who winked at me as he handed me a fresh straw for my Coke.

Once alone, I continued. "Sheriff Brady, remember him? He said I could probably get help tracking this witness down if I could talk to someone with a larger jurisdiction, like a federal or state agent."

"You mean like someone with the GBI...the Georgia Bureau of Investigation?"

"Yeah, exactly. But since this investigation isn't official, I've gotta figure out some angle to get the information I need." I sighed in frustration.

"Allie, you may not believe this, but I think I can provide that angle." Dave grinned and waved at somebody. "And here he comes now."

A young man, perhaps a few years older than Dave and I, approached the table. A sports coat slung over his shoulder, he loosened his tie and unbuttoned the top button of his oxford cloth dress shirt. As Dave stood up to shake his buddy's hand, I noticed the young man wore a shoulder harness with a pistol.

"Allie Sinclair, meet Walt Madigan!" Dave smiled and slapped his buddy on the back.

He had brown eyes, the color of caramel fudge. He wasn't as tall as Dave, but his broad shoulders and trim waistline made him look bigger. He offered me the most disarming smile. "*The* Allie Sinclair? The famous journalist? It's an honor to finally meet you."

I felt my neck color as he shook my hand. "Mind if I join you two, or is this a private party?" he asked with Southern gentlemanlike grace.

"Actually, Walt ol' buddy, I was just about to leave for a graveyard shift at the hospital. But Allie might agree to keep you company, at least for a while?" Dave glanced at me.

"I'm getting the better end of this deal!" Walt Madigan joked as he slid into the seat Dave vacated. "Can I at least buy this lovely lady a beer?"

Dave chortled. "Not unless her taste has changed in the last year. She likes that hard liquor, don't you, Allie?"

I blushed again. "Actually, I think I'll stick to *Coca Cola* tonight," I replied while studying Walt's eyes.

"Coke it is. Hey, McAfee! Another Coke for the lady and bring me my usual! Sorry you can't stay, Dave. You're lucky I'm here to help entertain your Flintville friend," Walt joked.

"Yeah, I bet you're sorry!" Dave quipped. "Actually, I think you can help Allie out in more ways than one." Walt looked a little embarrassed now, although I noticed a subtle glint in his caramel eyes. "Get your mind out of the gutter, you asshole!" Dave admonished. "Allie needs a GBI connection for a story she's researching."

Walt turned his gaze back to me. "Agent Walter Madigan, at your service. I'm here for as long as you need me!"

As I told him about my missing "witness," Walt talked me into having a cocktail. He suggested a Tom Collins, something that tasted more like lemonade than alcohol. I had three of them before the buzz kicked in. He then insisted we play pinball for an hour before he'd allow me to drive home. After beating the socks off me in several battles of *Eight Ball*, he walked me out to Aunt Bird's car, opened the door, and stood to watch me pull out of the parking lot.

The next morning, Agent Madigan called to say he'd located my missing person and insisted on accompanying me to the area. "That part of town is overrun with massage parlors, head shops, and topless bars. It's no place for a lady to travel alone," he explained when he called me at Mimi's. Since I hadn't gotten home until after midnight, I was still half-asleep. On the other hand, Walt, sounding cheerful and professional, didn't seem to be suffering one iota from our late night.

We met in *Manuel's* parking lot where I parked my car so I could ride with him in his official vehicle. "Manuel is a city councilman and a good friend," Walt explained. "Your car's safer here than at the police department."

Dr. Olin Fenwick, my missing person and the county coroner who'd conducted autopsies on Macy Dunn and Diddy, was living in a "flop house" on Ferris Avenue in downtown Atlanta.

We drove in silence as we listened to Elton John singing "My Song" on a local radio station. "So, I never asked last night," I began when a commercial came on. "How'd you and Dave meet?"

Walt, in a light blue oxford button down and paisley tie, smiled. "Dave was working night shift last summer when I brought in a wounded suspect. While the doc tried to save the sorry son of a gun, Dave and I talked football. I played high school ball for Coach Jimmy Gleason in Carrollton."

"I know Coach Gleason! Besides Bayshore down in Valdosta, he's the winningest coach in the state. What position did you play?"

Walt seemed impressed. "Dave told me you knew the game. I played defensive and offensive guard in high school. I was too small to make it in college football, so I chose baseball. I'll always love football, but baseball paid for my education at West Georgia College."

I chuckled. "You're not the typical college athlete."

Walt appeared confused. "Whaddaya mean?"

"You're not a conceited asshole!" I remembered Harrison Dix.

Walt laughed. "No darlin', I'm just a po' old country boy tryin' to do the best I can. When I graduated, I wanted to see what life was like in the big city. A recruiter thought I showed promise with law enforcement, so here I am. And here we are." He pulled into an empty parking space and hurried to exit the car so he could open my door.

Together, we approached a rather seedy-looking establishment with a faded sign reading "Price's Pawn Shop." Walt, lightly holding my elbow, escorted me down an alley adjacent to the shop. "The place is upstairs. The owner claims it's a boarding house, but the cops know it for a flop house. Drunks and addicts crash here."

He stopped and turned to face me. "Now, Allie, it's best you stay behind me and let me do the talking."

We climbed some rickety fire escape stairs. Walt pushed on a metal door and a bell attached to the door jingled. Inside was a small, filthy lobby. A man sat behind a counter smoking a cigarette and reading a porno magazine. He never even looked up. "A room for an hour is $3. It's $5 for a day."

My face colored when I realized why the proprietor thought we were there. Walt Madigan, the gentleman, seemed to disappear. He jerked the magazine out of the smoking man's hand and flashed his badge. "There's a lady present, you slime bag! We're looking for somebody."

Within seconds, Walt had the key to Room 210 where Otis Fenton, an alias according to Walt, resided. When he responded to Walt's knock, I knew in an instant it was Dr. Olin Fenwick. He had the same twitchy eyes and tobacco-stained fingers; he didn't recognize me.

"I ain't got no money, and I don't know nothing!" Fenwick whined as Walt pushed his way into the room.

"We're not after money," Walt explained in a controlled voice. "We're not here to arrest you, either, although I'm certain I could find reason for that. We just want some information."

Fenwick retreated to a nasty night table that held a bottle of whiskey. Hands shaking, he filled a dirty water glass to the brim. "I ain't got no information!" He trembled as he sucked the brown liquid from the glass.

I stared aghast at this broken down man who'd been a coroner for three counties, including Flint. "You remember doing an autopsy on Macy Dunn?" The words fell out before I realized I'd spoken.

A hint of sheer fear crossed his face. "That was about three lifetimes ago. What's it to you anyway?" He poured more whiskey into his filthy glass.

I clenched my hands. Walt noticed and took control of things. "Fenwick, if you give us some information, we'll leave you alone. Who are you hiding from anyway? Maybe I can help," Walt offered in an almost friendly tone.

Walt's demeanor caught Fenwick off guard. "That sonnabitch Royal! He ruined me!" he screamed into his liquor.

"Royal? As in John Royal?" Walt questioned as the fear returned to Fenwick's eyes. "What if I told you that John Royal was dead? He can't hurt you anymore, Fenwick. What if I told you that?"

His half-filled glass dropped from Fenwick's hands and shattered on the nasty floor. "Dead, you say? Oh God, don't lie to me!" Then Fenwick himself sank to his knees on the floor and began to sob like a baby.

Doctor Olin Fenwick signed an affidavit admitting he had altered the findings of Macy Dunn and Alfred Lemuel Sinclair's autopsies. Fenwick owed John Royal thousands of dollars in gambling debts from poker games. Obviously, all those nights when John Royal claimed to be working because he could not bear the sight of his dying wife, he'd actually been playing cards.

Fenwick wasn't certain how John Royal had come into possession of Diddy's syringe case, but he did remember explaining to Royal what caused a diabetic to need more insulin and how much insulin was a lethal dose. Now that I had the missing pieces, I could put the puzzle together myself.

John Royal knew Diddy had figured out who murdered Macy Dunn. The day Diddy died, he'd eaten lunch with the Kiwanis Club at the hotel, and he'd hung his coat on the hall tree in the hotel's lobby. Royal had probably excused himself from the club meeting, extracted the case from Diddy's coat, and inserted a deadly dose of insulin in Diddy's syringe.

How the syringe case came into John Royal's possession remained a mystery to me. Diddy was in the habit of leaving the newspaper's front door open, even on Tuesday when the office was closed. I couldn't help but think that John Royal had stopped by to make certain my daddy was dead from the overdose and then taken the syringe case as his souvenir. That was only a supposition, but it felt right to me.

My article, appearing in Monday's *Star*, contained no suppositions. It included only the facts with a copy of the signed confession of Dr. Olin Fenwick, alias Otis Fenton, who was now in the state's custody.

I didn't want to be in Flintville when Monday's edition came out. "Take some time off, Allie," Uncle Hoyt suggested. "You have your answers now, honey. It's time to let your daddy rest."

I took Uncle Hoyt's advice, and that Monday afternoon, I leaned against the same brick retaining wall outside of *Grady Memorial Hospital* as I had a few days earlier. David Banks, engrossed in animated conversation, almost tripped over my feet again.

"Allie! My God! Back so soon?" He smiled at me, and I knew he was kidding.

I returned his greeting with a genuine grin. "I came to thank you." I handed him a copy of the latest *Star*. "If it hadn't been for your help, I wouldn't have untangled things."

He smiled as he brushed my bangs out of my eyes. "Yeah, Walt gave me the short version. Allie, I'm glad I could help. It's the least I could do for you after I, um, after I..."

"Broke my heart?" I finished for him. "David, I believe the stars know what they're doing even when we fools don't."

"What do you mean?"

I smiled. "The stars knew that we were always supposed to be best friends, nothing more. Anyway, if we were together, I never would've met Walt Madigan."

Dave grabbed me up, twirled me around, and hugged me. "I knew the two of you would hit it off. So glad to be of service, Allie Sinclair!"

I laughed a totally relaxed belly laugh, a laugh I'd been saving for over a year now. "Can I employ your services one last time, then? I need your girlfriend to introduce me to somebody."

I headed west from Atlanta towards Carrollton, Georgia. Agent Walt Madigan had located another missing person for me. Essie Dunn was a junior at West Georgia College. She was enrolled for summer quarter and lived in Adamson Hall on the same floor with Lindy McMichael, Dave's girlfriend.

A resident advisor paged Lindy to the lobby when I arrived. I thought the meeting would be awkward, but she was so cute and sincere I understood why Dave had fallen for her. "I told Essie we had a mutual friend who was bringing her some news. She'll be down in a minute," Lindy explained.

The moment Essie Dunn walked into the lobby, I spotted her. She was a miniature copy of her sister Macy Dunn. "Essie, hi! I'm Allie Sinclair. Remember me?"

Essie, red hair framing her delicately freckled face, smiled. "You brought me chocolate cake and sat on our swing with me when Macy died."

For the next hour, we sat in the shade of a huge oak tree on campus. When I left Essie, she was fingering the little silver flute that had been attached to her sister's Peter Pan collar.

In the cold winter of 1974, I boarded a plane bound for New York City. Cece, ordered to bed rest for the last six weeks, would soon deliver her baby by C-section, and I would be there for the blessed event.

Aunt Bird, who'd planned to accompany me, was seven months pregnant herself. Doctor Justice and Uncle Hoyt told her she had no business traveling.

I teased, "I guess you and Uncle Hoyt should have stuck to sight-seeing while you were in Europe!" I couldn't have been more delighted at the prospect of having a niece and a cousin to spoil.

Walt saw me off at the airport. We'd seen a great deal of each other. He'd even helped me move into my apartment in Savannah when I went to work for the *Savannah Times* that fall.

"Don't you dare ride the subway by yourself while you're up there," he warned as he held me in his arms at my departure gate.

"Oh, hush your worrying and kiss me!" He obliged, and as always when our lips met, my heart skipped a beat.

Marcus, cigarette in one hand and bouquet of pink sweetheart roses in the other, greeted me at La Guardia. "My God, Allie. You look absolutely magnificent! You've been having sex, haven't you? I just know it!" He took a long drag on his Marlboro as I blushed. "I want to hear every single detail about this special agent. I just adore cops!"

"Hands off, Marcus! This one's all mine," I laughed as we headed to the hospital.

Forty-eight hours later on January 11, 1974, Allison Cecile Sinclair made her debut. Weighing in at just six pounds with sapphire eyes and a little blonde fuzz, there was no doubt she belonged to my sister.

"She's a new beginning for us Sinclairs," Cece beamed as she held the tiny pink bundle in her arms.

Brimming with tears, I leaned over to give both mother and daughter a kiss. "You're right, Cece. I think she's the next Sinclair star!"

2005
Epilogue

By the time I finished my story, the moon was high in the sky, and the September night had turned crisp. An hour earlier, Walt had rescued us from the chill with an afghan, crocheted by Mimi decades ago. He kissed both Emma and me goodnight and ambled off to bed. Walt had heard my story so many times, he had parts memorized. He understood I needed to tell my tale to Emma alone.

My daughter and I snuggled under the blanket. The fireflies had even retired, but the crickets and frogs harmonized with the creaking of the old swing as we rocked. Even though I couldn't hear her, I knew my soft-hearted Emma was crying, so we sat in silence for a while.

Once recovered, Emma, always the journalist, started with a question. "Mama, did you and Uncle Dave really have a 'thing' for a while? Dear God, you made the better choice. I mean, Uncle Dave's nice, but he's bald and got an old man's paunch!"

"Emmaline Madigan! Shame on you!" Of course, Emma was right. I did choose the right man, whose caramel eyes and broad shoulders still reduced my knees to Jell-O. "Between tennis and the gym, I guess your daddy's just stayed in a little better shape than Dave."

Emma chortled. "A little better, my ass! I've yet to date a guy who can beat Daddy arm wrestling. You remember when I first started dating? Daddy would pump iron in the basement and then greet my date at the front door. I'm surprised he didn't scare them off!"

"Your daddy is not all brawn and no brain. Just remember that!" After fifteen years as a GBI agent, Walt left to open his own security firm in Savannah. What had started as a one-man business had grown into the most reputable security company in the Southeast.

"I know how smart Daddy is! He can balance my checkbook in his head. If only he could spell," she kidded.

"Well, he's got me to spell for him, and I have him to keep me from bouncing checks all over Savannah. I guess we complement one another quite well."

Emma laid her head on my shoulder. "Complement each other? That's an understatement. Aunt Bird says you and Daddy've been joined at the hip for thirty years."

I hugged her close. "He's my best friend, Emma."

"Like your sister used to be?" she asked in a soft, quivering voice, and I knew she expected no answer. Instead we gazed heavenly, and for the umpteenth time in my daughter's life, I pointed out my special stars.

The next day, we waited until the last minute to leave for the dedication ceremony, but Cece had yet to arrive. She'd called earlier before boarding her plane but couldn't call again until she landed in Atlanta. Since Emma and I played major roles in the building dedication, Uncle Hoyt volunteered to wait outside for Cece while the rest of us entered the Sinclair Memorial Arts Center.

While I'd seen the building in its early construction stages, I wasn't prepared for the grandeur of the finished product. The center was erected on the spot where the Flintville High School music building once stood. The old high school, built in 1873, had been abandoned ten years ago for a modern structure on the outskirts of town. The city had purchased the property five years ago and built the arts center from the ground up.

"This place puts Flintville uptown!" Emma, her guitar in tow, exclaimed as we strolled through the spacious lobby. "Those two old biddies who financed this must have been loaded," she whispered to me.

A young woman I recognized as Frannie Parker's daughter rushed to greet us. The name-tag displayed on her bright orange suit read, "Janie Parker Roberts." Janie, with degrees in music and art, served as the director of the center.

"Mrs. Madigan, you're finally here. Follow me around back so you can enter on stage. The other dignitaries have already taken their seats." She looked around for a moment. "Isn't there supposed to be someone else with you?"

Aunt Bird intervened. "Yes, dear, but she's been delayed. Hoyt is waiting in the parking lot for her and will escort her in if that's okay."

Janie appeared relieved. "Certainly, Miz Ophelia. That's perfect. Now, maybe um, Mr. Madigan?" Walt nodded and smiled. "Yes, Mr. Madigan, if you could escort Miz Ophelia down the aisle to the front row, which is reserved for family. The orchestra is already warming up, and we want to start on time."

Janie corralled Emma and me down a side hall to a backstage entrance. The stage was crowded with dignitaries, two of whom I recognized. Reverend Elijah Atwell, who would offer the devotional and invocation, stood up and smiled as I entered the stage.

"Elijah! It's been far too long. How's your mama doing?" Old Moses had passed away several years ago, but Berthie, nearing eighty-five, still put up vegetables in the summer.

Elijah smiled and whispered, "She's sitting on the second row in a brand new hat. You can't miss her!" I peeked between the closed curtains and scanned the audience until I caught sight of Berthie, proudly surrounded by several great-grandchildren.

Ty Hastings left his seat and started to approach me. We were immediately shushed by Janie, who was listening to an earphone attached to her head.

"Please stay in your seat, Mayor Hastings. The orchestra will begin on the count of three, and then the curtains will rise. One, two, three!" she whispered as she glided off stage and disappeared.

I giggled to myself as I thought of Ty Hastings, one of my former cohorts from the long dissolved *B&B Brigade*, serving as mayor of Flintville. Both Ty and Stu Sims had settled in Flintville, where they co-owned the most successful realty firm in the tri-county area.

While the two real estate tycoons had grown rich off new developments in Flintville and neighboring counties, they'd also given back to their beloved community. Ty and Stu had developed a public park and recreation area along the banks of the Flint River; the park was awarded state park status. On the very grounds where Ty's family cabin and dock once stood was a bronze monument with an engraving that read *Teddy Gaddis State Park*. Somewhere nearby at the bottom of the river lay Teddy's dog tags.

While the orchestra filled the auditorium with a spectacular arrangement of "Georgia on My Mind," I gathered my thoughts. As Emma suspected, I'd written and rewritten my address, but instead of rehearsing it in my head for a final time, I discovered myself studying the audience.

Amid all the citizens in attendance, I found the faces of so many who'd been a part of my life in Flintville. On the first row beside Walt and Aunt Bird sat Roscoe Ray with his "adopted" parents. Catching my eye, Roscoe offered me the same excited grin I'd seen the day I first read him an episode of *Batman and Robin*.

My eyes wandered the second row. Beside Berthie and her Atwell brood, I found Stu Sims and his pretty wife, a South Georgia girl he'd met at college. She must be quite a cook, I thought, because she'd certainly fattened up skinny Stu.

Next to the Sims sat Dr. David Banks and his wife Lindy. Dave had served as Walt's best man in our wedding, although Walt had joked that Dave should have been a "bridesman" for me instead. He and Lindy still lived in Atlanta where Dave was considered one of the top trauma surgeons in the state. Their son Ted, who'd played running back for Georgia Tech, was now serving with the Army Reserves in Iraq.

Then of course there was dear Josie. Sitting next to Josie was her husband Zeke, semi-retired from his veterinary practice in LaGrange now that their daughter had joined the practice. Josie, thin and regal, had changed little over the years. We'd met a few months earlier to ride our five speeds along Atlanta's newly completed Comet Trail. She'd complained that having gears didn't give us as much exercise as our laborious uphill climbs on our old, gearless Schwinns.

Dr. Margaret Justice Powell was seated beside her aging father, who despite his years, still saw patients at their family practice. Margaret, who served as the practice's gynecologist, had added a pediatrician to the growing office when she married Dr. Frank Powell, a New Yorker who'd fallen in love with the South.

Across the aisle from Margaret, I spied someone I hadn't expected. Marcus Owens, rather thin but fit-looking, smiled at me. Not only had Marcus finally made the trip to Cece's hometown, but he'd also brought along his partner and savior. Frederick Martinez, a physical therapist and personal trainer, had nursed Marcus back to health after a heart attack two years ago, convincing Marcus to trade in his Marlboros for a treadmill.

I was so wrapped up in my reminiscing, Emma nudged me to stand during Reverend Atwell's invocation. The city manager offered some congratulatory words and a description of the center, which included the state-of-the-art auditorium where we were seated, an art museum, and a library that would serve as the home to

Flint County's archives. Throughout their speeches, Emma and I kept eyeing the back door in hopes that Uncle Hoyt would show up with Cece at his side.

I caught a glimpse of my handsome, blonde cousin, Lemuel Hoyt Lloyd, kneeling in the aisle with a camera in one hand and a notepad in the other. I knew Diddy was smiling down on Lem, my daddy's namesake, his sister's son, and the *Star's* newest editor-in-chief.

As my eyes roamed the magnificent forum, I breathed a quiet thank you prayer to Miz Gertie and Miss Melba Benton, both gone to a better place now. The last years of their lives, both ladies had resided in Flintville's newest assisted living village, where they became best friends. Aunt Bird said Miz Gertie's kind heart brought out the best in Flintville's crotchety old librarian Miss Benton, who by then was confined to a wheelchair.

When Miss Benton passed away and Miz Gertie followed a few months later, Flintville's citizens were surprised to learn both ladies had left the bulk of their estates to the creation of an arts center. Their one stipulation was that the center be named after the Sinclair family.

Mayor Hastings was winding down with his introduction of the keynote speaker, which happened to be me. "Citizens of Flintville, we're pleased and proud to have one of our native sisters, a Sinclair herself, to dedicate the Sinclair Memorial Arts Center. Please give a big 'welcome home' to Allie Sinclair Madigan!"

As I rose from my seat, I folded my rehearsed speech and left it in my chair. I decided that when it came to speaking to people I loved, I'd be better off winging it.

"Thank you, Ty, and thank you, Flintville, for welcoming me home. Flintville will always be home to me even though I've lived elsewhere for the past three decades. Thirty-two years ago, I served as the *Flintville Star's* interim editor while my uncle and aunt took a well-deserved vacation. I was fresh out of University of Georgia's College of Journalism and quite full of myself. I made lots of mistakes in those three weeks, but during that temporary stint, I wrote an editorial suggesting Flintville's need for a cultural arts center. It took three decades, but finally Flintville listened.

"I just wish both Gertie Stansell and Melba Benton could be here to see what their magnanimous gift has brought to the people of this town. I'm certain they're looking in on this celebration." I saw Roscoe Ray pull a handkerchief from his pocket.

"There is no greater tribute you could pay to both my mother and my daddy than honoring this center with their name. They, too, are shining down on us this day as we open a place where people throughout the county can enjoy the arts. I know Diddy would especially appreciate the archive wing, where copies of the *Flintville Star* will be stored."

I paused as I silently asked the Lord to get me through the next part. "The art wing will be a perfect venue for displaying works by both local and visiting artists. I'm so thankful that works by both my mother and Miss Benton will have permanent homes in that wing. In addition to those works, the collection entitled *Seasons of Georgia* has been donated to this building. I so wish that my sister could be here to share in the unveiling of her personal collection, which has received national acclaim and helped to put Flintville on the map. But as most of you know, my sister..."

Just as I thought I'd finish without allowing my voice to quiver, the center aisle entrance swung open, and there she was on the arm of Uncle Hoyt. Her stunning grace rendered me momentarily speechless. It was probably for the best, though, since all eyes had turned to watch her serene and stately trip down the center aisle.

Dressed in a simple blue sheath with her corn silk hair pulled back and tied at the nape of her neck, she looked so much like my sister, my Cece, that I almost called out to her. But as she and Uncle Hoyt slid in beside my aunt, I reminded myself that she wasn't my sister.

From my vantage point, I could see the tiny star of flint glittering from the silver chain around her neck, and I knew Cece was with us. "As I was saying, most of you know that my sister Cecile Sinclair passed away five years ago after a long and courageous battle with diabetes." I thought of those last few months when the disease she'd endured without complaint began to ravage her organs. When her kidneys began to fail, my sister made me promise to watch over her daughter, her beautiful daughter who looked so much like her mother.

"However," I continued. "We are thrilled that my sister's daughter Allison Cecile Sinclair has just arrived for this proud moment. Most of you know Allison as A.C. Sinclair, whose photographs have appeared in news magazine throughout the world. In the Sinclair home, however, she's our second Cece. My niece, Cece, has generously donated the Georgia collection from her mother's estate to the Sinclair Memorial Arts Center."

Fortunately, my announcement brought about a tremendous roar of applause delivering me from having to say more. Like her mother, our second Cece was quite modest about her work as a freelance photographer, or I would have explained her tardiness with pride. Commissioned by *National Geographic Magazine,* she'd been in Thailand creating a photo story of rebuilding efforts since the devastation from the horrific tsunami a year earlier.

As the applause diminished, Mayor Hastings approached the podium to introduce Emma. A stagehand brought Emma's guitar and a stool onstage, placing it behind a microphone.

Her caramel eyes, just like Walt's, gleamed with tears, but her voice was steady and strong. "I feel so blessed to have Sinclair blood. Mama says I inherited my singing ability from my great aunt, Ophelia Sinclair Lloyd. Mama has always called her the Sinclair rock. So, Aunt Bird, this song is especially for you."

As she sang the first verse of "Amazing Grace" without the accompaniment of her guitar, the hall reverberated with no other sound than Emma's voice. Slowly, she added the strings of her instrument to the second and then the third verse, the verse that truly told the Sinclair story:

Through many dangers, toils, and snares

We have already come.
Twas Grace that brought us safe thus far
And Grace will lead us home.

Far too soon we were offering hugs and goodbyes to Cece after sharing supper prepared by Aunt Bird. Cece's agent called saying she'd been offered a shoot in southern India where archaeologists had just uncovered the ruins of an ancient temple.

"But you just got here, Cece! Mama wanted to show you the Sinclair sisters' haunts tomorrow," Emma whined. Seeing my daughter, almost five years younger than her cousin, reminded me of watching my own sister take off once again as I wondered if we'd ever have time together. The two of them retreated to the side porch so they could catch up before Lem drove Cece to the airport.

My sister never returned to Flintville after Brad's suicide, and this was only the second visit for my niece. There'd been many reunions over the years, and our two daughters grew up together wherever we met—the Florida Keys, New York, Savannah—anywhere but Flintville. When Cece died, however, she requested her cremated ashes be sprinkled over the Flint River, making my niece's first visit to her mother's hometown a sad one. My sister's finest art, four series of paintings depicting Flintville, reflected the love she had for our town, a town that haunted her, too.

Once again as the stars filled the sky, I found myself alone in the swing on Aunt Bird's front porch. I could hear my aunt singing in harmony with Emma as they washed dishes in the kitchen. Walt and Uncle Hoyt had disappeared to the garage to tinker on my precious Studebaker.

"Mama?" I heard Emma call. "Are you awake?"

I opened my eyes. "I must have faded away for a moment. What time is it, honey?"

"It's after 10:00. Daddy told me to check on you and bring you a blanket." Once again she snuggled with me under Mimi's handmade afghan. I could tell by her silence that something was bothering her.

"Are you still upset about Cece leaving so soon? We'll be together in Savannah over Christmas," I reminded her.

"It's not that, Mama. I have some news of my own. I've already told Daddy, but he said I was on my own with you."

My heart fluttered in expectation, but the journalistic curiosity running through my veins urged me to listen. "Go ahead, Emma. Tell me."

"I know you'll be upset, but Mama, it's the assignment I've been waiting on for the past year. I have to go, Mama," she pleaded.

I steadied myself before asking the unavoidable question. "What's the assignment, Emma?"

She wrapped her fingers around my hand. "It's a six-week tour in Qatar." I felt the color drain from my face, but before I could protest, Emma continued.

"Now, don't get your panties all in a wad! I'll be with the backup crew; only the camera crew and reporters will travel into Iraq, I promise."

"But it's still the Middle East and a volatile area where anything can happen," I argued.

"It's what I'm trained to do. I'm a journalist just like you and just like your daddy. You go where the story takes you!"

The passion and truth in her words convinced me to accept the inevitable. Instead of continuing a senseless debate, I held my hands up in surrender. Then, I reached behind my neck and unlocked the tiny silver chain holding my precious star of flint.

"But, Mama," she protested. "You said the only way I'd ever get this would be if I raided your casket!"

"I've changed my mind, Emma." I fastened the chain around her neck. "You need it more than I do now."

I held her by her shoulders and looked deep into her glistening brown eyes. "When you get tired or lonely or afraid out there, just touch your star." I placed her fingertips lightly on the jewel. "It will be your safe harbor until you're home again."

"But what about you, Mama?" she asked in the tone of a little girl. "What if you need your star?"

"Don't worry about me, sweetheart." I pointed heavenward. "I know where to look if I need them."